CATALYST

HEART OF THE INFERNO SERIES

NICOLE FANNING

Nicole
FANNING

DELICIOUSLY DARK AND ABSOLUTELY THRILLING

Catalyst
Heart of the Inferno: Book 1
Copyright © 2021 Nicole Fanning
Second Edition

Edited by: Charly Jade
Proofread by: Mikayla Christy
Formatting & Interior: Charly Jade @ Designs by Charlyy
Cover by: Acacia Heather

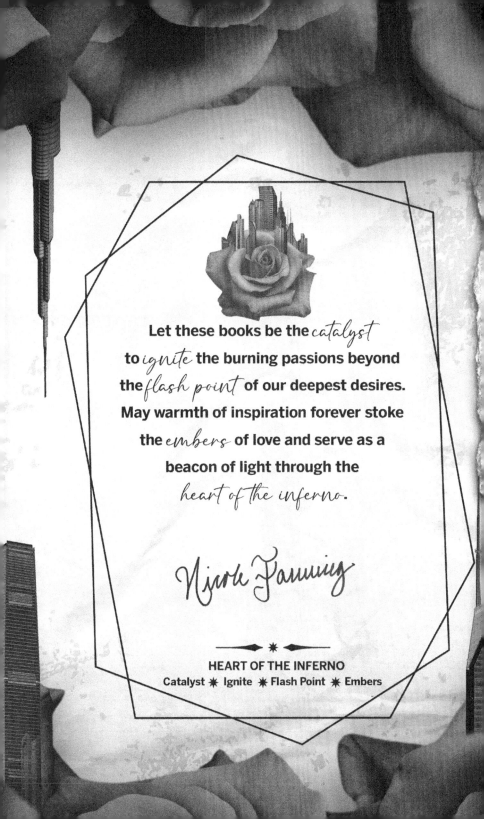

Let these books be the *catalyst*
to *ignite* the burning passions beyond
the *flash point* of our deepest desires.
May warmth of inspiration forever stoke
the *embers* of love and serve as a
beacon of light through the
heart of the inferno.

Nicole Fanning

HEART OF THE INFERNO
Catalyst ✳ Ignite ✳ Flash Point ✳ Embers

PLAYLIST

FIRE MEETS GASOLINE - SIA
STARBOY - THE WEEKND
JUNGLE - X AMBASSADOR
RIVER - BISHOP BRIGGS
SLOW HANDS - NIALL HORAN
JUST PRETEND - BAD OMENS
WONDERFUL TONIGHT - ERIC CLAPTON
INTO YOUR ARMS - WITT LOWRY
RIDE - SOMO
STREETS - DOJA CAT
LIKE THAT - BEA MILLER
RISE - DAVID GUETTA
I'M ON FIRE - AWOLNATION
BAD BITCH - BEBE REXHA
UNCHAINED MELODY - THE RIGHTEOUS BROTHERS
NEVER TEAR US APART - BISHOP BRIGGS
THE OTHER SIDE - RUELLE
SOMETHING IN THE ORANGE - ZACH BRYAN
TRUST YOU - ROSS COPPERMAN

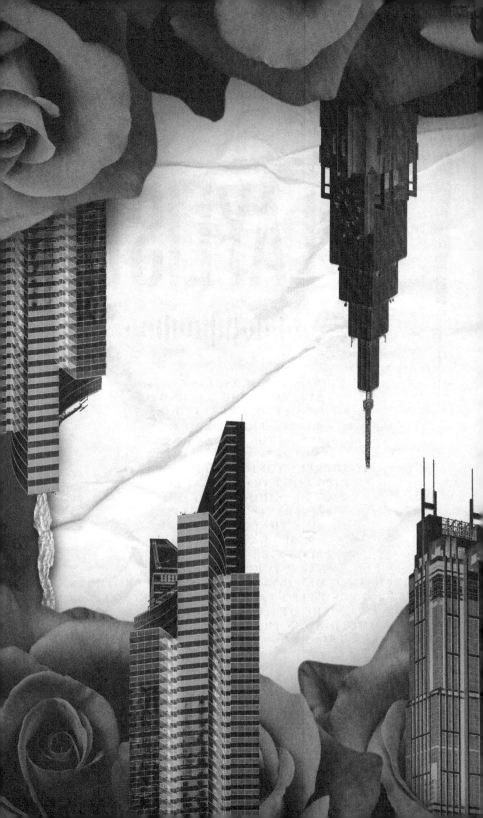

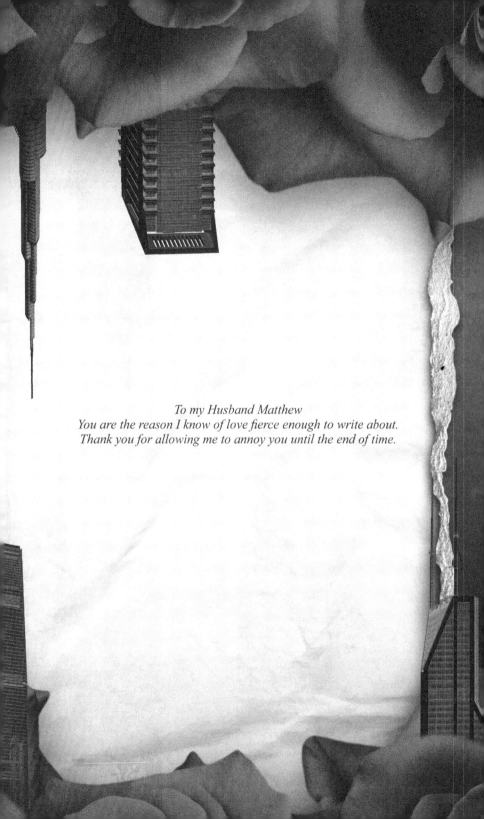

To my Husband Matthew
You are the reason I know of love fierce enough to write about.
Thank you for allowing me to annoy you until the end of time.

Content Warning

This book contains dark themes, and concepts.
The full list of content warnings is available:

Chapter One

THE ASSASSIN

I have a text.

8:35 p.m.: He's on his way.

Good. It's about time.

I lay my money down on the bar and make my way outside. Finding a solitary bench, I light a cigarette and wait, watching the hotel guests coming and going.

A group of giddy teenagers with colored braces taking pictures for their social media accounts. The married businessman with his tiny suitcase, getting a good 'last squeeze' of some slutty brunette's ass before hopping into a separate cab. An exhausted couple with out-of-state plates and two young kids, yelling at them to stay close. All of them caught up in their own lives.

Fuck them and their pathetic lives. Lives that mean nothing to me. Neither does his.

I hear the motorcycle approaching and take a drag on my cigarette as it pulls up into the valet. I shift on the bench making sure my gun is accessible.

I could do it here.

I know it is not part of the plan, but I could.

I could put a bullet in Chicago's favorite son and resident

billionaire playboy. Effectively ending his reign in this city.

It would be so easy. Just one bullet.

But I am not here for him today.

I look out over the top of my sunglasses just in time to see him getting off the bike. The woman he is with steps off too, and he helps her with her helmet, before pulling her in for a kiss.

Her.

The recent anomaly in the carefully tailored life of Jaxon Pace.

She stares into his eyes, and I wonder if she knows that this is not like him. That Jaxon Pace is not really a PDA kind of guy.

And yet here he is, fawning over her like a lovesick puppy.

Nauseating.

"Something to say?!" He yells at the orbiting staff, who are helplessly staring, and they scatter like roaches in the light.

I flip a page on my newspaper and bring my cigarette to my lips.

I could still take the shot.

One bullet, and the lengthy dynasty of one of the most prolific crime families in Chicago would come crashing down, collapsing in on itself.

But then, so would the plan. I am told the plan is better.

So, I will have to wait.

Besides, he is now surrounded by his usual brigade of bodyguards—bringing the total count of viable henchmen in the immediate proximity to five.

Significantly less favorable odds.

And I am not here for him.

I am here for *her.*

The mysterious paramour that has him so blindly captivated.

My organization has nothing on her and neither do the others. No dossier with her name on it exists anywhere in our dark and dirty world of crime and debauchery. The feds have nothing on her either; I've checked.

She is clean.

Well, except for the apparent company she keeps these days.

According to my sources he has been with her every waking second for the last four days and makes no effort to hide his affection.

Jaxon Pace's new addiction. His new drug of choice.

And he is hooked.

I can use that.

She could be remarkably effective if that pressure is applied correctly. This woman could perhaps be even more effective than a bullet.

Jaxon takes her by the hand and leads her inside.

A different kind of bullet. Yes, she is the play.

But since we have nothing on her, I need to know who she is first. Which is why I am here. My first emissary has failed, my first message has gone unnoticed.

No bother. I will send another.

And this time I will deliver it to her *myself.*

Chapter Two

JAXON

Four days earlier

My name is Jaxon Pace.

I am awake and I have made a few necessary observations:

One: There is a naked woman in bed with me. Two: I cannot dwell on said naked woman because I have a face-splitting headache which is causing the room to spin. And Three: This is not my bed, and this is not my house.

Technically this is not a house at all. This is a hotel.

I own a hotel. In fact, I own several hotels.

What was the name of this hotel again? Fuck.

My head is throbbing. Also, there is an alarm going off somewhere in the room, and I cannot immediately determine exactly where that is.

Great.

That is just what my extremely hungover, confused, naked self wants to wake up to—piercing obnoxious ringtones. Monotonous and unrelenting.

I rub my eyes, wishing I were still sleeping. But this stupid beeping is making that impossible.

Oh, for fucks sake.

I kick the covers off me and sit up with the intent to get off the bed and go smash the source of the noise to pieces. However, vertigo has other plans, and my headache takes the opportunity to punch me in the face again.

Perfect.

And then there is the beeping. More. Fucking. Beeping.

Who picked this stupid alarm tone!?

"Alright, alright, I'm up!" I shout at no one.

Well, I guess I could count the naked chick next to me.

I stare at her silhouette and try momentarily to think of her name, until I am reminded that thinking hurts with a hangover. There is also a decent chance I never asked her name in the first place.

So no, I guess we are not going to count her after all.

I scan the room, only slightly more awake than I was previously and I see a phone illuminated on the lounge chair across from me.

This is the source of the beeping!

I also take notice that a gun handle is poking out the side of the chair cushion—my gun handle.

Ah, that is right, I had business last night.

Naked Chick stirs behind me, and I chuckle briefly to myself.

Apparently, I had business and pleasure.

I grunt and stand upright, moving in the direction of the gun and the beeping.

I am going to shoot this fucking phone.

A few more observations come into view as I am now vertical. There is a lamp tipped over on the couch. There is a tray of food—room service. There is a gold sequined dress thrown across the armchair—likely belonging to Naked Chick. There is also a line and a half of coke on the table.

Well, hello there.

I lean in to examine it closer and see that it is clearly low-grade coke. Which means it is not mine, as I do not roll with anything less than premium.

I turn back to look at the woman in the bed.

Naked Chick just got a whole lot more interesting.

She has now rolled onto her back and lies in the middle of the bed with her fake tits straight up in the air. She is still out cold, and her face is completely covered by her hair.

I cannot appreciate all these thoughts as a whole because the goddamn beeping has not stopped. And I realize I am the idiot who is standing here staring at boobs and coke.

I yank my phone off the chair, and I see the name of the alarm register across my screen.

Jessica-7:30 a.m.

I look back at the clock.

7:05 a.m.

Shit.

Shit. Shit. Shit.

I rub my face at the same time I notice my tuxedo tie is on the glass decanter... my *empty* decanter next to the clock.

That certainly explains why my head is throbbing.

7:06 a.m.

Quit fucking around, Jaxon. Get moving.

I stare at the line of coke on the table before me, and briefly debate kick starting my morning with more than just a cup of coffee. But I know this would be a mistake.

Not today, big boy...

I brush the coke onto the floor.

I think we partied enough last night to not do shitty coke at 7:07 a.m. in the morning.

Coffee. I need coffee. And some Ibuprofen. And a bathroom. Not necessarily in that order.

7:08 a.m.

Actually, fuck all those things. I need to get the cokehead naked chick the fuck out of my room. *Now.*

My eyes strain in her direction, she is still snoring, those fake tits still pointing directly to the ceiling. It's a beautiful sight.

7:09 a.m.

Fuck, focus, Jaxon. Time is ticking.

She needs to go.

I have to piss first though. Immediately.

I stumble over to the bathroom while scrolling at my texts.

Ethan
6:20 a.m.: Sir, Jessica is inquiring as to your whereabouts. She is upset you did not come home last night.

Ethan
6:37 a.m.: Sir, I have tried to delay as much as possible, but she is demanding to see you.

Ethan
6:45 a.m.: Sir, we are on our way and inbound to Jefferson

in 30 minutes.

Water is dripping off my face when collectively my brain cells piece together this text thread.

Jefferson is the name of my hotel.

Jessica is going to be here at the Jefferson at 7:15a.m.

I look at the time now…

7:12 a.m.

Fuck.

I need Naked Chick out of my room… in three minutes flat.

I grab my bathrobe off the back of the bathroom hook, and stumble over to sleeping beauty. On her side of the bed, I find my boxer briefs and throw them on. Thankfully, I also find the condom foil which makes me breathe a sigh of relief.

But I still need her out of here.

I touch her shoulder, shaking her awake at the same time I glance at the clock.

7:13 a.m.

"Heyyyy, good morning." I say, trying to be friendly, but still practically pulling her upright.

She is disheveled and groggy, but I must admit she is a decently pretty girl. However, the coke residue around her nose snaps me back to the present and reminds me of the pressing issue.

"What time is it?"

She mumbles, trying to lay back down to go back to sleep.

"It's really fucking early. And I'm sorry, but I need you to leave."

She stares at me blankly, utterly stunned.

"Like… *now*," I say again.

I know this is probably a brutal way to wake up, but I cannot think of any other way to get this chick out of my hotel room, and I need her *out* of my hotel room.

"What? Are you fucking serious?" she says, her jaw hanging open.

"Completely. Time to go." I try to pull her up.

"Are you serious?" she repeats, glancing toward the clock and protesting.

Oh, for fucks sake… I do not have time for this.

"Yes, I am very serious. You need to leave. Now," I say flatly.

"Wow. Rude." She sits upright and uses the blanket to cover her body.

7:14 a.m.

"Yes I know," I say, handing her my robe. "Believe me, I'm well aware that I'm an asshole."

"Ya think?!" She snatches it from me, wrapping herself up angrily, while I grab her things from around the room.

At exactly 7:15 a.m. my phone lights up with another text

Ethan
7:15 a.m.: Sir, we are in the elevators on our way up.

Fuck. I really do not have time for this shit.

I turn back to her and see that she is trying to fix her hair in the mirror.

"Hey Sweetheart, let's go!" I yell, snapping my fingers. "What part of this do you not understand?! It's time to get the fuck out of my room!"

"Fuck you!" She yells back, storming for the door.

"You already did remember?" I say under my breath as I hand her the dress and purse.

Jesus, I can be such a heartless bastard sometimes.

"Pig!" She turns on her heel and walks toward the elevators.

I wait to make sure she makes it *on* the elevator, taking the opportunity to appreciate her thick backside for the last time.

Mmm, you're right. I am a pig... because while I do not remember the sex, that ass is fantastic.

I close the door and scramble to find my pants and collared shirt from last night. I straighten the room as best I can—so as not to draw too much attention to the debauchery that took place here, most of which I am still too fuzzy to remember. I fix the lamp, and I am halfway through tucking my shirt in when I hear a knock at the door. Out of instinct, I grab my gun from under the armchair cushion, and peer through the peephole.

Jessica.

I stuff the gun in the back of my pants and open the door.

"Daddy!"

A pretty little brunette launches herself into my arms.

"Jessibear!" I growl back at her, holding her against me while leaving the door open for my team to walk in.

Ethan, Josiah, Charlie, and Bruno enter the room. Ethan is in charge. Charlie has coffee and muffins. Bruno has a garment bag with fresh clothes. Josiah walks in, turns on the TV, and starts silently straightening the room.

This is what I pay them for. Keeping my shit together.

"Daddy, why weren't you at home this morning? You promised

you'd take me to my first day of school." My daughter pouts at me, bringing me back to the moment.

"I'm sorry, Baby," I lie. "I was working extra late last night, and had to get up really early."

"But you promised to go with me to meet my new teacher!" She says, her brown eyes piercing my heart.

Way to fuck that up bud.

"And I will, Princess," I say with a smile. "I will come with you to meet your new teacher, just like I promised. Daddy just needs a quick shower, okay?"

Jessica smiles, apparently satisfied, and wraps her tiny arms around me in a hug. As I squeeze her back, I happen to lock eyes with Ethan, who just shakes his head. She then wiggles her way out of my arms, takes a muffin from Charlie and settles in front of the tv, instantly distracted by whatever program Bruno chose.

Charlie hands me the coffee. The minute the bitter liquid touches my lips, I feel hope on the horizon.

It is like manna from heaven. Thank God.

"How much time do we have until the tutor arrives?" I ask Ethan.

"Thirty-five minutes."

I walk over to Jessica and kiss the top of her head.

"How was the Auction, Sir?" Charlie asks with a smile.

Oh, that's right—the Auction. That is where I was last night.

The Annual Children's Fund Auction

"It was good." I say, watching Josiah dump several empty champagne bottles in the trash can.

"Clearly," Ethan says snarkily.

Did I buy anything last night?

Fragments of the evening come back to me in a haphazard order. Images of Naked Chick, her boobs, and alcohol flash behind my eyes like an old movie reel.

Oh, that's right, I bought the girl.

Some of the Miss Illinois hopefuls had auctioned themselves off as 'dates' for the evening, in an effort to raise funds for the local children's hospital.

I had apparently just taken that a step further and brought her back to the hotel with me. Per usual.

What a morning.

I take another sip of coffee and shake my head, heading to the bathroom.

Ethan has already started the shower for me. I step in and feel immediately better than I have felt all morning. I stand there letting the water pound against my forehead, hoping by some miracle that it will seep through my pores and work to kill this hangover. My body is wrecked. I feel like I need forty-eight hours of sleep, twenty-four Ibuprofens, and probably a shot of penicillin, given how quickly Naked Chick hopped into bed with me.

But then again, I am, well... me.

I've never had a problem getting women into bed.

Ten minutes and a quick shave later, I am a new man and look a bit more like myself.

Normal might be a stretch though... especially with this group.

Josiah is still straightening up, quiet and observant like always. Charlie is sipping coffee and staring at his phone, and a six-year-old girl watches Dora the Explorer with a fascinated Bruno, who is a bit like a kid himself.

I step out onto the balcony to have a cigarette.

I have been trying to quit, but I feel like this clusterfuck of a morning warrants one. After all, I did pay five grand for a night with a beauty queen I just kicked out of my hotel room in less than four minutes flat.

So yeah, I think I've earned it.

I sit down on the chair and watch as the sunrise hits the city's skyscrapers with blinding illumination.

"At some point, I need to hear about your evening with Britta." Ethan's voice speaks from beside me, startling me.

This man is part ninja I swear. He's astoundingly quiet.

"Britta, eh?" I say, amused and somewhat disappointed I will not be able to refer to her as 'Naked Chick' anymore. "I wish I would've known her name this morning. It may have helped things move along quicker." I exhale deeply.

"I apologize for the disturbance," he says solemnly. "Jess woke up earlier than usual and was very persistent."

"It's fine," I smile, waving him off. "I was too drunk to remember most of my evening anyway. And from what I can remember, it was mediocre at best." I take another inhale.

Now I remember the nickname I gave her last night and it makes me smirk and shake my head.

Britta with the Tittas.

I stand up and walk to the glass railing.

Welcome to the shitshow. My shitshow.

"I had Travis track Britta down and make sure she has a room to go crash in until she is rested," Ethan says, lighting his own cigarette now. "I had him make sure she signed the waiver."

"Perfect," I say, leaning over the railing. "As always."

"And the tutor is waiting in the conference room downstairs."

Shit… the tutor.

"I have no idea how this is going to go, but I am fully anticipating a struggle," I say, sighing deeply and leaning forward on the balcony with my elbows.

"Maybe she's grown out of it. Six is a big year. My kids were shy at that age too," Ethan says.

"Right, but there's a difference between *shy* and completely *unwilling* to speak to women in any capacity."

"She speaks to Old Nan," Ethan says as optimistically as possible.

"Well, that's different. That's her nanny. Everyone speaks to Old Nan. I mean, the woman is like what, two hundred years old?"

Ethan chuckles.

"She's still a woman. I'm just saying, let's stay positive and just see how things go."

I sigh and light another cigarette, to the clear disappointment of Ethan.

"It's gonna be a day…" I say in my defense.

"It's always a fucking day with you," he says, rolling his eyes and staring out over the railing. Only he can talk to me like this.

Ethan has been in my life since before I was born. He is my right hand, and he was my father's right hand before me. He is an ex-navy seal sniper, trained in black ops, martial arts, reconnaissance and search and extraction. He's the kind of man you trust with your life. He is the only man I trust with mine… and Jessica's.

I take another drag and look through the window of my penthouse. Everyone is busy doing what they were previously, and Jessica is busy pretending to paint Bruno's nails while he is still glued to the television. My team is pretty straight forward, and with the exception of Charlie, they are all pretty quiet, but they are still good men.

Well not good men. You can't do what we do and still be considered good men.

But they have morals. They have a code. And any of them would die for me.

In *our* world that is as good as it gets when it comes to men.

"Jessica."

"No," Jessica says from behind my legs.

"Jess, come on."

"No."

"Jessica Elizabeth," I say, a bit more firmly. "*Now.*"

She hesitates a moment, then walks out from behind me, her eyes still focused warily on the woman at the conference room table. I kneel to talk to her.

"Jessibear," I whisper, "we talked about this right? You have to be a big girl now."

"I know, Daddy, but I don't want *her* to be my teacher."

"Well, unfortunately, you don't have a choice. You are six now. You are a big girl, and part of growing up is doing things you don't want to do. Trust me, I have to do it all the time."

"I know but—"

I raise my finger and cut her off. She lowers her eyes to the floor, respectfully.

"Yes, Daddy."

The defeat in her voice makes me feel like the worst father on earth. I sigh, taking her little hands in mine.

"Now, you're going to listen to the nice lady over there, do some schoolwork, and I will be back later," I say gently. "Then we will go get some ice cream, okay?"

She nods, but her eyes are still fixed on the floor, and she does not look up at me, effectively breaking my heart.

I lift her chin with my finger.

"I love you," I whisper to her. "Do you still love me?"

A small smile breaks across her face and she nods.

"Of course, Daddy."

"That's my girl," I say, kissing her cheek.

I stand up and take her hand, walking her over to the chair at the conference room table. I lift her into it, noticing Jessica apprehensively staring down the tutor.

"Don't worry, Mr. Pace, we will have lots of fun today!" The young woman says a bit over-enthusiastically. "I know we will all be great friends!"

I can see her blushing.

Oh Christ, not this again. Why do all the young women I employ want to fuck me?

"I don't really care about how much "fun" you have," I say curtly. "I care solely about my daughter's education. I trust you understand your role. Or do you need to be reminded?"

I really am an asshole.

"I... I do," she stammers, blushing harder now. "I mean, no, I do not need to be reminded."

"Good. I hope you also understand that I am leaving her in your care until I return, and until that time you are not to let her out of your sight?"

"Yes, Sir... I mean, yes," she squeaks out.

"Good," I say, turning and walking away. "Then we will all be good friends indeed."

Chapter Three

Natalie

Taillights. I am sick of taillights. I have been in Chicago for two hours, and half of that time I have spent staring at the taillights of the cars in front of me.

Well, this is delightful.

It also does not help that the rental car company at the airport was out of the four-door sedan I requested. And instead decided to upgrade me into this massive SUV that I feel incredibly unqualified to operate.

SUV? I am driving a freaking tank!

Finally, I see the hotel up ahead and slowly try to maneuver myself into the right lane so that I can turn. However, at the same time, the guy in the car next to me flips me off as I try to merge.

Jesus. I guess that is why it is called the Windy City and not the City of Brotherly Love.

I follow the signs towards the parking garage, but even this becomes a struggle because there is a lot of traffic heading into the garage. I pick the lane furthest away as it gives me enough space to finagle my big-assed vehicle into the lane.

Unfortunately, at the last second, I realize that I picked the wrong lane as I notice the sign above me says, 'Executive Garage.' But at this point there is no chance of me getting this tank out of this lane, and I accidentally mount the curb.

Ugh, screw this!

I decide I need to just focus on getting in the garage, and then I can figure out how to get back to regular parking.

But once inside, this proves to be more difficult than I expected, as this appears to be a completely separate garage and there is no entrance back into regular parking.

Well shit. Could this be any more frustrating?!

This has been such an incredibly stressful day, and I just need to stop moving for a moment and relax. So, I find a parking spot in the corner and just put the tank in park.

I sigh, resting my head on the headrest. My anxiety has been on edge since I boarded my flight in Miami. I have been dreading this trip for weeks—months really.

I know that all my family is here, and while I am looking forward to seeing them, there is one person who also happens to be here that I am not looking forward to seeing at all—my ex-fiancé, Colton.

I pull the visor down above me and look at my reflection. My eyes are red, and the bags underneath them are most certainly due to the fact that I did not sleep well last night.

Or really any of last week.

It really is just my luck that Colton also happens to be my cousin Ryan's best friend since grade school. He's also incredibly close with my family. So naturally, when Ryan got engaged, one of the first people he asked to stand up in his wedding was Colton.

And this wedding is in five days, here in Chicago. Which is why I am also here.

Lucky me.

I already know that everyone is going to be pressuring me to get back together with Colton. My mother, father, aunts, and uncles have all been very vocal in recent months of their hopes for a reconciliation between us. I guess it's technically no different from the reconciliation they've been pushing for over two years now.

I close my eyes and take a deep breath.

This is not going to be easy. None of this will be easy. But you can do this.

I have my reasons for leaving Colton and they haven't changed. Some things are just unforgivable.

I need to pull myself together. I have worked too hard to get over him, and I just need to rise above it.

And if none of that works, perhaps we will just tase his ass.
I laugh as I finger the taser in my purse.

A year ago, my mother, ever the worrier, suggested that if I was going to 'insist on being on my own' that I at least start carrying some sort of protection. She originally suggested I get a gun, but being that I'd never even held one, let alone fired one, it felt like too much of a stretch.

So, I had settled on a self-defense class and a taser. One shot had 100,000 volts and could take down a grown man. That was good enough for me.

I briefly consider the image of 100,000 volts shooting into Colton, and giggle to myself.

I should probably get checked in though.

I grab my purse and water bottle, and start getting my things together. However, just as I am closing the trunk, I suddenly hear a loud *boom* and the sound of hinges on a squeaky door swinging open.

"Get away from me!" A child's voice rings out through the garage.

I whip my head around searching for the source of the voice in trouble. The commotion is coming from the corner with the exit sign leading to the hotel entrance.

A little brown-haired girl is running between the cars, trying to get away from a big greasy man with a neck tattoo.

"Come here missy," he shouts at her. "Don't run, your dad sent me to get you!"

I step behind another car, surveying the situation.

What the hell is going on?

The hairs on the back of my neck stand on end. Something doesn't feel right about this.

"No! I don't know you!" She yells as she darts behind another car.

I don't know what's going on, but I do know this grown man is chasing this poor child and she is genuinely terrified.

"Get over here you little brat!"

Something is definitely not right.

He lunges at her, catching her in his arms. She lets out the kind of scream that sends chills down my spine.

"Gotcha!" He cackles to himself as she kicks and yells, but he quickly puts a hand over her mouth to silence her.

Now it is blindingly obvious: I am witnessing a child abduction.

I have to do something.

"Hey! Excuse me!" I bellow through the garage and begin toward him.

He stops and briefly turns to look at me, before deciding to ignore me.

"Put that child down," I say, trying to hide the fact my voice is shaking a bit. "I heard her, she doesn't know you!"

"Fuck off lady," he snaps. "If you know what's good for you, you'll mind your business."

He turns around and heads toward a large white van with tinted windows.

"I will not! Let her go now or I will call the police!"

He laughs and continues walking away from me. All the while the little girl in his arms keeps squirming and kicking.

What the hell do I do?

My body is shaking with adrenaline, but I know I have to hold my ground if I have any hope of stopping him.

"Hey! I said stop!"

But he's not listening. All of a sudden, I feel myself moving before I know what I am doing. I throw my water bottle at him, and by some miracle it whacks him square on the back of the head.

Holy shit!

He stumbles, a bit disoriented from the blow. He recoils and drops the little girl.

"Ahh! You *fucking* bit me! You little shit!"

She seized her opportunity! Smart girl!

"Come here sweetheart!" I call to her.

She bolts straight for me.

I take her hand and we crouch down behind a nearby car, away from the main alley. She looks up at me with absolute terror in her eyes, but I place my finger to my lips, signifying that we have to be quiet.

"That's it," the man says, pulling out a gun. "Now you're *both* dead!"

Holy Crap! Why wouldn't he just leave? Why is he trying to kill us?

I do not have time to process any of this because I'm now aware that we are in serious danger. I frantically look around for some way out. The problem is, the man with the neck tattoo and the gun is between us and the exit, which is at least eight cars away.

Our only advantage is he has no idea where we are in the garage. So still holding the hand of the little girl, I slowly move us along the front of another car, keeping him in my sights.

"I'm scared," she whimpers softly.

"It's okay, we are okay," I whisper, trying to calm both of us down. "We are going to be okay. We just have to be really quiet, and everything will be alright."

But I'm not sure that's actually true.

We are now trapped in a tiny garage with an angry kidnapper with a gun, who is actively searching for us.

"I'm not in the mood for your fucking games!" He yells, firing a bullet into the ceiling. The bullet hits the overhead light, causing it to shatter.

The little girl clings to me.

"Shh shh. It's okay sweetheart, we are going to be fine," I whisper, stroking her hair and quickly scanning our surroundings.

Think Natalie!

When the guy with the neck tattoo shot the light, he cut off half the light in the room, which is good for hiding, but has also made it harder to see.

I look at my car, but I know it's too far away.

I think about calling 911, but I know we don't have that kind of time. We need to get out of here *now*. The entrance door to the hotel is just a few cars ahead, but I would need a hotel key card to even open it.

I haven't even checked-in yet, and somehow I am in the garage with an armed gunman and a parentless child.

How is this shit even possible?

But, then I notice that next to the door is a fire alarm.

Oh my god! The fire alarm!

I know that big hotels like this have massive fire alarm systems and protocols. On top of making loads of noise, there is a chance that pulling it might even unlock it as it could be considered an exit door to the outside.

And even if that does not work, it will at the very least send a lot of hotel staff in this direction to evaluate the situation, which hopefully would be enough to scare this crazy guy off.

But we need to get there first, and the gunman has not made any signs of giving up his search for us.

Why is he so determined?

Now that I have a fraction of a plan, I need a distraction. I need to get him out of our way long enough to allow us to run to the door and pull the alarm.

Just as I am asking myself what I could use as a distraction, I look down and see an empty soda can by my foot.

This will do.

I move us along another car, keeping him in my sights but keeping us out of his. As he searches behind another car, I turn to the little girl.

"Do you see the fire alarm? When I tell you to run, you need to run to it and pull. Hopefully, it will make that door open, and if it does you run inside as fast as you can, until you find a grownup, okay?"

She stares at me, her big brown eyes filled with fear.

"We are going to be fine," I say, cupping her face with my hand. "You just have to get to that fire alarm, and I will be right behind you."

In truth, I'm not sure if both of us will make it inside before the gunman hears the door open, but my hope is that at least *she* might have a chance to get to safety.

Speaking of Mr. Neck Tattoo, he is moving row by row, checking one side of the garage then the other…and he is getting closer.

We're out of time.

As he approaches our side of the garage, I move us around the side of another car, and wait anxiously for the right moment.

I have to time this perfectly.

I wait until his eyes are looking towards our side of the garage before chucking the can as hard as I can in the opposite direction.

This is it.

I hear the can clatter off of another car and watch as he whips his head around.

"Where the fuck are you?!" He yells, sprinting to the other side of the garage, following the bait.

"Go!" I whisper to her.

She takes off running for the door, and I follow behind her keeping an eye on Mr. Neck Tattoo, who is still checking the other side of the garage. She hits the wall with the alarm and pulls it down. Immediately, screeching loud sirens and lights go off everywhere.

But the door has not unlocked.

"Damnit!" I whisper, as I yank it twice before giving up.

We are trapped.

Over the sound of the blaring sirens, I hear two shots ring out and the exit sign bulb over our heads explodes, sending shards of glass sprinkling down on top of us.

Neck Tattoo is shooting at us.

We have nowhere to run, so I push the little girl underneath the front of the nearest parked car, getting her out of view. I crouch down beside her shielding her with my body. I reach into my purse and put my hand on my taser. I fear he will kill us before I can use it, but that is all I have.

This is it. I am going to die here.

I wrap myself around the little girl, pulling her close to me as tightly as I can and brace myself when I hear footsteps approaching.

Suddenly, I hear a loud bang as the door opens, and more gunshots ring out. I close my eyes waiting for the bullets to hit us. But they do not.

There's more gunshots, squealing tires, shouting, and a crash. Followed by more squealing tires.

Then there is nothing but the sirens. My ears are ringing, and I have no idea what is going on.

I feel someone touch my shoulder, and instinctively I jump to my feet and fire my taser. It lands straight into the chest of a man, and he falls to the ground convulsing.

But this man is not Mr. Neck Tattoo.

This man is much younger and dressed in all black. Strong hands rip the taser from mine, and I find myself face to face with a much older man, who is significantly bigger than the guy I have just tased.

"You are *not* going to touch this child!" I yell with all of my remaining courage and punch the man square in the face. I feel his nose crack under my fist. I try to land another, but his hand catches mine before I can connect a second time.

"Ma'am! Please! I'm here to help!" He yells back at me. "We're all here to help!"

I look around and see several other men, all wearing the same outfit. My heart is pounding, my legs are shaking, and I can barely catch my breath.

I'm not sure if I'm actually safe, but I know I have just witnessed someone try to kidnap this child.

"Ethan!" The little girl shouts as she crawls out from under the car. She throws her arms around his legs and starts sobbing.

Okay, at least she knows him.

I stand there panting for a moment, the adrenaline coursing through my veins, and then suddenly my ears start ringing again, and my vision gets cloudy.

"Ma'am? Are you okay? Ma'am?"

The last thing I remember is the feeling of strong arms around me, and then everything goes black.

I wake up to a ceiling fan circling above me, and a terrible pain in my right hand. I'm lying on a leather couch, and there is a cool cloth on my forehead.

What the…?

"Ma'am?" A voice says, startling me.

"What's going on? Where am I?"

My right-hand hurts like hell. I stretch out my fingers.

"It's alright, you're here at the Hotel Jefferson."

Oh okay, well at least that's good, that's where I was trying to be.

"What happened?" I ask, sitting up.

I slowly start to look at the room around me and realize I'm in an office. The walls are a charcoal gray, and the wood furniture is a dark cedar. The place smells of sandalwood… and cologne.

"That's what we're trying to figure out."

I focus my eyes on the man in front of me. He's older, probably in his late fifties. His strong muscular frame is clothed in all black, minus a Hotel Jefferson name tag with 'Ethan White–Head of Security' written underneath. He also has a bruise forming on his left eye, and evidence of a recent broken nose that had perhaps been reset.

Oh. That's right…

It all starts coming back to me. The garage, the little girl, the neck tattoo, the gunshots, the taser and my fist landing a punch to someone's face. Presumably, *his* face.

"Oh my God," I say, wincing. "Did I do *that*?"

He stares at me for a moment before a small smirk breaks his lips, amused.

"Yes, first broken nose I've had in decades."

"If it makes you feel any better, you have a pretty hard face." I say stretching out my fingers on my right hand again which is incredibly swollen. "I am so sorry. I was just so rattled. I wasn't sure who you were," I say, my voice shaking.

"It's fine."

"That man… that man in the garage with the neck tattoo, did you see him?"

He nods.

"Yes, we did."

"He tried to kidnap that little girl, and I was just trying to stop him. But instead of him running off, he started shooting at us." I say, feeling the panic rising in my chest.

I start to hyperventilate, but the man in front of me raises his hand gently.

"Miss Tyler... it's okay."

"No, it's not okay...what the hell happened? I mean, all of that was real, right? Like, I was *shot* at today!"

"Take a few deep breaths."

Yes. That is the short answer.

All of that had happened, and I remember all of it now in vivid detail. The panic, the pounding of my heart, and the little girl clinging to me in terror.

"The little girl..." I ask. "Where is she? Is she safe?"

"Yes, Miss Tyler. She is safe with her father," he says with a smile, as he places a hand on mine. "Because of you."

Oh, thank God.

"Can I get you anything?"

"Wait, you called me Miss Tyler..." I say. "How do you—?"

"When you fainted, I brought you inside and found your wallet. We've already verified you have a reservation with us this evening."

"I fainted," I say more as a statement than a question.

Well, some gallant hero I am.

He nods as I stomach my embarrassment that I passed out in front of him, and he had to carry me through the hotel.

"I'm sorry, I had an early flight. I missed breakfast this morning."

...And dinner last night.

He stands up and silently walks out of the room. He returns momentarily with a bag of pretzels, a Sprite, and a small bag of ice.

"For your mean right hook," he says with a faint smile.

"Thank you."

I wrap my hand in the ice and wince from the pain. I realize that punching someone in real life has no comparison to practice-punching in self-defense class. None whatsoever.

I open the pretzels and pop one into my mouth, my hands still shaking.

"Now Miss Tyler—" he starts to say before I hear a commotion in the hallway.

Suddenly the office door swings open with a bang, making me jump, and causing me to spill a bit of the soda on the carpet.

"I want new cameras in the whole fucking building! *Immediately!*" The man in the doorway bellows down the hall. "And fire that fucking tutor! I want her out of this building before I leave this room!"

Then the door slams shut, making me jump again. The angry shouting man stands fuming with his back to me, his broad shoulders tensed against his suit coat.

"Miss Tyler," Ethan says softly. "May I present, Mr. Jaxon Pace."

Chapter Four

JAXON

How the fuck did this happen?

I take a few deep breaths.

I need to calm down before I put someone's head through a wall. I am ready to blow. I turn to the people in my office, and that is when her big green eyes suddenly meet mine.

A stunningly beautiful girl, with a small frame and messy blonde hair stares back at me, wide-eyed.

This is the woman who saved my child? No way. I do not believe it.

I mean, it's obvious some sort of altercation has happened—her jeans have grease stains on them, her hand is wrapped in ice, and her white button up blouse has dirt all over it. But there's just no way she could have pulled off what Ethan said she did.

She's just too… pretty.

"Sir, this is Miss—" Ethan starts to introduce her.

"Tyler." I finish for him.

"Nice to meet you." She smiles, looking at me warily.

Her gaze does not leave mine and it makes me slightly uncomfortable. So many thoughts are racing through my head, and I am immediately suspicious of her.

Is she from another 'family?' But if so, why haven't I heard of her?

Maybe she's an undercover federal agent?

Again, her eyes meet mine and I feel my blood heat in a way I have never felt before.

"Miss Tyler, do you remember anything about the man from the garage? Anything you can tell us would be helpful." Ethan says calmly.

"Um, he had a neck tattoo. It looked like some sort of snake or a dragon type thing," she says to Ethan. "Oh, and he had a white van with tinted windows."

She glances up at me again.

The magnetic pull I have to her deep green eyes makes me apprehensive. I see beautiful women all the time, but I've never experienced this effect. Something does not add up.

She must be connected to someone or something bigger. Why else would she be there in that garage when all of that was happening? And *she* was able to stop a kidnapping? All by herself? No, It doesn't make sense.

I feel like I'm supposed to believe that she somehow just 'coincidentally' found herself in my path.

But I will not fall for it.

I cannot be stupid enough to let my guard down for a pair of pretty eyes.

"Miss Tyler, what were you doing in my executive garage?" I ask, interrupting their exchange.

I need to know.

"I'm sorry?" she asks innocently, looking up at me.

Nice try, sweetheart.

"I think Miss Tyler was just about to explain…" Ethan tries to interject.

She's definitely too pretty.

She looks like she could be on television—maybe she's in the media?

"Are you a journalist? Were you there trying to get some inside cover story on me?"

"What?" she asks, confused. "No… I'm—"

"So, what are you, police? Undercover?"

I will break her.

"No, I'm a private nurse," she says flustered. "I'm just in town for the week. For a family wedding."

A nurse?! No fucking way.

Now I *really* do not believe her.

"Jaxon, perhaps we should just let the girl tell us what happened?" Ethan sighs sarcastically, I can tell he does not approve of my aggressive approach.

"What were you doing in my executive garage?" I ask again, this time more forceful.

"Excuse me?" she retorts, and I can hear the frustration mounting in her voice now.

A flash of anger streaks across her eyes, but this could just be an act.

"Oh, I'm sorry, do you not understand the question?" I snap.

"Jaxon…" Ethan cautions.

"We checked your information against what we have in the system." I say, leaning back against the desk and putting my hands in my pockets. "You booked a standard two-bed room for the week. That doesn't exactly speak 'executive' to me. And there are no business conference room reservations with your name on it. So, I will ask you again—what were *you* doing in *my* executive level garage?"

None of this makes sense to me, and I'm surprised Ethan is buying this bullshit. Regardless, I will get to the bottom of it.

"How dare you!" she scoffs, standing to her feet. "Are you seriously interrogating *me* right now? I can't fucking believe this!"

Neither can I.

"What. Were. You. Doing—" I start to repeat, slowly accentuating each word, but I am interrupted.

"It was a fucking accident!" She shouts at me. "I didn't mean to pull into *that* garage, but the traffic practically *pushed* me into that lane, and I didn't mean to end up there!"

What?

"But fortunately for you, that *is* where I ended up! In your executive garage, okay? I tried to get back to regular parking, but that was not an option once I was inside the executive garage."

Her face is red, and she is glaring at me.

"And then I saw what was happening and tried to help! Because I felt it was the right thing to do. That's all!"

She has to be lying.

"You expect me to believe that a—what was it you said again?" I ask, stepping closer to her. "A nurse? *Accidentally* just finds herself in my executive garage, thwarts a kidnapping against an armed gunman, by using a fire alarm, tases one of my men and breaks the nose of my head of security?!"

"Yes! Because that's what happened!" She shouts, stepping closer to me, her hands raised in anger.

I have to hand it to her, if she is lying, she is really committed to this story.

"And what, pray tell, made you even think to pull the fire alarm?" I ask, narrowing my eyes at her.

"Because, *asshole*, my best friend works for a hotel in Miami—and she told me once that big hotels like this have elaborate alarm systems, and I knew that at the very least someone would come see what was going on!" She shouts back at me.

"So—"

"So, instead of interrogating me as if I had anything to do with the attempted kidnapping of *that* little girl, I think you all should be thanking me!"

"We are," Ethan says, shooting me a look. "We are very *grateful.*"

How? How is any of this possible?

"And where is this child?!" She continues. "Where the hell are her parents?"

"You're looking at him."

The moment the words leave my lips, I admittedly feel a bit guilty. I trusted a stranger with my child, and she let me down. But at the end of the day, Jessica's safety is *my* responsibility, and I failed her.

Miss Tyler narrows her eyes at me.

"So… what you're saying is that she is *your* daughter?" she says quietly.

Shit.

"Yes."

"Miss Tyler, if we may—" Ethan tries again to diffuse the situation, but it's immediately clear that I have mistakenly dropped a grenade on this bonfire.

"Where the hell were *you*?!" She snaps, moving closer to me. "Why was this little girl roaming unattended, around a massive hotel, and running out an exit near a busy street?"

I swallow hard, struggling to come up with an explanation.

Wait a minute, when did this conversation get turned around on me?

"I'm in the process of getting to the bottom of that, I already fired her tutor, who was supposed to be watching her—"

"No! I'm not talking about a damn tutor! I'm talking about *you*! She's your child! She is your responsibility! And she was almost abducted right out from under you because of your own ineptitude and neglect!"

Her words are daggers propelling the guilt I already feel.

"I do *not* neglect my child!" I growl back at her, stepping towards her.

But Miss Tyler does not back down, instead she steps in front of me pushing herself back in my face.

"Says the man who almost lost her today to some thug!" she scoffs. "Where is she now, huh? Off with another 'babysitter' because you're too busy berating your hotel guests?!"

I try to come up with a reply but cannot.

The simple truth is I have nothing to say in rebuttal because Miss Tyler has rendered me speechless.

Well this has never happened before.

We both stand in silence before I relent, and just answer her question. I walk over to the door beside the desk and open it, motioning her to look inside.

She says nothing, instead glaring at me as if I am some hideous monster with three heads. However, at my insistence, she eventually steps over and looks inside. In the adjoining conference room, Jessica sits at the table, swinging her feet and happily coloring while listening to a movie on her iPad. Almost as if none of the afternoon's events had happened.

The resilience of children is astounding at times.

She looks up from her coloring and smiles at me.

"Hi Daddy!"

But the minute she sees Miss Tyler, on the other hand, her eyes get wide, and she immediately jumps up and runs to her, wrapping her arms around her legs.

What the fuck?

I lock eyes with Ethan, who looks equally stunned, as does a wide-eyed Miss Tyler.

"Hey troublemaker, are you doing okay?" She says to Jessica somewhat breathlessly.

Probably from yelling at me.

Jessica nods at her with a smile.

"Sweetheart, would you mind waiting just a minute for Daddy to finish his conversation?" I ask.

She nods, briefly smiling up at Miss Tyler again before releasing her and heading back to her crayons.

I close the door, finding myself back in the heavy awkwardness that now permeates the silent room.

Ethan crosses his arms and shoots a reproachful look at me. He's disappointed. *Clearly.*

"Well," he says softly, "now that we've covered that..."

"I... uh... well, I'm sorry." I say, clearing my throat.

For some odd reason, I find it slightly difficult to look up at Miss Tyler, that twinge of guilt returning.

But she says nothing and refuses to make eye contact with me either.

"Can I please," she whispers, sounding exhausted, "just check-in to my room? I've had an exceptionally long day."

"Yes." I say, shifting slightly. "But, I'd like to thank you. Please, let me upgrade you. We have some newly renovated suites that—"

"That's unnecessary," she snaps, cutting me off. "I didn't do it in hopes of a reward. This might shock you, but sometimes people do the right thing, simply because it's just the right thing to do. Besides, I've just seen what your gratitude is worth Mr. Pace, and I think I'd rather stick with my 'standard two-bed room' as you so politely put it."

She glares at me again before grabbing her purse and walking out of the office, slamming the door hard behind her.

"Well done, old boy," Ethan sighs, smacking my shoulder.

He quickly follows after her, leaving me standing in the middle of my office unable to move.

What the fuck just happened?

But I already know the answer to that question:

Natalie saved Jessica.

Jessica likes Natalie.

Natalie does not like me.

And not only does she not like me, she just *scolded* me like a child. No one has ever spoken to me like that, especially a woman.

I sit back on the edge of the desk, staring at the door.

I don't know what to think of Natalie Tyler, but I do know she's unlikely to leave my thoughts anytime soon.

Chapter Five

Natalie

"You are all set, Miss Tyler. We hope you enjoy your stay." The pretty desk clerk says to me as she hands me my room keys.

"Thank you," I nod as I put my license back into my wallet.

But when I look up, I find her still staring at me. In fact, all of the desk clerks are staring at me, but I am actively trying to ignore them and just leave as quickly as I can.

And why shouldn't they be staring?

I'm sure they've all heard what happened, or at least some version of the events.

I mean, I was the woman who set off all the fire alarms.

I am also still covered in dirt from hiding under cars, and I am praying that I do not see anyone I know. I am a spectacle and I need to get away from here.

I start to walk away before I remember something.

"I'm sorry, can you also please make sure that I have a 'Do Not Identify' note on my file? I don't want anyone, specifically another guest staying in the hotel, to be given my direct room number under *any* circumstances."

The girl who was just helping me looks confused, but just as I start to panic, an older woman steps forward with a smile.

"Yes, Miss Tyler, that is no problem at all. I will add that to your file."

I know it is extreme, but I do not need Colton knowing my room number and trying to pester me.

I walk my luggage towards the elevators, press my floor, and thank my lucky stars when the doors close, and I am alone.

Any more direct human contact today and I might just explode.

When I finally get to put my stuff down in my room, it almost feels surreal. I sit down on the bed and take a deep breath. There was a moment I was not sure I would even make it *here.*

To my simple, 'standard two-bed room.'

I cringe, remembering the snobby way Jaxon Pace said it.

Asshole.

I glance at my phone and see I have three missed calls from my mother.

Ugh, of course.

But I know that if I don't check in with her, she's likely to call a dozen more times, or file some missing person report.

"Hey where have you been?!" She asks immediately when she picks up the call. "Your flight landed hours ago, and no one has heard from you. I've been so worried! Is everything alright?"

I take a deep breath.

Over the years, I have learned how to handle these conversations with my mother. I know that if I tell her what really happened this afternoon, it will only make her more paranoid about my safety, and further convince her of my inability to take care of myself.

"I'm fine," I say, unzipping my suitcase. "I just got in my room. I got held up a bit."

That might be the understatement of the year.

As I say this, I flex my right hand again. The swelling has gone down a bit, but everything moves, so it is likely that nothing is broken, just really sore.

"Oh, that I understand, traffic was a nightmare!"

I put her on speaker and let her drone on about their flight and their trip as I continue to settle into my room.

"Well, hey listen, we are just getting ready to go out for a quick bite at this restaurant that Colton found…"

Her voice trails off, but the mere mention of his name makes me immediately flinch.

"Have you eaten?" she asks sweetly. "If not, you should come join us!"

Umm… no. Not today.

Especially given everything I have been through today.

"Nat?" she asks, and I realize I have not responded to her request.

"Sorry, no. I'm good. But thank you."

"Oh, come on. It will be fun!" She persists.

I can see we are starting already with this crap.

"Yeah, no," I say, a bit more firmly. "I'm just not feeling well, I have a bit of a headache."

"Colton said he's been trying to reach you, you know," she says, completely ignoring what I just said. "Have you... spoken to him?"

"No, mom, I have not," I say, my annoyance now clear in my voice.

"Natalie... maybe you should just—"

"Mom," I cut her off, exasperated. "I'm not doing this right now, okay? I am really not in the mood."

"Okay sweetheart, I don't mean to push," she says innocently.

Yes, you do. That's exactly what you were meaning to do.

"Enjoy your night, I will see you guys for breakfast tomorrow."

I fall backwards onto the bed as I hang up the phone. This day has been a hurricane of drama, and I don't have the energy to deal with anything regarding Colton because I'm still processing what happened a few hours ago.

Well, I'm trying to anyway.

I risked my life today, for a child I don't even know.

And that *man*! That snobbish, entitled, ungrateful, rude man having the audacity to accuse me of being involved in his daughter's attempted kidnapping?!

Jaxon Pace was quite possibly the biggest ass I've ever met. But, my God, he was...handsome.

No, not handsome. What am I? Sixty years old?

He was *hot*. Extremely hot.

Regardless of what a jerk he turned out to be, I am certain I have never seen a man so beautiful in person before. Tall and muscular, chestnut brown hair, a strong chiseled jawline. And those striking blue eyes, a bright icy blue, like the first frost on a winter's morning.

Well, I guess that makes sense, he certainly had been cold... frigid even.

But as much as I hate myself for dwelling on it, I can't get Jaxon's eyes out of my head. His gaze was paralyzing, making me feel things I had never felt before. Never before had a man had that effect on me. There was no denying he was sexy.

How can someone be so infuriatingly hot and cold at the same damn time?

Money, probably.

Just another entitled rich asshole with a power complex that helps him get away with talking down to everyone. I could tell that just by the way he had tried to intimidate me.

He had succeeded a little at first, especially with his looks disarming me so quickly, but in the end, I refused to give him the satisfaction.

"I want to apologize on behalf of Mr. Pace, Miss Tyler. I assure you, he didn't mean to be so crude. He isn't in the best frame of mind right now. He's just worked up from nearly losing his daughter."

That's what Ethan said when he caught up with me in the lobby. But I was worked up too, after trying to *save* his daughter.

He didn't need to be so angry, and he definitely had no right to make angry look so hot. That's just uncalled for, and mildly unfair.

I found myself staring at the way his chiseled jaw tensed, or the way his muscles strained against his shirt. It had made it difficult to think straight, and it felt slightly intoxicating.

No. Screw this, I do not want to think about him anymore.

I decide I need to wash Jaxon Pace out of my head. Immediately. Jaxon *and* all the grease and dirt I am still covered in.

I grab my toiletries bag and head to the shower, turning it on full blast. As the hot water fills the room with steam, I stare at myself in the mirror.

Jesus, I look like hell.

It's mildly disappointing, considering exactly how hard I had tried to look *good* today.

My brain taunts me.

And why is that Natalie? Was it just in case you ran into your ex-fiancé in the lobby?

It was true. I didn't want to see Colton, but if I did run into him, I wanted to like a full smoke show to try and recover some of my still-damaged pride.

But now, I realize how mildly desperate that sounds.

I step into the shower and hope it will wash off some of this truly icky feeling off my skin. A twinge of regret now teasing me.

Was coming here a mistake?

I had so many expectations for today. I had imagined it for weeks, preparing for every eventuality. But when it came down to the actual day, nothing had gone the way I planned. Not a single thing.

I wanted the Hollywood Movie Moment.

I wanted Colton to see me happy, confident, my hair flowing flawlessly in the wind, and in that moment some part of him would regret what he did to me.

I wanted some part of him to *suffer* for it. The way I had suffered.

Two years ago, I was in the middle of planning our wedding. The invitations had gone out, the cake had been tasted, the caterers had been paid.

But then three weeks before our wedding date, it all came crashing down... with a single text.

One text, from a number I did not recognize, popped up on his phone while he was in the shower. This tiny thing had led to the worst discovery of my life, and the end of my six-year relationship with Colton. Texts, pictures, hotel rendezvous receipts...

I discovered he had an entirely separate life going on right under my nose for years. Multiple affairs, with multiple women, from all over the city.

Meanwhile, this asshole slept next to me every night, and allowed me to plan our wedding, knowing full well he was cheating on me.

What followed was a literal nightmare.

My entire life fell apart in a matter of days. The wedding was canceled, the guests were notified, and I found I could not bear to live in a city that held so many memories of Colton.

So, I packed up my life, and moved to Miami where my best friend lived, and used the rest of my savings to buy a house there.

But when it came to telling my family about what had actually transpired with Colton, I couldn't bring myself to do it. He was part of my family, and while I figured they could deal with the end of our relationship, I feared the loss of him entirely would hurt them far more than it would hurt him.

In an effort to try and protect them, I decided instead to leave out the part about him sleeping with half the women in the city, and just tell them that it wasn't going to work out between Colton and I. I hoped this would deliver a less devastating blow.

But, they were devastated anyway.

And Colton, in true narcissistic fashion, didn't even own up to what he had done. He pretended that he was just as shocked as they were, and had no idea why I called off the wedding. He claimed I had simply gotten 'cold feet' and relished *my* family's sympathy.

Asshole.

I could never forgive him. Colton had broken us. He had broken *me.*

I needed to heal, and I found that the vibrant and sunny Miami was the place to do just that. I found a job, and made a happy, quiet little life for myself. And, since Colton never allowed a dog in the house, one of the first things I did was adopt one. A little one-eyed rescue Pug named Cyclops.

I was happy. And I was healing.

But my family, on the other hand, never healed. As time went on, it got harder and harder to tell them, so I just…didn't. And because they never heard the truth why we ended, they didn't get answers, and they didn't get closure.

Now I'm sure most of them just think I'm being unreasonable. They probably still hold on to the hope that Colton and I might still fall back in love with each other.

And Colton does too. I'm sure he's hoping that my family gathering for Ryan's wedding will provide enough pressure to give him a second chance.

But that's never going to happen.

I'm not the same person who left that small town two years ago. And I need to remember this.

I need to remember exactly why *I* came here: to see my family and celebrate with Ryan on his special day.

If I'm going to survive this trip in one piece, I need to stop feeling like I must prove how well I'm doing without Colton.

I have nothing to prove to *anyone*.

And, to be fair, I did some seriously badass things today.

On top of everything that happened in the garage with the little girl and the gunman, I scolded a man who likely makes ten times my salary with his eyes closed.

A very, very, good-looking man.

I take a deep breath as I stand letting the water cascade down my body, thinking about his eyes. I just can't seem to get them out of my head. Or the way his gaze had raked over my body. It felt almost *sinful*.

I run my hands through my hair, remembering the way his suit coat stretched across his broad shoulder blades and clung to his biceps. I also vividly recall how good his cologne smelled when we were standing inches from each other… or maybe that was his aftershave?

Oh my God, what am I doing?

I didn't spend the last two years of my life healing and repairing, to find myself obsessing over another impossible, self-absorbed, train wreck of a man.

I turn off the water and grab a towel, simultaneously scolding my brain for even allowing me to dwell on the gorgeous Jaxon Pace in any capacity.

It shouldn't matter if he's gorgeous, because he's insufferable. And he's a father for crying out loud.

Which likely means he probably has some equally gorgeous wife somewhere.

However, I did happen to notice that Mr. Pace was *not* wearing a wedding ring.

And, when I asked where Jessica's 'parents' were, he said "You are looking at *him*."

Which might mean he is a single parent.

Probably divorced then. Which isn't surprising considering what an ass he is.

But even if he were single, it's not like a guy like that would ever think twice about a girl like me. I'm sure that guys like him only date cheerleaders or beauty queens.

"Natalie Tyler!" I yell out loud, grabbing my hair dryer, having caught myself still thinking about Jaxon Pace. "Stop this now!"

I briefly consider breaking my foot off and beating my senses back into my mutinous brain, but think better of it considering my hand is still on the mend.

I can't afford to sacrifice any other body parts right now.

I have enough on my plate with just surviving this week to be thinking about a man I could never have.

"Get your shit together!" I say to myself, climbing into bed.

However, despite my resignation, I find myself Googling his name five minutes later. A barrage of news articles instantly pop up.

"Setting the *Pace*—Billionaire Jaxon Pace, 34, leads the way on new Eco-Friendly hotels by 2030."

"Most Mysterious Bachelor? Jaxon Pace keeps low profile!"

"Jaxon Pace rebuilds Veterans Memorial and pledges funding to local Children's Hospital."

Pages and pages of articles, praising Jaxon Pace for his philanthropy, speculating as to his relationship status, or talking about his various business accomplishments seem to go on forever.

He seems to be quite a guy.

Too bad he's also quite an asshole.

I finally turn out the light and settle under the comforter, vowing to put my thoughts of Jaxon Pace to bed at the same time.

But as I close my eyes, I find myself dreaming of his deep blue eyes, drowning me slowly in their icy depths.

Chapter Six

JAXON

I sit alone in my darkened penthouse living room watching the TV on mute. It is just past 11 p.m. and a 50-year-old bottle of Caol Ila Scotch sits beside me.

This is how I am coping.

My men are still tracking the perpetrator, but have no new information for me, so I have sent them away. Truth be told, I was mildly afraid I might strangle one of them in my rage.

I need to be alone. I feel murderous.

Someone tried to kidnap my fucking daughter today.

No matter how I try to recover from that fact, I can't seem to get past it.

Yes, I know Jessica is safe. But it's not enough.

Thankfully, once she was back at my side, she was fine, and had a relatively normal rest of the day. She's currently sleeping in her bedroom fifteen feet from me, silent as a lamb. I know this, because I have gotten up six times to check to see that she is still there.

She could've been somewhere else tonight, somewhere much worse...

I take another drink. I know, perhaps better than most, exactly how awful some people can be, and it's not helping me calm down.

I need to silence these thoughts. Therefore, I am drinking.

And what about *her*? The woman who saved Jessica today. Who put herself, woefully unprepared, between my child and an armed gunman determined to take her away from me.

What do I make of her?

Her file sits before me.

Everything I need to know about this woman is in this file. From her mortgage payments on her house in Miami, to her high school report cards, college transcripts, her extensive family tree, employment history, and a list of every man she's ever dated.

All things I now know, because I have spent the last few hours of silence reviewing every scrap of information Ethan could get for me on the mysterious Natalie Tyler.

Even though Ethan is not currently speaking to me, still furious over the way I had treated Natalie. *Strangely* furious.

But now, after pouring over all these details with a fine-toothed comb, and desperately trying to find even the smallest hint of dirt, I understand why Ethan thinks I was utterly in the wrong in how I treated her.

Natalie Tyler is 100% clean. And I am an asshole.

But we already knew that.

"Daddy?" Jessica's voice suddenly rings out in the dark room, making me jump.

"Hey, Jessibear, what are you doing up?"

But as she steps closer, I notice she has tear stains on her cheeks.

"I had a nightmare that the bad man tried to take me again," she says, her gentle voice cracking.

Her words feel like a searing hot knife plunging through my chest. I pull her onto my lap, wrapping her in my arms and wiping away her tears.

If I have any heart left at all, I can feel it crumbling to pieces.

My one job is to protect her...and I have failed.

"Sweetheart, the bad man will *never* take you away," I say, tucking her hair behind her ear and kissing her forehead. "I promise."

My beautiful girl yawns, clearly still exhausted. She wiggles out of my arms and lays down on the couch next to me, resting her head on my thigh. I pull the blanket off the cushion behind me and wrap it around her.

"Daddy?" she asks me softly. "Can Miss Tyler come to play with me tomorrow?"

What? Did she just...

My brain debates whether I just hallucinated what she just said, and I suddenly wish it was not impaired by alcohol.

"I don't know, Jess," I say softly, trying to reconcile the fact that my daughter is actually asking me this. "She might not want to."

"Why not?" she asks, rolling on her back and looking up at me.

Shit. How do I answer that?

"I think Daddy… made her mad."

"How?"

"Well, he hurt her feelings."

Drunk me is apparently a lot more honest than I anticipated.

"So just say you're sorry. That's what you're supposed to do when you hurt someone's feelings."

My child blinks up at me with an innocence I could not replicate if I tried. But her logic is infallible.

Damnit. She's right.

"I don't know how to do that," I say softly, stroking her hair. "I barely know her."

"You should send her flowers," Jessica says with a yawn. "Girls love flowers."

She closes her eyes and before I can even process what she just said, she starts to snore against my leg.

I look down at her.

She looks so much like her mother it hurts.

Her mother, Rachel.

Rachel was the last person I apologized to, and even then, I didn't get the opportunity to say it to her face.

I had to say it to her *headstone*. After she died.

But there's not enough scotch in this penthouse to unpack that this evening.

I stare at Jessica and down the rest of my glass.

There was no denying it, Jessica was right. Ethan was right. And I was wrong.

Natalie Tyler deserves an apology.

But how?

I look down at my sleeping child and smile.

"Flowers, huh? You know what Jess, that's a great idea."

"What the hell do you mean you can't give me her room number?!" I snap angrily at the front desk manager.

"As I said, Sir," Sally, my indispensable, but occasionally stubborn, hotel manager replies. "Miss Tyler has a 'Do Not Identify' request on her reservation file."

"What the fuck does that mean to me?!"

"It means, Sir," she says firmly. "That I cannot give you any of her information."

"That's ridiculous!"

"She doesn't want to be disturbed by another guest of the hotel, Sir."

"Sally, need I remind you that I *own* the hotel?!" I shout.

"And, Mr. Pace," she says sternly, "you also have an ongoing reservation in the penthouse."

I blink at her incredulously.

"Which means you're also, technically a *guest* of the hotel, Sir." She finishes, looking at me with satisfaction before crossing her arms across her chest.

Is she really having this argument with me right now?!

I truly do appreciate this woman. Sally has protected me, and my business, for the last eight years I have owned this hotel. She has always been someone I can rely on.

But right now, she is frustrating the hell out of me at seven in the morning and I want to hit something.

"Sally, I am just trying to deliver some fucking flowers!"

"Jesus, it's still early. Whatever could be the problem, Romeo?" I hear Ethan laugh behind me.

"Nothing!" I snap, my irritation boiling.

"Good morning, Mr. White. I was just explaining to Mr. Pace here that I cannot give him Miss Tyler's room number because Miss Tyler specifically asked for a 'Do Not Identify' to be added to her file upon check-in," Sally says politely to Ethan.

"Well, that sounds pretty self-explanatory. It also sounds like you've landed yourself pretty far in the doghouse with Miss Tyler there, bud." He laughs to himself. "But I suppose you're at least on the right track," he finishes.

"Do not fuck with me right now Ethan," I growl at him.

"Look, just leave the apology flowers here with a note, and Sally can have Miss Tyler pick them up from the desk whenever she sees her next, okay? Problem solved."

"Fine!" I say through gritted teeth.

CATALYST

I shove the flowers on the counter, and Sally pulls them behind the desk without a word.

"Now, it's time for racquetball," Ethan says, handing me my bag for our weekly game.

"Good, I want to kick your ass anyway," I snap.

"You can try, lover boy."

I might hit him for real today.

I yank the bag out of his hand, and we start down the hallway towards the racquetball courts.

However, as luck would have it, we have barely made it halfway when I see Natalie Tyler leave the gym.

She is engaged in a lively conversation with another woman, and I watch as something makes her laugh.

Fuck, she's even prettier when she smiles.

"Well, wouldn't you know. It looks like you might get your chance after all," Ethan says with a nudge. "I think I'll take the long way to the court."

He smiles with a wink, turning left down another hallway.

Instinctively, I slow down trying to put myself in her path, but immediately my throat goes dry.

Shit. What do I say?

I try to think of something clever, but I am distracted by how good she looks right now, especially in the skin-tight workout outfit she's wearing. A thin sweater covers her black crop top and her leggings hug every inch of her delicious curves, leaving extraordinarily little to the imagination.

There is no denying Natalie Tyler is a beautiful girl.

But she is approaching quickly, and I still have no idea what I am going to say.

Focus dude.

"Miss Tyler," I say loudly, as I stop in the middle of the hallway and cross my hands in front of me.

Good job, Jaxon. Real fucking subtle.

She sees me, and a look of surprise crosses her face. Followed immediately by one of disgust.

The two women approach me, although Miss Tyler looks like someone is twisting her arm off in the process. The woman she's with looks up at me, then glances back at Miss Tyler with an excited smile.

"Um, I've got to run Nat. I've got a call with the florist," she says, tapping her shoulder. "The rehearsal dinner was moved to Thursday, but we will send a card to your room with the details."

She excuses herself and walks away, smiling up at me as she walks past.

Now that is more of the reaction I'm used to.

Miss Tyler on the other hand, looks at me as if I'm some heckler that won't stop pestering her. She narrows her eyes at me and crosses her arms across her body.

"Mr. Pace," she says, her tone icy and cold.

Yikes. This might be harder than I thought.

Her immediate hostility has me on the backfoot, but somehow that just makes me even more determined to try to find a way to disarm her.

"Who was that?" I ask politely.

"Not that it's *any* of your business," she says, sighing deeply, "but that's my cousin's fiancé."

"Is that the wedding you referred to yesterday?"

"Yes," she says, sounding annoyed. "Now, what do you want?"

"Well actually, I was trying to find you, to…um…"

"To what? Tell me my car has been towed?" she snaps sarcastically as she narrows her eyes at me.

"Er, no, I…"

I have clearly underestimated how upset I made her yesterday, as this conversation is not going well.

Fuck, maybe flowers were not enough.

"I, uh, well, I've had some time to think about our conversation yesterday and I'd like to apologize. I was wondering if perhaps I could make it up to you over dinner?"

Good save.

"No," she says flatly.

Wait…what?

"No?"

I am completely stunned. People do not usually refuse me. Especially women.

Shit…Okay, what do I do now?

I scramble to think of something else.

"Okay well, I do understand you're busy… perhaps I could upgrade your room?"

"That's unnecessary," she says just as dismissively. "As I said yesterday, I'm quite happy with my perfectly *standard* two-bed room."

I think I have established that she's still *very* pissed at me.

Is this how this usually goes? Because this sucks.

"Look, I just want to apologize."

"That's also unnecessary Mr. Pace."

Now I'm starting to get frustrated.

"Okay, Miss Tyler, what exactly do you—" I start to say, but I'm suddenly interrupted by a blond-haired man with unremarkable features, who comes jogging up to us.

"Nat! Oh my God, I finally found you!"

Who the fuck is this clown?

Natalie Tyler's face is unreadable. At first she looks surprised, perhaps even uncomfortable. I briefly catch her glance my way, before smiling at the annoying cretin rudely disrupting our conversation.

"Sorry… am I interrupting?" The man says, looking at me, then back at her.

Yes, actually.

I notice that she is blushing now.

For some reason I recognize him, though I have no idea why. I try to remember the details of her file from last night.

But she wouldn't blush like that if he were just a relative.

Women usually blush when they're embarrassed, or there's some sort of a romantic connection. But I notice her stance has become more rigid and defensive.

He isn't her boyfriend, because according to social media she doesn't have one. I do remember seeing something about an engagement—a canceled engagement.

And that's when it hits me.

This is the ex-fiancé.

"No, you're not interrupting," Miss Tyler's voice jolts me from my mental rabbit hole. "Mr. Pace was just *leaving.*"

I stare at her, her eyes finding mine, and then briefly looking away. But then she looks up at me again.

Hmm…It seems I make her uncomfortable too. But in a different way.

Realizing she is not going to give me the forgiveness I seek, I pause, taking a good long look at Mr. Unremarkable.

She could certainly do better than this twat.

"Correct. I will be off. Have a lovely day, Miss Tyler," I say with a smile, excusing myself and walking away.

Let's just see what she thinks when she sees the flowers.

Perhaps she will say yes to dinner then.

I turn to go meet Ethan at the court but then I see that he is already walking down the hallway toward me, and he looks absolutely furious.

"We found the van from yesterday," he growls. "And we may also have a lead on the kidnapper's location too."

Finally, some good news.

Chapter Seven

Natalie

"Miss Tyler!"

Across the lobby the front desk manager, who also happens to be the older woman who helped me at check-in yesterday, calls me over for the *second* time today.

Oh great, now what? Is Jaxon Pace suing me for turning down his bouquet of white roses?

"Yes?"

"Hello, Miss Tyler, I just wanted to let you know," she says a bit flustered. "The gentleman who sent you the flowers this morning has gone ahead and sent you two dozen more."

Are you kidding me?

"Please, send them back. Just like the others."

"Well, that's just it, Ma'am," she says politely. "We can't. The florist will not accept them back. Also, the gentleman who sent them said that if you don't accept *these* then he is going to start sending a *dozen* more bouquets every hour, on the hour, until you do accept."

Really?!

"So that just leaves us with all these flowers you see…"

This stubborn asshole.

Jaxon Pace has to be bluffing. I mean, it's not as if he's going to keep sending flowers to his own hotel if I refuse to accept them.

"He won't do that, I promise. Please just tell him I'm not interested in his flowers… or his apology."

She opens her mouth to protest but I turn on my heel and head for the door.

Do not play chicken with me, Jaxon Pace.

According to what Colton told me this morning, the bridal party has opted for dinner at some fancy farm-to-table restaurant on the water. Afterwards, they also plan to hit up a nearby club for drinks and dancing. He also asked me, repeatedly, to join them.

But I'm not planning to attend.

Tonight I have a date with my favorite cousin—Steph. We have not seen each other since I left for Miami, and despite not knowing any of the gritty details, she still loyally stuck up for me after the break with Colton.

Steph is gorgeous. She's tall and slender, and even though she possesses the trademark blonde hair of the Tyler clan, she's hacked it off in some cute little bob cut, much to the disapproval of her mother.

Actually, knowing Steph it was likely specifically *for* the disapproval of her mother.

Which is one of the things I love most about her. She's fun, and feisty, and has the personality of a rottweiler, refusing to take crap from anyone.

So naturally, when I told her that Colton cornered me outside the gym this morning and asked me to join him tonight, she insisted we deliberately blow them off. She also insisted we make our own plan for a night on the town, just in case anyone in the family tried to guilt trip me into changing my mind.

We wander the downtown area, taking in the sights and window shopping a bit before finding a quiet little diner to grab a bite to eat. Afterwards, we got some hot cocoa by the pier and decided to meet my younger cousins for Glow in the Dark bowling.

When we leave the bowling alley our arms are thoroughly sore, but I feel lighter than I've felt in months.

This is why she's my favorite cousin. She's just easy to be around.

We are standing on a street corner waiting for the light to turn green when my phone lights up.

Colton
11:45 p.m.: Where are you? I thought you were going to come out. Come join us at Xenas for a night cap!

Steph is already reading the text over my shoulder.

"Fuck that," she says, rolling her eyes. "I heard there's a place that does Drag Queen Bingo up the street, and that sounds like *way* more fun!"

And as always, she's right.

While neither of us were particularly good at bingo, the comedian who ran the event had us in stitches the entire time.

We stayed until closing, and then we giggled all the way back to the hotel a little past two a.m.

Steph finds a bench in the valet area and sits down.

"I'll catch you in the morning, Cuz," she says, waving me on. "I'm going to smoke and call my girlfriend."

"I can wait," I protest. "I don't want to leave you out here by yourself."

"Please, I'm fine," she says, rolling her eyes. "We're in a hotel. How much danger can I be in?"

Girl if you only knew...

But, to be fair, I hadn't told Steph anything about what happened yesterday. I hadn't told anyone actually.

"Well, at least text me when you get back up to your room, okay?" I say, heading for the doors.

"Yes Mommmm!" She calls playfully as I head inside.

But as soon as I open the lobby doors, I can smell them.

Flowers. Hundreds of flowers. White roses to be exact.

And they are *everywhere.*

My heart immediately starts pounding.

Glancing around the room I notice there's six vases of white roses on the counter behind the front desk, and several more on the mantle of both giant gas fireplaces.

But it doesn't stop there.

More vases of white roses sit on every end table and console in the entire lobby. To my right, gorgeous bouquets of white roses decorate every credenza table down the hall, all the way to the ballrooms. To my left, they are on every table in the restaurant, and there's even some in the bar.

Oh my God...He really did it.

Jaxon Pace really *had* sent a dozen bouquets every hour, on the hour, exactly as he promised.

I doubt there's a single white rose left in Chicago.

It looks as if the hotel staff has just been placing the vases wherever they could find a flat surface.

But then, in the vase closest to me, I notice something that makes my heart stop in its tracks: there's a dedication card sticking out.

In fact, every bouquet has one.

No...He wouldn't.

I walk over to the table and yank out the card, my cheeks heating and my heart thumping loudly in my chest.

To the valiant Natalie Tyler,
Please accept this in honor of my full gratitude, and sincerest
apologies.
-J

My jaw hits the floor.

I quickly sprint over to the vase on the other end table and pull out its card, gasping when I see that it too has the same exact message written on it.

Oh my God...

Jaxon Pace has not only littered this entire hotel with white roses...he has put my *name* on every dedication card.

Every. Single. One.

I cannot believe this!

I immediately start to panic, realizing that if anyone in our massive wedding party just happens to get curious and look at one of these vases, I will have so much explaining to do.

"Miss Tyler!"

The front desk manager, Sally, practically shouts my name across the lobby, again, and this time she looks thoroughly annoyed. All the clerks behind the desk glance at me too.

"That's *her*!" I hear one of them say a little too loudly.

Oh shit...I'm in trouble.

I walk slowly over to the counter, feeling like a child who's

CATALYST

been summoned to the principal's office.

"Good evening, Miss Tyler." The manager says with a forced politeness that looks almost painful. "I don't mean to persist, and I know you mentioned that you wanted us to refuse, but as you can see the gentleman *has* made good on his promise. And, as I also understand, has another dozen bouquets scheduled to arrive in under forty-five minutes. Per this promise"

Oh my God...

She holds up her finger, and sneezes, wiping her nose with a tissue.

"My apologies, my allergies are going a bit crazy at the moment with all of the pollen in the air."

Shit. That's my fault.

"At this point," she continues. "We're unfortunately starting to run out of places to put them."

I immediately feel bad.

The look on the poor woman's face tells me that she's had to deal with this situation the entire time I've been gone, and she's now understandably frustrated.

"I don't want to tell you what to do, but—"

"It's fine," I say quickly. "I'll accept it…Er, them. The flowers, that is. But if I do, I'll need you to promise me that you'll take all of these cards out of these vases. Like immediately. My whole family is here and—"

"Deal," she barks, interrupting me.

She picks up what I can only assume is the latest bouquet delivery and sets it on the counter before me. However, this vase, unlike the others, has a bright red bow attached to it.

"The gentleman is in the bar," she says, wiping her nose again, without looking up at me.

"Which gentleman?"

That sounded weird...

I don't want this woman thinking I have a *plethora* of gentleman callers. But, then again, it *is* my fault her hotel lobby is covered in white roses, so I doubt I'll be able to salvage her opinion of me anywhere in the future.

"*The* gentleman," she sighs, motioning around the room. "The one who sent all of these. I think he's expecting you."

Well, that's convenient. Has he been waiting for me?

I turn to head towards the bar, but I hear her clear her throat loudly.

"Miss Tyler…" she says, placing her hand on the vase I forgot on her counter.

Whoops.

I walk back over and grab it, flashing her an awkward smile.

"And if you're going in to speak with him, would you also please let him know that you've accepted. Perhaps he can still cancel the three a.m. delivery?"

"Yes of course," I say, a soft blush settling across my cheeks.

I head for the bar.

Behind me, Sally wastes no time telling the bellhops to start removing the dedication cards from all the vases.

As I open the door, I find Jaxon Pace alone, sitting at a high-top table in the center of the room. An open bottle of wine and two glasses sit before him.

Tonight, there is no suit coat and tie, for the billionaire hotel owner, but rather a simple white dress shirt with the neck casual and open. A thin pair of reading glasses shield eyes that are buried in a book.

He looks... inviting.

My cheeks heat as I just stand there taking him in.

I may still be furious with him, and royally annoyed that he would stoop to this level of pettiness, but part of me is mesmerized. Perhaps it's because he looks relaxed and unguarded, not the foreboding bundle of rage and suspicion I saw yesterday.

He's just beautiful.

"You came," he says softly, without looking up from his book, which appears to be a historical account of Hannibal Barca.

"You knew I would," I say, stepping further into the room.

"Honestly, I wasn't so sure."

"Yes, you were," I say, setting the vase of white roses down at a nearby table before taking a seat at his. "Otherwise, you would've just asked for *one* glass."

Nice try, Mr. Pace.

He chuckles softly and looks up at me over the rim of his glasses. When those devastating eyes of his meet mine, my blood heats inside my veins.

"You are quick," he says bemused, setting down his book and glasses.

"And you, Sir, are very persistent."

"That is true," he reaches for the bottle, and pours me a glass of wine. "But I don't usually have to work so hard."

Taking the glass from him, I raise it in a toast.

"Then I suppose I shall toast all your ex-lovers, for they must all be very, collectively, unsatisfied."

He smirks.

"Oh, I think they would certainly disagree, Miss Tyler," he says as our glasses clink. "I always aim for satisfaction."

Oh shit...

The look in his eye makes me feel like Little Red Riding Hood the moment she realized that *she* was about to be devoured.

"So, you wanted to see me," I ask, swallowing hard.

"Whatever gave you that impression?"

I toss the dedication card I stole from the vase on the table.

"I don't think you understand, this would have been incredibly difficult to explain to my family."

"You mean you haven't told them about our little *tryst*?" he says sarcastically.

"Is that what you'd call what happened yesterday? You know, where you went full attack dog on me, and we berated each other in your office?" I say, a coy smile on my lips. "No. I tend to leave my masochistic exploits with billionaire dickheads out of conversations with my loved ones."

He narrows his eyes at me and leans into the table.

"And is that because you'd rather recall them in private? Perhaps when you're alone in the bathtub...thinking of *me*?"

Did he really just say that?!

I swallow hard, realizing he's trying to undress my wit.

"How did you know?" I say playfully, brushing my hair behind my ear.

He laughs and I join him, but then we both fall silent.

He sets his wine glass down and spins it slowly with his fingers before looking up at me.

"The man who interrupted our conversation earlier..." He says quietly, cutting me with his icy blue eyes. "Is he your lover?"

I chuckle again.

"My *lover*? No, he is not."

"What is he to you?"

I must admit, Jaxon Pace looks absolutely lethal right now.

His face is serious, yet somehow playful. A combination I am sure only he could pull off. I'm curious as to why he's asking me this, but my body betrays me, and I feel strangely compelled to answer him.

"He's just my ex."

"I see," he says, casually taking a drink. "And do you still have...?"

He doesn't have to finish the question, because I already know what he's asking.

"I'm fairly confident that's none of your business." I say with a grin, narrowing my eyes at him. "But no, I do not still have feelings for him. Never again."

I can't be sure, but I swear I catch a faint smile tugging at the corners of his mouth.

"Why do you want to know, exactly?"

He pauses a moment before shrugging.

"Just curious."

But...why?

Even though part of this feels like casual flirting, it also somehow feels like a battle of wills, and I am unwilling to surrender. But, if I'm going to gain any traction, I can't be the only one getting interrogated.

"And you?" I ask.

"What about me?"

"Well, is there a *Mrs.* Billionaire-Dickhead who would be upset about you having a drink with me, alone in a bar, well past closing time?"

"Ouch. You wound me, Madam," he says, shaking his head. "To assume I would do such a thing to my missus. How little you must think of me, Miss Tyler."

"I wonder why *that* could be?" I say, gently teasing.

"Fair enough," he sighs deeply, nodding gently. "I guess I didn't make the best of impressions."

"Not really, no."

A serious look suddenly crosses his face.

"I *am* sorry," he says, softly clearing his throat. "For how I spoke to you yesterday. And for how I treated you. You didn't deserve any of that, and I could never hope to repay you for what you did for me, and for Jessica."

The gravity of this moment is palpable.

It's obvious that Jaxon Pace has uncharacteristically let his guard down. And despite being determined to despise him, I do believe the sincerity reflected in his eyes. He looks anxious, and I realize now how unfamiliar this must be to him.

I suppose when you have money and good looks like his, you probably don't have to apologize for much.

My brain yells at me to say something after my reflective pause grows into the minor silence lingering between us.

"Thank you," I choke out. "I do accept your apology."

His eyes hold me, threatening to burn through my corneas to my brain and imprint themselves forever.

"But, I also can't have any more roses butchered in my honor, or your front desk lady might have me murdered in my sleep," I say with a smile as I tear my eyes from him, afraid I might give myself away. "And also, it's just Natalie," I say, swallowing hard. "You don't need to keep calling me Miss Tyler."

He chuckles and takes another sip of wine.

"Hello, Natalie. I'm Jaxon. And now that we've got that out of the way, and I've been forgiven, perhaps now you will accept my invitation to dinner?"

Dinner? Whoa.

My pulse bolts from the gate like a racehorse in the Kentucky Derby, and I have to take a sip of wine to buy me time to catch up with it.

His eyes feel like magnets into my soul, and it is a bit intimidating.

"That depends..." I say slowly.

"On?" A wicked grin tugs at the corners of his mouth and makes it impossible to look away from him.

"On whether you intend on suffocating me with enough flora for a small continent again if I decline," I say with a wink, impressed that I am actually flirting somewhat successfully.

He chuckles and takes a drink, a smile unashamedly spreading across his face.

"No promises."

God he is sexy when he smiles.

"You didn't exactly answer my question," I state, diverting my eyes to my own wine glass.

"No."

"No?" I ask, confused.

"The answer to your question. No, there is no, what did you so eloquently call it? A Mrs. Billionaire-Dickhead? Or anyone else waiting for me this evening."

His devilish grin has returned and threatens to undo me. I think my heart skips a beat, but I just nod and take a sip of wine.

"Sounds like a very quiet evening for you then."

"Well, I do need a few nights off here and there."

He sits back in his chair and his shirt tenses on his skin, teasing his broad chest and shoulders.

"Oh, I see, you must have all your girlfriends on a *rotation* then."

"Nah, I don't really do the whole girlfriend thing."

Oh. Right.

I bite my lip absentmindedly, immediately catching Jaxon's eyes drifting south to my mouth.

"So, what are you like, saving yourself for marriage or something?" I joke, awkwardly trying to cover my disappointment.

What the hell was that Natalie? That was awful.

"Oh, I'm a big advocate for sex," he says, finishing his glass. "Marriage, on the other hand? No, not quite as much."

My momentary high evaporates instantly.

This is a man with a fear of commitment. And now I further understand that his dinner invite, and the steamy looks he keeps shooting my way, are because he just wants to fuck me.

He just sees me as an easy target.

"I suppose marriage is not a very lucrative proposition for someone in your position," I say feebly, trying to reign in my bitterness, and the fact that my thoughts are spiraling.

But if I'm honest, I'm mostly just disappointed in myself for thinking for one minute that maybe…

No. We are not even going to go there.

"Well, it's—" he begins to say something, but I interrupt him, feeling the immediate need to be as far away from this room as I can possibly get.

"Actually, Mr. Pace, I really should get going," I say, standing up and downing the last of my wine.

I can feel my body tense, my 'flight' response activated.

I have no business sharing wine and flirting with a man who is hopelessly out of my league, and who clearly sees me as just another conquest.

"I do accept your apology, so there's no need to continue to send me anymore flowers. Especially since they are stressing out your staff."

Jaxon looks utterly confused.

"I'm sorry, did I say something that upset you?"

"No. Not at all," I say, grabbing my coat from the back of the chair. "As I said, no more apologies."

I give him an empty smile.

"Natalie, I—"

"Thank you, Mr. Pace, for the wine," I say with finality, as I turn and leave the bar as fast as my legs can carry me.

I deliberately avoid all the curious glances from the front desk and head straight for the elevators.

How could I be so stupid?

I hate myself for it, but I can feel the emotions rising in my stomach. By the time I reach my room I have tears welling in my eyes. I hate myself for even entertaining the fantasy that maybe Jaxon Pace was flirting with me, and there was an actual connection. I hate myself for letting my guard down.

I am an idiot.

Suddenly my phone lights up, and I see Colton is calling.

Ugh. He's the absolute last person I want to talk to.

I briefly consider just letting it go to voicemail, but I feel as though it will only continue to get harder and harder to avoid him.

"Hello?" I say, trying to sound fine while wiping the hot tears from my eyes.

"So, what do I have to do to get you to stop treating me like I have the plague?" Colton asks.

The sounds of people talking lively in the background, indicating that he's still out with the bridal party.

At the same time, however, I hear a slight knock at my hotel door.

Who could that be?

"What?"

"I want to see you, Nat. I've tried calling and texting. Do I need to get a boombox and go stand outside the hotel?"

I smirk to myself, reminded that occasionally Colton can be funny.

There is a second knock, and this time I get out of bed.

"I'm sorry, I've just been super busy since I got here."

"Okay so what about dinner tomorrow night?"

"I don't really think dinner is—"

"How about just a drink—tomorrow at like sixish? We can just go to the bar downstairs, and I dunno, share some shitty germ-infested bar peanuts."

"Hah, fine. But you can keep all the gross bar peanuts for yourself."

"Excellent. It's a date."

"It's *not* a date, Colton," I say firmly, heading for the door.

"Fair enough, it's a non-date, date."

"Goodnight, Colton." I roll my eyes as I end the call.

Reaching the door I look through the peephole, but see no one outside. Reminding myself that it can't possibly be Colton, as he just called me from a bar downtown, I decide to open the door.

And there, on the doorstep, is a vase of white roses, with the red bow.

The *same* vase I presumably left in the bar downstairs… with Jaxon. A handwritten card sits underneath it.

Natalie,
I'm not sure what I did this time, but I'd like the chance to apologize for that too.
Have dinner with me.
-J

Chapter Eight

JAXON

"Get him out of here."

After removing my blood-soaked leather gloves, I start unbuttoning my dress shirt, which is also ruined.

Levi hands me a fresh shirt.

"What's *left* of him anyway..." Ethan grunts from the corner of the room, that's otherwise silent as a tomb.

I glare at him, but say nothing, as most of my men are still here. I take a moment to survey the scene as I change.

Blood is everywhere; the result of a rage-fueled beating I inflicted as I extracted information. Josiah and Samuel untie the arms of the attempted kidnapper from the chair in front of me and drag his limp body out of the room, leaving me alone with Ethan.

He didn't really give us much information though...

"I'm sorry," I sneer at Ethan venomously, "do you not approve of my methods? Should I have just talked nicely to him? Offered him a cup of Earl Grey and had a polite chat with him over some biscuits?"

"That's not what I said," Ethan says quietly.

"No, but you seem to have opinions about the way I handle things lately!" I snap. "That man put his fucking hands on my daughter! *My* daughter, Ethan! Do you understand?! I can't even bring myself to even think about what he planned to do with her if he had been successful! And it is a miracle he wasn't, because apparently everyone else in charge of her security was too busy fucking off instead of doing their goddamn jobs!"

"I understand your rage."

"No," I whisper, shaking my head. "I do not think you do."

"I absolutely do. But this... this was different," he says, pointing to the blood on the floor. "And you know it. You weren't in control, Jaxon."

"This was not different," I scoff dismissively. "This is the way of our world, and you know that."

Ethan says nothing.

"I was completely in control."

"You cut off his fucking hands!" Ethan suddenly shouts at me, clearly unable to control himself any longer.

I take a deep breath and raise one finger in the air.

"Ethan, I have love for you," I whisper. "But if you value your head, do *not* raise your voice at me again."

"Someone has to!" He snaps.

"This was necessary!" I shout. "Any of the other families would've done exactly what I did to him... or worse."

"We're supposed to be better than that."

"This fucker reaped what he sowed! He didn't deserve better than anything I gave him, and I will not hear another word about it!" I growl lethally.

Ethan sets his jaw, and just stares back at me silently. He wants to say something, but doesn't. But even still, the look on his face irritates me, his disapproval evident.

Worried I might actually hit him tonight, I turn and storm out of the room, my rage boiling as I wander through the warehouse. My cleanup crew walks past me, heading towards the shower room where we just conducted the interrogation.

"Boss." Travis nods at me.

I say nothing but nod back at him.

Sorry in advance boys, it's a bit of a mess.

I take the long way out of the warehouse, hoping it will calm me down, but when I reach the cars outside, I'm still fuming.

"We're going alone! Everyone else can follow!" I shout to my men, before stepping inside the Range Rover to wait for Ethan.

Fucking Ethan. How dare he?

What pisses me off the most is that I know on some level he is probably right, even if I don't want him to be.

So what if he's right? He's always fucking right...It's annoying.
Except, apparently, about apologizing to Natalie.
That was a massive failure.
And the whole fiasco with her this evening has not done anything to improve my mood. If anything, all it did was push my teetering self-control over the edge. Not that it was very 'controlled' to start with, but tonight my rage was primal. I rarely even stopped for air between blows.
But I refuse to feel bad about the fate of that man.
He chose his fate when he chose to target my child.
He put his hands on Jessica... so he *lost* those hands.
Unfortunately, the only information he ended up giving us was that someone had ordered him to lift my child from the hotel, threatening his life if he was unsuccessful. He claimed that while he did not know who this person was, he was certain that they didn't work for any of the other crime families, suggesting this was a private party.
A fact I found extremely hard to believe. New crime families just don't appear out of thin air in this city. The structure of our syndicate doesn't allow for that.
He said his employer had given him specific information about my whereabouts that day and Jessica's, almost as if they had eyes in my hotel. And if that's true, it means that I have a glaring security leak.
I have full faith in my men and our organization. However, the majority of my hotel staff aren't involved in *this* side of my business.
Any one of them could've been approached, with threats or cash, and asked to give away Jessica's whereabouts that day.
This is not a pleasant thought.
But, none of my thoughts are very pleasant as of late.
Ethan walks up to the car and gets inside, but says nothing as we pull out of the shipyard. After a few minutes of absolute silence, he pulls out his cigarettes, and hands me one. We smoke in silence before the phone rings inside the car.
"This is Ethan, go ahead."
"Sir, there is a Britta Demoines that is trying to reach Mr. Pace on the hotel mainline. Would he like to speak to her?" Sally from the front desk asks politely.
"Britta who?" I ask.
"Hello, Sir. She says she met you at the Annual Children's Fund Auction?"

Britta with the Tittas. I remember her now… well, kind of.

While I am not overly excited about the prospect of a second round of mediocre sex, I do wonder if it might take my mind off of this evening's events with Natalie. But before I can even open my mouth to answer, Ethan suddenly ends the call.

"What the hell?" I ask incredulously.

"What happened with Miss Tyler tonight?" he asks quietly.

"What the hell are you doing? What is this?"

Did he just cut off my phone call? Does he have a death wish tonight?

"Jaxon, will you relax? I am trying to fucking help you. What the fuck happened tonight?"

"Are you serious right now?!" I yell back at him.

"Yes, because something clearly happened." He continues ignoring me. "Yesterday you wanted to know everything but her fucking blood type, and tonight you waited around the hotel for her, only to show up hours later pissed as hell and beat the face off a hostage! And cut off his goddamn hands."

I'm stunned. I cannot believe this man right now.

He is the bravest motherfucker in Chicago.

"So, what the fuck happened?" he asks again.

"I don't know what the fuck happened!" I shout angrily. "I apologized like you said I should. I sent her flowers. A whole truckload of flowers. She met me for a drink, things seemed to be going well and then all of a sudden, she got all pissy for no reason and left without a word!"

"What did you say?" he asks, a slight smirk on his face.

"What did *I* say? Are you actually suggesting that this is *my* fault?" I ask indignantly.

Jesus…this must be how Natalie felt yesterday.

But it's this thought that suddenly stops me in my tracks.

I understand now why she had been so pissed at me yesterday, as it certainly doesn't feel good to be accused of being the problem. But unlike yesterday, I really don't know what I said tonight that upset her so much.

"What did you *say*," Ethan says, emphasizing the last part. "Women are a different breed, Jaxon. You'll find that they're all about the *words*. They have meaning, and you have to be careful to use the right ones. And you have to be more careful not to use the wrong ones."

"I don't fucking know what I said! All I did was ask about that guy I saw her with earlier. She said he wasn't important."

"But you know differently." Ethan interrupts me with a glance.
"What?"
"You know from her file that's her ex-fiancé. Whether or not he isn't important to her now, doesn't mean he is not important, overall. Remember that."
Jesus. When Natalie said that, I hadn't dissected it that far.
"Go on," Ethan says.
"I think she asked if I had anyone," I say, slapping my hand on my leg.
"And you said?"
"That's not really my thing. I don't have relationships."
"Bingo," Ethan says with a chuckle. "Rookie mistake."
"What? I was being honest."
"You were being *too* honest."
"That's a *thing*?" I snort. "Christ, maybe I don't know what I'm doing."
"You don't."
"Excuse me?"
"None of us do in the beginning."
"That's comforting," I say sarcastically.
"Look kid, I was married for twenty years. Trust me, there is always a *thing*," Ethan laughs. "You're bound to fuck it up some way or another."
Fuck.
"I was trying to tell her that I don't have anything serious. I didn't want her to feel like I was just trying to, you know, fuck her."
"But you did anyway," Ethan says, with a shrug.
"I mean I would, obviously," I say, looking out the window. "I don't know… I guess I started enjoying myself a little. She was fun, feisty, and smart. I actually started trying to just get to know her a little. But somehow, I still fucked it up."
"Women are different. They are incredibly sensitive to what you say and *how* you say it."
"Fuck this, dude," I said, rolling the window down. "I don't understand this shit."
"It takes practice."
"Yeah, that sounds exhausting. Call Britta back, at least we both understand what the expectations are there."
"I can promise you don't want Britta," Ethan says, rolling his eyes. "Miss Tyler is just out of your league. Something you haven't experienced before."
"Out of *my* league?" I scoff at him. "Please."

"I said what I said. You should count yourself lucky she even gave you the time of day, especially after what she did for you and how you treated her."

"I tried to apologize! I've been trying all damn day!" I shout, completely frustrated. "How can that be so fucking hard?!"

"The problem is, you're expecting it to be *easy*," Ethan says. "The fact is, you fucked up. Which means that you're supposed to grovel a bit and ask for forgiveness. It's supposed to be uncomfortable for a minute. So maybe, if you do more of that, and less parading like such a self-righteous prick, you'll get a different result."

I say nothing. When he puts it like that, I sound like an obnoxious child throwing a temper tantrum.

Maybe I am.

"You just have to try with this girl, man. She's making you work for it," Ethan says, with a smile. "Which is something you haven't experienced before. But trust me when I say, the best ones always make you work for it."

I open my mouth to say some snippy comment, but when I glance at Ethan, I understand that he's not actually referring to Natalie, he is referring to his *wife*.

Ethan lost his wife Eliza and their two children in a car accident with a drunk driver, almost nineteen years ago. In one terrible moment, he lost his entire family.

He was practically inconsolable. However, whenever he speaks about her, it feels as if she's still alive somewhere, just waiting for him to come home. After all this time, it's clear how much he *still* loves her.

I know that look myself. After all, my father adored my mother the same way. He talked about her after she passed away, and I know he loved her the same way.

Which might be why it's hard for me to admit that I've never felt that way before.

I mean, I *had* loved Rachel, in a way. But definitely not like that. I didn't do much right in our relationship, so even when we were together, all I usually felt was guilt. But even though it was no secret that things were not always easy between us, I had been devastated when she died.

It wasn't love, but it was the closest I've ever felt.

These days, I don't keep anyone around long enough to develop any kind of attachment. Britta is just the most recent conquest in a long line of one-night stands. Which were fun for a little while, but were devoid of any such feelings or emotions. I found that was usually easier for everyone.

But, as much as I don't want to admit it, especially to Ethan, another night with Britta doesn't sound as appealing as it usually would.

"Come on Jaxon... I've never known you to give up so easily before," Ethan teases. "You just have to work at it."

"She hates me dude," I laugh sarcastically. "She despises me. Probably thinks I'm just another scumbag with too much money. How the fuck do I work for something like that?"

"You just have to try."

"You keep saying that, but I sent nine-hundred roses to her today and that still was not enough. I made this big gesture, and she's still pissed at me."

"This isn't about how big of a gesture you make Jaxon, it's about what *kind*."

A moment of silence fills the car.

"Yeah, I literally have no fucking idea what that means," I say, chuckling out loud.

This time Ethan chuckles too, the tension between us finally dissipating.

"You just need to understand that your regular approach isn't going to work here, and despite your intentions, you made her feel like all you're trying to do is sleep with her."

I share a look with Ethan.

"I mean, as I said, I'm not opposed to that scenario..."

"I think it's safe to say, with everything we've learned about her in the last twenty-four hours, Miss Tyler is not going to jump in bed with you. She's not Britta," Ethan admonishes. "So just scrap that playbook. Think of Miss Tyler as an investment. Invest for once."

"Again, she hates me. I asked her to dinner, and she said no. How am I supposed to invest if I can't even get her to give me the opportunity?"

"Have faith that the opportunity will present itself. Then just don't fuck it up when it does."

"Again, I still have no idea what that means."

"I'm confident you'll figure it out."

The phone rings inside the car again and Ethan answers. "This is Ethan, go ahead."

"Sir, I think we were disconnected," Sally says gently. "What did you want me to tell Miss Demoines?"

"Tell her," I say with a pause. "I'm unavailable. Indefinitely."

"Yes, Sir."

I hang up the call and light another cigarette.

I can't believe I'm turning down guaranteed sex for this.

"I'm proud of you," he says.

"Shut the fuck up," I snort. "Seriously. I've had just about enough of this shit. In fact, as soon as we get back to the hotel, we're going to finish our racquetball game. I still owe you an ass whooping."

"And, as I said before," he says with a laugh. "You can *try*, lover boy,"

The late-night workout with Ethan helped to release some tension, and by the next morning, I'm in moderately better spirits.

To be fair, it was the combination of the workout, a fifth of whiskey, a good wank, and a few solid hours of sleep.

As I make my way across the lobby with my coffee, however, I see a commotion at the front desk.

A young brunette is accompanied by a tall blonde man, and several older adults. She's crying and talking frantically with the clerk behind the desk.

I recognize her. She's the woman walking with Natalie yesterday.

She's the bride in the Tyler-Godfrey wedding reception we're hosting here.

Sally is on duty, and she and the clerk are trying desperately to calm the woman down, but she's practically hysterical.

"I don't know what to do!" She sobs. "First the florist says they can't make our centerpieces because they're completely out of white roses," she says to the man with her, presumably the groom. "But I see plenty of white roses here!"

She motions angrily around my lobby, which is outlandishly filled to the brim with the 900 white roses I sent to Natalie.

Whoops.

Sally shoots an angry look in my direction as I cross behind the desk, heading toward my office.

I quickly skirt past and down the hall.

"And if that's not enough of a disaster, now the band has strep throat!" I hear her weep. "The wedding is in four days! Four days!

What do we do? How are we supposed to find any band in four days?!"

My hand is on my office door knob when I stop in my tracks. A wicked smile spreads slowly across my face as Ethan's words from last night echo in my head.

"Have faith the opportunity will present itself."

"Excuse me," I say, walking back down the hallway and into the lobby. "Perhaps I might be able to *help* with that."

Chapter Nine

Natalie

"So, the museum is closed for the whole month?" Colton whines. "That's such bullshit."

"Yeah, I'm bummed, I guess they had a really amazing Greek exhibit—" I start to say but I'm immediately cut off by Colton.

"I mean, like really, though, who really wants to spend the day in a museum. Looking at a bunch of pottery and coins that a bunch of old ass savages used to own?"

I mean... I did.

I look out the window. I've forgotten how exhausting his company can be at times.

"So how have you been?"

"I'm good, I've been working as a private nurse for this elderly man up in Boca—"

"Gosh, Nat, you look so good though. Have you lost weight?" Colton interrupts again, changing the subject.

"Thanks? Perhaps some but not much..." I say shifting in my seat, watching Colton look me up and down. His gaze on my body makes me immediately uncomfortable.

"I mean, don't take this the wrong way or anything but I've

always thought you would look incredibly good if you were down to like a size two or four. You just have such a pretty face. It would complement you well."

"Yeah, I guess I've never really focused on my jean size."

Now I feel self-conscious. I hate how he can make me feel so unworthy in an instant.

It's not like Colton is a total heartthrob. He's just slightly better than average. I also find it slightly ironic that he's asking me about my weight when in fact, I think he's put on a little weight himself. His face seems puffy, and he has bags under his eyes.

Yet here he is, making me feel awkward and uncomfortable—like always.

Typical.

"So," he says, taking another drink and leaning into the table. "Do you have a boyfriend now?"

The smile on his face immediately annoys me.

This entire conversation feels like nails on a chalkboard, and my relationship status isn't really any of his business.

No asshole, it's been really hard to date, because it's really hard to trust, because of what you put me through.

"Not anyone in particular, I'm just having fun dating," I say with a smile.

In truth, however, it has been months since I have been on any kind of date with a man.

"Hah, I call bullshit. No one ever really enjoys dating, it's a goddamn nightmare," he says smugly, taking another drink.

Well, that's comforting, considering we dated for six years.

"I take it you aren't seeing anyone?" I ask, sitting back in my seat. I watch as he shifts in his chair.

"No, I've been trying to just really focus on myself, ya know? I've just been so busy with my career, and I've just been taking time off from dating. Really trying to get my head right."

"What do you mean?" I ask, sensing that he's clearly uncomfortable with this personal question being turned around on him. "Surely there has to be someone in your life?"

"Nope. Not a soul," he says, scratching his chin. "You know, after we ended, I couldn't cope for a while. Honestly, it just never crossed my mind."

Even though it's obvious he's trying to look sincere, I can't help but notice the hairs on the back of my neck stand up. This was oddly something that happened in our relationship whenever I felt he was being dishonest.

I do not believe this well-rehearsed sob story for a minute, but I do like hearing him say it, even if I hate that I like hearing him say it.

"That is kind of why I didn't bring a date to the wedding..." he says. "I'd be lying if I said there wasn't some part of me that's hoping for a... truce between us." He plays with the tag on his beer bottle and looks up at me.

A truce? Really? That's the best you could do, Colton?

I freeze, unsure of what to say in response.

It's been two years since I've seen him, and for months I've explicitly planned for this moment right here.

Of course, I wanted him to agonize over losing me, and I wanted him to beg me to take him back; not because I wanted to be with him again, but because I wanted the satisfaction of turning him down. I wanted to be the one who had control over this situation, because I felt like I had no control whatsoever in his betrayal.

I wanted him to feel what I felt. But now, I feel nothing.

"Colton, I..." I start to say.

"I know, I know, it's crazy," he says, taking my hand in his. He pauses to stare at my chipped nails, and I immediately pull my hand away.

"I have a manicure appointment tomorrow," I snap, feeling my cheeks get hot.

God, I hate when he does that. How does he make me feel so... shitty?

Colton always seems to find a way to make me feel insecure about myself. As if I suck at being a woman, and that perhaps if I had been thinner, prettier, or more perfect he wouldn't have cheated on me. Somehow, twenty minutes alone with him and I feel as if I am, once again, not enough.

"Look, Natalie, I just want to put it out there. I mean, we had some good times, right?"

"We did. Once," I say shortly.

"That's what I mean. We *work*, Natalie. And we both know your family *adores* me—"

This comment instantly enrages me.

"Yeah, and why is *that*, Colton?" I snap. "Is it perhaps because they have no idea you were cheating on me with like seven different women?"

I can't stop the words as they fall out of my mouth, but I relish the surprised look on Colton's face.

"Natalie—"

"And on that note, do you have any idea what it's like to be ostracized from your own family? For two years? For two years my entire family has been under the impression that I just got cold feet and randomly decided to uproot my entire life and move across the country."

He attempts to speak but I quickly cut him off again.

"And why do they believe that? Because that's the made-up nonsense *you* told them. Not the truth. Nothing even remotely close to the truth that I discovered Emily, or Taila, or Vanessa's chat histories, nude pictures and homemade sex tapes on your phone from when we were together."

"Nat…"

"Do you think they would still adore you if they knew?" I whisper venomously across the table at him.

"Nat, I know, I know. I fucked up, baby, but—"

"Do *not* call me baby!" I snap so loudly the woman at the table next to us looks up. "And yeah, you're damn right you fucked up. You fucked us up."

I am now furious, and my hands are shaking, but I refuse to back down now.

Colton just stares at me trying to think of something to say.

The absolute nerve of this fucking clown!

"Did you know I had to eat the cost of our wedding?" I whisper to him, leaning into the table.

"No, I didn't—"

"Who do you think covers that when you pull out of a contract three weeks before the wedding? Did you even offer to help? Of course not!"

"You moved away! How was I supposed to reach you?"

"My phone number never changed, Colton! You are just a cheap asshole who was too much of a sissy to face up to his mistakes!"

He opens his mouth to say something, but I put a hand up to silence him. This might not be how I intended this conversation to go, but now that it is happening, I can't stop it.

"The *truth* here is that you left me trying to explain to my entire family why we were not only not getting married, but also no longer together! And at the very least, if you intended on remaining close with them, you could've just admitted that you had screwed up somehow! You could've at least owned up to your fault in this! But instead, you made up some ridiculous story in which you are the victim, and you play on my own family's sympathies!"

He reaches across the table a third time and this time I slap at his hand.

"Nat, I was devastated! I was just not thinking clearly, and just trying to mitigate the damages and maintain some sense of my dignity in the process!"

"Dignity?!" I whisper forcefully across the table. "What dignity did you afford to me? The woman you slept in bed next to after you spent your days fucking half the city!"

"Natalie, please believe me when I say I truly regret what happened, and I want to fix this. There's nothing I won't do to fix us!" he says desperately. "Trust me."

I cannot stop myself from laughing out loud.

"*Trust* you? Hah! Colton, you lied to me every single day! Your relationship with Emily alone spanned almost three years of our relationship. At what point did you plan to tell me about her? Perhaps when we were walking down the aisle? Or maybe on our honeymoon?!"

"Look I—"

"The fact is you broke us. You broke the foundation of everything I thought we were. There's no fixing that. But somehow, I still got stuck cleaning up the mess you made," I say, my voice cracking.

Fuck, I said I was not going to let him see me cry.

"Natalie, baby, I know what I did was fucked up," he says, seemingly unfazed by what I just said to him.

"I said do not call me baby! We are done here," I say, standing up from the table. As I do, I notice my mother, seated in a booth, quickly put her face back in a book she is clearly pretending to read.

When did she get here?

I see her look up expectantly from across the room. Then I understand—she must have known that Colton and I were meeting here. Because he *told* her.

Somehow this infuriates me more.

"Natalie, wait—" Colton tries to stop me, but I'm already headed out of the bar.

Fuck this. Fuck all of this. Fuck all of them.

I am halfway across the lobby when I hear my mother call my name.

"Natalie."

I try to ignore her, but she tries again, this time a bit louder.

"Natalie!"

I stop and turn around, shaking my head as I do so.

What could she possibly have to say?

I specifically begged her not to get involved with this.

"Is everything okay?" she asks innocently. "You seem upset?"

"Yeah, Mom, I'm fine," I say sarcastically.

I try to turn back around and continue back up to my room, but she gently grabs my arm.

"Did, um, everything go okay with Colton? I saw the two of you chatting, and I know you said you didn't want to talk to him, but sweetheart he's been so excited to talk to you."

My family's love of Colton is nauseating at this point.

"Why don't you come up to my room and have some wine with me, hmm?" she says, brushing a hair out of my face. "We can talk about it?"

The very *last* thing I want to do right now is talk more about this. I just want to leave. I want to leave this room, this hotel, maybe this city and state altogether. "No, Mom, I can't," I say, pushing her hand away.

"Oh, why not? It's been forever since we've been able to have a face-to-face chat," she says persisting.

God I just don't want to do this right now.

"I said I can't, Mom. I'm sorry, I have..." I scramble to find something to finish that sentence with and decide just to lie. "Plans tonight."

I immediately realize, however, that this is a terrible lie because what plans could I possibly have tonight, in a city where I don't know anyone? Everyone in the family has already heard that Steph is down with a migraine today, and she's the only person I would've made 'plans' with anyway.

"Plans? What plans?" she says, astonished. "Who do you have plans with?"

"With *me*."

A low but commanding voice speaks from behind me, making me jump. I turn to see Jaxon Pace standing there, with his hands in his pockets.

What the...?

"Um...I'm sorry, who are...you?" I watch as my mother stumbles over her words, visibly stunned by the presence of this mysterious stranger.

A mysterious stranger who *also* just happens to be debilitatingly handsome.

Jaxon stares at me, and as our eyes lock, I realize he's already pushed me off the dock. I can't exactly negate his help, not now, especially since I don't have a backup option.

"Yes, Mom, I forgot, I had um…" I mumble, glancing nervously up at Jaxon.

"Dinner plans," he grins, finishing my sentence.

"Dinner plans," I say almost breathlessly. "Yes!"

My mother looks utterly confused.

"And I'm sorry, but you are?" She smiles, draping her hand across her chest, obviously finding Jaxon attractive.

I guess I can't blame her for that.

It doesn't hurt that he looks impossibly good at this moment, his bright blue eyes contrasting nicely against his dark gray suit, and his subtle facial hair seems to define his muscular jaw even more than usual.

"Jaxon Pace," he says charmingly. "I'm the owner of the Hotel Jefferson. Pleasure to meet you."

"Oh, my, well," My mother says, batting her eyelashes at him, swooning. "It is certainly a pleasure to meet you too, Mr. Pace."

"And you are?"

"Natalie," my mother says, leading me.

"Sorry, this is my mother," I say, awkwardly. "Mom, this is—"

"Mr. Pace," my mother says, smiling wildly and extending her hand to Jaxon. "We covered that already."

"Impossible," Jaxon says firmly, taking her hand.

"What?" I ask, confused.

"Forgive me," Jaxon smiles, delicately putting his lips to her hand, kissing it politely. "You just look far too *young*."

"Oh, goodness!" My mother giggles, blushing.

Oh my God…really mom?

I roll my eyes and have to look away, trying to stifle my amusement at the two of them.

"So this is your hotel?"

"Indeed."

I feel my mother place a hand on my arm as she continues speaking to Jaxon.

"How wonderful. I was telling Natalie here what a *gorgeous* hotel this is!"

You were?

"…And the fresh flowers everywhere," My mother continues shamelessly. "My gosh, they are just such a beautiful touch!"

"Well, thank you. I'm thrilled to hear that. I think so too."

He straightens his suit coat, covertly winking at me.

"However, Natalie here never mentioned that she knew *you*."

"Oh," Jaxon smirks, feigning surprise. "How disappointing."

"How did the two of you become acquainted, exactly?" My mother asks me.

I panic.

I still haven't told her about the events of yesterday, the taser, or the little girl. I don't think she could handle it.

But Jaxon answers for me.

"We met this past spring," he lies, smoothly. "I have an elderly uncle in Miami, and Natalie's hospital sent her to evaluate him. She did a phenomenal job. And when I heard she was going to be in Chicago, I insisted that we have dinner so I could repay her for her kindness."

He locks eyes with me and smiles wickedly.

"And I am a very hard man to refuse."

Yeah, and incredibly persistent.

"Oh, I bet!" My mother giggles, scrunching up her nose playfully.

Jaxon's gaze momentarily shifts to something behind us, but then he quickly looks back to my mother and smiles.

"I do apologize for stealing Natalie away like this, but we have a dinner reservation," he says apologetically, checking his watch. "And if we don't leave right now, we might lose our table."

"Oh right!" My mom says excitedly. "Of course!"

She gives me a quick hug, stopping to straighten my hair.

I can't help but notice that she's beaming ear to ear, like she is sending me off to prom.

"Well, you kids have fun!"

"Natalie?" Jaxon says motioning me forward with his hand.

I pause for a moment, debating if I should continue with this ruse. However, at the same time I happen to turn and see that Colton has finally come out of the bar and is making his way over to us.

Off the dock it is.

I take a step towards Jaxon.

"Please get me out of here." I whisper so only he can hear me. "*Now.*"

"That was the plan," he whispers, glancing back in Colton's direction.

Then to my utter surprise, I feel him place his hand on the small of my back. Shivers immediately erupts down my spine as I feel him gently propel us forward toward the doors.

But I do not object.

All of the front desk staff watch as he gracefully leads me across the lobby and opens the door for me.

The moment we step outside, the cool Chicago breeze brushes against my face, and I feel as if I can finally breathe again.

"This way," Jaxon says, nodding to the valet guy.

When he turns back to me I can tell he wants to say something, but I beat him to it.

"Thank you," I say sincerely. "You can't possibly know what you saved me from back there, but it was uncomfortable. If you want, you can just take me to the garage and drop me off. I can sneak up to my room."

He stares at me, and gently bites his lip, apparently deciding against whatever it was he was going to say.

Another cool breeze catches me off guard and I shiver just a bit.

"You're cold."

"Oh, no, I'm—"

But before I can even finish the sentence, Jaxon has already removed his jacket and placed it over my shoulders.

My objection dies on my lips once I'm wrapped in the warmth of his jacket, feeling his arm around me, holding me close.

Why does his cologne smell so amazing?

Suddenly, I hear a rumble, and within seconds a gorgeous black Lamborghini pulls up in front of us.

If I weren't clenching my jaw together to keep it from chattering, I'm sure it would have detached itself and fallen to the pavement. The valet hands Jaxon the keys and he opens the door, as if this is just a regular old Ford Taurus.

"Seriously?" I say to him. "Don't you own any normal cars?"

"I suppose," he says, chuckling. "I own a dealership. At least I think so. Or maybe it's a fleet of dealerships? I can't remember."

I sit down as the door closes, but I'm too stunned to move.

The car's interior is beautiful, which I guess I should expect considering the vehicle is worth three times my yearly salary.

Jaxon hops in next to me and shuts the door. His hair is slightly messy, there's a wild look in his eye, and the boyish grin on his face somehow makes him look even sexier.

"Do you need help?" he asks.

"Um, no," I say, "I mean I don't think so?"

I'm still stunned from the last ten minutes, let alone being ushered into a Lamborghini.

"Hmmm… are you sure? Because you look confused," he says, raising an eyebrow at me.

"Well, yeah, I guess I am little…"

He suddenly leans over the armrest, putting his face only inches from mine.

"I've got you," he whispers, his blue eyes locked on mine.

Oh my...

My heart begins to pound, but before I know what's happening, he reaches past me, grabs the seatbelt, and fastens it in place...right between my legs.

"Um," I say, nervously clearing my throat. "That's not what I meant."

"Oh?" he says, settling back into the driver's seat.

"Well, I thought you were just going to drop me at the back of the hotel? I hardly think I need a seatbelt for that."

"Fuck that," he snorts.

"Wait...what?" I ask, confused. "What are we doing?"

"I said we were going to dinner, so we're going to dinner," he says, revving the engine and shooting me a wild grin. "And pissing off your ex."

Chapter Ten

JAXON

"How did you know… about my ex?"

We've driven a few blocks before Natalie breaks the silence between us in the car.

Shit. I let that slip. I have to start buttoning up my game.

"I overheard you telling him off in the pub," I say gently.

"Great," she quips sarcastically. "I didn't even notice you were in there. Was I that loud?"

I can tell she's embarrassed, and part of me wants to confess that it really wasn't that obvious.

But, then I would also have to confess that I had actually been listening via the new security system I had installed today. And since I just succeeded in finally getting her to agree to dinner with me, I decide to keep my creepy methods of discovery to myself.

"You weren't loud at all, I just happened to catch the end of him saying he knew that he fucked up, and saw you storm off. That seemed pretty self-explanatory."

Annnnd perhaps the file in my office with your name on it.

"That obvious?"

"Let's just say I've had my fair share of women yell at me over the years, so I can read the body language pretty well."

"Shocking, Mr. Pace," she sighs with a smirk. "But yes, I may have read one or two tabloid articles about you."

She researched me. That's...interesting.

"And what impeccable truths did they render?" I say with a chuckle.

"Oh, you know, Billionaire. Playboy. Dickhead. The standard."

"Hey now, don't judge. Chicago deserves a resident billionaire, playboy, dickhead like all the rest of the major cities. I make the old gal feel like she's made it to the big leagues."

"Fuuuck me," Natalie sighs, collapsing back against the seat, shaking her head.

"Madam!" I gasp cartoonishly. "We just met!"

My ridiculousness makes her laugh, which admittedly is a beautiful sound. However, I also now realize she thinks I overheard her have a public argument with Mr. Unremarkable, and she's royally embarrassed.

"Natalie, I promise it really wasn't that bad," I say quietly, turning the corner.

"Promise?"

"Yes."

I glance over at her, catching the look of sad innocence flashing in her eyes before she looks out the window.

"Where are we going?"

To be honest, I haven't thought that far ahead. I wasn't even sure she would actually get in my car given how aggressively she had turned down my advances before.

"Anywhere you want."

"I thought you said you had a reservation?"

"I don't need a reservation anywhere. I have a table any time, in any restaurant, whenever I want it."

"Is that what life is like when you're the resident playboy dickhead of the city?" She asks, raising an eyebrow.

"Resident *billionaire* playboy dickhead," I say, correcting her with a grin. "And yes, or at least it has been in my usual experience."

"Why do I get the impression that with you, Jaxon Pace, no experience is 'usual?'"

"Probably because I have supersonic hearing and I kidnapped you in my Lamborghini."

She laughs again, and this time I notice the smile across her face as she glances out the window. The sunlight catches her face and I find myself staring.

Fuck, she really is beautiful.

Her features, especially when she smiles, are absolutely stunning.

Realizing that I would not be doing myself any favors by crashing the car the moment I get her in it, I turn my attention back to the road.

"What do you feel like eating?" I ask, clearing my throat.

"This is your show," Natalie shrugs. "Surprise me."

I smirk.

Revving the engine in my beast of a car, I suddenly jerk the wheel to the right, cutting off the car in the lane next to me in order to turn down a side street.

"Now you're talking, Miss Tyler."

"Oh no," she giggles. "What have I gotten myself into."

I wink at her and press my virtual assistant button on the steering wheel.

"This is Ethan, go ahead," he responds immediately.

"Ethan, please call Marco and inform him that I'm coming for dinner… with a *guest*. Arrival time is ten minutes."

"Copy that," he says, ending the call.

"Is Marco a restaurant?" Natalie inquires.

"No, Marco is a person," I say, enjoying the confused look on her face. "He's my chef. Well, one of my chefs."

"One of my chefs…" Natalie repeats, rolling her eyes. "Of course, you have more than one chef. More than one car, more than one bodyguard, more than one chef."

"Hey now, don't go getting all judgmental on me now missy, we were making progress," I say, wagging my finger back and forth.

She laughs again, and for some reason I find myself smiling.

"You're right, you're right. You just rescued me from my overbearing family and insufferable ex. I have no room to judge." She puts her hands up in protest, and I finally feel her start to relax a bit.

Which helps me to relax as well.

"That's right, and you, madam, should be ashamed of yourself."

"Me?" She scoffs, incredulously.

"Yes, you! You just got into a car with a man you barely know, without even a hint of restraint!" I say, playfully scolding her. "What did your mother tell you about getting into cars with strange men?"

"Make sure you have your taser with you," she says sarcastically.

I glance over at her, narrowing my eyes suspiciously.

"*Do* you have your taser with you?"

"No."

This time we both laugh.

Strangely enough, I've forgotten what a good laugh feels like, as it's not something I get often in my line of work.

We turn a corner, and the marina comes into view.

"Where are we?" she asks as I throw the car in park.

But I say nothing, biting my lip. Instead, I get out and walk around to her side of the car. I open her door and extend my hand to her, pulling her up and practically into my arms.

The realization that Natalie Tyler is so very close to me suddenly makes my heart start pounding. I reach down and straighten my jacket around her shoulders, if only to savor this moment a little longer.

The pull I feel towards her is magnetic.

Light from the sun setting over the water catches in her green eyes, highlighting every fleck of gold and amber. Her soft supple lips, combined with the intoxicating scent of her perfume, has me completely mesmerized. And, because I still have her pinned between me and the car, I suddenly find it nearly impossible to resist cupping her face and kissing her right here.

What is this?

But just when I think I'm losing my mind, I catch Natalie's eyes drifting to my lips, and the soft blush settling across her cheeks.

Whatever this is, she's feeling it too.

She tears her eyes away from mine, and tucks her hair behind her ear bashfully.

"Seriously though, Jaxon," she says softly. "Where are we going?"

"Hopefully to a boat, or this date just got really weird." I joke.

"Boat? You didn't say anything about a boat, or about this being a date. Or is that just what you call it when you spontaneously kidnap women in fancy cars?" she says, squinting her eyes playfully at me.

"Well, I did say I wanted to apologize, so I figured go big or go home. And I've just found that typically when you own the boat and the fancy car, you can call the kidnapping whatever you want," I say, extending my arm to her.

"Oh I see! Well then, lead the way, good sir."

She takes my arm as we walk down the dock, and I swallow hard, feeling my pulse quicken.

"Monsieur Pace!" A hearty warm welcome comes from a short portly French man shouting from the deck of my Yacht—The

Ismena.

"Marco," I say as we step aboard.

He steps forward to embrace and even though I don't normally let people touch me, Marco's cooking is superb, so I tolerate it.

"It's been so very long since I have seen you, my friend!" he says, looking Natalie up and down and taking her hand. "And with a guest! Who is zis gorgeous mademoiselle? Elle est magnifique."

"Bonjour monsieur c'est agréable, de vous rencontrer," Natalie says smile, nodding to him.

Holy shit, she speaks French?

And if *I'm* surprised by this, it's nothing compared to Marco, whose face lights up like the 4th of July.

"Elle parle Français?! Magnifique!"

He embraces her again, kissing both of her cheeks and then clasps his hands together in sheer joy.

"I like zis one." He winks at me. "Please make yourself comfortable with a drink, and I will have dinner out immediately."

He snaps his fingers and scurries off toward the kitchen shouting more directions in French to the terrified assistant cooks scrambling to keep up.

"I, uh," I say, clearing my throat. "Had no idea you could speak French?"

"Well, to be fair, Mr. Pace, we barely know each other," Natalie says, smiling at me. "I assume there's a great number of things you don't know about me."

That is certainly true…and really sexy.

I suddenly feel the need to loosen my tie a bit around my neck, as my temperature inexplicably rises.

My eyes follow Natalie as she scans the Ismena.

"This really is a beautiful boat, Jaxon."

"Thank you. Would you like a drink? Or a tour?" I offer, motioning toward the bar on the back of the boat.

"Both?"

"You got it, mademoiselle."

After the drinks are made, I take the opportunity to show her around the yacht.

As I walk the length of the boat, I realize that I haven't spent much time here in recent years. But then again, I don't really spend much time anywhere besides the hotel these days.

We're out on the deck, and I'm walking her through the boat history, when I notice Natalie is shivering, her arms wrapped tightly across her body.

Shit, she's cold.

After all, beneath my jacket, she's just wearing a thin sweater and that deliciously short skirt that kept tempting me in the Lamborghini.

"I apologize, I'm going on about mainsails and I forgot that the breeze off the water is chilly," I say, wrapping an arm around her and bringing us indoors immediately.

At least she's letting me *touch* her now, a prospect that felt impossible yesterday.

"No, no, it's fine!" she protests. "Honestly, I didn't even notice."

"Uh huh," I say with a smile.

When we step back inside, I take the thin jacket and trade it for a thick cashmere blanket from off the back of the couch, wrapping it around her shivering shoulders.

"There's nothing on the ship worth catching a cold over." I say, staring into her deep green eyes.

"Thank you," she says, smiling up at me through her lashes.

"After all, I don't think that would go down in history as a very memorable date."

"Oh, this will certainly be memorable, Jaxon," she winks, biting her bottom lip.

I want to bite that lip. More than that… I want to throw her on that couch, kiss them raw and hear them moan my name.

Jesus, Jaxon… reign it in.

My dirty thoughts catch me by surprise. While I'm used to women jumping into bed with me, Natalie has refused all my advances, save today, and I find that… kind of intriguing.

However, I realize now that I am blatantly out of practice on how to behave when sex is not the goal of the evening.

Well, at least not the *main* goal, anyway.

I finally got her alone, I can't let my dick do the thinking.

But her pretty face, tantalizing curves and gentle smile are making that incredibly difficult.

Fortunately, Marco comes out to tell us that dinner is ready and asks where we would like to be served.

"Inside is fine, the lady is cold."

"I will get ze staff to turn on the fireplace too, eh? More romantic," he says quietly to me with a wink.

Naughty man…he's trying to get me laid too.

Natalie giggles, clearly amused too.

We have a seat and Marco's sous chef serves a bottle of red wine and plates our meals. I wait for him to leave before raising my glass in a toast.

"To apologies, and kidnappings both failed and successful," I say with a smile, and Natalie smiles too.

I take the first few bites and I remember why I love Marco's cooking so much.

"Oh, my word, this is delicious," Natalie says in delight. "I might have to steal Marco from you."

"I'm sure if you gave him the option, he would leave me in a heartbeat for you."

We both chuckle but then silence settles over the table again. Small talk isn't something I've done in quite some time.

"So," I say, swallowing hard. "Tell me about *you.*"

"What do you want to know?"

"Everything."

The sun has set, and we're on the second bottle of wine, when Natalie suddenly looks up from her storytelling and smiles.

"Thank you, for this, Jaxon."

I wish I could explain the way her enjoyment makes me feel, but I catch myself getting distracted simply by the way her smile lights up her eyes, illuminating her full beauty.

"The pleasure is mine. I hope this was a satisfactory abduction."

"Certainly. But only because of Marco's food," she says with a wink, taking a sip of wine.

"He's a hard man to compete with. He always finds a way to steal my thunder."

She giggles, and I stare at her, watching her hair flowing in the breeze as she looks out over the water. She looks so relaxed and happy. There's something peaceful about just watching her like this.

I don't know if I've ever felt peace before like this.

However, old habits die hard, and I'm still actively fighting the urge to flip this table over and ravage her.

Instead, I take another sip of wine.

"This was a massive improvement from my night," she smiles.

"Really, thank you."

I nod gently.

"Look, I know this is not my business, or my place to say anything," I say, pouring her another glass of wine. "But your ex seems like a dick."

She blinks at me, surprised.

Crap, was that too aggressive?

I can never tell because I spend nearly all my time with men who kill people for a living... and we don't waste time dwelling on pleasantries or politeness.

But Natalie just smirks and raises a brow at me.

"This coming from the billionaire, playboy, dickhead," she says into her glass of wine, her eyes catching mine.

"Which is why I'm quite familiar with the type. And that guy is definitely..." I say, shaking my head.

"An asshole," she says, finishing my sentence. "I know. He's an arrogant asshole."

"Forgive me, but I just don't see you as the type that tolerates arrogant assholes," I reach for my wine. "Speaking from experience of course."

"Yeahhhhh...." She winces with a smile. "You know I have been thinking, and I probably owe *you* an apology for that."

"No, you don't. You were completely in the right, and I was wrong. If anything had happened to her..." I shake my head, gripping the wine glass tightly.

Natalie sets her glass down and clears her throat, her face suddenly serious.

"Jaxon, I am sorry though. I was mad, but I feel like I may have gone too far. Now that I've spent some time with you, it's clear you put so much detail into everything you do."

All of a sudden, she reaches across the table and places her hand on mine. My heart rate skyrockets as my eyes find hers.

"I have no doubt that applies to the wellbeing of your child above everyone else." She sighs and lowers her eyes. "I had no right to accuse you of neglecting her. I'm sorry for that."

I am stunned. Too stunned to speak. But I also might be distracted by the feeling of her hand on mine before she bashfully pulls it away.

"My life...well, it's been a bit of a disaster as of late, and with everything that happened yesterday in the garage," she says, tucking a lock of her blonde hair behind her ear.

She shudders, and immediately brings me back to the

conversation at hand.

"Natalie, no, please don't apologize for being angry with me. I was an ass. I had no right to attack you the way I did, and it was disrespectful, rude and frankly embarrassing."

Our eyes lock, and I swear I feel like my whole body is on fire. Again, I seem to forget what I was saying entirely.

What is this? What is happening to me? Get it together.

"As for feeling like a disaster, well, that I can relate with. I feel that way all the time. The joys of being a single dad. Jessica has practically grown up at that hotel, and I'm still grappling with the fact that something like that could happen there." I shake my head as I glance towards the fireplace. "It's just… unsettling."

My mind drifts back to the questions I had last night.

Who could have done that? Who can't I trust right now?

"Do you have any idea who was trying to come after her?" she asks, practically reading my mind.

But then she shakes her head as a look of embarrassment shoots across her face.

"I'm sorry, what am I doing? That's really none of my business."

"Well, considering you risked your life for her, I'd say it's a fair question," I shrug. "But unfortunately, I don't have any answers, only have more questions."

Also, it was worth mentally noting that the only person who could *give* me any more information is dead.

But Natalie doesn't want to hear about that.

It certainly would not help with improving her perception of me.

"And the police aren't doing anything to help?"

Hah, the police. That's cute.

"Not anything worth mentioning," I reply.

"I hope they find something," she says, aggressively cutting another bite of steak. "The world is crazy, but there's no reason to hurt children. Anyone who does that is absolute trash. I think they deserve to die."

"I agree," I say, trying to hide my smile.

I think I like feisty Natalie.

"So… changing the subject entirely, what did he do?" I ask, genuinely curious. "The ex, that is."

This question makes her laugh.

"Are we back to that? Is this really the conversation you want to have right now?"

"Yes. We've already covered my fuck up…" I say with a wink.

"Let's move on to his."

"Well, what do men usually do to fuck things up?" she asks sardonically, throwing her head back playfully.

"Oh, sweetheart," I chuckle. *"That* list is long and arduous." I clink my glass against hers in a toast. "Believe me, men never short of material to fuck up with."

"Noted," she laughs.

"So he fucked up?"

"Well, he fucked other people. For years. While we were together." she says with a sarcastic laugh. "So, yes, he did."

"Ouch. Yeah, that's pretty *fucked* up," I say, emphasizing the word with a wink.

She giggles.

"And yet... you're laughing about it!"

"I'm not laughing!"

But she is, and it's quickly becoming my favorite sound.

"I guess it's just so ridiculous that it's almost comical now." She sits back in her chair and folds her arms across her chest. "Or maybe I've just reached the point where I can look at it and think 'wow, I almost settled for *that*.'"

"Yikes," I say, pouring another glass of wine for both of us. She takes her glass and wraps the blanket around her tighter.

"I feel like I would have forgiven him for a singular indiscretion, but when I found out it had gone on for years, with multiple people... there's just no forgiveness for that."

Now that I understand. All too well.

"Did I tell you we were actually engaged?" she says softly.

No, but it's something I already knew—from your file.

"No, you didn't," I answer truthfully.

"I think that's what stung the most. Here I thought we were building our life, and he was off building a harem."

A part of me feels a twinge of guilt as she says this. My own sins claw tauntingly at the mental box I've put them in, trying to get out.

"He was my first real boyfriend," she continues, setting the glass down. "He had all the *firsts*, you know."

"The firsts are important for sure," I say carefully. "But they aren't everything. If you learn to experience life, you will find that there are plenty of firsts still to be had."

She looks up with me, a gentle vulnerability in her face.

"Have you dated anyone since you broke things off with him?" I ask. "Gotten back out into the world?"

She bashfully tucks a strand of hair behind her ear.

"I tried a few times, but it never went past the first few dates. It's hard to move on when you have so much…"

"Baggage," we both say at the same time.

"Baggage is something I understand," I say softly. "Some things just stay with you. They linger."

"Exactly," she says, biting her lip. "And I didn't know enough about what I was doing to make an accurate assessment." She takes another sip of wine, and stares into the glass. "Sometimes, I wonder if I just needed Colton and I to *be* something because I thought that's what everyone expected we *should* be. Does that make sense?"

"Yes. It does."

It makes perfect sense.

I remember having these same conversations with my father about Rachel. My father didn't hate Rachel, but he never truly felt that she was the *one* for me in the long term, just the one in front of me at the moment.

"Maybe it's my fault for pushing us to get married. Or who knows, maybe I was just terrible in bed," she says sarcastically. "Again he was my first, so…"

Her voice trails off, but I notice the nervous way she is fidgeting with her hands on the blanket.

"I'm sorry, I really shouldn't be saying all of this, I think it may be the wine," she says softly.

And maybe it is the wine, but I instinctively reach across the table and place my hand on hers.

"Natalie," I say, unable to stop myself. "I'm not going to claim to be any kind of expert on this subject, and believe me, I've fucked up myself. A lot. Probably more than anyone you know, but I can promise you that *you* were not the reason he did what he did."

I shock myself, unsure why I'm saying all of this to her.

Clearing my throat, I glance down at my hand on hers before finding her eyes again.

"I wasn't kidding when I said that we men have a million ways to fuck things up."

Rachel's face pops into the back of my head, and I close my eyes trying my best to shut it out.

"Sometimes it's intentional, sometimes it was just the circumstance of the moment." I pause, realizing she has not pulled away and her hand is still underneath mine, her soft skin under my fingertips distracting me momentarily. "But the ugly truth here is that no one forces us to do what we…do. It's always a *choice*. And sometimes those choices destroy us."

Jesus. What the fuck is in this wine?

That was way more emotional than I wanted to get.

"You sound like you know this from experience…" Natalie says softly, her eyes also settling on our hands on the table, but she still does not pull away.

But I do, now feeling the weight of my own demons.

"I have more than a few regrets in my life," I respond, sitting back in my chair. "Collateral damage, if you will."

If she only knew…

The look on her face is incredibly hard to read, and I briefly regret my openness.

I know by now that Natalie Tyler is a smart girl, and I'm sure she's put my veiled statements together. I'm also sure that by now she's realizing that I'm just another scumbag, and regretting ever letting me kidnap her for dinner.

As she should.

Because I *am* just another scumbag.

"I assume," Natalie says gently. "That you're referring to Jessica's mother?"

I stare at her for a long moment before nodding.

"Rachel," I say, swallowing hard. "And yeah, I screwed things up royally with her."

"Was she your wife?" Natalie asks.

I hesitate, unsure if I should try and unpack this box of demons with a woman I barely know.

Do we really want to go here?

I've gone years without doing so for my own safety.

"I don't mean to pry," Natalie says sincerely. "But if it makes you feel better, I promise you couldn't feel more pathetic than I do right now. And I hear misery loves company."

She smiles, and completely disarms me.

Fuck it. Why not? What do I have to lose?

It's not as if Natalie could possibly think any less of me than she already does.

I refill both our glasses.

"Rachel and I were never officially married. We'd been seeing each other on and off for several months when she got pregnant. We had a lot of pressure to get married, but Rachel didn't want to get married solely because of the baby, so we agreed to just put it on the back burner and figure it out later."

Natalie takes her wine and sits back in her chair. Intently

listening, her eyes fixed on me.

"But then my father died when I was twenty-seven, just a month after Jessica was born. I had to step into the empire he created. It came with a lot of pressure, and a lot of hours, and a lot of...vices."

As I take a sip of wine, flashbacks of clubs, and drugs, and naked women partying with me until the late hours of the morning come flooding back to me.

"She was struggling with being a new mom, and I was zero help. I slept around, and I was never there when she needed me. And when I was around, we fought about all the other things. Eventually, she finally had enough of my shitty behavior and left. Moved across the country. But just as she was getting settled on her own, she died in a house fire."

"Oh my..." Natalie says, raising her fingers to her mouth.

"The one great regret of my life is profoundly Rachel. She deserved better. And I never got to apologize to her for it."

Natalie says nothing, but her eyes are glued to me, and filled with pity.

My face heats, and I am immediately embarrassed.

I don't want her pity because I know I don't deserve it.

Fuck, what am I doing right now?

I have no idea why I am saying any of this.

"Excuse me," I say politely, standing to my feet. "I think I just need some air."

"Jaxon, I—" she starts to say quietly as I head outside onto the deck.

My head is spinning.

I can't believe I told her all of that. I literally just unburdened myself with a woman who just told me about the massive agony her ex-partner's infidelity caused her.

What the fuck was I thinking?

Suddenly, I hear footsteps sound on the deck behind me and turn to see Natalie with the blanket draped around her shoulders, standing there.

"Jaxon... I'm so sorry," she says gently. "I didn't mean to bring up something that is so clearly painful for you."

I shake my head.

"Don't be," I say, painting a smile on my face. "I got carried away."

I chuckle to myself.

"I'm clearly not very good at small talk."

"Or perhaps you just had a human moment," she says softly.

"Regrets are normal. We all have those you know."

The concern in her eyes is both disarming and uncomfortable.

"Just like Colton," I say, trying to turn the conversation away from me.

But Natalie's face is unchanging, still filled with empathy in those deep green eyes.

Well, this took a depressing turn. Great job.

"I'm sorry," I say, embarrassed. "It's been six years, and I still don't know how to talk about it."

She steps towards me and places a hand on my arm.

"But…you *are* talking about it, and that's what is important. It's the only way you can learn from it and move past it. I understand that this isn't easy for men." She smiles. "Especially men like *you*."

Men like me? Sweetheart, you don't know any men like me.

But her touch feels like electricity is pulsing through my bones, and I breathe in sharply from the impact.

"Perhaps it's not my place to say this, but the guilt you feel means you did at least learn something from this horrible chain of events. And maybe it means you have a chance to make a better choice next time."

Wait. What? Did she just…

"Natalie, I don't think there will be a next time for me."

"What do you mean?"

I sigh.

"I truly didn't mean to offend you last night. I just know how it usually goes with women in my life," I say, taking a deep breath. "It just doesn't…last very long."

She looks at me, but unlike last night, I see understanding in her eyes, instead of anger.

"Which is fine if that's what you want. But you must decide if that is all you want."

I chuckle to myself, shaking my head.

"I don't know what I want. So, I just stopped wanting."

So many thoughts are flooding my brain, none of them forming complete sentences.

"It's a lot to unpack with someone. I usually just don't."

"I understand that," she says with a smile.

"You do?" I ask.

"I do. Part of me wants to move on, and part of me doesn't know how," she says with a shrug. "Baggage."

"Hah, what a pair we are."

"Damn you," she says with a smile, looking off over the water.

"What?" I ask, confused. "What have I done now?"

I really need a manual for this shit...

"I was more than content just writing you off as just another asshole."

"Aren't I?" I scoff sarcastically. "Billionaire. Playboy. Dickhead. Remember?"

"Yeah, you are all of those things," she says, looking at the ground. "But that's not *who* you are. It's just what you want people to *think* you are."

Her eyes catch mine, and suddenly I am unable to move.

"What do you mean?"

"I mean, I see now there might be more to you than you let on."

Oh sweetheart, you have no idea.

"And now I see the scary façade you put on is actually just to conceal the fact you *do* have a heart beating somewhere in here." She steps forward and puts her hand on my chest. "Otherwise, you wouldn't have regrets. And you wouldn't care as much as you do. And you wouldn't have gone out of your way to do any of this tonight, or share this with me, just to help *me* feel less pathetic and alone in my misery."

Is that what I'm doing?

I have no idea anymore. I have no ideas whatsoever. My brain is completely devoid of thoughts entirely with her scent filling my nostrils. All I can think about is how pretty her face is in the harbor lights, while she stands here trying to piece my soul back together.

God, there really is no way around it... I want her.

I can't deny it, nor can I remember the last time I wanted anyone like this. I slowly touch her arm, my heart racing in my chest beneath her palm.

"Look, I don't know what type of man you've been, or what sins you've committed in your life. But, you said it yourself that all of this comes down to choices, right? Well, from what I can tell, you're at least trying to be a better man."

"Natalie, I am not a *better* man..." I start to say, but her hand is still on my ribs, and I feel my blood heating under her fingers.

My futile efforts to grasp control fail simultaneously, and my cock swells inside my pants. I simply cannot help the way my body responds to her.

"I don't believe that," she says, looking up at me through her lashes. "You lived through a major tragedy. And all you have done is try to protect and take care of the people around you. You might act cold, but you have a good heart."

"Natalie…" I say, trying to keep my composure, but her mossy green eyes staring into mine tempt me past the point of resistance.

In an instant, my mouth is on hers, crushing her lips to mine. I knock the blanket to the ground and my hand instinctively is in her hair, gently pulling her curls towards me, listening to her breath catching in her throat.

Her body collapses into mine, but then I feel her pull away.

Shit, have I gone too far?

I freeze instinctively, my hands still in her hair, and my breathing heavy. But then she presses her lips back to mine, her fervor matching mine.

Any remnants of self-control evaporate instantly.

Natalie, I promise you, I am not a better man. Because I want to do a million sinful things to you.

I wrap my free hand around her waist and pull her closer to me, brushing my fingers along the skin on her lower back. Slowly kissing her neck, and she moans out loud, turning me on even more. I flip us around, so that she is pressed up against the railing. I press my tongue into her mouth and enjoy the feeling of her tits pressed against me, and my throbbing cock pressed against her.

Fuck, I need her. Now.

I fully intend to throw patience out the window and ravish her, but out of the corner of my eye, I see Ethan step aboard the Ismena, his face dark.

And immediately I know something terrible has happened.

Chapter Eleven

Natalie

The tension on board The Ismena is so thick, it lingers around us like fog. Jaxon, who moments ago had seemed ready to take me passionately right there on the deck of the ship, is now cold and buried in his text messages.

This is awkward. Maybe I should go?

"Jaxon, I can call a cab if you need me to—" I start to suggest.

"I'm so sorry, Natalie." He interrupts, momentarily looking up from his phone.

The pain in his face is evident.

He runs a hand through his chestnut-colored hair.

"Believe me, this isn't how I wanted things to go this evening."

Oh my...how did he want it to go?

I want an answer to that question, and my body wants to return to what we were doing five minutes prior.

I try to think of something to say, but I find all my words have disappeared as I stare back into his eyes—eyes that have the power to hold me for eternity and spike my blood.

But his attention is pulled away from me and back to the apparent crisis at hand.

"Do we have the camera footage? Did anyone *see* anything?" Jaxon growls at Ethan, his anger visible on his face.

He looks terrifying.

"We will know shortly, Sir. We have men on-site investigating as we speak."

"And Jess—" he says looking up at Ethan.

"I came directly to you as soon as I secured Miss Pace," Ethan says with a steady nod.

"Miss Pace." That must be Jessica.

Jaxon's relief is evident but short-lived. His frigid expression returning almost instantly, chilling me to my core.

Something very bad must have happened.

Jaxon dials a number and walks outside. I watch as he slowly walks back and forth along the length of the deck, speaking on the phone to someone. I have no idea what is being said, but all I can tell is that I would not want to be on the receiving end of that phone call.

But even angry he's still a sight to behold. His neck and jaw are tense with stress, but they still look as though they have been chiseled straight out of stone. His collared shirt clings to his well-defined arms and his tie sits loosely at his collar bone.

I feel slightly guilty—ravenously watching him move, thinking selfishly to myself about how badly I want to rewind the clock and go back to when his hands were on me. He may look absolutely intimidating right now, but he is an extremely attractive man.

An extremely attractive man whose kiss had set my very bones on fire.

I have never felt a kiss like that before.

It felt like sheer electricity coursing through my veins and crackling on my skin. I was drawn to him, like a moth to a flame, and in that moment, I wanted to throw caution to the wind and just let him have his way with me.

But the moment had passed.

It's obvious he clearly has some major problem on his hands now just by looking at Ethan, who stands silently appraising me.

His expression is blank, but I can tell even he is on edge, so I don't bother trying to make conversation. The lines on his face, and the scars on his hands tell me that if he felt I was a threat to Jaxon, I wouldn't be allowed anywhere near him.

Jaxon Pace is definitely complex, that much is certain. I've known him for just over forty-eight hours, and in that time, I've seen his daughter almost kidnapped, and now some sort of serious altercation at one of his warehouses.

There is so much drama in his life.

And then there's the ridiculous world of luxury this man orbits in, which is well beyond my comprehension. I'm out of my element here, and acknowledging this, I suddenly feel stupid.

What am I doing here? Why am I allowing myself to get distracted with this man's life?

It's not like I live in Chicago or even anywhere remotely close to the city. I live in a different state, 2000 miles away, and I'm only in town for a few days. I'm just a guest at his hotel. I truly have no business entertaining this fantasy, and no business kissing him. And I certainly have no business picturing him shoving me up against a wall and ripping my clothes off.

But… he kissed me.

He made that choice, not me. Even if I had been wanting to do it myself, Jaxon was still the first to act on it.

And holy shit, what a kiss it was.

I shiver, not from the cold, but from the memory of his lips on mine, and his hand wrapping around me.

"We need to return to The Jefferson." Jaxon's voice startles me as he walks back indoors. "Immediately. It's not safe here."

I nod silently, trying to stay calm, but also trying to silence my thoughts about the kiss we shared, which now appears long forgotten.

I follow Ethan off the yacht, with Jaxon close behind. I regret not being able to say goodbye to Marco or compliment him on the delicious dinner he prepared for us.

"Jaxon, you said it's not safe. Am I in any…danger?" I ask softly, almost terrified of the answer.

But in an instant, I feel his hand on the small of my back again and his breath on my neck.

"Don't worry, right now, you're the safest woman in the city," he whispers against my skin, setting me ablaze. "You're with me."

Shivers erupts down my spine, and my insides clench hearing him say this to me.

However, this would perhaps be more romantic if Jaxon were not also simultaneously looking around the marina scanning for some potential threats.

We don't head back to the Lamborghini, but instead to a black Range Rover SUV with a driver. He opens the door to the backseat and helps me inside, before walking around and getting in himself. As we pull away, I notice another SUV pulling out of the marina behind us.

"Don't worry, they're with us," Jaxon says, reading my thoughts, but not looking up from his phone.

We have extra security now?

He dials a number and holds the phone to his ear. "Good evening Sally, please proceed with what we discussed."

He hangs up the phone without saying goodbye.

What the...?

I am watching all of this unfold but understanding nothing, and I feel suddenly as if I probably should've just stayed in my hotel room and watched cable.

But that fucking kiss...

It lingers on my mind, and it feels as if it was imprinted in the marrow of my bones.

I sigh softly.

Stop it, Natalie. You're an idiot. I'm sure Jaxon Pace kisses seventeen women a week.

Screw this, I need to get a handle on my emotions and stop acting like a fragile little flower trembling in the wind.

"Natalie..." Jaxon's voice cuts the tension in the car and my self-deprecating inner monologue. "I want to thank you for a wonderful evening. I'm sorry that—"

"Jaxon, it's no problem," I say, cutting him off. "I understand that you're a businessman, and something has come up and you have business to handle." I continue, trying to hide the way even his voice affects me.

I swallow hard.

"I appreciate you distracting me for a little while. Dinner was amazing. Please be sure to express my gratitude to Marco."

He stares at me in silence, with a look that is both intimidating and incredibly visceral—like a lion about to pounce on a gazelle. I'm aware that I'm the gazelle in this scenario, and I'm also aware that I can't breathe when he stares at me like this.

What is he thinking? Is he going to kiss me again? Or touch me?

But unfortunately, he does neither.

His phone buzzes and he's instantly pulled away again, breaking the trance between us.

Good job there, Nat. You really kept it together.

I slump into the window, my mind running in circles.

Before long we're back at The Jefferson.

The driver pulls up right in front of the valet. I try to open my door but another tall man, with dark skin and olive-green eyes, beats me to it.

"Miss Tyler, the concierge has requested you stop by the desk before heading up to your room," he says softly.

"Thank you, um—"

"Charlie," he smiles.

Well, at least he seems friendly.

Jaxon walks around to my side of the car and stands beside me.

"Again, Natalie, I'm sorry for this disruption to the evening," he says with a sigh. "I will be in touch."

He looks as though he wants to say more but chooses not to. His mind appears to be somewhere else. I feel awkward as well, so I just smile at him.

"Thank you again for dinner," I say politely.

He pauses a moment more, his eyes raking my body as I stand paralyzed, unable to move under the weight of his gaze.

"I *will* be in touch," he repeats firmly, a darkness in his voice lingering in the air between us.

But before I can dissect it, he is back in the car, and being driven away by Ethan.

"Do you need help, Miss Tyler?" Charlie asks me, bringing me back to the present.

I shake my head.

"No, thank you," I say with a forced smile. "I'm fine."

He nods, then heads back over to the valet booth, where a couple of adolescent boys shoot glances my way. I realize I probably look ridiculous, getting dropped off by Jaxon Pace outside of his own hotel.

What they must think of me.

I straighten my shoulders and head inside. Once again, I cannot wait to take a hot shower and wash away my thoughts of Jaxon.

But I have to stop by the front desk first and thankfully, I don't see Sally anywhere.

I'm not sure I can face her after the flower fiasco.

"Hello, I was told that you wanted to see me?" I say to the pretty blonde attendant, as I step up to the counter. "You had something for Natalie Tyler?"

But then, out of nowhere, Sally appears.

Uh oh. What have I done now?

"Ahh yes, Miss Tyler," she says politely. "I regret to inform you that we had a minor incident in the room above yours with the plumbing."

"What?" I gasp.

"Not to worry, we caught it just in time so nothing in your room was damaged, but we obviously had to make repairs on it immediately," she continues.

Are you kidding me? Could this night get any worse?

"And, with that in mind, we've gone ahead and reserved another room for you. It's one of our finest *suites*."

Wait... what?

"I do, again, apologize for this inconvenience, and if there is *anything* we can do to make your stay with us more exceptional, please don't hesitate to ask. Anything at all."

I am speechless. I just stand there staring at her, shocked that they had already handled all of this in the short time I was gone.

"Of course, I will just go back and gather my things immediately," I finally manage to say.

"Oh, don't worry, your things have already been moved, with the utmost of care, into your new room," she says while handing me a new room key.

"Um, okay. Wow," I say, taking the key from her. "What floor am I on?"

"Floor forty-four, Ma'am. The only difference is you will be using the private lifts, just to the left of the bar over there," she says, pointing to another elevator hidden around the corner.

I just stare at her, my mind still trying to catch up with this development.

"Also, I think you have a couple of messages," she says, walking over and sifting through some papers that lay organized on the back counter.

She hands me two envelopes.

"Umm, thank you, Sally."

And then it occurs to me: Jaxon said her name in the car tonight on his phone call right before we arrived.

"Sally, please proceed with what we discussed."

Suddenly I understand: *Jaxon* is responsible for this.

"Please, at least let me upgrade your room."

That was what he said to me yesterday when he was trying to apologize.

This. Damn. Man.

It is blatantly obvious now that he just faked a "room disaster" to get his way. I briefly consider protesting, but I can tell that even though Sally appears sweet and professional she would certainly never dare to disappoint Jaxon.

Unbelievable. This evening is unbelievable.

This man is unbelievable.

But I am too tired to argue, so instead, I just turn around and head for the lifts she described. I scan my card and step inside. The elevator is gorgeous, and there is even a small loveseat inside. I see there are only two floor buttons on the keypad. Floors forty-four and forty-five. I press forty-four and I decide to take a seat on the chair.

Is this real? Was any of tonight real or have I just had too much wine?

I look at the two envelopes that Sally handed me and open the first one, which is a card from Ryan and his fiancé with the details of their rehearsal dinner on Thursday.

I open the next one, but inside is just a blank piece of paper. No note on either side, and nothing else in the envelope.

Hmm, I guess it must have just been a mistake.

The doors ding softly and open into a foyer, illuminated with soft lighting from an overhead chandelier hanging over a small table, decorated with a vase of white roses.

That's the vase with the red bow.

On the table is another envelope, however, this one is a thick stock letterhead, and *my* name is handwritten on the outside.

It's from Jaxon.

I pick it up and realize that even the envelope smells like him, the smallest hint of his cologne lingering on the paper.

He wrote this himself. In his own hand.

I slowly open the envelope as I walk further into the foyer…

Natalie-
I can be very persistent when it comes to things I want.
-J

He included his phone number. His *personal* number.

As my brain tries to catch up with my racing heart, I look up from the letter in my hand, and my jaw drops when I see the view I have just walked into.

Floor to ceiling windows, probably twenty feet in height, lead the way to a massive balcony. Outside I can see an outdoor bar and sitting area complete with a jacuzzi and fireplace.

To my right a formal dinner table and chairs sit adjacent to a kitchen outfitted with granite counter tops. Further still, the living room boasts a variety of custom sofas and lounge chairs all positioned in front of a huge gas fireplace, glowing warmly in the corner.

As I take a step to my right, I find myself walking into the main bedroom. A huge platform king bed with fluffy white sheets faces windows staring out into the night, boasting the Chicago skyline lit up like Christmas and another cozy gas fireplace warms a smaller sitting area.

I am utterly speechless.

Jaxon has not gifted me a suite.

Jaxon has gifted me a *penthouse*.

Chapter Twelve

JAXON

"I need to know who these fuckers are!" I shout in the car. "There's strict protocols in place to always prevent this situation from happening!"

"Only one of *our* men could've accessed the loading bay," Ethan says gravely, confirming what is already preying heavily on my mind.

"So, we have a rat… and two dead men," I growl.

This night just keeps getting better and better.

The phone rings on the vehicle intercom and I answer.

"Talk to me," I snap.

"Sir, we have secured the area, and the team is in the process of scanning the vessel."

"And? What the fuck are we dealing with here?"

"Sir, I'm not sure. This…" I hear Samuel take a breath hesitantly. "This appears to be something *new*."

"What do you mean, Sam?"

"Sir, I will show you when you get here, but there appears to be a new player in the game."

What the actual fuck is he talking about?

"But," he continues. "We have one of them. We found him hiding in the storage bay of the ship."

Ethan shoots me a look and shuts off the call.

Good. Very Good.

I dial Levi.

"Levi, I want checks done on all our other yards, immediately. Change the access codes and assign one surveyor per location— Alpha level only! Redisperse if necessary, but I want everything locked down! No one in or out without checking in with the base!"

I need to secure my ships, and I need to protect my men.

We pull up outside the warehouse where four of my men are waiting to surround me.

In an imminent threat situation, this is standard procedure: Ethan runs point, and the rest of these assholes have my back. We walk into the main area of the loading dock where I see one of my ships, The Passenger, sitting silently in her hold.

Because this particular ship was carrying Victor Black's drugs, this tells me that this wasn't just a random warehouse robbery attempt.

No. This was done by someone who *knew* the cargo.

Samuel greets us. He's a tall, reasonably fit redhead, with freckles covering most of his pale skin. "Sir, this way."

He takes us to the foreman's office, where the body of my warehouse foreman lays slumped over in his office chair, covered in blood and glass from the shattered warehouse viewing window.

"Talk to me, Sam."

"Sir, we believe this was intended to just be a robbery of the cargo. From the surveillance footage we can tell that the intruders gained access to the building, and then immediately came up the stairs and fired two shots through the glass, instantly killing the foreman."

"Just a robbery of the cargo."

If that were true, I find it oddly convenient that the foreman would be the first to die, as he would be expected to be the first to alert base if someone were able to gain access to our warehouse. I watch as Sam's eyes hit the pavement.

"There's more, Sir."

He motions for us to follow him further down the catwalk, where there lies a linen rucksack… with boots sticking out from under it. As he pulls back the cover, I freeze.

Bruno lies lifeless on the catwalk, covered in blood. Two bullet wounds in his chest, and his eyes staring off toward nothing.

No. My eyes must be playing tricks on me.
The knot in my stomach tightens.
This kid was just that… a kid. He was watching TV with my daughter two days ago for Christ's sake.
This is my fault. I fucking knew better.
After Bruno's parents died, we were the only family he had. Like me, this was the only life he had ever known, as his parents had both been involved in this business. Something told me that he was too young to get involved but he kept insisting he was ready. I'd given him warehouse duty to keep him out of trouble.
And yet trouble still found him.
Fuck, Bruno.
"Sir, it appears Bruno heard the shots from his post and ran up to assist the foreman," Samuel says, a quiet rage and sadness behind his voice. "Where he was killed."
I say nothing.
My words have all escaped me. Staring at Bruno's lifeless body I feel as though I fired the bullets myself.
His death is on me.
I look out over the edge of the scaffolding at The Passenger resting comfortably in her hold. Around her, crates and cranes sit non-operational for the time being.
I know my warehouse security is the equivalent of Fort Knox. Too many safeguards exist for any of these potential eventualities.
Too many for this to be just a random event.
Someone fucking planned this.
Someone who *knows* our processes, our cargo, and our access codes, planned and executed a hit on my warehouse and my men. And I am seething.
"You said we have one of them?" I say, slowly turning.
"Yes, Sir."
"Where. Is. He?" I growl.
I want vengeance. I want blood. And I am going to get it.
Samuel stares back at me, and nods to the boat.
Despite the thirty men now crawling and scanning this place top to bottom, the warehouse is silent as we walk downstairs, and aboard The Passenger. The tightly packed hallways on the ship echo our every movement, and all around us crates upon crates lie untouched.
Seems strange for a burglary.
In the bow of the ship, we find *him.*
A skinny white man, tied to a chair, his head hanging towards his

lap as he mumbles to himself. I see the sweat on his brow, and the unusual way his body twitches at every sound. These are symptoms I have seen before. He is obviously out of his mind on drugs.

My men have clearly already tried to extract *some* information from him, based on the blood on his shirt and pants, and the fresh bruises forming on his face.

Bruno was one of them. They are just as angry as I am.

"He hasn't told us anything." Levi steps up next to me. "Except mumbling some fucking nonsense about a two-headed dragon."

I notice he has a tattoo on his left forearm. A black ink circle encompassing a dragon with two heads. It occurs to me that the kidnapper had the same tattoo. Which is all the confirmation I need.

I step forward in front of him.

"Look at me," I growl.

The man ignores my request and continues to mumble and tap his fingers on the chair.

"I said look at me!" I thunder at him, my voice echoing loudly in the metal hull, rattling the walls and causing the single lightbulb above us to flicker.

The man recoils in his seat and goes silent. Slowly he lifts his head to stare at me. One of his eyes is blue, the other is brown. Although, the brown eye is completely bloodshot.

Likely a *gift* from my men.

A string of three tattooed teardrops trickles down under his bloodshot eye, and he has a swastika-shaped scar on his forehead, as if it had been carved into his skin.

This man is an ex-con, and the three tears symbolize each stay he has had in the joint. Prison trash.

Prison trash that somehow made it into my warehouse and shot up my men.

This infuriates me even more.

It's no secret the men I employ are dangerous men. Nor is it a secret that we work in a dangerous and frequently illegal enterprise. But I do not employ petty thugs like this.

And they don't deserve to die at the hands of scum.

Bruno did not deserve to die, at all.

Swastika Face tries to lower his face again, but I catch his chin in my hand and grip it so hard I can almost feel it crack.

I force him to look at me. His eyes anxiously shoot to me momentarily but then he tries feebly to look away.

"You will look at me, asshole, or I will cut off your fucking eyelids and make you eat them!" I shout.

I see a flash of fear work its way across his face as his eyes slowly find mine.

"Good. Now we understand each other," I say, letting go of his blood covered face.

The man starts to tremble, looking about nervously.

Levi passes me a chair, which I drag slowly and deliberately across the floor. The piercing echo of its legs scraping against the metal floor sounds like nails on a chalkboard.

I watch as the man jumps as I drop it in front of him. Gripping the back, I straddle it so that we're face to face.

"I'm a busy man, so let's get right to it. You're going to tell me what you and your buddies were doing in my warehouse."

He is silent.

Remembering that Bruno's lifeless body lies above me, rage suddenly floods my veins.

Fuck this shit.

I yank my gun from its holster and shoot him in his left foot, shattering the bones to pieces. Reverberations from the bullet echo around the room, as do the screams of my new little prison pal.

"Do I have your fucking attention now?!"

"I don't know anything! I swear, I don't! Argggh!"

"See, I don't believe that," I say, pointing my finger and wagging it in his face. "Those teardrops on your cheek tell me you've spent some time in our dark little world, and I believe a seasoned criminal like yourself knows that snitching on his masters could get him killed."

I nod to Ethan who hands me his tactical knife, and my leather driving gloves.

"And, believe me, I understand that prospect seems scary. You are right to fear your employers. They *will* kill you."

The man continues to whimper and moan in agony as I slowly pull my gloves on, one by one, before flicking open the knife. I press the blade to his forearm, cutting him only slightly to demonstrate how sharp the blade is.

"Arrrgh!" he cries, trying to look away from me, but I grab his sweaty face in my hand.

"But I want you to understand," I growl. "You should fear *me* more."

His eyes flash with panic and pain.

I step directly on the bullet wound in his foot, applying my full weight and listening with satisfaction as my little Nazi friend starts screaming his head off.

"Two of my men are dead," I seethe, covering his mouth. "So, I promise, I will make death a fucking *luxury* for you."

He continues whimpering, fear dripping off him like the sweat dripping off his forehead.

"You're going to tell me what you know, or I'm going to carve you up like a Thanksgiving turkey. And as for your masters? Well, they won't be troubled. Because you've always been dispensable to them."

Swastika Face starts crying. He strains against the ropes holding him to the chair, reeling from the pain I'm inflicting and shaking, terrified at the prospect of what is to come.

As he should be.

While I consider myself a fair man, I have no mercy when it comes to my family. Or my men. Those who have dared to cross me have found that I have no pity. No sympathy. No remorse. I'm not even human.

I'm a *Don*. Doing a Don's job: protecting what's his.

The way I see it, Bruno's life was cut short by this thug or thugs like this. We will never get him back. So, this man is going to answer for that.

"We can do this the easy way, or the hard way. Either way, no one is coming to your rescue tonight."

I step on his foot again.

"Oh, God!" He screams.

"God will not save you here, friend," I snort. "Trust me when I say there will be no final confession for you, unless you confess to *me*."

"Look man, it was just a job!" The man screams, his whole body shaking. "Just a robbery."

"I know it was a fucking robbery you moron!" I spit in his face. "Who ordered it?!"

"I don't know his name. I met him the day I got out. He said if I did a job for him, he'd hook me up with some smack. That's all!"

"Then how do you explain this?" I snap, grabbing his arm. "Did you just coincidentally pick the same tattoo as the man who tried to kidnap my daughter two days ago?"

"I don't know what you're talking about!" He whines, looking away uncomfortably.

He's lying.

"Oh, I think you do," I say venomously, pulling out my gun again.

"Look man, I don't know anything about a kidnapping, I swear!"

But I don't believe him.

I lock eyes with Levi, who steps forward and holds the man's hand down on the arm of the chair.

"No! Don't! Please! I don't know anything!" he whimpers. "I don't!"

I take the knife and press it above the knuckle on his index finger, smashing the blade down hard and pulling it through the tip. Shattering bone and nerve endings all at once.

His blood curdling scream rips through the hull of the ship.

"What were you doing in my fucking warehouse?!" I shout at him.

He continues screaming, and I am losing my patience.

I lean in as if I am going to split another fingertip, and he suddenly decides to start talking.

"He made me join it!" The man screams. "The man has an organization called the Two-Headed Dragon, that's the name. He said we weren't allowed to talk about it with anyone or they would go after our families and friends."

"I want a name!"

I see him make a conscious choice not to answer this, despite his body convulsing with pain.

We can come back to that. He has nine more fingers.

"How many men came here tonight?!"

"Six! We had six…" he breathes, still crying. "And someone on the inside."

"Who?" I ask, grabbing his hair and pulling his head up.

He thrashes about wildly, trying desperately to get out of the chair, but I give him no relief, pressing my weight into his bleeding hand.

"Who the fuck let you in!?" I thunder.

His wild eyes stare at me, before slowly drifting up to a corner of the room.

I follow his gaze… and it lands on *Samuel.*

Two things happen in the blink of an eye.

First, all my men in the room draw their weapons and point them directly at Samuel.

And two, Samuel pulls his own gun, puts it in his mouth, and pulls the trigger.

His head explodes all over us.

The ringing from the gunshot in the metal hull echoes in the room, which promptly erupts into chaos. The men are screaming in disbelief and horror.

"What the actual *fuck*?!" I yell, completely stunned.

I turn back to the man in the chair, his face now stained with the blood of my bodyguard, who just blew his own brains out.

A twisted smile forms across the convict's face, as he starts laughing.

"You have no idea what you're getting involved with… they are commmmming!"

Suddenly he starts screaming, the insanity behind his eyes wide with fury.

"All hail the two-headed dragon! All hail the two-headed dragon!"

Fuck this.

I put a bullet in his head.

When the ringing from the third gunshot stops, I can hear my men muttering amongst themselves. Their trust in each other is visibly shaken, and their suspicions are rapidly escalating. The chaos in the room is suffocating, and I fear this situation could quickly become a bloodbath.

I need to get them out of here.

"Enough!" Ethan yells, apparently having the same idea.

All conversation screeches to a halt, as seven men stare at me, likely just as confused as I am.

"Everyone out," I whisper.

Without a word, they file past Samuel's corpse, lying in a pool of his own blood.

One of my best men, for over a decade, just took his own life right in front of me. And I have no idea *why*.

"What the fuck Ethan?" I whisper breathlessly.

He just shakes his head, unable to reply.

I stare down at Samuel, then to the convict in the chair, whose head hangs off the back, a bullet hole between his eyes.

"What the fuck just happened?" I repeat. "And what the *fuck* is the Two-Headed Dragon?"

It's just after midnight, when I sit down on the couch in my study to review the surveillance footage.

I've had a shower and poured myself a drink, but it has done nothing to calm my racing mind.

The footage reveals Sam, using his fingerprint scan plus four-digit code, to let six masked intruders inside. I watch as they make their way to the holding bay where one of them immediately goes upstairs and shoots the foreman. Bruno appears on the screen, rushing in to help.

…Only to be shot twice by the coked-out Nazi.

Well what do you know.

I wish I'd made him suffer more.

All of the events I'm watching on the footage, happened exactly the way Samuel said it did. *Before* he shot himself.

And despite my obvious disappointment in Samuel's betrayal, it's clear from watching the footage that he wasn't aware these intruders planned on killing anyone.

My stomach twists, watching him try frantically to resuscitate Bruno on the catwalk, sobbing over his body.

What really doesn't make sense, however, is what the intruders did next. After eliminating the only two possible targets, they had plenty of time to move the product off the ships. But they didn't.

They didn't even *try*.

Instead, a masked man, dressed head-to-toe in black clothing, looks up directly into the surveillance camera, and holds up two fingers. Then he fires his gun into the ceiling, signaling it was time to go.

And then they just left.

Everyone except our Nazi friend, whom I assume stayed behind to try and get some of the goods he'd been promised.

"This doesn't make any sense, Ethan," I say, stopping the tape. "Who puts this much effort into breaking into a secure facility for a robbery, only to leave two dead men, and the goods behind?"

"Someone who wasn't interested in the robbery," he says as he exhales the smoke from a cigarette. "Only in making it look like one."

Why would someone do that?

"There's something else," Ethan says, producing an envelope. "We found this in Samuel's pocket when we stripped his body."

Inside the envelope is a blank piece of paper, with the words "*Illuminate Me-S*" written faintly in the corner.

"It looks like nothing," Ethan says, gently taking the paper from me and turning it, so I am looking at the surface. "But if you look at it carefully, there is a faint embossment."

It's then that I see it—a two-headed dragon, identical to the tattoo the cokehead, and the kidnapper sported.

"Did Sam write that?" I ask, pointing to the only words on the paper.

Ethan nods.

"Jaxon this is way too organized to be just a random hit from one of the lower-level gangs. This is professional, with damn near surgical precision."

"You think that's what Sam was talking about?" I ask.

"I think we at least need to acknowledge the possibility we are dealing with a new player of some kind," Ethan says gravely.

Great. Just what I fucking need right now.

I take another drag on my cigarette and sit back in my chair.

"A new player." I repeat aloud. "As if this city isn't crowded enough already."

We have worked so hard to establish and maintain the fragile peace we have, and that peace hangs by a thread between me and the other Dons. And between me and Victor Black, the alliance is shaky at best.

I glance down at the blank paper on the table and pick it up to examine it again.

"Illuminate me."

An idea comes to mind.

I grab my lighter, and wave it beneath the paper, careful not to set it on fire. I'm hoping maybe the heat will bring forth a message, concealed in some sort of invisible ink.

Why else would Sam have written "Illuminate Me."

But unfortunately, nothing happens.

I guess not.

"And we have no chatter, or intel on this Two-Headed Dragon. Or what it is they're after. Or why they are targeting us," I say this not as a question, but as an acknowledgement.

My phone buzzes in my pocket. I have a text message from a 786 number.

MIAMI

After all, I saw it in a file I read recently.

But before I can open the text, I notice the glow from my phone has caused text to appear on the paper I am holding.

"Illuminate."

I say out loud, turning on the flashlight on my phone, and

watching as the paper immediately lights up with text.

You will have visitors at the Reuben Street Warehouse on Wednesday night at 9pm. If you value the lives of your wife and son, you will grant them access. Do not test us.

My blood runs cold.

This message was meant for Samuel, and it was a threat to his family. By the Two-Headed Dragon.

"If Samuel was being threatened, why wouldn't he have told us?" I ask Ethan.

I run my hand through my hair, sighing heavily.

"Like, that's what we *do*. That's all we're supposed to do. It's our fucking job to protect each other in this family."

Ethan sighs.

There's more...

"When we were cleaning up Samuel's body, we found clear track marks on his arms." Ethan's face is a mixture of both concern, and sadness. "It's unsure at this time whether it was heroin or meth."

Well, that explains his desire to keep it from us.

But something still nags at me.

"Samuel was the first to greet us when we arrived at the warehouse." I lean forward on my knees and stroke my chin. "I mean he walked us around, he explained what happened... the whole time knowing he was on the security cameras, and that we would eventually see all of this. He knew that ultimately, we would find out he was somehow involved."

Ethan pauses to look at me.

"Sam knew our ways," I continue. "He knew we would review the security footage the same way he knew we would interrogate our little pal. And considering how far gone our little Nazi friend was, even before we got persuasive, Sam must have known the guy would crack and blow his cover."

"You think Sam *planned* to end it there." Ethan finishes.

"I think he was in over his head, and I think he knew he had fucked up the moment he opened that door for the robbers. I don't believe he ever intended for anyone to die."

Especially Bruno.

I refuse to believe anything else. But this realization chills me to my core. From the moment I brought Bruno into the family, Samuel had taken to him, and looked after him like an older brother.

Technically, Bruno wasn't a member of my Alpha Squad.

Alpha Squad status in the Pace Family Mafia was an honor bestowed on only the elite, and reserved for the best of the best. The six men chosen for Alpha were handpicked to be my personal protection. Each man was in charge of a different aspect of my business, and commanded their own team however they saw fit. They were the men I trusted most in the world, and I rarely trusted anyone.

Under Samuel's watchful eye, I allowed Bruno to shadow the Alpha Squad occasionally, to give him a sense of direction and perhaps a goal he could work towards.

Both of them had lost family members in the line of duty, and they connected instantly. This, combined with the fact that Samuel was one of my oldest and most trusted men, had been a big part of why I felt so comfortable with letting Bruno do warehouse duty when he was not with me.

"He probably thought this was just going to be a robbery, skimming a little off the top," Ethan says, his lips pursed. "But then it clearly went south quickly, and at that point there was nothing he could do."

"Maybe *this*," I say, picking up the paper again and staring at it. "Was the only thing Sam *could* do. He knew how all of this would play out, and he purposefully left it for us to find. His final act was his way of telling us."

"Or *warning* us," Ethan says, taking the paper from me and examining it again.

"Every dealer in this town knows me, and they know my rules about my Alpha Squad," I growl. "If Samuel was using, there's only one person who would be willing to risk their neck to supply him."

"Black," Ethan says quietly.

"And he knows my fucking policy when it comes to the men on *my* protection order."

That fucker. I know he's involved.

I stand up and walk to my bar, needing another drink.

"I want all the Squads drug tested, Ethan. Alpha, Beta and Zeta. All of them. First thing in the morning. No exceptions."

"Yes, Sir," Ethan responds firmly.

"Ethan, we've been over this. *You* don't have to call me Sir when it's just the two of us. It's unnecessary. You know this. I'm not your Don here," I say, motioning to the room the two of us are standing in.

This is a courtesy I afford only to Ethan, given our relationship.

"You are always my Don," Ethan says as I turn back around toward the bar. "Otherwise, I wouldn't be here at all. I'd be throwing back drinks on a beach somewhere."

I smirk to myself, pouring my drink before turning around to face him.

"You know what I mean," I say, taking a drink.

"Forgive me," he says with a smile. "But it felt necessary."

"And why's that?"

"You were a Don tonight. A *real* Don."

"Oh, so you *do* approve of violence?" I smirk.

"*Calculated* violence," he says, crossing his legs. "It must serve a purpose. Otherwise, we're all just savages. Your father taught me that. You sounded a lot like him tonight. More than ever. He'd be proud."

I try to offer a drink to Ethan, but as always, he refuses.

Ethan governs himself according to his own set of rules, one of which being that he won't drink while working.

Which is one of the many reasons I can be more relaxed with him.

"I'll make sure everyone tests in the morning."

"I can't have loose ends like that. Especially on my Alpha Squad," I say quietly. "I want you *personally* to look into all the recent interactions and dealings of everyone on Alpha Squad. Quietly. If everyone checks out, have them perform the same evaluation for their Beta and Zeta teams. Hopefully, it will create a sense of accountability. I need everyone on the lookout."

I walk over to the window, staring into the backyard while I take a drink.

"I need to know if Black has hooks in any of my men. And I know how persuasive he can be."

Unfortunately, I know better than anyone.

Ethan stands up and walks over to me slowly.

"Jaxon," he whispers, "You can't keep beating yourself up about that shit any longer. It's in the past, leave it there."

I turn to face him, studying the concern in his face before placing my hand on his shoulder.

"That's what I need you to find out," I say quietly. "I trust *you*, Ethan. I need to know who else I can trust."

He stares at me for a long moment before nodding, his gaze falling to the floor. Understanding that I need to be alone, he heads for the door.

"You know," he says, pausing in the doorway. "I know Samuel's betrayal is a shock. But the men respect you. They respect this family. You've given them plenty of reasons to do so in the last few years. Tonight, you just gave them another one. You *can* trust your men, Jaxon."

I stare at Ethan. He knows exactly why I am hesitant to trust anyone in my life. But especially my men.

"Sam's family—" I start to say, changing the subject.

"I'll make sure they have whatever they need. Including protection," Ethan finishes. "We will look after them. As always."

I nod and watch him leave.

Taking another drink, I look back at the security footage playing on a loop in my study and decide I've had enough.

I shut it off and head upstairs to the bedrooms, stopping briefly to check on Jessica, who is sound asleep, surrounded by all her stuffed animals.

As I step into my room, I walk directly out on the balcony, lighting another cigarette as I do.

Clearly, I am doing great at quitting.

As I stand there staring out over the lake, I cannot stop thinking about Sam.

Fucking, Sam.

I have no doubts now, that he absolutely knew the moment I arrived that he planned to end it there. As payment for his sins against me, and against the Family, but especially against Bruno.

But how long had he been under Black's thumb?

I know *exactly* how crushing that thumb could be.

After all, it had been Black who had encouraged me to experiment with his wicked concoctions when I had first taken over from my father. The pressure to succeed, and to gain the respect of my men, had me burning the candle eighteen to twenty hours a day. With a brand-new baby at home, sleep was never restful.

Enter Victor Black.

He pushed 'uppers' at me as a way to cope. But soon thereafter, had me addicted to practically everything he supplied, including some of the weird combinations he had his chemists put together.

With all of the uppers, downers, and inbetweeners, it was safe to say I was always on a high of some kind.

I found myself a man of two extremes—rage and lust.

A man out of his mind, needing a warm body to punch, or fuck.

Which is how I hurt Rachel.

In my defense, I never laid a hand on her in anger. Ever.

I just laid my hands all over *other* women. Repeatedly.

Until one day she finally had enough of my bullshit, and left in the middle of the night.

I kept tabs on her obviously, as she was still the mother of my child, and she had left Jessica behind with me. But Rachel and I never *spoke* again. Which meant that I never got the opportunity to apologize, or make things right with her, before she died.

Tonight was the first time I have really thought about her in years. And I opened-up about her to Natalie tonight, a lot more than I ever intended.

I still can't believe I did that.

Openness is not really something I do.

But there is something about that girl I can't explain.

Natalie wasn't *trying* to pull information out of me, or interrogate me, but she had me so comfortable I just started spilling my guts. And once I started it was like a tap I could not turn off.

Thinking of Natalie, I pull my phone out of my pocket and open the text from the Miami number.

MIAMI
12:15 a.m.: You, Jaxon Pace, are impossible. But thank you for this room. It's incredible. As was my evening. With you. For some strange reason, I can't stop smiling.

I chuckle, and flick my half-finished cigarette off the balcony, before walking back inside.

I left her at just past nine in the lobby of The Jefferson, and Charlie had confirmed she made it up to the penthouse safely. That tells me that she's probably been thinking of me for hours, and finally broke down and decided to text me.

I find myself smiling. Thinking of Natalie provides me the first relief in hours.

But then I shudder.

If she knew what those hours had entailed...

If she knew I had tortured and eventually murdered a man, and watched another blow his brains out, she would probably run screaming for the hills.

As she should. And I should let her.

Then again, maybe not.

She *had* been willing to fight a man in a parking garage to save Jessica. She tasered one of my men, and cracked Ethan's nose, unsure if they were friends or foes.

I don't know her very well, but there's certainly a fire in her I haven't seen before.

And it was that same fire that set me ablaze onboard The Ismena tonight.

I wanted her. Desperately. I loved the way she kissed me, and the feeling of her curls in my hands as her body was pressed against me. A stunningly perfect body, that ached for me the same way mine ached for her.

I've never felt that kind of... desire before.

Sure, I've seen beautiful women before, and I've definitely fucked my fair share of beautiful women before.

But none of them, not a single one, has *ever* come close to making me feel what I felt tonight. It was like some surreal combination of having a relaxed dinner with a friend...while *also* wanting to bend her over and fuck her six ways from Sunday on every surface on the ship.

I glance at the clock.

12:37 a.m.

I suppose that's still an acceptable window to text her back.

Me
12:38 a.m.: I enjoyed this evening. And I very much look forward to making you smile again. Soon.

I smile to myself as a delicious and equally devious idea pops into my head.

Oh, Miss Tyler, what I have in store for you...

Chapter Thirteen

Natalie

I awake to the sun blasting through the gigantic bedroom windows.

As beautiful as the penthouse is, the reflection of the rising sun against the building across from the hotel is blinding. I stumble out of bed and try fruitlessly to yank the blinds closed. But unfortunately for me, they are electronic, and I can't find a keypad on a wall anywhere. So, I just gave up.

I debate laying back down in the heavenly down sheets, but now I am utterly awake.

Coffee. It's time for coffee.

Something tells me that in a penthouse like this, with every possible need accounted for, there probably exists a semi-stocked kitchen.

And I am right.

In this kitchen I find a variety of coffees and teas, along with fresh fruit and muffins. In the fridge there are hard boiled eggs, as well as an assortment of omelets and sandwiches, all pre-packaged and ready to eat.

What a hard life these spoiled rich people live.

I grab a muffin and make myself a hot cup of coffee, then step out onto the balcony. After all, what is the point of being given a penthouse suite forty-four floors up if you're not going to appreciate the view of the city on a spectacular morning like this?

I find a delectably soft cashmere blanket on one of the couches and settle in with my breakfast. The thought that has gone into this penthouse experience is astounding. They have literally thought of everything someone could want when staying here.

As I sip my coffee, the steam rising in the crisp late summer air, my mind wanders and replays the events of the last two days. Regardless of what happens next, I think it is safe to say I've shattered my expectations for this week already.

Colton was an ass, but I had expected that. My mother was impossible, but at least I knew her intentions were good, and I know how to handle her. Steph was amazing as always, and ever my rock.

The only thing I had not expected was meeting a certain sexy billionaire who had been shaking up my life for the last forty-eight hours.

I mean, that kiss though…

Even the next morning, my whole-body shivers just thinking about it. And him.

The practical and inherently negative side of my brain tells me not to get too excited, because Jaxon probably wines, dines and saliva-swaps with dozens of socialites a month.

Whereas the whimsical, curious, and inherently hopeful side of my brain reassures me that no matter what Jaxon's intentions may have been at the start of the evening, that kiss took us both by surprise. It was real.

I felt it in my bones, and I'm certain he did too.

Jaxon is still an enigma to me. I understood that Rachel, his late girlfriend had passed, and apparently he's pretty guilt-ridden over her death, but why? And why, with such a small child, money, and the good looks to break a thousand hearts, would he not at some point in the last six years, have settled down and gotten married? Surely there was no shortage of women in Chicago, or in America for that matter, that would not trample over each other for the chance to bag a man like Jaxon?

Considering all of that, why would he bother wasting an evening with someone as boring as me?

I'm not special by any consideration, except maybe to a few select members of my family and friends. But I don't have anything incredibly unique or exciting about me. I'm just a private nurse whose biggest adventure was leaving the state I had grown up in all my life.

Oh, and it took my fiancé cheating on me for me to do so.

Jaxon Pace, on the other hand, lives in penthouses, drives $250,000 sports cars and casually eats his Wednesday night dinner on his private yacht.

We are from two completely different worlds.

I tell myself that at some point I need to make my way back to reality. Even if my *current* reality involves me watching the sun come up on a penthouse balcony.

Jaxon wanted to make a statement, that much was clear. But the intentions behind that statement were not.

Was he just trying to flex his power and money? Was he just trying to seduce me?

Or, perhaps, was he just trying to thank me?

But, even then, he didn't have to step in and cover for me yesterday with my mother. And he didn't have to take me for that cozy dinner aboard his yacht. And he definitely didn't have to give me a penthouse.

If thanking me was all he really wanted to do, he'd already more than accomplished that with 900 white roses and drinks in the bar Tuesday night. There was no need for him to take it a step further and do any of the things he did yesterday.

Let alone all *three*.

And he certainly did not have to kiss me.

I touch my fingers to my lips, caressing where his had been the night before. I remember the fervor with which he kissed me, and how I had kissed him back. It was more than just lust or passion. No, it was *need*. As if the rest of the world could fall apart around us, and Jaxon wouldn't have cared at all.

I've never felt a kiss like that in all my life.

Right, but he probably just wants to sleep with me.

I try not to let rationality take too much of my bliss, but I have to admit, it's probably true. Because I can't help but feel men like Jaxon Pace, who are naturally charismatic and sparkly, belong in the spotlight with other sparkly people.

Not with someone as unpolished and boring as me.

Speaking of unpolished, I look down at my hands and remember my half-polished nails are well overdue for a manicure. Which was something I hoped to accomplish before the rehearsal dinner this evening. I savor the view one more time before dragging myself back inside.

After pouring myself another cup of coffee, I head into the bedroom. I still cannot believe this is *my* bedroom for the next few days.

Last night, I toured the whole penthouse, finding that this suite housed three massive bedrooms, each with their own adjoining bathroom. There were other rooms as well, such as a small gym, a study, and a movie theater and in the living room there was even a baby grand piano.

In my bathroom, there was a selection of high-end shampoos and conditioners, as well as bath bombs and a full bubble bath selection, presumably for the impressive standalone tub that sat in the middle of the room.

There also was a full 'dressing room' attached to the world's biggest walk-in closet with a tri-fold mirror.

Sally hadn't been kidding when she said my things had been handled with care, as the hotel staff had folded and pressed all my laundry, before putting them into the drawers of the dresser. Apparently they also found my dress for the wedding and hung it up in the closet, while also laying out a very plushy robe and slippers.

The few things I brought with me for a week-long trip looked so miniscule in such a giant closet, that simply *had* to be bigger than my first apartment with Colton.

Speaking of Colton, I notice I've missed a text from him as I head to the shower.

Colton
8:15 a.m.: Hey good morning! Sorry about last night, I did not mean to get pushy. About to head down to breakfast, do you want me to bring you anything? #roomservice

I cringe, thinking of how exhausting his company had been last night, and how smart I'd been to put the "Do Not Identify" notice on my room.

Regardless, for now I decide just to ignore his text completely. Which is at least an improvement from the nervous wreck I'd been about seeing him at the start of the week.

I wonder why yesterday felt so unsatisfying?

I mean, I got what I wanted from him—regret, misery, suffering. He literally sat across from me last night saying everything I wanted him to say, and yet when he did I just felt numb. I still feel that way now.

However, I'm distracted by a new text…from *Jaxon*.

I feel my heartbeat quicken in my chest as I see his name on my phone.

Jaxon
8:26 a.m.: Good morning. I hope you slept well.

It is only seven words, but those seven words send a warm feeling radiating down my spine. I stare at the text for at least five minutes, realizing that Jaxon had thought of me, already.

Perhaps I had even been the first thing on his mind this morning.

I try to come up with a response, but everything I type does not sound right.

8:35 a.m.: I did. I think I understand why the rich always look so good—they sleep like royalty.

Is my first text to him, but I quickly delete it.

Too sarcastic and it sounds like I am trying too hard to be funny.

8:36 a.m.: I did. How about you, sexy?

Is my second attempt, but I delete it just as quickly.

Far too… aggressive. Damnit why is this so hard?!

I decide that I'm spending entirely too much time thinking about it and just go with the safe reply.

Me
8:45 a.m.: I did, I hope you did as well?

Wow, Natalie, your originality is shocking.

"Ugh," I grunt, throwing my phone down and forcing myself to go take a shower.

I promptly spent the next twenty minutes standing in the hot water thinking of a hundred more interesting or flirtatious ways I *could* have answered that text. But, I chickened out, and just stuck to the 'safe' choice, like I always do.

Recently this has become my biggest pet peeve with myself: I avoid taking risks.

I would even go as far as to say that lately, I specifically avoid risk at all costs, trying to control or at least be prepared for every eventuality that could possibly happen.

It's exhausting. Especially when I haven't always been this way. In fact, I had actually been quite a wild child in my youth and teenage years.

My therapist in Miami seems to think this is perhaps just some residual trauma from what happened with Colton. She reasons that because Colton's betrayal had been out of my control, it destroyed my sense of confidence overall.

So because of Colton, I now have some stupid complex where I have an irrational fear of spontaneity, or being caught off guard.

Perhaps that's why every interaction with Jaxon has felt so alien to me from the start. Nothing on earth could prepare me for that man.

And he's definitely not the safe choice here.

But... I *like* that about him.

Every moment with him feels like a complete headrush. My heart starts racing when he looks at me, his gentle touch spikes my blood, and his kiss makes me feel as if every single inch of me was on fire.

However, Jaxon needs a woman who can keep up with him. One who is brave enough to take risks.

Or at least one that knows how to flirt.

By the time I am done with my shower, I'm beyond annoyed with myself.

I pick up my phone, but I can't even bring myself to look at my messages. Instead, I toss it back on the bed, reasoning that if he responded at all, it was only out of courtesy.

I remove the towel from my hair, shaking any excess water out as I walk into the kitchen.

"Natalie, why are you so boring? Why can't you ever do anything bold?!" I say aloud, grabbing a yogurt and a bottle of water from the refrigerator before slamming it closed. "Ugh!"

"Um, I'd say you're pretty bold..." A young man's voice suddenly comes from behind me in the living room, making me jump.

I scream and drop the water bottle, and the yogurt, causing it to explode all over the floor.

"Oh my god! Who the hell are you and what are you doing here?!" I yell.

Instinctively I grab a large steak knife from the block on the counter and try to find anything to cover my naked body with. But all I can find is the small hand towel on the stove.

Who is this and what the fuck is he doing in the penthouse?!

"Please, Miss Tyler, I'm not here to hurt you!" he shouts, looking away while still trying to be cautious of the panicked naked lady wielding a steak knife. "Mr. Pace said you'd been informed of my arrival!"

"Oh my God," I gasp, still fighting to try and maneuver the tiny towel over my body. "*What?*"

Perhaps I should've looked at my text messages!

"Could you put the knife down? Please? I can explain."

"Um, sure."

I try to drop just the kitchen knife but when I do, my towel accidentally goes with it.

"Eek! No! Don't look!"

I abandon all hope and scramble out of the kitchen.

As I run quickly down the hallway, I swear I hear him chuckling to himself as I slam the bedroom door behind me.

"Oh my God…" I breathe.

I'm absolutely mortified, and quickly rush to my phone.

Jaxon
8:46 a.m.: I did, thank you. By the way, I've assigned Charlie to be your penthouse butler. He will be coming by at nine to help with any needs or errands that you might have.

Great. Simply great.

I've been in the penthouse not more than twelve hours and I've already flashed the fucking butler!

To make it worse, the more I think about it, I realize I recognize the man in the kitchen as the young man from the valet last night.

Charlie.

I'm so mortified that I'm not sure that I can face him.

Shit, I have to.

Despite my sheer embarrassment, I throw on the plushy bathrobe and walk out, finding Charlie in the kitchen cleaning up the water and yogurt. When he hears the door open, he comically covers his eyes.

"Is it safe, Miss Tyler?" he chuckles, a huge grin on his face.

I laugh, grateful for his efforts to diffuse an awkward situation.

"I suppose. Unless you're a package of yogurt," I giggle, my cheeks turning red.

"Yeah I don't know how we're going to get it off the *ceiling*," he says looking up.

"What?!" I panic, my eyes darting to the ceiling above us.

Holy shit! If I ruin Jaxon Pace's penthouse, I—

But my panicked thoughts are silenced when I hear Charlie laughing.

"Oh my God," I finally exhale, touching his shoulder gently and looking away. "You're just messing with me!"

"I mean, there's probably some up there, but your secret is safe with me, Miss Tyler."

We lock eyes again, and this time we both laugh.

"I'm so sorry for…er, well, ya know…flashing you," I glance at him apologetically. "I'm royally embarrassed."

"No apologies, necessary! I didn't mean to intrude or startle you." He shoots me a sympathetic glance before winking at me. "If I'm honest, it certainly made my morning!"

I laugh again, shaking my head and feeling the blush dissipating from my cheeks.

"Mr. Pace said he was going to tell you of my arrival."

"Technically he did," I say, scrunching up my nose. "I just missed the text because I was in the shower."

Charlie nods. The two of us stand in silence for a moment before I sigh.

"I feel like I should warn you now that I am not used to all of this. I've never stayed in a place like this, and I've definitely never had a butler. I don't even know what a butler *does* to be honest with you."

Charlie smiles warmly.

"I've got you. My goal is just to help with anything you need. Basically, because the penthouse suites are pretty far from the lobby, we try to have someone on hand to help with minor conveniences. So if you want food ordered in from a specific restaurant or you need water bottles, toothpaste, or extra *towels*," he stops to wink at me, making me blush again. "That's something you could send me to get for you."

"Oh my, well, I've never had anyone to wait on me like that. I'm not sure I could ever ask you to do something like that for me."

I stare at him uncomfortably.

"Try not to think too hard about it. I'd just be doing my job, ma'am. I'm here to make your experience at The Jefferson the best it could possibly be."

I nod.

Does he just sit in the living room all day waiting for me to give him instructions?

I'm not entirely sure how I feel about someone being in the suite with me the whole time. I'm a bit of an introvert, and I do like my privacy.

"And, um, do you just, stay… *here*?" I ask.

Charlie shakes his head and quickly produces a small business card from his pocket.

"No, ma'am. There's a separate staff elevator for housekeeping and such, and I have a room on this floor just outside the door. You can text me at this number, or just dial nine from any of the phones in the suite, and I'll be on my way with whatever you need in a heartbeat."

His jovial expression and demeanor, even despite the chaotic moments prior, helps me relax. Overall, he just seems like a really nice guy.

I like him.

"I don't think I have anything right now… oh wait!" I say excitedly. "How do I shut the blinds in the bedroom?"

"There's a keypad in the nightstand next to the bed."

I did not think of that.

"Greatttt, so now I feel embarrassed and stupid."

"Please don't. I understand that this is a lot to adjust to," he chuckles, before leaning in to whisper. "And if it makes you feel better, Mr. Pace struggled with them too after he moved into the other penthouse upstairs."

I laugh.

"You know, Charlie, it actually does."

"I will get out of your way and let you get back to your day," he says as he heads to the foyer.

As he walks toward the door, a question pops into my head that I decide I desperately need answered.

"Charlie, do you butler a lot? For Jaxon's… *friends*?"

I say it in a way that I hope he understands that I really mean Jaxon's female friends. I know I shouldn't ask, but I want to know how often he pulls this 'penthouse' card of his with women.

Charlie pauses a moment, a grin tugging at his mouth.

"Actually, no. This is the first time Mr. Pace has made a request like this, of any of us." He appraises me softly, and his eyes silently assure me of the truthfulness in his answer. "I think he just wants to make you happy."

I am speechless, and I smile up at him with my cheeks burning.

"Please, let him know that I am."

Charlie smiles and nods. "Do let me know if you need anything,

Miss Tyler."

I glance down at my hands and then I am reminded I need a manicure, and I am unfamiliar with this city.

"Charlie, this might be out of your purview, but do you know where I could go around here to get a manicure?"

"The hotel has complete spa services…" he says slowly, but I shake my head indicating I do not want to do that. I just have the sneaking suspicion that Jaxon would probably try and comp any services I ordered.

"…But if you're looking for something offsite, I might recommend 'The Golden Lotus' which is a salon about two blocks north."

"Thank you!" I smile at him.

"My pleasure."

He nods, then shuts the door and I am left standing alone in the foyer by myself, with a shameless smile on my face.

"This is the first time." I guess maybe I am a little special after all.

I ponder Charlie's words, and the fact that floor forty-five is evidently Jaxon's personal penthouse, as I walk back into the bedroom. I collapse onto the bed and I open my text thread with Jaxon.

Me
9:26 a.m.: Well, I missed this text, so poor Charlie got an eyeful.

The reply is almost immediate.

Jaxon
9:26 a.m.: Lucky guy. Maybe I should rethink my career choice. Do you have plans tonight?

My heart starts pounding in my chest.
Jaxon is asking if I have plans tonight.

Me
9:27 a.m.: I have the rehearsal dinner at Campeggio's from 5-6:30 p.m., but my schedule is free after that…

Jaxon

9:28 a.m.: Well, now your schedule is booked. I'll pick you up at 6:45. Wear pants. I'm not the butler, after all.

I stifle a laugh, but I am conscious that my hands are shaking as I text back.

Me
9:29 a.m.: Pity. Pants it is.

And just like that, I have my second date with Jaxon Pace.

Chapter Fourteen

JAXON

I carry my sleepy daughter down the staircase, with Ethan and Josiah following close behind.

"Why are we going back to the hotel?" Jessica asks.

"Because Professor Murray is going to be tutoring you there during the week from now on. But tomorrow is Friday, and we will come home tomorrow, I promise," I say, setting her on the bench and kissing her forehead. "You remember Professor Murray, right?"

"He was my teacher last year," she says, scrunching up her face. "He smells funny."

Her honesty makes me want to laugh, but I suppress the urge.

"Jessica," I admonish gently, "that's not very nice, and what did we talk about last night?"

"School is important, and I need to show respect to my teachers."

"Good girl. Now put your headphones on."

"He really does smell funny though!" she says defensively.

Again, I try not to laugh, instead shooting her a look that says this subject is closed. She sighs in defeat and pulls the headphones over her ears. I put on a cognitive learning program for her, and she gives me a thumbs up, signaling that she can hear the music.

The headphones she wears are top-of-the-line noise canceling, so that I can keep her safe from the conversations I occasionally need to have around her.

"It's all the Aspercreme," Ethan says humorously. "That's what she smells on Professor Murray."

"Yeah, that would be my guess, too." I chuckle to myself.

The front doors open, and I see Levi and Max waiting a few steps ahead by the cars. I take Jessica's hand and help her into her car seat, her attention completely focused on whatever is playing on her iPad. Which is good, since I've learned my child is remarkably perceptive, and I do not need her noticing my entire team on high security alert right now. I do not want to add more stress to her life.

In the last forty-eight hours, our team has seen a break-in at my warehouse, the death of three of my men, and the nearly successful kidnapping of my daughter. Moving her back to the hotel, where I spend most of my time during the week, is the safest option for her right now.

I am not taking any chances.

As we drive back to The Jefferson, Ethan and Josiah update me on my ships. Eight of my nine Chicago–bound freighters are safely in their moorings, cargo intact. However, the ninth ship, 'The Pilgrim,' which was scheduled to dock five days ago, is still unaccounted for.

"What was the cargo?" I ask.

"Spices," Ethan responds softly. "The kind Black uses…"

He means drugs.

"The usual?"

"Hallucinogenic."

"How much?"

"Three metric tons."

Jesus Christ.

"And we just *lost* her? This massive freighter just disappeared? What about the Echo software we installed on all of our transports?"

"Yes, we can confirm the ship's hull was outfitted with an Echo, and while this is a bit odd, this is exactly the kind of event this software is designed for," Ethan says.

"Even if we don't know what kind of event this is," I say through gritted teeth. "What can we expect?"

Ethan pulls up the stat sheet on the Echo software on a tablet and hands it to me. "The moment the ship enters any port within ten miles of a cellphone tower, the Echo will activate and will ping its location. Then our teams can respond."

"Did Samuel know about the Echo software?" I ask. "Is there a chance he could have told someone about it, and *if* the same perpetrators are involved, could it already be deactivated?"

Ethan defers to Josiah, who oversees all our Northeast Shipping.

"No, Sir," Josiah responds from the driver's seat. "The Echo program was marked situationally classified. Only myself, Ethan, and my two Beta commanders knew that these ships were outfitted with the Echo devices. Samuel joined the warehouse team after the software was installed."

"And what's the status of our warehouse security eval?"

"All passcodes and communication channels have been changed, Sir, and the Beta team has been scrambled to all facilities to oversee operations for the entire east coast."

"Good."

I wish I could say this news makes me feel better, but not by much. Samuel's betrayal has been preying on my mind all night.

I shoot a glance to Jessica, who is humming along to the music on her iPad.

How many times had I trusted Sam with her protection?

Had my trust in him contributed to the kidnapping attempt?

This thought makes me uncomfortable. Samuel was on my Alpha Team. He had alternated between the warehouse surveillance, and my protection detail. He knew a lot of information that would be valuable to anyone trying to harm us, and who knows what details he had already divulged to my enemies.

All because of an addiction.

This is not supposed to happen at the Alpha level. In our world, drugs were easily accessible at any given moment. So naturally I understood some of my men indulged themselves. Many of them, in fact. I did not have rules regarding drug use, nor did I restrict or monitor their activities.

After all, this is not the fucking police academy.

They need to be in charge of their own person. I expect my generals to teach their recruits moderation and balance when it comes to the vices of our world. This was the tradition that the Dons of old had passed down from multiple generations. It was what my father had taught me. As long as you could still perform your duties, no one asked any questions about your proclivities.

Over time, new recruits would develop a tolerance, and respect for their role on our team. If they continued to show reliability and reasonable restraint, they would be given greater responsibilities.

They could even be considered for Alpha Squad.

However, Alpha Squad was different. It was the highest rank in our family and was reserved for the men I trusted most.

These became the men solely responsible for my protection and Jessica's. For them, there *were* rules, and there was a zero tolerance for drugs, as I needed these men to be sharp, alert and of sound mind. I needed them to protect my family.

Although, they are my family, too.

No matter how angry or disappointed I am at Samuel, I cannot deny I feel slightly disappointed in myself.

At the end of the day, Sam did not feel he could come to me for help to get himself straight, or to help protect his family. This is simply not acceptable, and something I should not see if my organization was one-hundred percent healthy. If my men cannot trust me to do everything in my power to protect them, why should they do the same for me?

"I want to address the men," I say to Ethan. "Let's assemble Alpha-Zeta at the house tomorrow afternoon."

"What for?"

"We need to discuss what happened with Samuel. Stop the infection before it spreads. I want to remind them that above all, this family exists to look after each other. I do not want anyone suffering in silence like Sam was."

"Yes, Sir." He nods.

My thoughts are interrupted, however, with a text.

Charlie:
10:02 a.m.: Sir, Miss Tyler just left the Penthouse. I believe she said she was going to get a manicure. I sent her to the Golden Lotus.

I smile.

I bet she decided to go offsite on purpose.

And I bet she did so because she rightfully assumed that I had already alerted my staff to comp all services to her.

What a coincidence that I own the Golden Lotus, too.

Me
10:03 a.m.: Thank you. Please let them know she is my guest, and to treat her accordingly. They are not to alert her, but they are not to charge her card. Have we spoken with Robert yet?

Charlie
10:04 a.m.: Already done, Sir.

After I get Jessica settled with the Aspercreme Professor, I join my team in the penthouse study.

"So, what do we know about this Two-Headed Dragon?"

Max speaks first. "After our chat with the twitcher from last night, I did some digging. Our people on the ground say they have seen a few guys with this tattoo showing up in the homeless circles and outside the jail, offering shelter, food and work."

"Quite an offer if you are homeless."

"It seems pretty obvious they are specifically targeting these groups for that reason."

"The most vulnerable, and the most unstable," Ethan comments.

"What's more is that there is talk among those circles that anyone who has taken the Two-Headed Dragon's offer has not returned. I've also heard word from our people in the Old Town district that there has been an increase of delivery trucks going in and out of an underground garage near the Little Tokyo Restaurant."

Levi takes over. He dims the lights and points to the TV screen, where images of the parking garage, the Little Tokyo Restaurant, construction barricades and armed men guarding delivery trucks appear in rapid succession.

"Jesus, since when do weekly grocery deliveries warrant armed escorts?" I ask.

"By men all wearing the same tattoo as our prison pal from the other night," Ethan says looking at me, and I see that he is correct. At least a dozen men in this photo have the same tattoo.

"What do we know about that garage?" Ethan asks.

Levi puts the blueprints up on the screen. "It's pretty standard, built in the late 1950s, it was functioning until the early nineties, when the surrounding businesses tanked, and was subsequently declared a city blight zone in the last ten years. This entire area has been largely unoccupied due to the decay of the surrounding structures."

"Seems pretty occupied now," I say.

Every photo Levi skims through shows armed men and security barricades blocking the view of the garage below.

"What info do we have from the ground?"

"We are working on that now, Sir," Max says. "We are sending in two operatives to survey the restaurant this afternoon."

"Hold on a minute," Ethan says. "Can you bring up the blueprint of the garage again, Levi? Enhance that righthand corner, my eyes aren't what they used to be." He stands and walks toward the screen to get a better view. Levi zooms in on the corner Ethan requested, and a blurry icon comes into focus.

"What is that?" I ask.

"If I am not mistaken, that symbol means that that garage is an old air raid shelter," Levi says after closer examination.

"Apparently your eyes are better than you thought," I say to Ethan. "What does that mean?"

"It means that the garage could potentially have entrances that go deep underground, possibly even into the subway rail system nearby."

"That's certainly convenient," I say sarcastically.

It is well known that whether you are moving product, selling product, or in need of a quick getaway after executing a hit, having access to or control over quick transportation is essential to any successful illegal enterprise.

Because of this, we make sure to know and control all of these entrances to the subway.

"I think we have a better understanding of how this new gang sprung up so quickly," Ethan says, shooting a look at me. "They are using the subways."

I light a cigarette and stare at the screen. "We need to confirm that. That's strictly our turf."

I turn to Travis, the latest Beta that has been promoted to Alpha after Samuel's departure. "Travis, I want to see the maps and the development blueprints for that whole area," I say as I exhale. "I want to know every doorway, tunnel, exit and fucking broom closet within a ten-mile radius of that garage."

"Yes, Sir," he says enthusiastically.

"Max, we should confirm if they have already gained access to the subway system. Send a couple of guys into the tunnels in city uniform and tell them to check everything from that direction. Every staircase, every platform, every service entrance. If they are using it, we need to find that access point."

"Yes, Sir."

"Levi, we need to get eyes in the sky as quickly as possible. Let's get some surveillance units up and functioning on the surrounding buildings tonight. But do it discreetly. Use the street patrols and dealers. Once we have some footage, we can see about making some possible IDs and know who we are dealing with."

"We could also see if our friends on the force could swing by and do a spot check on those trucks," Ethan suggests. "See what 'groceries' they are shipping."

"Agreed, but make sure they only do it outside of the perimeter, I don't need any city workers getting killed or drawing too much attention. We don't want to alert them just yet."

"Yes, Sir."

"We need to move quickly, but silently. I want to know who they are, how they are getting around, and what they are supplying. Once we know that, we cut them off. And we cut them off hard," I say as I put out my cigarette forcibly in the ashtray. "Let's get to work gentlemen."

The men start to file out of my office, but I stop Ethan in the doorway as he is leaving.

"Let's also set a meeting with Black."

"Tonight?" He asks.

"No, not tonight," I say, clearing my throat. "Tonight, I have plans."

He throws me a smirk before walking away. I turn back to the TV and the blueprints.

A new mafia clan.

Something we have not seen in this city in close to three decades. Around here, new clans did not just appear out of thin air, and there was a reason for that. It was a fragile ecosystem carefully curated and monitored by the bosses to maintain order.

My father had worked to keep that balance his whole life. When the Mexican Cartel had tried to expand into our territory, he fought against it. Teaming up with the other three bosses that once controlled the city to fight back—and won. Peace had followed; the golden days of the alliance.

But like him, those days were gone. Black and I were the main two bosses left, with a handful of smaller clans making up the rest. All of them paid homage to us, as we controlled the city. They do this because they understand that these days, clans are more likely to die than thrive, and survival is only for the strong… and the wicked.

I check my watch.

Lunchtime.

Lunchtime for me means scotch, so I walk over to my bar and pour myself a drink.

Never a dull moment around here.

I am in the middle of rubbing my forehead and questioning my decision to give up cocaine when my phone buzzes.

Natalie
12:30 p.m.: So… do I get any sort of hint as to what we are doing this evening?

She is anxious to know my plans.

I smirk as I take a drink, knowing that if it were entirely up to me, this evening would involve a lot less clothing. But I know that Ethan is right: I can't let my cock do the thinking when it comes to Natalie. At least not entirely.

Me
12:35 p.m.: Nervous?

Natalie
12:36 p.m.: A little. I mean, you did kidnap me for our first date.

Me
12:37 p.m.: Well, considering I asked nicely this time, I think that means kidnapping is off the table.

Natalie
12:38 p.m.: Well, that's not necessarily comforting considering how extravagant your table is, Jaxon.

Me
12:39 p.m.: I'm simply happy you are finally admitting last night was a date.

Natalie
12:40 p.m.: I cannot tell if you are the most interesting man I have ever met, or the most frustrating.

Me
12:41 p.m.: I'll settle for both. And fine, I will give you a

hint.
Your hint: "We will travel the world, without leaving the city."

Natalie
12:42 p.m.: That's not a hint… that's a riddle.

Me
12:43 p.m.: Then a riddle is what you get.

I laugh to myself, picturing the frustration on Natalie's face at this moment. If she's going to make me work for it, then this evening needs to be an experience that only I can deliver.
After all, that is more my *style anyway.*

Chapter Fifteen

Natalie

Jaxon
12:41 p.m.: I'll settle for both. And fine, I will give you a hint.
Your hint: "We will travel the world, without leaving the city.

What the heck does that mean?
Does "travel the world" mean he is planning to fly me somewhere? No, because he said, "without leaving the city."
I leave the massage room excited and anxious, and head for the manicure area of the spa, deciding that Jaxon Pace is indeed the most frustrating man I have ever met. All of a sudden, I hear my mother's voice echo across the room.
"Oh, my goodness, Natalie! Over here!"
"Mom?"
What is she doing here?
However, with just a quick glance around the room, I realize almost all my female family members are here. Aunts, cousins, and obviously my mother, occupy nearly every manicure station.

Of all the damn spas in Chicago…

About a dozen appraising looks shoot my way, but at least my mother seems genuinely excited to see me.

"What a coincidence!" she says excitedly. "I know you mentioned you were going to find a place to get your nails done, and when I told the girls over breakfast, they thought it was a wonderful idea!"

"Yeah, I'm surprised no one let me know it was going to be a group thing," I say sarcastically. "An invite would have been nice."

"Well, it was kind of a last-minute decision." My mother smiles and tries to deflect politely.

"And it's not like you've attended any other family events since you've been here," My Aunt Kathy sneers beside her.

She shoots me the kind of disapproving look that she has perfected her entire life. A judgmental shrew that likes to stick her nose in everyone's business and has an opinion about everything. She is by far my least favorite aunt.

"Oh, put a pin in it, Mom." I hear Steph snap from behind me and I turn to face her. "No one asked your grumpy ass for input."

I shoot Steph a smile.

I just love her and her sass.

How she could be related to Aunt Kathy has always been a mystery to me.

"I'm just saying," her mom says defensively, "she hasn't really shown her face much since she got here."

"Well, maybe that's because she doesn't like you."

Steph wraps her arm around my shoulder and pulls me away.

"Ignore her, her back has been hurting, so she has been even more unbearable these days."

"Thank you," I say, rolling my eyes.

I settle comfortably in a pedicure chair while Steph camps out next to me, telling me about her latest girlfriend. I am doing my best to listen, but grumpy Aunt Kathy ends up in the pedicure chair next to me and is talking so loudly it is proving difficult.

"I'm constantly in a state of pain these days from my sciatica," she groans. "Like I was explaining to Colton yesterday, it just feels like someone is stabbing me in the hip over and over."

I try emphatically to pretend that I'm not listening, but the mention of Colton's name draws my attention.

"I feel so bad for Colton, the poor boy told me that he partially tore the rotator cuff in his shoulder playing tennis with the Governor's son." My Aunt Carol joins in. "I ended up giving him one of my Percocet just so he could sleep last night."

"Oh, I know, isn't that just awful? I gave him one of my Vicodin this morning," I hear my mother say. "That's a horrible injury, I have a friend from church who said her son accidentally tore his rotator cuff on the job and has not been able to go back to work for two months."

"But you know what, look, Colton is still here isn't he?" Aunt Kathy brags. "Nothing could keep that sweet boy from being here for Ryan. I *respect* that. No matter what life throws at him, Colton *always* does the right thing, even though he certainly hasn't had an easy go of things these last few years…"

I can't be sure without turning around and joining the conversation, but I feel as though my aunt is not-so-subtly referring to me, and I feel my face getting hot. Listening to my aunts blow smoke up Colton's ass is infuriating.

I promise Colton has had a much easier time than I have.

I don't know what it is about him, but he still has my family wrapped around his finger. Which honestly was something I used to love about him. I used to love the way my family loved him, but now their love of him feels increasingly suffocating. I was the one who got hurt, and yet I am the bad guy in the eyes of my own family…the heartless, petulant woman that broke *his* heart?! Unbelievable.

Even now, I wonder how they would respond if I suddenly just whipped around, and told them all the truth? If I told them everything he did to me, and just shatter their glorified image of their golden-boy Colton.

Aunt Kathy would probably fall into the pedicure bowl.

"Hey, are you okay?" Steph says, shaking me from my thoughts. "You look a little pale there, Tyler."

"Yeah, I'm fine." I try to give her a half-smile.

"When did you eat last? I feel like you are all skin and bones these days. You *are* eating right?" Steph narrows her eyes at me.

"Yeah, I ate this morning around eight."

"Girl, that was like six hours ago," Steph snorts. "Let me go see if I can find you a candy bar or something."

"Wait, Steph, you don—"

Arguing with Steph is pointless, as she is gone before I can even protest. So instead, I collapse back into the pedicure chair and enjoy the amazing foot massage my nail tech is giving me. It's so good I could almost fall asleep.

"Did you hear about the band? The bride just found out they

all have strep throat! She was practically hysterical yesterday morning." I hear my Aunt Carol continue with her gossip, and I hear my mother gasp out loud, but continue drifting off to slumberland.

"Oh my!"

"I know! But then I guess, miraculously, the owner of the hotel happened to overhear, and he *personally* offered to find her a replacement!" Aunt Carol continues.

Annnnnnd suddenly I'm wide awake again.

"Wow, really?" My mother gushes.

"Yes! Apparently, he also said the hotel would cover the entire cost, so the whole thing is on house!" Aunt Carol whispers excitedly.

"Oh my gosh, that is incredible!"

I fight to keep my jaw from dropping to the floor.

Jaxon... Jaxon did that.

I grab my phone from my pocket.

Me
2:16 p.m.: Did you really offer to pay for the band in my wedding??

Jaxon
2:17 p.m.: You're getting married?!

Well, you kind of walked into that one Natalie.

Me
2:18 p.m.: You know what I meant.

Jaxon
2:19 p.m.: I might know. I also might have pulled a few strings... pun intended btw.

Me
2:20 p.m.: Why would you do that?

Jaxon
2:21 p.m.: Who wants to go to a wedding without music?

Me
2:22 p.m.: That's not what I said.

Jaxon
2:23 p.m.: Who was it that said, "Sometimes people do the right thing, simply because it is the right thing to do?"

Whoa.
I smirk, impressed with his creativity to use my own words against me.

Me
2:24 p.m.: Not sure, but whomever they are, they sound pretty smart. Well, thank you. That is incredibly generous of you.

Jaxon
2:21 p.m.: I hope it is obvious by now, Miss Tyler, that I can be very generous. Among other things.

Me
2:22 p.m.: Such as?

Jaxon
2:22 p.m.: I guess you'll just have to wait and see.

I suddenly feel my cheeks heat as I bite my fingernail, picturing quite a few other things that he could be generous with.

"Hey! Stop that! You just had them painted!" Steph says, jumping back into the chair beside me and tossing a candy bar into my lap. "And why do you look as though you're up to no good over there, missy?" she asks as she raises a brow at me.

I open the candy bar while trying to hide the fact that I am blushing and smiling ear to ear.

"No reason. Thanks for the chocolate!"

"You'll have to wait and see…"

Something tells me the waiting was going to be the hard part.

A few hours later at the rehearsal dinner I find I have a front row seat to a dramatic story retelling, courtesy of Colton.

"…And then I just scooped him up in my arms and pulled him back into the boat…"

I just roll my eyes and sip my wine. I guess it should not matter that he's already told this story at least a dozen times in the last six years, because my family is still listening intently and staring at him like he is the messiah.

The short version of his parable? Messiah Colton saves a little boy from some rapids. It's an excellent story.

But Messiah Colton's version is also complete crap.

The true version of this story is much different, because in that version Colton did extraordinarily little to help the child drowning in the rapids, and I was the one who saved the kid.

In my junior year of college, I spent two weeks of my summer break visiting Colton in Utah. Colton was working there as a tour guide for one his uncle's white-water rapids rafting businesses.

To be fair, when it came to playing the part of the tour guide, he was surprisingly good. After all, he has always loved any opportunity to be in the spotlight.

However, when it came to actually navigating the rapids, Colton had absolutely no idea what he was doing, and he almost killed all of us on the raft that day.

For starters, he neglected to check the vest of the only child on board, a boy, probably younger than ten. However, I noticed before we left and corrected this mistake, which probably saved the kid's life. An hour later, Colton lost control of the boat and it tipped halfway over, accidentally dumping the little boy into the raging rapids.

To this day, I do not know what made me jump in after the kid. I was not even the best of swimmers. But something in me just reacted, and I was in the water before I even knew what I was doing. After getting smashed into a few massive rocks, I was able to reach him, and slowly got him over to the shoreline.

But it took over three hours for Colton and the parents to get back to us, and when he eventually did, he was more worried about his reputation. Which ended up being a pointless concern, because even though he never actually got in the water that day, he was still hailed a hero by the parents.

He even made it into the town newspaper for his "heroic water rescue." At the time I did not care that he took credit for my actions, because I loved Colton. I wanted him to get all the praise and glory because I knew that the attention would make him profoundly happy.

It had only bothered me when Christmas came that year and he told this story to my family for the first time. Because instead of telling the *truth* of what happened that day, he just recited what had been written in the newspaper about him. He did not even give me the credit with my own family.

But then again, he's always been pretty adept at changing the story around when it suits him.

Especially when it makes him look better. I take another sip of my wine, as my family chuckles along to his fictional narrative.

"Oh, my goodness! You could have been killed!" My younger cousin Chloe reacts to Colton's fairytale.

"That's true! But sometimes you can't be afraid to take risks for the things that matter!" he says, and then turns to me with a wink and an overly dramatic and public toast of his glass. All eyes suddenly turn to me, and I hear my relatives cooing and murmuring.

God damnit, Colton.

I want to clobber him, but instead I return his toast, which seems to satisfy the crowd.

"Sorry love, I just couldn't resist," he whispers as he sits back down next to me, looking thoroughly pleased with himself.

"Clearly. It was almost convincing too," I say sarcastically without meeting his gaze.

"What was?"

"Nothing." I roll my eyes and take another sip of wine.

"Hey, I have a question for you." He turns to me and leans in so close that I can smell the alcohol on his breath, and I have to pull away. "And I really hate to ask."

His demeanor changes instantly to something more serious, and I feel him hesitate, as though he is contemplating whether he wants to ask this question at all.

"Okay, and that is?"

"So, I don't know if I told you, but I really hurt my shoulder last week playing tennis with my friend," he starts. "He's actually the son of the Governor..." His eyes search my face for a reaction, as if he expects one.

"Okay?"

Where is he going with this?

"Right, well, I wasn't able to get in to see my doctor before we left for the wedding." He glances quickly across the table. "And I know you mentioned you were a nurse for the elderly or something like that? So, I was just wondering if perhaps you happened to have any pain medications on you? Like Vicodin or Percocet?"

"Didn't my mother already give you something for that?" I ask softly so that only he can hear me.

Why is he asking me for pain medication?

"Well, yeah, but it's really killing me, and I don't want to bother her again with this."

"And I thought I heard Carol say she gave you something too... Percocet, right?" I say, remembering the conversation from earlier.

"You know what, never mind," he says, smiling again and placing his sweaty hand on my arm. "I didn't mean to trouble you with it, I'm sure a hefty dose of Ibuprofen and an ice pack or two can get me through until I get home."

He takes a giant swig of wine, and changes the subject, suddenly trying to be his charming self again.

"Did you ladies have a good time at the salon today?"

I briefly debate trying to pry further into his pain medication request but decide against it.

"Yes, it was lovely. My mother got her nails painted purple."

"Oh my, something *other* than red? Someone needs to slow that wild woman down!" he says softly.

"Shh! Don't make a big deal over it or someone may call and report her!" I say, whispering into my glass of wine.

Colton follows that up with quietly imitating a police siren, which makes us both laugh.

I forgot how much fun we used to have at family functions like this, making fun of the rest of them.

Back when it was just the teenage backyard barbeques with my cousins, where we first shared stolen glances and flirty handwritten notes. Or back when we were broke college students, and he could remember my birthday without a calendar reminder.

"I miss this," he says, echoing my silent sentiments. I smile at him.

"I know. It's been a while."

It's moments like this that I wish there was hope of us still being friends. We had shared so many years together, and so many memories, it would just make things like this easier on both of us. But mostly me.

"Hey Colton! Tell them about that time you went streaking across the field at halftime during the big game with State!" My cousin Ryan, the groom, suddenly interrupts us.

The table erupts with raucous laughter, excited for the next Messiah Colton parable. Everyone except for the bride that is.

I can't tell if she has either had too much wine, or not enough.

Regardless, she seems ready for this rehearsal dinner to be over. She glances my way and I mouth *"I'm sorry."*

To which she smirks and just shrugs her shoulders.

Boys will be boys, I guess.

Ryan, Colton, and all the groomsmen are soon completely engaged in another story at the end of the table.

As I reach for my wine, I see Colton's phone, which he left on the table next me, light up with a text.

Emily
6:15 p.m.-Incoming Text

The moment I see her name, I feel like my stomach does a backflip.

Emily. It cannot be.

I glance up at Colton, who is completely immersed in another tale, then back at the phone. I can hear my heartbeat in my ears.

He wouldn't still be texting that Emily...would he?

But also, how many other Emily's could he know?

I continue staring at it and in that moment, brashly decide I must know. So, I covertly slip his phone off the table and into my purse, and head immediately for the bathroom, my legs trembling beneath me.

It can't possibly be that Emily...he was just saying he missed me, and yesterday he was begging for me back.

I try to talk myself down, wondering if I should just go back and ask him directly. However, if it *is* her, I know that if I ask Colton outright, he will never give me the truth. There is only one way I can know for sure.

Colton has not changed his password, so opening the phone is easy. It automatically opens the text from Emily. The first thing I see is her contact photo.

Holy shit...it is her.

Emily
6:15 p.m.: Hello? What's the plan? Are you at least coming back to my room tonight?

Emily
6:00 p.m.: This is bullshit Colton, I appreciate the free ticket, but I came all the way here for you, and you haven't even invited me out to meet anyone.

Emily
2:00 p.m.: Look, I loved our little 'afternoon delight.' I just wish you didn't keep me locked away like I'm some secret or something.

Emily
8:00 a.m.: Good morning sexy, I just landed in Chicago!

My stomach flips a thousand times, and my whole body is shaking. It is true. Colton is still talking to the same Emily that he had been having an affair with during half our relationship. And if that is not enough, it appears he even bought her a plane ticket to come here.

He actually brought her to fucking Chicago.

I start casually scrolling back through the text history. However, I instantly regret this decision when I realize they have spoken every day for months, maybe years.

It appears they never stopped speaking, at all. I am stunned. For three days straight, he has been blowing up my phone, begging me to give him another chance, and now I come to learn that he never stopped talking to the very woman that ended our relationship.

Now I feel like the third glass of wine was a terrible idea. My head is spinning. I feel sick. Like actually sick. In fact, I am going to be sick.

I spin around, barely making it to the toilet before I vomit up the contents of my stomach. When I finish, I find myself fighting back tears, as my brain tries desperately to reign in my sanity.

No, absolutely not, Natalie. You are not going to cry over this asshole.

He does not deserve that. And neither do I.

I have had enough of crying over Colton to last a lifetime. And ultimately, whomever he chooses to speak with is none of my business anymore. We are no longer together.

But I still feel stunned to my core and take a few deep breaths to try and steady myself.

His phone buzzes in my hand, but this time I see a new message from a new contact.

Edgar-Hookup
6:23 p.m.: Sorry man, I don't refill until the 10th. I can hook you up with everything you need then, probably about 40

of the V-10mg.

Upon review, there are more texts just like it, spanning the last eight months. Conclusion? Colton has been buying prescription painkillers, in bulk.

He doesn't have an injured shoulder...he has an addiction.

Suddenly, it all makes sense—the weight gain, the sweaty palms, twitchy movements, and constant bags under his eyes—these are all indications of a person struggling with *withdrawal*. It would also explain him shamelessly hunting for pain medication amongst the wedding guests.

Unbelievable.

I take a moment to process all of this before I decide to just put the phone back in my purse.

You know what? This isn't my circus, anymore.

All of this is Colton's problem—not mine.

And as painful and nauseating as this experience is, in some ways it feels like just another reminder of why I left him. He is a cheating, lying, manipulative, and apparently now pill-popping narcissist, that I cut out of my life intentionally.

I need to remember that intentionally, too.

As I walk out of the bathroom stall, I suddenly hear my phone chime, and pull it out of my purse.

Jaxon
6:45 p.m.: I am outside, are you ready?

Holy shit. In all this mess, I completely forgot about Jaxon!

I am not ready to see him just yet. I quickly fix my makeup, brush my teeth, and fluff my curls before walking back out to the table. Thankfully, Colton is still down at the other end of the table, completely oblivious to the fact that his phone was even missing the entire time.

I set it back down on the table when no one is looking, then say my goodbyes to my parents, before making my way over to the bride.

"Thank you for dinner. Sorry they are so ridiculous," I say with a smile, motioning toward the end of the table.

She laughs and shrugs. "Oh, it is fine, what can you do?"

All of a sudden, I see her eyes widen and hear her gasp softly, as her attention turns to something just behind me. Or *someone*.

I already know who it is.

Jaxon.

I turn and see him standing in the doorway, running his fingers through his hair. His intimidating frame is sporting dark blue jeans, a gray long-sleeve tee, and a leather jacket. Our eyes lock, and my pulse quickens the minute I see a positively wicked grin skate across his face. I feel the heat in my cheeks intensify as he steps toward me.

The room behind me grows silent, as the rest of the guests quickly become aware of his presence. I decide that I don't feel like having any awkward conversations about this handsome stranger.

"Can we go?" I whisper.

"Of course," he replies softly.

I see him give a slight nod to the room behind me, acknowledging them before leading me out of the restaurant. When the cool air hits my face, I remember I can breathe again. Which is something I seem to forget whenever I find myself in Jaxon's wake. He steps past me towards a beautiful vintage Harley, which has two helmets sitting on the seat.

Oh my... this must be what he meant by "wear pants."

"I'm sorry, I hope I wasn't interrupting," he says, far too innocently for me to believe him.

"I dunno, I'm starting to think you kinda *like* interrupting," I say, squinting my eyes at him and watching him grin back at me mischievously.

"You may be right. I certainly like stealing you away." He winks as he settles on the bike.

"On a motorcycle, too." I nod toward the bike.

"Well, you asked if I had any normal cars," he says, displaying the bike with pride. "Besides, I have found there is no better way to navigate Chicago city traffic at this hour."

"While I agree city traffic is horrendous, I don't think this necessarily qualifies as a car, Jaxon."

"Would you just get on the damn bike?" he says with a wink, as he hands me a helmet. He looks unbelievably sexy, and more relaxed than I have yet to see him be.

"Now might be a good time to tell you I've never been on a motorcycle before..." I say nervously as I reach for the helmet, but he grabs me and pulls me close.

He slides a hand up the outside of my thigh and effectively turns my legs to mush.

"So, are you saying I get to share a *first* with you, Miss Tyler? Good." His voice is husky and deep as he brushes a hair from my face, his scent intoxicating me.

Oh my... did he really just say that?

This is definitely not ordinary second 'date' behavior, at least in my experience. But, then again, something tells me Jaxon couldn't be ordinary if he tried.

My heart thunders in my chest, and my breath evaporates as he leans in to kiss me, but just before our lips touch, I hear Colton's voice call to me from the sidewalk.

"Natalie?" he asks loudly, "What's going on here? Who is *this*?" His mouth is hanging open as he motions to Jaxon incredulously.

Jaxon just shoots an arrogant smile at Colton and chuckles, deliberately ignoring Colton's question. He winks at me and nods toward the bike, making me smile. I put on the helmet, and after steadying myself on his shoulders, I mount the bike, climbing on behind him.

"*This* is my date," I say boldly once I have settled on the bike. "And by the way, I think Emily would like to see you tonight... she did come all this way, after all."

I watch with satisfaction as all the blood drains from Colton's face. He opens his mouth to say something, but Jaxon purposefully starts revving the engine on the bike, drowning him out entirely.

"Hold on!" he yells, and we pull away from the curb.

My stomach lurches, and I wrap my arms around his waist tightly. We merge into traffic, leaving Colton on the sidewalk looking flustered and frustrated.

The sun is setting in the city, casting a gentle shadow as we weave in and out of the cars, making our way through the bustling city streets.

My heart is pounding, and part of me is terrified, and yet somehow, I inexplicably trust that I am safe with him.

"The safest woman in the city"

I slide my hands inside his jacket and squeeze him a little tighter, feeling his ab muscles tighten under my hands. I breathe in, inhaling the scent of his leather jacket and his cologne, convinced I had never smelled anything so intoxicating.

Jaxon smells like heaven, and a little bit of sin, but all I know is that I have never felt so alive.

Chapter Sixteen

JAXON

I pull the bike down a quiet street looking for a parking spot. However, when I realize this means Natalie will finally have to *release* her tantalizing grip on my body, I selfishly consider scratching my original plan and just driving around town until we run out of gas, just to feel her arms around me.

However, I decide not to be selfish and park. I help her off the bike and we start down the sidewalk.

"Jaxon… I feel like I am constantly asking you this, but where are we going?"

"What, you haven't worked it out yet?" I say teasingly, pulling her close and wrapping my arm around her waist.

I have to admit, I am thoroughly enjoying the feeling of her body against me. I see her blush from my boldness, but she does not object, instead a warm smile settles across her cheeks.

"Seriously though, I don't understand," she laughs, still looking around trying to guess our destination.

"You're about to."

We turn the corner, and the Art Museum comes into view.

"But… it's closed," Natalie says.

"You know that for certain?"

"I know because I really wanted to see it and even tried to get tickets when I got into town. But they told me they are closed for the next few months for renovations."

"Okay, you are right. They are," I say with a grin.

We circle around to the back staircase where Travis is waiting patiently for me.

"I'm so confused, how are we going to visit a closed museum?"

"Nothing in this city is closed for me, love," I say as Travis opens the door and we step inside the darkened corridor of the museum.

"Jaxon!" Natalie whispers forcefully. "Are we really supposed to be here?" Her voice trails off, however, as she immediately becomes distracted by paintings on the walls.

"Mr. Pace! We are so fortunate to have you join us this evening!" A short, tiny man with thick glasses greets us.

"Robert, how are things?"

"Things are quiet, Mr. Pace," he says with a smile. I see his eyes fall to Natalie, and slowly canvas her body.

His eyes linger a bit too long for my taste.

"But then, what better way to see a museum, eh?" He winks at her.

She gives him a polite smile.

I briefly contemplate making him pay for that wink.

If he were not forty years my senior, and responsible for laundering all of the money for the syndicate, I probably would. But it wouldn't be a fair fight. Also, because of his role, Robert is considered "Switzerland" among the clans. He keeps himself neutral, unbiased, and silent in all our non-financial matters, a fact which makes him absolutely indispensable.

And utterly *untouchable*.

…Unless I want to start a war.

Fortunately for me, and all the young women of the city, he's safely tucked away in a stone building filled with moth-eaten original manuscripts and trinkets.

And happy as hell about it.

"We can show ourselves around," I say, motioning for Natalie to head down the hallway.

As she turns away, I see Robert lick his lips, raking her backside with his eyes. Now *this* I cannot ignore.

"Robert," I snap, careful to not alert Natalie.

Instantly he throws his hands up in submission.

"A man can dream, right?" he chuckles and walks off down another darkened corridor.

Fucking animals.

I find Natalie and the two of us start our tour. It doesn't take long before I find myself getting an art history lesson on nearly every painting in the museum.

Natalie's knowledge is astounding, but my brain is starting to hurt.

That's what I get for taking an art lover to a museum.

Information I picked up reviewing her file.

Natalie approaches another canvas, and I can hear her telling me something about the artist's apparent revelation that influenced his work, but I've stopped listening.

All I can focus on is the light dancing in her eyes, and the way her hands start waving about excitedly the faster she speaks.

Then she moves a few feet to the next frame and starts all over again.

God, how does she have this much passion for a bunch of oil paintings?

But I'm quickly beginning to understand that every single thing she does seems to have a passion behind it.

Natalie is bursting with *life*. I, on the other hand, am not.

The only passion I see is in the bedroom, and my day-to-day is more about survival and preservation of the status quo, than appreciating the experience.

"Jaxon?"

Her question jolts me from my thoughts and unfortunately exposes the fact that I haven't been paying attention.

Shit. Busted.

"Crap, I've just bored you to death..." she says, her hand instantly covering her face. "I'm so sorry, I didn't even realize, I got carried away. I suppose this is why no one wants to go to museums with me anymore."

"Don't be sorry. I was just admiring your enthusiasm for brush strokes."

"No, no, I'm sorry," she whispers, still embarrassed, glancing sheepishly at the floor.

Damn it, Jaxon, look what you did.

"Hey now, what did I say?" I step forward and gently touch her chin, lifting her gaze to meet mine. "Don't be sorry. It's fine, I promise. Please forgive my inattentiveness."

Her smile returns, and a blush settles across her cheeks. Her soft lips entice me, and I desperately want to kiss her.

Be patient.

I'm clearly not trying to adhere to any etiquette standards for a second date, nor am I above finding any excuse to touch her. But if I kiss her now, I'm not sure I will be able to *stop.* Which would effectively end the museum tour she's enjoying so much.

Try to control yourself for once.

"Now what were you saying about Monet?" I ask, taking her hand and walking further down the corridor.

"Well, did you know that at one point in his life, Monet was once so frustrated that he jumped off a bridge into the Seine?"

"I did not," I answer truthfully.

She immediately jumps straight back into our history lesson. This is by far the most educational date I have ever been on. Not that I have been on many dates, at all.

When was the last time I was actually on a date?

Usually, the extent of my interaction with women involves alcohol and fucking. It's an exchange that is silently agreed upon in the first few minutes, and the entire interaction lasts a few hours at most. Which is usually more than enough time to get bored with whatever vapid social princess is on my menu for the evening.

And the truth is, if I wasn't actively trying to "work for it," my plan probably would've involved naked extracurriculars with Natalie too.

Lord knows I want to.

The way those jeans of hers snake around her hips has been toying with me since I first saw her. She has a very svelte frame, but she has curves, too. I like that on a woman, as opposed to being stick thin. I want something to touch and grip on to.

What I wouldn't give to have her perky ass bent over my desk, my hands in her hair while I ram myself into her...

I need to stop thinking about these things, as I can feel my cock swelling in my pants just thinking about her like that. But I don't actually want her to see me like that.

I mean, yeah, okay, I definitely *do.*

But I also want to be more than some beast who is *only* good at fucking. And inexplicably, Natalie makes me feel as if I *should* be more than that.

It's evident to me that Natalie is far more elaborate than I am. She has so many more layers than I have, which awkwardly makes me feel slightly inadequate by comparison.

Maybe *that's* what Ethan meant.

Perhaps Natalie *is* out of my league.

On top of being courageous and kind, the girl is also smart and funny. She speaks French, and based on our tour also apparently has a thorough understanding and love of the arts.

Natalie is *interesting*.

I can do this. I can be more than just a good lay.

At least, for *now.*

"So, are you going to tell me why you actually brought me here?" she asks suddenly, pausing in front of the main staircase and catching me lost in my thoughts again.

"What do you mean?"

"I mean, you don't have to keep thanking me for saving Jessica," she says, tucking a strand of hair behind her ear. "You really don't have to keep doing this, Jaxon. You have already done *so* much for me, and for my family."

"Natalie, that's not what this is," I say cautiously. "I just wanted to…"

I don't know how to finish this sentence.

The real reason I brought her here was because I knew she wanted to come here. Which sounds way too unselfish to actually be *my* reasoning, so now I'm confused. It feels like a hundred reasons all at once, and suddenly I'm nervous that none of them sound like something I would say.

"I just want to spend time with you. Get to know you a little more."

"But why?" Natalie asks softly.

"Why does anyone do anything?" I chuckle.

"That's fair," she shrugs. "I guess I just assumed you could be spending your evening getting to know some spoiled debutante who is actually local. You know, instead of getting an art-history lecture with an out-of-towner."

She crosses her arms and leans on the banister, a coy smile on her face.

"Perhaps I like getting lectured."

"Oh, I see. So, you like slow and painful torture. You really *are* a masochist, Jaxon Pace." She winks at me, biting her lip.

Oh, those lips…

This time I cannot help myself.

I pull her into me, pressing my lips to hers, and cupping her face with my hand.

"Guilty," I breathe against her lips. "Call me a glutton for punishment."

She feels so good in my arms, and I want her desperately. I run my fingers along her chin, and gently kiss her cheek, feeling her breath quicken. The way her body responds to my touch makes mine respond in kind and I crush her lips to mine once again.

"So... then why didn't you just try and take me back to your penthouse?" she asks breathlessly when I finally allow her up for air.

Can she hear my thoughts?

The look in her eyes tells me she's imagined the same scenario I've been picturing since last night on my boat. Just knowing this threatens to undo me, and I can feel my cock throbbing in my pants.

I could do it. Holy fuck I could do it.

I could end this tour right now, take her straight back to The Jefferson, and fuck her righteously.

But then...all of this would be over. And for some reason, I'm not ready for it to be over. So instead, I kiss her gently on the lips, while consciously fighting the selfish impulse to rip her clothes off in front of Monet.

"Perhaps," I say, stroking her cheek with my thumb. "I have an appetite for something *different* this evening."

She looks at me, struggling to contain her own desire.

If I don't put some distance between us, I will cave.

"Forgive me," I say, stepping back slightly. "I feel very... out of practice here."

"I know the feeling," she says softly.

"And I understand a lot has happened in the last few days..."

"Just a little," she replies with a smile.

"I realize that it would probably be easier if I just backed off and didn't complicate your life any further."

Natalie says nothing. Her expression is unreadable, but her eyes are locked on mine, burrowing into my soul.

"But," I say quietly. "I just can't seem to stay away from you."

"Then don't," she whispers. She pauses a moment then leans in to kiss me again.

Fuck it.

I thread my fingers in her hair, surrendering to this raging fire between us and kissing her deeply.

No! I have to calm down or I will blow it completely.

Gently, I find a way to tear myself away, knowing that my resolve to keep her clothed is fading. I stand there with my forehead pressed against hers trying to calm down.

How does she make me go 0 to 100 so fast?!

"I'm sorry," I whisper. "Again."

"No apologies necessary," she says with a tantalizing smile. "Remember?"

"I feel like I keep crossing some invisible line. I guess I don't know how to do this anymore," I say quietly, scanning her eyes. "Admittedly, it's been years since I've been on a real date. Is there usually this much restraint required?"

"I don't know. I've never felt like *this* on a date before. Even when Colton and I were dating, I never felt..."

"*This.*" I finish for her.

She nods in agreement.

But what *is* this? Is it just chemistry? Or maybe an overdose of pheromones?

I take a deep breath and smile, extending my arm to her.

"We still have lots more to see, shall we continue?"

She nods with a smile and takes my hand. But then she stops, turning to me with a serious expression on her face.

"Jaxon, can I ask you a question?" She asks softly.

"Of course."

"Well, I guess it's more of a request really..."

"Even better," I grin, pulling her back to me and kissing her hand. "I like those. Anything you want, it's yours."

"Regardless of what this becomes," she says, taking a deep breath. "Whether we end up just being friends, or maybe something more...will you promise to just be *honest* with me?"

I can't tell if it's the sincerity in her voice, or the silent vulnerability behind her eyes, but this statement breaks my heart.

This is her ask?

Fuck, what did this asshole do to her?

But as I stand there judging Colton, I'm reminded that at one point in my life I was the asshole, too.

I lied to Rachel. A lot.

I hurt her. A lot.

Yet here I stand, condemning Colton, while staring into the eyes of quite possibly the most interesting, and innocent, girl I have ever met. A girl, who doesn't know a fraction of my darkness; who could've asked me for anything money could buy, and I would have given it to her without so much as a second thought.

...And all she asked for was my *honesty*.

And now I don't know if I can *keep* the promise I just made. Honesty isn't something I give freely without consequences.

Sure, sometimes non-syndicate civilians, or "Regs" as we call them, find out about the mafia. It's always a risk, but we have ways of mitigating those risks. Most people can be bought off, or at least intimidated into keeping their mouth shut, because at the end of the day, most people prefer ignorance when it comes to this sort of stuff.

From the moment I was born I've lived a double life. By day I'm a single-father billionaire hotelier, and by night I'm the Don Supreme of our crime syndicate. I'm well accustomed to the ways and risks of our world, and have to be careful with my honesty in order to protect my family

"I will do my best," I say quietly.

She stares back at me, perhaps not completely satisfied with this answer.

"Look, Natalie, I don't—"

"No, it's okay. I understand," she whispers, shaking her head. "Really, I do. I realize we barely know each other, and I have no business asking you to share everything with me."

You don't want to know everything, I promise.

"That's not it," I say, trying to think of a better way to say this. "It's not the *ask* that is the problem, it's the execution."

"What do you mean?"

"What I mean is that I don't normally do *this*," I say, motioning between myself and her. "So, I have no frame of reference for what you want, and don't necessarily know how to give it to you."

"Oh."

"My life is complicated, but it's complicated that I understand. My family, I understand. Business, I understand. Sex, even that I understand." I swallow hard. "But this…this is new territory for me," I say softly.

"This?" she asks.

I run my fingers through my hair, trying to gather my thoughts.

"Wait, do you mean…dating?" she whispers.

I just stare at her, taking in the softness of her features, and the adorable blush warming her cheeks.

"I mean, er, I'm not suggesting that's what *we* are doing," she scrambles nervously.

Look at that, I guess even Natalie gets flustered sometimes.

"I mean, any kind of relationship," I say softly. "I just don't have them."

"As in…*ever*?" She asks.

This might be harder than I thought.

I take her hand and pull her over to a bench in the gallery.

"Remember when I told you about the girl named Rachel?"

"Jessica's mother." Natalie nods.

"Yes. Well, she was the first and last person I was in any kind of relationship with. And I fucked it up. All of it. Horribly. We were quite different people, and it was often a struggle. We just kind of fell into some tangled mess together, and then Jessica happened, and everything that comes with having a child with someone."

Natalie's eyes drop from mine momentarily.

"I guess what I'm trying to say is that I don't try to date because I never understood *how* to date," I sigh. "And, I also understand how complicated my life is, so it usually just becomes a situation where I don't see a woman after…"

I clear my throat, seeing her face appraising me and feeling slightly embarrassed.

"Well, you obviously understand, I don't need to explain."

Natalie's silence is killing me. I want to know what she is thinking, though I suspect it's not a great reflection of myself.

"So, how does Jessica react? You know, seeing all these women coming and going from your home?" she finally asks.

"She doesn't. I don't allow her to see any of that," I say firmly. "And I don't allow any women at my home. Ever."

"Oh right, the hotel," Natalie says, looking away from me.

Fuck, this is going off the rails.

"Look, Natalie, I'm not some womanizing asshole."

Yes, I am.

"I don't have some revolving door of women that I sleep with and never call again."

Yes, I do.

"That's not my goal."

Well, at least that part is true.

"And in some fucked up way, all of this is connected to honesty for me," I sigh. "I've never put much effort into being honest and open about my life because I don't put much effort into anyone—friendships or dating. And because I'm also not entirely sure *how* to bring them around Jessica, I just don't bring them around her. Which ultimately makes non-commitments the only viable option for me."

Natalie nods slowly, inciting me to continue.

"I mean, she doesn't remember her mother, and I don't want to put that kind of pressure on her or any woman in my life." I realize this somehow got incredibly serious, and I might just be rambling at this point.

Why am I doing this?

I'm usually a steel trap. But for the life of me I don't understand why I just keep divulging personal information to Natalie.

She could easily put my best interrogators to shame.

"Fuck, look, I'm sorry. I realize none of this is an appropriate answer to your question, and I just went way off on a tangent," I chuckle to myself.

I stand to my feet and turn to face the closest painting just so that I don't have to face her disapproval.

"See? I told you I have no idea what I'm doing."

I'm embarrassed, and regret everything that just came out of my mouth.

I probably should've just tried to fuck her.

"I just don't know the limits anymore, like what is too much honesty, and what is too little," I whisper to myself.

Suddenly, a hand is on my back—her hand.

"We said no apologies," Natalie says softly. "And for the record, Jaxon, you just *did* it without even realizing what you were doing."

"What?" I ask.

"I asked you to be honest with me, and you were."

I turn to face her, and she takes a deep breath before continuing.

"Look, I don't need to know all the details of your life," she says gently. "And I don't need them to be pretty or perfectly wrapped up in a bow. I get that life is messy and difficult. And I understand that honesty might not be easy for you."

"No, for the record, it feels pretty terrible actually. It's like a magnifying glass on all of my failures."

"I get it," she says with a smile. "Lucky for you, I also fully understand what it's like to feel like you've failed at something."

"I doubt that sincerely," I say with a chuckle. "Pretty sure you might *actually* be a saint."

In fact I know you are. I've seen your file.

She chuckles too.

"Oh, I promise I'm not. I've made a lot of mistakes. You talk about being out of practice? I get that. I am no expert when it comes to relationships. And I don't have many friendships with men."

Oh, I'm sure they all want to be your friend.

"Fact is, I'm still learning too. Which is kind of the reason I was asking. I just want to know that if I'm going to be getting to know you and letting my guard down with you, that you will tell me the truth. It's just something I need, so that I don't get hurt."

"I have no intention of hurting you…" I say slowly, trying to keep my thoughts together but faltering at her close proximity to me. "But I also want you to know, I don't have the greatest track record when it comes to screwing shit up... even with the best intentions."

"And I want you to know that I appreciate your *honesty*," Natalie says with a smile. "I know this is really heavy."

"But somehow you make it feel lighter." The words escape my lips before I even register what I said.

What the hell?

I quickly scramble to cover the cheesy response I just gave.

"I'll do my best to be honest with you, if you can do your best to be patient with me."

"Fair trade, Sir," she breathes hard, her eyes falling to my lips.

I know what she wants.

So without hesitation, I kiss her passionately.

There are no words to describe what I feel at this moment. Or maybe I've just forgotten them all.

"What are you doing to me?" I whisper when I finally pull away, my fingers lingering softly on her face.

"Me?" she says giggling as she pulls away. "You think this is easy for me?"

"What do you mean?"

"What do I mean?" she says, laughing harder. "I mean I'm just as emotionally battered as you are, and I'm just a normal human. I don't have any extravagant gifts to distract you with."

She straightens her shirt, avoiding my gaze.

"You've got sportscars, yachts, penthouses and private museum tours," she shrugs bashfully. "I feel a little out of my league here."

Ethan would disagree with you.

"You gave me a second chance after I was an asshole to you. That's more than most people would have given."

Her eyes fall to the floor, but then find mine again.

"And, you've given me a few moments of peace from my normally out-of-control and fast-paced life." I say, kissing her softly. "Believe me when I say, Natalie Tyler, those are truly extravagant gifts in my world."

She smiles, and I swear she puts all the Old Masters to shame.

Chapter Seventeen

Natalie

My hand is in his as we slowly tour the museum's treasures. And while some are rare, some are expensive and some are priceless, there is one treasure that I am beginning to find the most beautiful of all…Jaxon Pace. The man himself.

I learned that he is Greek, and that his great-great grandfather was an immigrant to America. He tells me of his childhood, of his fond memories as part of a large extended family, and of his parents who have both sadly passed on, along with many of his aunts and uncles.

He tells me of his first business ventures and triumphs and vast successes. How he built his hotel and shipping empires, expanding them both well beyond what his father had accomplished.

I hear about the joy he felt on the day Jessica was born, and his life as a single dad. He even tells me more about Rachel, although these memories come with a lot of regrets, and guilt from things he did in his past that hurt her.

Although this was not the most pleasant of subject material, I was certain I was witnessing a level of openness that was very foreign to him. Which made sense when I learned that his days mostly consisted of business dealings and boardrooms.

When I asked if he had a best friend, or any friends at all, he just shook his head. That was when I realized he never talked about any of the guilt and remorse he felt concerning Rachel and her death.

…With anyone.

Some part of me felt honored that he would share these things with me of all people. However, there was still a part of me that was worried about getting close to someone who openly admits past infidelity.

But somehow, I trust him.

There was a sincerity in his voice that felt genuine, and I could tell he was making an effort to give me the honesty I asked for. Despite feeling like I had a thousand logical reasons not to trust the enigmatic Jaxon Pace, I did.

I've always believed that people can change. I mean, we all do it naturally.

I know I certainly have in just the last few years on my own. And perhaps, in some ways, maybe it *took* regret, or pain, or even loss for me to make those changes.

Or maybe it was just as Jaxon said last night on the Ismena— maybe everything really is just a *choice*. Maybe all that stands between you and the best version of yourself, is a choice.

I mean, my life started changing for the better the moment I stopped being a bystander, and no longer let myself be a victim of the choices of others.

The question is: could Jaxon be faithful?

What are you doing, Natalie?

But I know the answer to that already. I am getting far too ahead of myself.

As Jaxon walks us into a room filled with period artwork from the 17th century, I take a minute to recalibrate my disobedient heart.

I am not his girlfriend, and we are not dating.

We are just two people enjoying an evening, and a bunch of priceless relics together, learning about each other. What he could be should not be my concern right now. In fact, it *cannot* be my concern right now.

Maybe I need to stop overthinking and just enjoy it.

So that is what I endeavor to do.

I told him about my life, about Miami, and how much I love my new job that constantly has me in new places, meeting new people.

I told him about how the sunshine and vibrant colors and cultures of the city are healing and intoxicating.

I told him about my one-eyed rescue pug named Cyclops, who was waiting for me back home. And how I loved rainstorms and watching old black and white movies with a cup of tea.

It certainly felt like more of an actual first date than our wine and baggage filled disaster of an evening on his yacht. And yet, for some reason, I felt like I had known him my whole life.

Jaxon Pace was still a mystery to me, but he felt like more of a friend than a stranger, which was different than anything I had experienced before.

"Ah, here we are," Jaxon says enthusiastically, as we turn a corner into a massive display room. "I thought I would save the best for last."

It's then that I notice the room before us is filled with Grecian artwork, pottery, weapons, and statues.

Oh. My. God...

The Grecian exhibit I had been so excited to see!

"Jaxon! This is incredible!" I exclaim, bringing my hands to my face.

As a child, I had grown up in a small, boring little town that did not have many children my age. But it had a library. It was here I spent most of my summer days, and where I had first fallen in love with Greece. I had pored over every book they had on the country and had memorized all of the mythology like the back of my hand.

Now, here I am, standing in a room filled with artifacts from a beautiful ancient world, and I am completely overwhelmed.

How did Jaxon know this was the exhibit I wanted to see the most?

I glance up at him and I see the sly smile across his face.

However he knew, I was certain he had no intention of telling.

"Well, go on," he encourages.

I don't need to be told twice, bolting like a horse straight out of the gate. I immediately dart to the nearest display of Greek swords and daggers spread across a table. Coins and fabrics, used and worn thousands of years ago, were scattered across the tables, calling to me, singing of their mysteries. One by one, I moved from table to table and toured the vast display cases, quite literally lost in time.

I am utterly lost in this beautiful world when a new voice echoes through the room.

"Excuse me, Mr. Pace, I have that item you requested."

I look up to see a pretty brunette in a skintight pencil skirt standing in the doorway with a basket in her arms and a huge smile plastered on her face.

"Thank you, Felicity," Jaxon says, evidently knowing who she is.

I watch as she tucks her hair behind her ear, clearly captivated by him.

"If you want, I can set it up for you?" she sighs sweetly, savoring every second of eye contact with him. And apparently unaware of my presence, as I remain covertly tucked behind a gigantic statue.

I feel my blood boiling watching her flirt with him.

How is he going to respond?

"Sweetheart, would you like a glass of wine?" Jaxon's voice suddenly booms across the room, startling me and causing me to bump into the sword table behind me.

Sweetheart!

I notice the wicked grin painted across his lips, and that his eyes are focused on my hiding spot, as if he knows *exactly* where I have been standing the entire time. He did that on purpose.

I can feel the blood rushing to my cheeks, but I step out from behind the statue, doing my best to hide my bewilderment at being referred to as *sweetheart*.

"Yes, I would love one."

I smile as I approach Felicity and Jaxon, watching him rake me with a look so tantalizing I feel a tingling in my bones, and I can't help but blush. Felicity is blushing too, at least until she looks in my direction, and then her gaze immediately turns to ice, as she begins to sulkily take the wine and two glasses out of the basket. It's obvious that she knows who Jaxon is too, but did not know I was here with him, and she seems royally disappointed about it.

No dear, that second glass isn't for you.

My own petty possessiveness surprises me, and stuns me a little, as I have never been that kind of girl. I try to shake it off, as Jaxon takes the wine bottle from her.

"Thank you, Felicity, I think we can manage from here. Please give my thanks to Robert for making this happen," he says.

"Yes, thank you," I say, trying to be nice, and not fault her for finding him attractive. But she refuses to look at me. Instead she walks out of the room with her nose in the air, almost as quickly as she appeared.

And here I thought that I was being petty.

"Jaxon, how is it that you can have wine delivered to you in a museum?" I ask with a smirk. "A museum that is *also* technically closed to the public?"

As he twists the bottle opener, I see his muscles flexing in his long sleeve tee, and suddenly feel as if it has gotten warmer in here.

No wonder Felicity couldn't keep her eyes to herself.

"Oh, I can have anything I want," he says with a wink.

Is that so, Jaxon Pace?

"Anything?" As I pose my question, I lean over the table purposefully, so that my breasts press against the front of my black button up and fall directly within his line of sight. I see him look up to answer, with assumedly some witty remark, only to become instantly distracted and drop the wine bottle opener altogether.

Hah! Success!

"I got it," I say, seizing this opportunity to bend over and retrieve it, also teasing him with a view from behind.

But when I turn to face him, and my eyes meet his, my heart skips a beat. He looks as though he wants to rip every piece of my clothing off and fuck me ravenously. Right now.

And I would be lying if I said I didn't want that too.

"You were saying?" I say sweetly, handing him the bottle opener.

"Lifestyles of the rich and famous, baby," he says with a smile.

Sweetheart. Baby.

The pet names have not gone unnoticed.

I step around the table as he pours two glasses for us.

"Maybe we should invite her back, Felicity seems... disappointed," I say teasingly as I reach for my glass, but Jaxon grabs my hand and pulls me into him for a deep kiss.

He cups my face with one hand while the other slips under the back of my shirt and presses against the skin on my back. I give into the kiss, placing my hands on his muscular chest.

"I don't give a fuck about Felicity," he says against my lips when he comes up for air, silencing every thought I have rolling around in my head.

I slide my hand up his chest to his neck, and thread my fingers through his dark chestnut hair. A sigh escapes his lips, telling me Mr. Big Scary CEO enjoys this attention.

I can feel his desire pressing against my leg, and it makes me hot between my thighs.

I want him too. *Badly*. I picture myself feeling his bare chest under my fingers, trailing sweet kisses down his stomach, listening to the sounds he makes while I explore his body. I want to smell the way his cologne mixes with his scent and lingers on his body.

I feel my libido taking over, and quickly pull my lips from his, frightened by what I feel for him, and how desperately I want him.

I breathe heavily, trying to get my desire under control, but keeping my fingers on the back of his neck and my body pressed against his.

"What... are you doing to me, Natalie?" he whispers against me, echoing my thoughts exactly.

"I don't know... this is new for me too."

And it is. I feel excited, embarrassed, and terrified all at once. Obviously, I've experienced an attraction to men before, but nothing like this. This near primal desire I am feeling for him feels nearly radioactive, and I have never felt this *need* for someone before.

But if my short experience with him on the Ismena taught me anything, it's that once I cross that line, there is no turning back. Jaxon would not hold back, nor do I think I could either. My bones feel as if they are literally on fire for him and threaten to set everything around us ablaze.

He presses his forehead to mine, kissing me gently, and I can feel him breathing deeply. When we finally pull away from each other, I can visibly see him battling the same feelings.

It's at least comforting to know he wants *me* just as badly.

...Or dangerous.

"You," he says with a smile.

"You," I say, smiling back at him.

He hands me a glass of wine, then wraps his arm around me, pulling me close again, and leads me forward.

"Come," he says, his voice raw. "There is something I am excited to show you."

He leads me to a glass display case in the only corner of the room I have yet to explore. Inside is a necklace of dangling, teardrop-shaped sapphires as big as dimes, arranged in a cascading pattern, and surrounded by small accent diamonds.

"The Sapphires of Troy"

I say reading the placard aloud.

Jaxon looks at me over the top of his wine glass. "Have you ever heard of Helen of Troy?"

"Yes, of course. I wrote a full editorial analysis paper on the Iliad during my undergrad."

"So, you're familiar with the story of Helen and Paris?"

"The doomed lovers, yes. Heartbreaking ending."

Hopefully not a foreshadowing of where this is going.

"Ahh, well, with all respect to Homer, I wonder if you would let me share with you an alternative version of the tale of the fabled pair. A local folktale, from my ancestral homeland, that has been passed down for generations, and the one that my mother told me when I was a boy."

"Oh my, yes, I would love to hear it!" I say excitedly.

"So, we know that when Paris first saw Helen, he fell immediately and irrevocably in love with her. So much so, that this Prince of Troy stole her away across the sea, risking his entire kingdom in the process. There he married her, and on their wedding night, he presented her with a necklace of the most beautiful diamonds in all of Greece."

"Sadly, as we know, their honeymoon was short lived. And while Homer says Paris died in the war, my mother's tale says that when the city fell, Paris and Helen fled—leaving everything behind but the diamonds still around her neck."

"They fled into the hills, where they learned to live off the land as peasant farmers. Far from the pleasures and beauty of the palace, all they had left in the world was each other. But to them, that was enough. That is, until they welcomed a daughter, Calliope, into their lives. The three of them lived a simple life and were poor in everything but love."

"It is said that many years later, when Paris died, Helen was inconsolable. She built a funeral pyre for her husband on the beach. When it was completed, she took the gems that had never left her neck for a single day and gave them to Calliope for her wedding day. She cried out to Aphrodite, asking for the Goddess to bless her daughter with a love as true as she had known with Paris. She then lit the pyre that held her beloved husband, and as the flames went up, Helen laid down beside him, unable to part with him, even in death."

"As Calliope wept at the loss of both of her parents, her cries were heard by some fishermen in the bay. Her tears were so plentiful, and heartfelt, that they stained the jewels around her neck, and turned them blue."

"According to legend, Aphrodite, moved by this final display, took pity on Calliope, now alone in the world. She commanded her son, Cupid, to strike the heart of the handsome young fisherman below, causing him to leap from the ship and swim to Calliope. Struck by her beauty, and Cupid's arrow, the man consoled and comforted her, taking her to his home."

"He eventually went on to marry her, and they were blessed with a happy marriage and a daughter of their own."

"Many years later, on her daughter's wedding day, she passed the gems on to her, and her daughter then passed them on to her son for his new wife on her wedding day. The condition was that the gems were blessed by the Gods and should always be passed to the next generation of the family."

"The members of this family, known as the 'Peripateo' family, are said to be blessed in love. And the gems themselves are believed to bring good fortune and love to anyone who wears them on the day they are wed," Jaxon finishes with a smile.

"Oh my God... that is beautiful. I've never heard this version."

"Nor would you. I only know this story because it's the story of *my* family. You see, my great-great-grandfather changed his name from Peripateo to Pace when he came to the States."

I stare into his gorgeous empyrean eyes, and I feel as if time stands still around us as I am immersed in this beautiful heritage.

"So, what you are saying is that these are *your* family's heirlooms? That means... they must be centuries old."

"Yes, these gems have been in my family for almost twelve generations. All the women in my family have worn these on their wedding day," Jaxon says, staring at the gems in the case.

Whoa.

"Then... what on earth are they doing here?" I ask softly.

Jaxon shrugs, still staring at the sapphires.

"I guess after Rachel passed, and my life changed directions, I just accepted I would probably never marry, myself. One day they will belong to Jessica, but they were just collecting dust in a closet, which would have broken my mother's heart. I figured since I'm a loyal patron, I might as well loan them to the museum specifically for this exhibit and allow the world to see them."

On hearing this, my heart breaks for him. Despite the cold, and sometimes terrifying demeanor of this beautiful man, there were still hints of a sad little boy, trying to plug the holes of his emotional boat.

The most beautiful...

The most interesting...

The most frustrating...

And quite possibly the loneliest man I have ever met in my entire life...

An hour later we pulled back up to the valet at the hotel.

As soon as I step off the bike, I find Jaxon in front of me removing my helmet. Without warning, he wraps his arm around my waist and kisses me very hard. And *very* publicly.

And even despite the realization that some of my family members could be lingering in the lobby, I don't care. I can't fight it, and I will not even try. It's becoming painfully obvious that I am utterly powerless to resist Jaxon Pace.

As he pulls away, my heart warms to see the boyish grin across his face, a carefree respite from his usual intimidating frown. I linger in his arms, feeling a smile spread across my face, too.

When he turns to speak to the valet, however, I suddenly notice how many people are staring at us. The valet guys are snickering at each other, a couple of housekeeping ladies changing shifts are whispering nearby on a park bench, and while they did not seem to speak, I even caught the eyes of more than one of Jaxon's security detail.

Oh no, I wonder if Charlie told everyone what happened this morning?!

I blush and stare quickly at the ground, embarrassed, letting my hand fall from his chest.

"What's wrong?" he asks, turning back to me, the boyish grin now replaced with a face of concern.

I cannot have that.

"Oh nothing, I was just thinking that this bike is amazing! No wonder you like this so much!" I say with a smile.

I feel confident in my deflection, as years of embarrassing interactions with Colton had left me incredibly good at hiding my true emotions with a smile.

But the frighteningly observant Jaxon is not fooled at all. "Fuck the bike." He says as he pulls me to him and runs a finger along my chin. "What is it?"

I hesitate a moment, but from the look in his eye I understand that he will know if I try lying to him a second time. "Everyone is staring," I whisper.

"Of course, they are," he scoffs. "Have you seen yourself? You're gorgeous."

"No, I mean, do you think Charlie told everyone he saw me... *naked*?" I whisper bashfully.

A smirk creeps across his face, and he leans down to gently kiss my cheek.

"I promise you, Miss Tyler," he whispers so lethally it sends shivers down my spine. "Charlie knows better."

"Something to say?!" Jaxon's voice suddenly thunders across the entire atrium, making me jump. "No? Then I suggest you all turn around and get the fuck back to work!"

No one needs to be told twice, and I hear several muttered apologies as they scuffle to disappear, or at the very least look busy, their eyes anywhere but on us.

He could certainly be frightening when he wanted to be.

"Better?" he says with the same smirk.

"You're absolutely terrifying babe," I reply, winking at him.

"Oh baby, you have no idea what I'm capable of." He chuckles, kissing my hand, and pulling me toward the doors.

I bite my lip.

It does feel good to be with him.

I feel absolutely untouchable.

"Daddddy!" A voice yells, and all of a sudden Jessica comes catapulting across the lobby and launches herself at Jaxon. He scoops her up in his arms and plants a kiss on her cheek.

"How was school today, Jessibear?" he asks her.

"Boring!" she says, rolling her eyes and touching his face.

He is beaming from ear to ear, the frightening CEO long forgotten.

Jessica's eyes then settle on me, and she smiles, burying her face in his chest, but still glancing up at me.

"What's going on, troublemaker?" I ask her, tickling her leg. "Do you remember me?"

She giggles in that adorable and addictive laugh that children have.

"Yesss! You're Miss Natalie," she says, now bashfully hiding behind her curls and looking up at her dad.

"Very good!" I smile back at her.

She leans in and whispers something in her father's ear, who smiles and then looks at me. "Yeah, I think she's pretty too," he says, his eyes paralyzing me.

I feel my cheeks get hot as I blush.

"Do you want to go get ice cream with us?" Jessica asks innocently, making Jaxon chuckle.

"Hold on now, you little extortionist, no one said anything about ice cream. It's well past bedtime already. We need to go home."

"But I thought you said I could play with Miss Natalie again?" Jessica pouts, her face full of precious disappointment.

What did she say?

I swear if Jaxon is capable of blushing, then he surely is.

"I'm pretty sure I said *maybe*, and not tonight," he says quietly.

"Awwww!" she pouts, disappointedly.

"Tell you what," he says, putting her down. "How about you help me take Miss Natalie to her room to say goodnight?"

Jessica pouts at him, unsatisfied with this negotiation.

He looks up at me, his face practically begging me for help.

"You know, I sure would feel better if I had a big brave bodyguard like *you* to escort me," I say as I squat down beside her. "What do you say? Are you up to the task?"

I extend my hand to her, her dark brown eyes lighting up excitedly as she enthusiastically clasps my hand in hers.

"Aww," I hear one of the women behind the desk sigh.

I just try to ignore it, but the momentarily disarmed Mr. Pace whips his head around to glare at them and clears his throat, causing everyone to scatter.

Whoa. He just silenced an entire lobby with a cough.

Jessica, unfazed by her father's aggressiveness, pulls me excitedly toward the elevator, and we all pile in. Ethan silently joins us too, while the rest of Jaxon's men post up on the couches in the lobby.

He sure has very dedicated security.

I sit down on the couch in the elevator, and Jaxon takes a seat beside me. He reaches for Jessica but she playfully avoids his clutches. She giggles and shakes her head, pointing to me instead.

"What about me?" Jaxon pretends to pout.

Jessica shakes her head again, giggling harder.

"Ask first," he says, cautioning her.

"May I sit on your lap?" she asks bashfully.

"Of course!" I say, lifting her into my arms.

Jaxon silently mouths "*I'm sorry*" before gently placing his arm around me.

"So tell me, what's your favorite subject that you're learning about?" I ask Jessica as she settles on my lap.

"Ummm science."

"Ooh, science huh?"

"Yup! I wanna be a scientist when I'm big. Or a doctor. Or a movie star!"

"That's quite a list!" I laugh.

"What do you do?" she asks, twirling her hair with a toothy grin.

"Me? Well, I'm a nurse."

Her eyes suddenly get really wide.

"So do you...do you give people *shots*?"

"Sometimes," I shrug. "But only when they need them."

"I hope I never need them. I hate shots," she says, scrunching up her nose and wrapping her arms around her tiny little body.

"Me too!" I whisper in her ear, making both of us giggle. Jaxon chuckles and looks at Ethan, and I almost swear I see a flash of a smile on Ethan's face, too.

"Daddy takes me for ice cream whenever I get a shot."

"This kid and ice cream..." Jaxon says, putting a hand over his face. "I swear she does eat more than ice cream."

"Not if I can help it!" she says excitedly.

This makes all of us laugh.

The elevator dings and the doors open to my floor. Jessica hops off my lap and we walk into the lobby of the penthouse.

"Daddy, I don't wanna go home yet," she says, tugging on his arm. "Can't we stay a little longer?"

I look at Jaxon, who looks completely unsure how to handle this situation. I think we both had different plans for this exchange, than what is allowed in front of a six-year-old.

Especially one who isn't used to seeing women interacting with her father.

"Tell you what," I say, squatting down to Jessica's level. "If you're a good girl and go home, brush your teeth, and go to bed for your Daddy, I promise we will get ice cream together soon. Sound fair?"

"Okay! Goodnight, Miss Natalie!" She exclaims and throws her arms around me, hugging me close.

My heart might have stopped beating. And by the look on Jaxon's face, I think his might've too. He steps forward, a stunned expression still on his face, and wraps me in a hug, kissing my neck discreetly.

"Those are some powerful negotiation skills," He whispers. "I'm impressed."

His voice is soft and enticing, but his eyes reflect his true intentions so clearly it makes my bones feel jiggly.

"Oh baby, you have no idea what I'm capable of," I say with a wink, echoing his statements from earlier.

"Well, I certainly hope to find out," he says, kissing my hand, and making my breath quicken again.

Then he steps back on the elevator and disappears.

"Good evening, Ma'am!" Charlie's friendly voice comes from

behind me, surprising me a little, as my thoughts are lost in Jaxon.

"Oh, Charlie, hello!" I say with a smile.

As I stare at his jovial expression, I feel momentarily guilty for assuming he would have gossiped about seeing me naked this morning. I can't explain why, but seeing him now, I knew Jaxon was right—he would never be so crude.

"Can I help you with anything, Charlie?" I ask, but he smiles as if I have just asked him something ridiculous.

"No, Ma'am."

"No Ma'am," I say with a smile. "It's just *Natalie*."

"My apologies, Miss Natalie. Can I take your coat?"

I'm not sure "Miss Natalie" is better, but okay.

"I've had housekeeping start the fire in the master bedroom and turn down the sheets. They also set up a fresh tray of fruit and cheese in the kitchen."

"Holy smokes… thank you."

I think Charlie can sense how overwhelmed I feel, so he smiles.

"I'll be in my room all night. If you need anything at all, don't hesitate to ring me."

"Thank you, Charlie, for everything. I'm so appreciative, I don't know why Jaxon thinks I deserve all of this."

Charlie grins and looks at the ground.

"With all due respect, I saw the smile on Miss Jessica's face. I know *exactly* why," he says, making me blush instantly.

Suddenly, we are both distracted by a knock at the door. I move to open it, but Charlie beats me to it, stepping in front of me in one motion. His stance seems distinctly more rigid and cautious as he opens the door slowly.

"A message for Miss Tyler from the Front Desk," A porter says, handing Charlie an envelope.

Charlie thanks him and then closes the door just as slowly as he opened it. He takes a good look at the blank envelope on both sides before handing it to me.

Is this standard butler procedure?

I mean, it is not like I would know from experience, but it does seem a little weird to me.

"For you, Ma'am."

"Natalie, Charlie," I say, rolling my eyes. "If we're going to work together, you can't keep calling me Ma'am."

He nods with a polite smile, but it's not nearly as jovial as earlier. Shrugging it off, I open the envelope. However, inside I find just another blank letter. I turn it over in my hands, checking it completely for any kind of writing.

"Huh. How odd."

"What is it?" Charlie inquires.

"I think someone may be playing a joke on me."

"What do you mean?"

I walk over to the kitchen counter where the rehearsal dinner invite sits, and the other blank message sits underneath today's paper.

"This is the *second* blank message I have gotten from the front desk," I say, handing it to him.

"Miss Tyler—" Charlie asks before I playfully raise an eyebrow at him. "I mean, Miss Natalie, would you mind if I take both of these? I want to show them to the front desk and see if I can figure out what is happening."

"Be my guest." I shrug with a yawn, wrapping my arms around myself.

What a crazy day today has been.

"I think it's time I head for bed, Charlie. Or at least I should head in that general direction."

"In that case, might I suggest one of the bottles of wine?"

"Wine?" I ask.

"I've heard the Cabernet is pretty decent."

"You know what, I think that is a fantastic idea."

Chapter Eighteen

JAXON

"Does Miss Natalie live at the hotel too?" Jessica asks as I tuck her into bed, back at the house.

"No, she does not. She is just visiting for a little while," I reply with a smile, but I am aware that she has been talking about Natalie nonstop since we left the hotel.

"Where does she live?"

"She lives in a place called Miami."

"Where is Mom-ami?"

"It's in Florida... a little far from here," I say with a chuckle.

I can see the wheels turning in her little head.

"But... we are going to get ice cream, right?" she asks with a yawn, her eyes finally drooping. I smile and kiss her forehead.

"Goodnight, pumpkin. I love you."

"Night, Daddy. I love you, too."

I stay for a few more moments watching her drift off to sleep and contemplating my own anxieties. When I know she is really asleep, I shut the lights off and close her bedroom door.

The fact that my daughter seems to think I live at the hotel is sitting off with me. It feels so cold and impersonal.

What's more, Jess has brought up an uncomfortable truth about Natalie.

While I can't deny the chemistry between us, and how easy it feels spending time with her, she is *not* local. She is technically just a guest in my hotel, visiting Chicago.

What if she just… leaves? And that's it?

A prospect that has never bothered me before with any of the other women I have been involved with, now seems to leave a truly unsettling feeling on my skin. I do not *want* her to leave. I spent hours with her tonight, sharing things that I have never talked about before and I just enjoyed being with her.

It felt natural.

Further still, Natalie was the first woman Jessica tolerates being around. And not just tolerates, but seems to actually like, as the child has not stopped talking about her since the day they met.

On the other hand, it's not as if Natalie should be obligated to stay, simply because my child likes her. I couldn't put that on her, that would be remarkably unfair. That's not Natalie's responsibility.

But this attachment is everything I feared when it came to this sort of thing. The fear of *more* loss.

I can't stop the anxiety rising in my chest. If Natalie decides to just walk out of our lives, it would only make things harder on Jessica… and it would be entirely my fault.

After all, I knew the risk when I asked to see her a *second* time.

Had I been thinking clearly, I would have just let things go after the argument in my office. Or even after the yacht dinner.

But I didn't *want* to. I wanted to see her again. I wanted to see her tonight, and even now I crave more time with her.

So, I went after it like I always do.

Pursuit in itself is not new to me. I am used to going after the things I want. And I'm used to getting what I want. However, that's much easier when what I want is just a quick piece of ass, and for the woman to fuck off into oblivion when I've had my fun.

But this is different. I am getting attached. I can feel it.

I actually enjoyed our 'date' this evening. I enjoyed her on my arm, and the feeling of having her attention and being able to give her a piece of happiness. I enjoyed what it felt like to *have* someone again.

But now my selfish indulgence could not only backfire on me, but it could also hurt my daughter in the process.

Which is why I avoid this shit altogether.

Walking down the empty hallway, I glance into a few rooms on the upstairs floor. All of them vacant but for the furniture and decor. Occasionally one of my men would crash in one of these guest bedrooms after a long shift or a drink too many, if Ethan deemed it necessary. But these were the only guests these rooms ever saw.

No wonder my child thinks I live in a hotel. I do. And sadly, so does she. This house is just another hotel. It's certainly nothing like it had been when my parents were alive.

I had grown up as an only child too, but at least I had both my parents, grandparents and even aunts and uncles around for a time. This house was constantly filled with the sounds of conversation and laughter, or the smell of my mother's cooking.

My dad had conducted business here, just as I do, but his relationships with his men had been more... personal. They often had drinks, and would watch football together, and there was always a poker table set up in the basement.

This is not the case anymore. Not since I lost everyone. I still had a few extended cousins in Greece but given how quickly I had gone from boy to man when my father died, I never really had the time to form any relationship with them.

My parents were dead. Rachel was dead. My only connection to the 'personal' felt as if it had died with them.

For the most part, I am happy being alone. I value the separation of *family* from *business*. To me, it helped to create a respect among my men, one that perhaps had become too lax in the days when my father was Don.

...And what ultimately led to his death.

After all, my father had been betrayed, by one of his men. After my mother died of cancer, my father had slowly started to drift away from the kind and respected Don he used to be. He drank aggressively, gambled more, and dabbled in the party drugs of the day. Toward the end of his life, he had more frequent outbursts, often which left me or Ethan consistently picking up the pieces and trying to get him sober.

One day, after a particularly bad night, he tearfully told me he was at rock bottom and needed help. I promised I would get it for him. But unfortunately, I never got the chance. He died the next day.

To this day, I still don't know for sure who it was, or *why*.

All I know is that it was someone my father trusted. Lured him out of the house and shot him in the back three times. On our front lawn. Which was where Ethan found him choking on his own blood.

I didn't cope. I didn't know how. I just buried it and committed myself to changing things. To make our organization stronger so that this could never happen again.

My approach to the work became more about respect and fear. The way I saw it, my father died because he became too friendly with the people responsible for the success of his businesses, and his protection. I would not make the same mistake. I could not.

After all, I had Jessica. She was *all* I had.

But what have I sacrificed in return? What has it all been for?

I sit down on the edge of my bed, but I know sleep is impossible. It's times like this I wonder just how much I have actually protected Jessica, and perhaps how much I have hurt her.

All these thoughts of Rachel I have had as of late, have just reopened old wounds that have never healed. She begged me to leave all of this behind. She pleaded with me to let someone else take over and leave with her and our daughter for a better life.

But I refused. I felt like I couldn't just leave all of this. I knew that the men in my organization were not ready to change leadership, and I truly felt I could be exactly what the family needed. And I was, for a time. Until I got lost in the vices of this life and became more obsessed with power and pleasure. Ethan, again, pulling me back from the brink and the same destruction of my father.

In my selfishness, I didn't see how badly I was hurting Rachel, the only person I had left in the world, until she was walking out the door completely fed up with my bullshit.

All I wanted to do was make things better for her and for us, but I had failed. I got caught up in the work and the lifestyle and Rachel suffered because of me. She suffered because she didn't have a partner. She suffered because she had to watch the drugged-up, exhausted, and increasingly angry father of her child refuse to acknowledge that what he thought was best, might not actually be best at all.

I failed Rachel. And at this moment, I sincerely wonder if I am failing Jessica, too.

I may be fine with my solitary life, but at least that was by choice. Jessica is not getting a choice in this.

Fuck it's remarkable she's as balanced and happy as she is.

Her distrust of women is probably due to the fact that she never knew her mother and didn't have any women in her life besides her nanny. All she has ever known is a life of big, scary intimidating men.

Fuck sleep.

I head downstairs to the bar and pour myself a drink.

I find my cigarettes in my jacket pocket in the kitchen and see Ethan sitting out by the fire pit. I decide to join him, and I light a cigarette, sitting down across from him.

We sit in silence until I light the second cigarette.

"What's on your mind boss?" he asks quietly.

I debate ignoring him, but I don't actually want to be alone with my thoughts tonight. I want to talk to someone.

"I worry that I'm failing Jessica," I say after a long pause. "She thinks we live in a hotel. She has no other children or women in her life. What kind of life is that for a child her age?"

"The best life you can give her."

"Well, if that's true, Ethan, then it's mildly disappointing."

"She has *you*," Ethan says firmly. "That child adores you."

But is that enough?

"Yes," Ethan replies, somehow reading my mind. "It is enough."

"What, are you a clairvoyant now?"

"No, but I know the look of a father wondering if he did enough to protect his children," he says with a laugh. "I've been staring at him in the mirror for forty years."

I just stare at him, unsure of what to say in response.

"I know what you're feeling. Every parent feels this way. And I'm sorry to be the one to tell you this but it never goes away."

"That's not very comforting."

"Comfort is not really one of my skills."

"Clearly," I say with a half chuckle.

"Jaxon, you are always going to wonder if you're doing the right thing, or enough of the right thing. It's normal. It's the only indication that you *are* doing the right thing."

I take a drink and stare into the fire.

"Rachel…" I say slowly. "Rachel asked me to leave all of this behind and just leave with her. She said it was the only way to really protect Jessica. But I refused. Now I…"

"And now you are second guessing if that was the right choice?"

I say nothing, but I know Ethan understands.

"Jaxon, you can only do the best you can with what you have," Ethan says slowly, lighting another cigarette of his own. "You knew that with your father gone, the entire organization would crumble in the state it was in. You stayed to fix that."

"Yes, at first," I say, shaking my head. "But then…"

"You just got a little lost," he says softly.

"A little?" I scoff.

"You were young. But you did the best you could."

"If that was the best I could do, then we have passed from mildly disappointing into *severely* disappointing," I say quietly.

"Hindsight is always easier my friend."

"It doesn't feel easier."

"What you're talking about is regret. And no, regret is harder."

I take another drag, watching the flames crackle in the fire.

"But you cannot live in the past, Jaxon. You have to keep going and move forward."

I sigh deeply. "I'm not sure I know *how* to do that."

"Well," he says with a nod, "we could start by talking about this new girl of yours?"

"She's just a girl," I whisper.

"Just a girl you've seen every night for the last four days," Ethan says sarcastically.

"I'm still being careful," I lie.

"No, you're not," Ethan says with a smile.

"I am."

I'm really not though. Which is part of the problem.

"And so, what if you weren't?" Ethan replies.

"You don't have to worry, Ethan. I think I've decided I'm done. I don't think I'm going to see her again."

"Hmm," he says with a sigh. "Well, then that's too bad."

"Huh?"

"That's a mistake," he says, taking another drag of his cigarette. "But I figured this was coming."

His tone catches me by surprise, almost as if he is disappointed.

"Excuse me?"

"Jaxon, the minute that girl told you off in your office, I knew it."

"You knew what?" I say staring at him.

"That you had finally met your match. And it was going to shake up your world... and scare the piss out of you in the process."

For some reason, his insinuation that I am afraid makes me feel like he thinks I am weak, which does not sit well with me.

"You think I'm afraid?" I ask incredulously.

"Yeah, I do, actually."

"I'm sorry, were you or were you not just sitting there, telling me that it was normal to worry about this stuff?" I snap. "What the fuck?"

"No, I said it was normal to worry as a *father*. But this is different. This is you being afraid of the connection and vulnerability that you feel with this girl, and now you want to pick up and run."

"I literally don't understand you right now, Ethan."

I don't want to fight with this man.

I don't understand where he is going with this?

I also don't like him inferring that I am a coward who is running, and I can feel my blood pressure rising by the second.

"I've been watching you do it for years," he says quietly.

"What the fuck are you talking about?" I snap. "Do *what*?!"

"You keep everyone at a distance, you don't let anyone in," Ethan says, waving his hand in the air.

"You, of all people, know *exactly* why that is... why do you suddenly have a problem with it?!" I yell back at him.

"Keep your voice down!" Ethan snaps at me angrily

Is this fucker serious right now?!

If this were anyone else telling me to keep my voice down in my own house, I'd have punched his teeth in already.

"Jaxon, listen to me. I love you like a son, but sometimes you are as stubborn as a mule." Ethan says, shaking his head. "I've watched over you since you were born. And believe me when I say, you have been surviving on life support for the better part of the decade—convinced it's the only way to live."

What the...?

"But now, you have a shot at something. Something that might actually be real with this girl, and instead of trying to flush it out, you are trying to run from it because all these feelings and emotions scare you."

I don't even know what to say, I just stare at him in silence.

"I've seen more *life* in you in the last four days than in the last five years combined," Ethan says, his tone softer. "I just think, if you let her go now, you'd be making the biggest mistake of your life."

I am so confused.

"How can you say this to me? How can you suggest that this can continue between Natalie and me? How can inviting anyone, let alone someone as clean and perfect as she is, into this life be a good thing? Look at how much it has cost everyone around us? It demands everything from us!"

"You are right, it demands everything from us, but that doesn't mean you have to give it everything, Jaxon!" Ethan says, shaking his head. "This is what you still need to learn about this life."

"Ethan, Natalie is just another liability. You know this. I have responsibilities here. I need to protect myself. I need to protect

Jessica. I need to protect this family," I say, pointing toward the fire and shaking my head.

"You've protected enough! You've protected this family enough. Look where we are now! This family is stronger than it has ever been, and it does not need you to *protect* it anymore. You *are* the Don! You carried us, and got us through, and now this family exists to protect *you*!" Ethan says aggressively.

"But the work isn't done! We still have enemies. More by the minute! I don't have the right to be selfish, just out there…"

"What Jaxon?! Actually *living*?!" Ethan shouts cutting me off, his boldness stunning me into silence once again.

In all the years I've known him, he has *never* spoken to me like this.

"Listen to me, the work will never be done, do you hear me? We will always have enemies!" he snaps back at me.

But suddenly he pauses and takes a deep breath, shaking his head.

"But dammit, maybe I think that somewhere in this chaotic, violent and dangerous life we live, you deserve to have a *life* worth living too," he says quietly. "Something more than just this half existence you're so used to."

What?

My anger evaporates in an instant.

"Look, my boy," he says, his tone softer. "I do know what it's like to worry constantly, fearing the day the wolves might come to tear your life apart."

I am shaking but every muscle in my body is frozen in place.

"But what I have learned is there's no avoiding worry, and there's no stopping fear. No matter how much you plan and protect, the wolves are always in your shadow, and the fear will never truly leave. It's the curse of anyone who has lived through real tragedy like we have. Tragedy can always happen, and you cannot defeat the fear of losing something or someone you care about."

"But, if I cannot defeat the fear?" I ask, barely above a whisper. "What am I to *do*?"

"You *live*."

"What?" I gasp, stunned.

"You will never eradicate fear from your life through force, so you have to learn to live with it," Ethan says with a sigh. "And the only way to do that is to build a life outside of the dark work we do. Something that's good, that allows you a safe place to rest and recuperate. Something that makes all the bullshit we have to weed through everyday worth it."

I stare at him, unable to look away.

"The only parallel to the darkness we deal in, is a light bright enough to guide you home, no matter how lost you may feel," Ethan says, holding my gaze. "I'm talking about a real family that you can come home to."

"But what good am I to that family if I can't protect them?"

Ethan smiles at me. "Strength that is derived from fear or anger can never be as powerful as strength derived from having something to actually live for. Something worth fighting for. Something good and precious like that will make a man do things he could never imagine possible. It makes him strong. It makes him brave. And I know that you, Jaxon, will always be brave enough to protect your family. You will always have the strength to fight for what truly matters." Ethan's eyes hold mine with intensity.

I stare at him for what feels like an eternity before I get up and walk over to the couch he is sitting on and sit down beside him. I know that he would only be arguing with me, or saying any of this, if he truly was trying to stop me from making a mistake.

We sit in silence a moment before a chuckle escapes my lips.

"So effectively you are telling me to get a life… that's rich."

He starts to chuckle too. He puts his hand on my shoulder. "Can you just fucking listen to me for once?"

"I listen to you all the fucking time. And if you think I need a life, well, guess what? You do too, old man."

"I'm just that, an *old* man now. I've lived enough. Trust me." He turns to me. "And sure, fucking whores and partying until the sun comes up has it's perks. But at some point, a man can't be satisfied with that, and he just wants more."

Fuck he might have a point.

I have been attracted to Natalie because she is *more.* She's more than any woman I have ever met, and this is the first woman I think might actually be out of my league.

"This girl," he says slowly. "She's special, Jaxon. Don't throw it away."

"Even if I agreed with you on that… How do I know she can handle who I am? And this "dark life" as you put it."

"You won't know until you know."

I sigh, feeling slightly discouraged with his answer.

"But," he continues, "I will say, that any woman willing to risk herself *for* your child, might just be worth the risk *herself.*"

My mind is racing.

"Jaxon, you have good instincts. Just take your time. Feel it out. You'll know how to proceed, if and when the time is right."

"Yeah, well, I'm not really good at the whole 'patience' thing though," I say, lighting another cigarette, only to have it instantly swatted out of my hand by Ethan.

"You said you were quitting," he says with a smug grin.

I just keep staring at him, stunned.

The nerve of this fucking guy.

"It's a process. Give me a break," I say, pulling out another one. "Don't push your luck tonight."

Ethan laughs and throws his hands up in defeat, sitting back against the couch.

"Can we get back to real business? Did you do the digging I asked you to? Has everyone been tested?"

"Everyone has. And everyone is clean. Maybe it was just Samuel that slipped up."

"Maybe."

Even though these results should thrill me, I still can't help but feel suspicious. Especially when it comes to a slippery fucker like Black. I wouldn't put anything past him.

"But speaking of drugs..." Ethan says, handing me an envelope that has been sitting beside him on the couch the entire time. "It seems Natalie's ex-fiancé, Colton, has been asking the local dealers around town for some party favors—molly, ecstasy and painkillers."

As he speaks, I open the envelope and see that it contains pictures of Colton outside of one of Black's clubs, buying drugs.

Fuck. This is not good.

Black's men are vicious, and just as likely to rob and kill you as they are to sell to you. Knowing what I know about him from Natalie, and what he did to her, I personally couldn't care less if Colton suddenly disappeared off the face of the earth. But I know on some level Natalie would. And that is something I do happen to care about.

"This fucking asshole." I sigh looking through the photos. "He has no idea who he is dealing with. Or who he is putting in danger."

"Well, if he keeps going the way he is, he is about to find out."

Chapter Nineteen

Natalie

After Charlie leaves, I find the Cabernet and sit by the fire in the bedroom, replaying the day's events. I am tired, but not physically. My mind is racing and ablaze with thoughts of Jaxon, and the incredible evening we had just had together.

However, once my glass is empty, I find that I am still wide awake and anxious, so I decide there is only one thing that can possibly help—that gigantic stand-alone bathtub.

As I strip down, I pull my phone from my pocket and place it on the bed. This is the first time I have looked at it since Jaxon stole me away on his motorcycle.

Which, for the record, was pretty frickin' hot…

But given that I have now gone nearly five hours without even glancing at it, I find that I have seventeen missed calls and ten text messages.

One call from Steph.

Two calls from my mother.

Fourteen calls from Colton.

All but one of the text messages were from Colton as well, and the one rogue text was from Steph.

Steph
7:00 p.m.: I'm assuming you are busy with that handsome hotelier. And yeah, your mom totally spilled the beans to everyone about him, so just an FYI: You are so on my shit list for not telling me first. Love you, text me when you come back down for air LOL!

I laugh out loud and pour myself another glass.
I still can't believe I just left in front of everyone like that tonight!
That was incredibly bold by my standards. I had finally stepped outside my comfort zone and tried something new.
Too bad I didn't get to see Aunt Kathy's face when I rode off with Jaxon.
But being the good girl that I am, I decided to send both my mother and Steph a text letting them know that I am indeed safe and back at the hotel in one piece. There is no need to make anyone worry, and I figure this is the least I can do before someone in my family ends up inquiring about me at the front desk, embarrassing me further. However, I do not feel the need to text Colton, as I owe him no explanations whatsoever.
Steph texts back almost instantly.

Steph
11:26 p.m.: Pity, I was so ready to write your biography if you ended up as some penthouse plaything, locked in a sex dungeon somewhere. I want more deets tomorrow. Non-negotiable.

Penthouse plaything... hah! If she only knew!
I am still laughing to myself when I notice another text coming through behind it.

Colton
11:28 p.m.: Nat, please call me. I just want to talk to you.

Nope.
Not even remotely interested in listening to Colton try to explain away what I saw on his phone. I just don't care to hear his lies anymore. I know the truth, and none of it really matters. He's a grown man, and can make his own decisions, and those decisions are none of my concern, no matter how shocking and disappointing

they may be.

As the bath water runs, I sit on the edge of the tub and just stare at my reflection in the mirror. I am exhausted, and the last few days have been a complete whirlwind, but I look… happy.

Is that possible?

Considering the roller coaster that started tonight at the restaurant, I feel like I should be more of an emotional wreck, but I couldn't feel farther from that at this moment. My cheeks are rosy, my eyes seem brighter, on top of sporting this ridiculous smile that has not left my face in hours.

Even when I had first prepared to come here and spent hours trying to make myself look like a bombshell, I had not even come close to seeing the glow radiating off of me.

I feel good.

Free almost, like an invisible elephant has been lifted off my shoulders. If I'm honest with myself, I had completely different intentions coming to Chicago for this wedding. I wanted revenge. I never wanted to get back together with Colton, only to make him regret what he did to me. And based on the look on his face when I left him this evening, and the barrage of text messages sitting unread on my phone, it seems like I have accomplished exactly that.

But I can feel the shift in me. I feel so much lighter after just a few hours with… *him.*

Jaxon.

The billionaire, the hotelier, the man.

Never in a million years could I have imagined meeting Jaxon, let alone penthouses, yacht dinners, motorcycle rides and private museum tours. But what somehow eclipses all of these experiences combined, is how he makes me feel. As if I am his unattainable prize, and that I am sexy, irresistible and… powerful.

I have never felt a pull like that to a man before. Any man.

And he feels it too, he told me so tonight.

I throw my hair in a bun and slip into the steaming hot tub.

But why me, though?

It is the question I have been asking myself for the last few days, and it might as well be tattooed behind my eyes. On paper we make no sense, as we come from completely different worlds. But I can't deny the chemistry between us, and I have to acknowledge what I am feeling. The man just *does* things to me.

He makes me feel as if every cell in my body is betraying its own natural design and pulling me to him like a magnet. Jaxon can make my heart pound with just a look and make my knees tremble with a kiss. And his touch makes me... *hot.*

I run my hands over my body as the warm water caresses my skin. I cannot stop thinking of the smell of his cologne, or his lips on my neck, or his touch igniting fire in my blood.

I gently brush my sensitive region with my fingers, feeling the budding sensation burning through my stomach.

It has been a while since...

I tease my fingers along the area again. The ripples in the water bubble against the walls of the tub, sending low waves of pleasure my way. I lay there trying to calm my racing heart when I hear my phone chime on the edge of the tub by my feet. When I casually glance at the screen, I nearly drop the whole thing in the water...

It's him.

Jaxon
11:37 p.m.: Are you still awake?

Me
11:38 p.m.: Yes, I couldn't sleep.

Jaxon
11:39 p.m.: Me either.

Attached to this message he sends a picture of his hand holding a glass of whiskey, in front of a fireplace.

I smile deviously to myself.

This is my chance to be bold and take a risk.

Me
11:40 p.m.: Funny... I had the same idea...

With my response, I attach a picture of my crossed legs poking out of the bathtub, and my hand holding my glass of wine.

His response comes almost instantly.

Jaxon
11:41 p.m.: You win. Are you thinking of me?

Me
11:42 p.m.: Yes, if you must know.

Jaxon
11:43 p.m.: I must.

Me:
11:44 p.m.: Do you like the view from your penthouse, Mr. Pace?

Jaxon:
11:45 p.m.: I do. But I think I could make it even better for you.

Me:
11:46 p.m.: And how do you plan to do that?

Jaxon:
11:47 p.m.: By burying my face between your thighs.

I choke on my wine, and before I have even recovered, the phone starts ringing.

Holy shit. I can't not answer, I was just texting him!

I take a deep breath and answer.

"Hello?"

"Evening…" His voice is smooth and deep.

"To what do I owe the pleasure?"

"Well, I figured since you were thinking of me, a phone call is the least I can do… in the name of pleasure."

Thank God he cannot see my face right now…

"How thoughtful of you, Mr. Pace."

"Tell me, Natalie… are your nipples hard?"

"Jaxon!" I gasp as my jaw drops, utterly floored by his boldness. "I don't…"

"I asked you a question." His voice is dark and raw.

"I know, but it's a very… interesting question. Jaxon, are you just calling me to… get *off*?" I ask tentatively, scared of the answer.

Jaxon lets out a deep sigh and hesitates a moment before responding to my question.

"No, Natalie," he says quietly, sounding mildly disappointed. "While I am admittedly a selfish asshole, I'm not that desperate. I called to make this about you."

Oh my.

"I'm sorry," I say softly.

"Don't be sorry," he says firmly. "Just touch your nipples and answer my question." His voice is low and lethal, and it sends a wave of shivers down my spine. I hesitate.

I mean, on one hand I was just thinking of him... like *this*.

But am I really going to just talk to him...like *this*?

"Should I let you go?" he asks gently, his voice hesitant.

Fuck it, I said I was going to be bold, so now is the time.

"No... please don't," I say barely above a whisper.

"Okay, then don't make me ask a third time." His voice alone is sexy as hell, a mix of serious and a wicked playfulness that makes my body shiver. Part of me is curious about what would happen if he *did* have to ask a third time.

"Okay..." I say, touching my hand to my breast. I run my fingers across my nipple and gasp at the sensitivity that shoots through me.

"Good girl," Jaxon says deviously. "How do they feel?"

"They are... hard, and *so* sensitive." I hate how breathless I sound, and my head is spinning with this intimate line of questioning. No one has ever talked to me like this before, and my body feels feverish with excitement.

"Of course, they are... you are aroused. Now, run your finger along the outside three times, then squeeze your nipple gently."

Oh my God.

"Okay..." I follow his instructions slowly, feeling my heart rate increase. My breasts feel so warm, and my nipples are engorged. "They feel incredible."

"I bet they do. I can't wait to have them in my mouth."

"Jaxon!"

"Natalie, please know I want to have every fucking inch of you in my mouth..." he says darkly. "Starting with those delicious, perky tits you were deliberately teasing me with earlier this evening." His voice melts me through the phone, and I cannot help but squeeze my breast, a soft moan escaping my lips just imagining him doing exactly that. "Are you ready for the next step?" he continues.

Oh my god...next step? Is this really happening?

"Yes," I breathe, my heart now pounding in my ears.

"Keep one hand on your breast and put your other hand between your legs... I want you to touch your pussy for me."

I cannot breathe. He is *really* saying this to me right now.

"Jaxon..." I mutter softly.

"Natalie, if you make me ask again, I swear I will drive over there right now and give you these instructions in person," he growls.

Holy shit.

I can't deny a part of me wants that scenario, or at least to test his seriousness. But I have already played this game once... and lost.

"Natalie, palm your fucking pussy lips for me."

Oh my God. How is this man saying this to me right now?

He is so sexy and so commanding I can't help but obey. I trail my hand down my body, feeling my clit throbbing between my legs, anxious for action, and electrified by his dark and dangerous voice giving me these instructions.

"Okay... I'm doing it," I say, my hand placed gently on the outside, causing my body to tense with desire.

"Squeeze."

I obey, and gently squeeze the outside of my vagina with my whole palm. The increased blood flow to the area makes my whole body react, and my nipples feel as hard as glass.

"Oh my God..." I cry out, unable to stop myself and closing my eyes. Jaxon's voice cuts through the darkness, dripping with desire, every word heating me from within.

"Natalie, do you know how badly I wanted to bend you over that table in the museum today? How desperately I wanted to feel your pussy in my hand. Just like this."

This is my fault for teasing him. But fuck, this is so sexy.

I can feel myself getting wetter by the minute, and I can barely control my breathing or any of the emotions running through me.

"I wanted that, too," I whisper.

"I know you did. Keep going. Swirl your fingers around slowly."

"Jaxon, I don't know..."

"Do you want to stop?" he whispers.

No, I do not. That is the very last thing I want to do.

"No, it's just... I've never done this on the phone before."

"That's okay, baby, you are doing great. Does it feel good?"

"Yes... it feels incredible."

"That's how it's supposed to feel. God, I can't wait to have my hands on your pussy like this. I can't wait to touch your body and feel you leaking out between my fingers..."

"Oh, my fucking God," I whisper, his words intoxicating me.

"That's it. Picture it for me, Natalie."

Oh, trust me, I am.

I feel as though my veins are filled with molten lava, setting my whole body ablaze.

"Jaxon... are you touching yourself too?" I ask breathlessly.

"No, sweetheart, I already told you, tonight is all about *you*."

His reassurance is all I need to stop questioning and just give in to what I am feeling.

"Oh my…"

"Now, listen carefully. Slip your fingers just inside the lips. I want you to put one on either side of your clit…"

"Yes…"

"I am dying to have your clit in my mouth, pinned under my tongue, teasing you mercilessly."

My body is electrocuted with his words, and I shudder. "Oh my God, Jaxon." I grip the side of the tub with my free hand.

"Those are exactly the words I want to hear, Natalie, but with my face buried in your pussy. I want to taste you so bad, feeling your juices on my tongue… Do you want that?"

"Yes…" I say, my voice trembling.

"Say it for me, Natalie…"

"I want you, Jaxon…"

"What do you want me to do, baby?"

"I want you… to taste me…"

I have to be hallucinating. This can't be real life.

I can't believe Jaxon is saying these things to me, but it feels amazing. This is definitely better than a thousand 'solo sessions' and I can feel my orgasm quickening between my thighs.

"Slow and easy, just like that. Make soft circles around your clit. I want you to imagine it's my mouth on your pussy, pleasuring you and sucking you dry."

I moan, unable to control what is happening inside my body. "Do you want me… to go inside?" I whisper.

"Oh no, gorgeous, I want to be inside you myself… in person."

That does it, I feel myself begin to climax and my legs start shaking uncontrollably. My heart hammers away in my chest and I feel my body tense.

"Jaxon…"

"That's it, baby, just give in to it."

"*Fuck!*" I yell as my orgasm explodes within me. My whole body seizes, and the ripples from the water in the tub seem to intensify the experience, extending it longer than I have ever remembered.

Was that supposed to happen? Did Jaxon know that would happen?

I lay there for a moment catching my breath, feeling the aftershocks still coursing through my body. There is silence on the phone, and immediately I feel bashful.

Holy hell. What the fuck was that? Did that really just happen?
"Jaxon?"
"Yes, baby girl?" he says softly.
Baby girl.
"I was worried you left."
"No, I'm not going anywhere."
Oh, my goodness…
My stomach does a backflip and I wish I could melt through the phone and be wherever he is right now.
"How do you feel? Are you ready for bed now?" he asks gently.
God, why does he sound sexier somehow? Is that even possible?
"I feel amazing," I say quietly. "But if I'm honest…"
"Always."
"I also feel a little guilty."
"Because of me?" His voice is oddly soft, barely a whisper, as if he's nervous as to what my answer will be.
"No, I just feel guilty because I didn't… make *you* feel… the same." I cringe as I say the words aloud, but relax as soon as I hear Jaxon chuckle, sounding a bit relieved himself.
"Natalie, as I said, this wasn't about me," He says warmly. "This was about you."
"I know, I just feel a bit… selfish."
"You feel selfish because I wanted to get you off tonight?"
"Well, it just feels one sided. I got something and you didn't."
"My dear, pleasure doesn't always have to be an even exchange, it's not a currency. It's a gift you share. And sometimes it's enough to just make someone else feel good."
Holy shit, is he even real?
"Trust me, I enjoyed that just as much as you did."
A smile cuts across my face as my cheeks heat. "I highly doubt that," I chuckle softly. "I've just never done that on the phone before."
"Well, that makes two of us." he says quietly.
What?!
"Stop. That's not true."
"Natalie, you specifically asked me not to lie to you," Jaxon says, his tone becoming serious again.
"I only meant that you were… *really* good at it," I say embarrassed.
"I'm even better in person," he laughs, a naughty confidence in his voice. "Perhaps I will get the chance to show you sometime."
"I don't doubt it," I giggle. "And maybe you will."

Did I really just say that??

"Jaxon, I know I have perhaps taken up a lot of your time lately," I say nervously. "But can I see you?"

"Tonight? Are you already ready for round two?" he chuckles, sounding genuinely surprised.

"No! I meant tomorrow!" I laugh, hearing him laugh in the background too. I am grateful he can't see the ridiculous blushing grin on my face.

"Unfortunately, I do have several meetings tomorrow, and some business to take care of tomorrow night."

"Oh, I see. That's okay, I understand." I try to sound understanding, but my smile fades in a wave of disappointment.

"But, if you're up for something late at night, maybe we could have a drink together after I finish my evening meeting?"

My heart instantly soars, and my grin returns as I dip slowly back down into the warm bath water. "Late night is actually perfect for me. I have the bachelorette party with the girls tomorrow night, but I'll be more of a chaperone than a participant, so I will still be awake."

"From experience, being a participant is always more fun," He says, gently clearing his throat. "You're not driving, are you?"

"I don't know yet for sure, but I might have to. I don't think anyone planned transportation, so some of us may have to volunteer. We have brunch tomorrow morning at the hotel restaurant, and I think we are going to sort all the details out then."

"Hmm. I see."

"However, as much as I don't want to say goodnight, I should probably get out of this tub. I'm starting to get pruney."

"Well, I can't have that," he chuckles. "Goodnight, Natalie." The warm sincerity in his voice sends shivers through my body.

"Goodnight, Jaxon." I say softly.

As soon as I hang up the phone, I break into a fit of giggles that carries me all the way to bed. When I climb under the soft comforter my eyelids are heavy, but I decide to send Jaxon one last text goodnight.

Me
1:15 a.m.: I know you said last night that you wanted to make me smile again, and I just wanted to let you know that at this point, I do not think I can stop. Thank you, AGAIN, for yet another incredible experience.

Jaxon
1:17 a.m.: And again, Miss Tyler, it's truly MY pleasure. ;-)

If this is a dream, I never want to wake up.

Chapter Twenty

JAXON

"Good morning gentlemen."

I speak from the balcony over the foyer of my house to all my point men and top recruits below.

"I've asked you all here in person to discuss a few updates with you. First order of business, I know that all of you were asked to complete tox screenings, and I believe you have the right to know *why*. As you all know, our organization doesn't exactly operate within the realm of law, nor are any of us shining examples of sober living."

A small chuckle goes up from around the room.

"You were not tested to see *if* drugs were in your system, you were tested to see *whose* drugs were in your system. Unless you are Alpha level or above, how you handle your business is your prerogative. We all indulge ourselves and enjoy a little fun occasionally, perks of the trade."

A soft chuckle goes up from around the room.

"However, a shipment was stolen from one of our secure stock yards," I say, the room falling silent again. "And a second burglary was attempted and damn near successful. The men who did this cost more than one man his life. With that said, we gather together today to toast our fallen brothers."

I raise my glass of whiskey.

At once, all the men in the room with their right hand balled in a fist, beat their chest three times together in unison, then raise their glasses to me in a silent toast. As their Don, I beat my chest once in response, then take a drink with them.

Then I continue. "These men also had a clear point of entry into our warehouse…one of our *own*." I watch the looks of surprise streak across almost all of the faces in the room before continuing.

"Samuel served on my team for over a decade. I trusted this man with the protection of my life, and the lives of other men. Which as you know only happens in this organization when they prove they know the rules, and the limits." I nod.

"After ten years of impeccable service to this family, Samuel began using altered heroin supplied to him by one of Black's dealers. We know this because we know all of Black's drugs possess a chemical signature that is unique to him. These alterations are designed to require consistent and accelerated usage, and its potency is unmatched. Once his body was hooked, so too followed his mind. And from there followed the deaths of two of his teammates."

I see a few men in the room shaking their heads. I know this is hard for them to hear, but it's imperative.

"Those of you in this room represent *all* levels of leadership in this organization, either by rank or by example to your fellow recruits. And as we have said before, this organization exists in and around the vices of men. We consistently have access to, and indulge in, those vices from time to time. But we know the rules, and we know the limits. However, our youngest recruits may not."

"It's important to remember that the young men joining this organization usually don't have other career options, or they would have chosen something else instead. Nevertheless, they are chosen, vetted, and trained under your leadership. We need to be sure part of that leadership is teaching them by *example* when enough is *enough* and when it's entirely *too much*. It is vital to our success, but above that it is vital to their survival."

I rest my hands on the banister before continuing.

"I know personally how easy it is to head down the path that our Samuel found himself on. And if it wasn't for the help of several of you in this room, I may have met the same fate he did."

I take a deep breath, and look around the room, preparing to say something I have never said before to my men.

"Which is why here and now I want to make it clear to all of you, that if you find yourself in a position where you are compromised, you come to me, or to Ethan *directly*. If you find one of your men is unable to perform his duties on a regular or semi-regular basis, you send them to me, or to Ethan *directly*."

"We have resources at our disposal to help get you back on track, and to provide protection for your families should they be threatened. We are here for your protection and preservation. Which is what makes us different than the other organizations in this business. It also makes us better. We will get you help and anything you need. That is what we are here for. It is why this *family* exists."

I steady myself. This is by far the most empathetic and personal I have been with my men since becoming their Don. But I see the humbled looks of acknowledgement around the room.

"Gentlemen, we may be conducting dirty business in a wicked world, and all of us may be devils ourselves, but we are *not* monsters," I say pausing. "We are family."

Suddenly, my men below unexpectedly beat their chest twice in response. I feel a sense of pride wash over me. These men have been the only family I have known for the last five years. It feels good to feel as though I am finally doing right by them in more than just their paychecks. I shoot a glance at Ethan. His words from last night were the right words, and they were enough.

"Make no mistake, Black's product infiltrated this organization, and three of our men are dead because of it." I pause, letting my words settle in the room.

"In the past, we held a loose arrangement with their dealers, under the pretense our men didn't waste their time sampling this rat poison. But we are past that point now. Effective immediately, Black's products are prohibited for internal use or sale. Billy and Walter, I want you to get in touch with our contacts on the East Coast, and our friends from South America. Have your teams draw up negotiations for new supply lines for any transportable goods. You can work with Rodney and Dex on any new facilities or transport that needs to be set up."

"Yes, Sir!"

"Rodney, I want your team to do full surveillance evaluations on any personnel and security for those facilities and transport."

"Yes, Sir!"

"Amos, your team will assist, but I also want a survey done on all of our current international coastal warehouses, transport vehicles and storage facilities. I want to know what we can improve."

"Yes, Sir!"

"Trevor and Darrell, I want your teams to draw up in-depth portfolios on all Black's local dealers south of Grant Park and west of the river. I want to know every single one. Foot soldiers, lieutenants, generals—all of them. I want to know *specifically* who was selling to Samuel and harassing his family. When you find them, bring them to the warehouse so they can answer directly to me."

"Yes, Sir!"

"Everyone else is to stick to their regular responsibilities. Any questions?" I ask.

"Yeah, who's the pretty blonde with the fine ass you've been spending so much time with?" Wesley, one of the younger members of the security squad, shouts.

A few laughs go up around the room, along with a whistle or two, but only from the younger men, all of whom are obviously Zeta. My Alpha team, however, knows better than to make a joke like this. Their eyes suddenly lock on Wesley like he is prey.

He did not just fucking say that.

I smile and rub my chin, considering how to respond as my blood begins to boil in my veins. However, before I can, I am interrupted…by Ethan.

"Excuse me, recruit?!" Ethan's voice booms. "Do you think that's how you address your Don?!"

The smile and color drains instantly from Wesley's face.

"No, Sir," he stammers nervously. I see him glance around the room at all the hostile faces glaring at him, realizing his mistake.

"I'm sorry I can't hear you!" Ethan yells, his face red. "What did you say?!"

"No, sir!" Wesley shouts. "Sorry, sir!"

"That's right you're fucking sorry!" Ethan continues. "You have the fucking audacity to disrespect your commander after you just failed him?!"

"Sir?" Wesley asks, confused.

"That pretty blonde had to do *your* fucking job, Wesley! You had one job, protect this family. Tell me, is Jessica part of this family?!"

"Yes…"

"Yes what?!"

"Yes, Sir! It's my job to protect Jessica, Sir!" Wesley stammers.

"So, can you explain to me how someone almost kidnapped her right out from under your watch?!"

"No, Sir…I…don't know, Sir!"

"You don't fucking know! Well, ain't that the fucking truth!" Ethan crosses his arms in front of Wesley but does not relent. "Do you want to know who stopped Jessica's kidnapping?! That pretty blonde that you just disrespected!"

"Yes, Sir! Sorry, Sir!" Wesley's brow begins to sweat.

"You should be fucking sorry! And you should remain fucking sorry until you can pull your head out of your ass!"

Ethan turns to face the rest of the crowd and moves between them as he continues to shout loudly.

"That pretty blonde is to be known from this moment forward as Miss Tyler! And I want you all to understand that she did more than all of you men that day!" Ethan snaps, driving his point home. "You who swore to protect your Don and this family above all else, *failed*! All of you should be embarrassed!"

My Alpha team watches their commander silently with respect.

"As far as I'm concerned, every man in this family owes Miss Tyler a debt of gratitude that can never be repaid!"

My heart swells, listening to the sincerity in Ethan's voice.

"None of you will ever disrespect her in my presence again! Is that understood?!"

All my men including the commanders on Alpha, beat their chest twice silently, in response to my second in command.

Ethan pauses for a long time in front of Wesley, staring him down. Wesley looks as though he is about to shit his pants.

Well done, Ethan.

He straightens his jacket, and then finds his way back to his spot in the room before I shoot him a nod.

"Miss Tyler is my personal guest. If she approaches any of you or your staff, you are to assist with whatever she requests with polite expediency. But under no circumstances are you to embarrass me or discuss the business of this organization." I continue. "And on a personal note, I want it known that if any of you find it impossible to keep your eyes to yourself or make her even slightly uncomfortable with classless ogling of her fine ass, I'll personally relieve that man of his eyesight."

Wesley continues staring at the floor, looking as though he has seen a ghost, or if he might spontaneously become one.

Much better.

"That will be all."

They all file out of the foyer and back to their tasks in complete silence. Wesley being one of the first to bolt out the door.

I watch them with satisfaction. At the end of the day, I want my men to understand that while there is *nothing* I won't do for them, I will not tolerate disrespect. This is the new compromise I decided upon last night. A combination between the Don my father was, and one I am. As the last of the men file out of the room, Ethan approaches me on the balcony.

"I think that went well," he says with a smirk. He looks invigorated, as if he did not just make a twenty-five-year-old, two-hundred-pound hitman shit his pants.

"Where did that come from, eh?" I say, returning his smirk.

"Hey now, I've said before it's a bad idea to poke the bear," he says with a shrug. "You would do well to remember that from time to time."

I chuckle and he just wink back at me.

This fucking guy.

"Why are you here?"

"There's something you need to see," he says, producing another envelope and handing it to me.

"What? More pictures of Colton buying shitty molly?" I scoff.

"Not exactly. Charlie called me late last night. He asked me to come by the hotel and said that this was delivered to Natalie's room from the front desk just after you left yesterday."

I pull out the letter. It's an exact copy of the one that was found in Sam's pocket. Completely blank, with the only distinguishable emblem being the Two-Headed Dragon embossed on the outside of the envelope.

I look up at Ethan, my mind ringing, and my anxiety spiraling.

This can't be.

I use the flashlight on my phone to illuminate the message.

"Who are you?"

My blood chills in my veins, and I freeze instinctively.

"It's actually the *second* one she's received," Ethan says, jolting me from my bones and handing me a second letter. "The message is identical on both."

Fuck.

"Charlie was there when she received the second letter. She didn't know what she was looking at and told him it was odd. She then showed the first letter she picked up from reception. Naturally, he's concerned, and doesn't want to leave his shift."

"How?" Is all I can utter.

"We are looking into it. I personally interviewed the porter this morning. He said someone else delivered that message, but they were in our uniform. He saw the man on his way out of the door but says he did not recognize this man. He just assumed the guy was new."

Fuck. Fuck. Fuck.

"Why are they going after her? We know they are watching me, but if they've been watching me, they would know I've only known her a few days."

"And in those few days you've been with her every moment you're not actively working."

I glare at Ethan, but he puts a hand up telling me to relax.

"I still support this, mind you," he said sternly. "I'm just stating the obvious, and it's my job to be observant."

"Goddamn it," I whisper, crunching the paper in my hands angrily.

The last thing I want is to make Natalie a target.

"I want a security detail on her at all times, but they are not to make their presence known to her, at all. Send Josiah to relieve Charlie so he can get some rest, but when he is rested, I want him to run point, and tail her. He's not to take his eyes off her if she leaves the penthouse."

"Already done."

"Thank you."

Ethan suddenly looks at me in shock.

"What?" I ask.

"Nothing, just weird to hear you say that."

"Yeah well, I'm trying a new thing where I'm not just a total dickhead *all* the time."

Ethan laughs, but I can tell he approves.

"Oh, and I want the hotel to provide a limo in my name for the Tyler bachelorette celebrations tonight. I don't want anyone drinking and driving this evening. Let's just handle that for them."

"Understood." He nods.

"Make the driver one of ours."

"Of course."

"Good. Then I'll be with her after my meeting with Black, so I will see if any further 'messages' arrive. And who delivers them."

The very thought of seeing that fat fuck makes my blood boil. I turn and start walking away.

"Do you think he's behind this?" Ethan says after me.

"I don't know. But I have found that somehow, all the dirt in this city always leads back to Black."

Chapter Twenty-One

Natalie

Friday morning arrives much later than yesterday. Which is most assuredly because I figured out how to close the blinds the night before. When I finally force myself out of bed, and walk into the bathroom, I suddenly burst into a fit of giggles seeing the bathtub.

With my empty wine glass on the floor next to it.

Oh my God. That really happened. I had phone sex last night.

I take a quick shower, laughing to myself the entire time, replaying all the events of the night before. When I emerge from the bedroom, I find Charlie waiting for me in the kitchen just past ten, with a fresh breakfast tray.

Astonishingly, I am actually able to convince him to sit and have a cup of coffee with me. As we chat, I learn about his family in Haiti, and he tells me about the treacherous journey he made to America when he was just a teenager. His dying mother's wish was for him to come here and find a better opportunity.

However, upon his arrival he sadly learned that the relative he planned to live with had also passed away. Now only seventeen-years-old, he was stranded in a foreign country. He was jobless, homeless, and penniless, regrettably no better than he had been in Haiti. He panhandled for money just to eat and found himself regretting his decision to come to the States at all.

That is, until he met Ethan, who introduced him to Jaxon.

"Mr. Pace was the first man who saw me for what I was—a lost and lonely young man, hungry for a chance to prove what I could offer. He gave me an opportunity when no one else would, and he believed in me. I will forever admire him for that."

It's evident in the way he speaks about Jaxon that he has a strong respect and reverence for him, it warms my heart.

"I admire him too," I say, trying to hide my rosy cheeks.

Charlie laughs and takes a sip of coffee. "I can see that."

"Oh no! Is it that obvious?" I say with a laugh.

"Don't worry, I won't tell anyone," he winks. "Although, I don't think you need to worry too much, I think it's safe to say at this point that the feeling is mutual."

"What do you mean?"

"Just that I have never seen Mr. Pace act like this. He seems unusually relaxed since you've come around."

"Oh my, this is how he behaves when he is *relaxed*?" I laugh in surprise. "God help us all!"

We both laugh again, and my heart feels distinctly lighter.

After our chat, I said goodbye and took the elevator downstairs.

There is no hope of me fighting the ridiculous smile that has plastered itself on my face. That is, until I am ambushed walking into the restaurant by my cousins and the bride.

"Natalie! Oh my God! How could you not tell us?" the bride, Michelle, demands with a smile.

"What?"

"The guy last night? The one who picked you up from Campeggio's? He's the *owner* of the hotel!" Michelle laughs in happy amusement. "He's the same man who helped us with the band fiasco!"

"Ahhh right," I say smiling. "I probably should have mentioned that. I guess I just forgot." I blush and swallow hard, kicking myself for not anticipating this conversation after I chose to ride off publicly with Jaxon.

"Oh, I see, so you just *forgot* to tell us that you're gallivanting around town with a billionaire?" Steph says, stepping forward and wrapping me in a hug.

"Well, I didn't think the *billionaire* part was as important."

"Ummm yes, it is," she says with a wink.

My younger cousin, Chloe, walks up to me and tugs on my arm, her eyes as big as saucers. "Natalie, he is *so* handsome!"

"He really is hunky!" Michelle says, slapping my arm. "Good for you girl!"

Oh God... it's starting.

I start to panic, feeling increasingly overwhelmed.

I really wanted to keep this separate from my family, until I had a better understanding of what's going on with Jaxon.

I just don't need another very public scandal with the men I am connected to.

"Alright ladies, give her some space," the matron of honor, Rebecca, says firmly, evidently noticing the pack of them pouncing on me. "Let's take a seat and order some food. We have bachelorette plans to discuss!"

The lure of food thankfully gets me off the hook, and my cousins head swiftly to the large table prepared for our party. As I sit down, I see my phone light up in my purse.

Colton
12:30 p.m.: Nat, I know you're mad, but can we PLEASE just talk about this? I am begging you. I promise it's not what it looks like!

For some reason, his text infuriates me.

Not what it looks like? Is he joking? Or does he think I will still believe this nonsense?

I am so sick of this charade, and this onslaught of nonstop text messages. I had hoped that he would just give up at some point, but I realize now that I have to say something back to him, or he may never stop. So, I take a deep breath and finally decide to respond to Colton once and for all. I take a moment to gather my thoughts completely, as I want to make sure that I am crystal clear.

Me
12:32 p.m.: Colton, I don't care what it "looks like" anymore, because I know what it is. Stop bothering me. Emily is clearly who you want and cannot live without. BE WITH HER. Because while I can forgive you for that, I cannot forgive you for bringing your mistress to my cousin's wedding, while trying to plead my forgiveness. Let me save you the trouble: DON'T. BOTHER. There's nothing left for me to forgive because there is nothing here for you anymore.

Colton tries calling my phone, but I decline. Further still, I decide it's finally time to do what I should have done a while ago, and *block* him. I have had enough of Colton's drama interfering with my day.

I am going to have a good day today.

A few minutes later, I just sat down with a delicious looking plate of french toast, when my phone chimes again.

Seriously?!

Rolling my eyes, I snatch it up aggressively, annoyed that somehow Colton is still able to text me after I blocked him. But I'm pleasantly surprised when Jaxon's name appears instead.

Jaxon
12:43 p.m.: Good afternoon, I trust you slept well.

Me
12:44 p.m.: I did. Did you?

Jaxon
12:45 p.m.: Actually, I did get a few minutes.

Me
12:46 p.m.: That doesn't sound too restful, might I recommend a nice BATH? I hear it's good for relieving some tension.

Jaxon
12:47 p.m.: I will keep that in mind. Although, on balance, I have a few other ideas for a good release.

His inference makes me shiver, remembering the things he had said to me last night.

Me
12:48 p.m.: Now I am curious, care to share?

Jaxon
12:49 p.m.: Perhaps later. For now, please enjoy this surprise in my absence.

Me
12:50 p.m.: Surprise?

Suddenly, a man, dressed in a black-on-black suit approaches, and I notice that he looks like one of Jaxon's men that had been with us the night we left the marina. The man heads directly to the head of the table where the bride and matron of honor sit talking and laughing to each other.

What's going on?

"Ladies, I have been asked to inform you that Mr. Pace has arranged for one of our hotel limousines to be the transport for your celebration this evening." His voice is rugged, but he sports a smile. Squeals and gasps of astonishment go up immediately from around the table.

"Oh, my goodness! That is amazing! But why would he do that?" Michelle excitedly exclaims.

The man says nothing, but his eyes catch mine for a second, and he smiles with a slight nod.

Oh my...

All the heads at the table begin to turn towards me and I feel my face get hot instantly.

"Your driver is Ramon. Just ask for him at the valet whenever you are ready to go, and he is yours for the entire evening. He will also not accept your gratuity, as he has already been taken care of," the man says to Rebecca, then turns and walks away without another word.

The table erupts with conversation, everyone chattering amongst themselves, and frequently shooting looks at me.

"Oh, Natalie, this guy is really into you!" Michelle says excitedly from across the table.

"Yeah, that is so considerate of him! Now all of us can just enjoy the night together! How did you meet him?" Rebecca asks, and the table instantly grows quiet, as apparently this is the question on everyone's mind right now.

"Well, um, you know, we just bumped into each other one day," I say with a chuckle, and completely aware my cheeks are turning the color of ripe pomegranates.

"My goodness! What a lucky bump—*sheesh!*" Michelle jokes, and the whole table laughs.

I smile and chuckle along with everyone else, grateful to have the collective attention off of me. When appropriate, I grab my phone to text Jaxon.

I can't believe he did that!

Me
12:55 p.m.: Oh my God, Jaxon!

Jaxon
12:56 p.m.: For the record, "Oh my God, Jaxon" did sound incredible on the phone last night. But I bet it's even better in person.

I smile ear to ear, while feeling my body clench as his words shock me, yet again.
How does he do that?!

Me
12:57 p.m.: Well, thank you…for ALL of it.

Then a wicked smile crosses my face, and I decide to be bold.

Me
12:57 p.m.: … But perhaps 'Thank You' would sound better in person too?

Jaxon
12:58 p.m.: Oh, my dear… I can't wait to find that out myself.

I giggle to myself, but as I look up, I see Steph grinning at me like a madwoman from across the table.
Eeek! Busted.
She gets up and makes her way around the table to the seat next to me, which is currently occupied by her younger sister, Bethany.
"Beat it squirt," she quips cantankerously, evicting Bethany from the chair. She sits down, pours herself a mimosa, and leans back in the chair, all while sporting the same wild grin as before. "Sooo, Natalie, this new beau of yours is causing quite a stir," she says motioning to the table, where I notice that all the conversations swirling around me are all about Jaxon.
"Have you seen him? He's *gorgeous*!"
"He's *always* surrounded by like five scary looking dudes!"
"He's loaded, like really loaded!"
"Yeah, I think he was on the cover of Forbes last month!"
"Did you see him on that motorcycle yesterday? And I saw him pull up outside the hotel the other day in a Lamborghini!"

Oh my… he really is causing a disturbance.

Every conversation around me right now is about the man that has been occupying my nights, and my thoughts, for the last four days.

"Steph… this is…"

"Completely terrifying given your immediate history with that douche canoe Colton? Yeah, I'd say understandable," she says, stealing the rest of my french toast with a shrug. "But, even despite that, I would still argue that this is probably fucking good for you." She takes a sip of her mimosa and looks at me above the glass.

"But…"

"Look, Nat, fuck all of these people," she says, waving her hand around toward the table.

"Steph! 'These people' are our *family!*" I whisper back, but still laugh at her crudeness.

"So what?" Steph leans in so only I can hear her. "As far as I am concerned, each and every one of them can all get on the first train to Fuckoffville, with any negative opinions about this guy trying to make you happy."

"Wow… your compassion is overwhelming," I laugh, rolling my eyes at her, but starting to feel a little better.

"Cousin, I saw your face, and I'm not an idiot. I know you were texting *him*. And you looked H-A-P-P-Y which is something I have deeply missed seeing on your face."

I smile back at her, unable to say anything.

"And it's certainly more happiness than Colton ever gave you," she says, grabbing the bunch of grapes off my plate and popping one into her mouth. "So, I would say that's a massive improvement just on principle."

"But, what if this doesn't…" I trail off, unable to finish this sentence, because I don't want to think about this possibly blowing up in my face.

What if this situation with Jaxon is pointless and does not actually become anything at all?

"So, what if it doesn't?" she replies. "That shouldn't stop you from just enjoying and appreciating the experience." Steph places her hand on mine. "Nat, everything doesn't always have to work out all the time. You are single and you are experimenting. You are getting to know someone on a deeper level, and that may or may not work out with some fairytale picture of the two of you getting married and riding away to your castle to pop out a few little crotch goblins." She smiles at me. "Yes, of course, that is a beautiful picture, but it is just one of *many* possible pictures."

"That's true. I guess that's just the one I always imagined."

"Right, but how did that turn out last time?" she says, her face sarcastic, but her tone is gentle. "I'll tell you—it was nothing like you imagined it would be. You were so caught up in making sure it was a fairytale that you ended up finding yourself in a nightmare. Now here you are, thirty-years-old and you haven't even tried anything else. Or *anyone* else."

Shit. She is right.

"I realize I am more comfortable with the more 'casual' relationships than you are, but even I struggle with the desire to put a title on everything. Sometimes it works, and sometimes you just want different things." Steph takes a deep breath and looks around the table before looking back at me. "And it's not a bad thing to want commitment and security from someone you care about either. Just don't make that the end-all be-all of what you're trying to accomplish."

I smile at her, knowing that despite her bluntness and personality, she is speaking straight from her heart. As she always does.

"All I'm saying is just let it be, let it simmer, and just feel it out."

I squeeze her hand, letting her know I understand. She is telling me to just go with the flow and see where it takes me.

"Don't judge a painting while the artist is still holding the brush... or you might miss out on something beautiful altogether."

Steph has a point. Perhaps, for once in my life, I need to let go of the need for control, and just see what happens next.

I left our brunch in a haze. On one hand, I was ecstatic that Jaxon had made a semi-public display of affection toward me. But on the other hand, I had a thousand doubts about this entire situation, and I was worried that I could get hurt.

As I walk across the lobby toward the elevator, the girl behind the desk looks my way, and then quickly looks away.

"Good morning, Miss Tyler," one of the bellhops says cheerfully as I pass in front of him.

I also happen to notice that there are a few of the bodyguard suits lingering around the lobby.

I wonder if Jaxon is here?

He said he had business to handle today, but he never said where.

I have some time to kill, so I decide to go check out the setup of the wedding venue for tomorrow. I walk down the long corridor toward the ballrooms until I arrive at the one with "Tyler–Godfrey" written on the sign outdoors. I find the door is open, and I let myself inside. The hotel staff had been setting up centerpieces and cutlery, but conveniently appear to be finished for the day and are walking out the service entrance in the back of the room. Which means I have the ballroom all to myself.

Perfect timing.

The room is dimly lit, but it smells of flowers and fresh linen. I wander slowly through the tables, taking my time browsing the beautiful floral arrangements and charging plates.

I remember what it was like planning a wedding.

I also remember hating it frequently because Colton insisted it was entirely my 'show' and offered no feedback. He told me he didn't have time to get involved, and his lack of interest had just fueled my own, leading me to resent wedding planning entirely. However, it's obvious that *this* bride must have loved every moment of her wedding planning. It showed, as everything was planned perfectly, down to the last beautiful detail.

I am admiring one of the centerpiece flowers when I hear the door to the hallway close loudly, making me jump.

"Hey, Nat," Colton says awkwardly in the doorway. "One of the girls said they saw you come this way."

Oh, for fucks sake.

"Well, I still have nothing to say to *you*," I say firmly, and then turn to leave through the opposite door. "I thought I had made myself abundantly clear in my text this morning."

"Nat, will you just *listen* to me?!" Colton practically shouts, the desperation apparent in his voice as he walks toward me quickly, cutting me off. "Please?"

"No, Colton," I snap acidly. "I will not!"

"Nat, please!" he begs, catching me by the arm. "I just want to explain what you saw."

"No, you want to lie and manipulate your way out of trouble by trying to convince me of some alternative truth you have concocted!" I shout back at him. "But I no longer have any interest in who you are fucking, or your fictional narratives, Colton! Just leave me alone!"

"Natalie!" Colton yells, still refusing to let me out of his grasp as I try to wiggle my arm free.

"Let go of me, Colton!" I yell at him, but he doesn't release me. *What the hell?!*

I'm so frustrated and angry that I can't get away from him that I slap him, hard, across his face. Thankfully, this momentarily stuns him enough to let go of me.

"I don't know what the hell you were thinking! Bringing *that* woman here for this wedding, but I don't care anymore! I don't love you anymore, Colton, I can barely even tolerate you! It is over! We are done! Leave me alone!"

I head swiftly for the door, needing to be as far away from him as possible. All of a sudden, a sharp pain radiates on the back of my head, as Colton grabs me by my hair, yanking me back. I am so stunned that I don't even feel him wrap his arms around my body and his hand around my throat. He turns me around, forcing me to face the ballroom, keeping his back against the door, effectively blocking the exit.

"Colton! What the fuck are you doing?! *Oww!* You're hurting me, let me go!"

"Nat, please, just listen! Goddamnit *listen*!!" He suddenly roars in my ear, causing me to freeze, as my head starts spinning. "That is all I want." His voice is suddenly calm and his hot breath on my neck makes me want to vomit.

I am truly terrified of him at this moment.

"Now, I can tell you're a bit preoccupied with your new fancy man candy, I get it. But I promise that men like that only want one thing from girls like you," he whispers against my ear.

I can feel the tears now streaming down my face, not only from the pain Colton is causing me, but also from his words stabbing at my insecurities, threatening to obliterate my fragile optimism regarding Jaxon.

"You don't know anything about him…" I say, trying to muster what remaining courage I have.

"I know that what he sees in you is just another piece of doe-eyed ass that just fell conveniently into his lap." He releases his painful hold on my hair, and gently strokes it. "But I still love you, Nat. I know we've had our problems, but I do not love Emily. *You* are everything that I want."

"Let me go!" I yell back at him. "I don't want you, Colton!"

"See, I know that's not true, Natalie. I know you—"

Suddenly the door behind us opens, and I feel him stumble.

"Sir, step away from Miss Tyler!" A loud male voice shouts from behind me.

At the same time the other door to the ballroom opens, and I see the big man in the black suit from brunch walk toward us with his gun drawn. Colton releases me, and I crumple to the floor, clutching my neck. "Get on your stomach! Now! Put your hands on your head!" he shouts.

I sit shaking, trying to get my breath back, and watching as a terrified Colton falls to his knees, trying to follow directions.

"You like to put your hands on women motherfucker?!" The man from brunch shouts at him, shoving him onto his stomach.

"Gentlemen please, I...I...don't know what you think was happening but—"

"Shut the fuck up!" The other security guard shouts. "Or I will happily tase your ass into silence, do you understand me?!"

"Miss Tyler, are you okay?" the man from brunch asks. "Do you know this man?"

"Yes… and yes," I stammer, still shaking. Colton is now pinned to the ground beneath the knee of the other security guard, pressing him forcibly into the carpet.

"Did he hurt you, Miss Tyler?" Another voice, this one more familiar, asks softly from behind me, and I turn to see Ethan standing there.

Ethan.

"It's nothing…" I say softly.

Ethan is at my side and helps me to my feet, but I stumble, my legs still trembling. He instantly catches me around the waist and walks us toward a table. "Would you like to sit down?" he asks gently.

I nod. Adrenaline is coursing through my body, and I feel my teeth begin to chatter.

What the fuck just happened? Why would Colton do that?

"Take him to security," Ethan says, waving at the man pinning Colton down. "Then wait for me. And only me."

"Please," I say as Ethan helps me into a chair. "Don't arrest him. He's the best man for the wedding my family is hosting here tomorrow." The words just fall out of my mouth before I can stop them, but Ethan puts a hand up to stop me.

"We are not going to arrest him, only have a chat," He says calmly, although I do catch sight of his face as he looks furiously at Colton being led away.

I momentarily breathe a sigh of relief, but then everything starts bubbling to the surface.

"He's my ex," I say quickly to Ethan. "And I think he's on drugs, or something, I'm not sure, but he is not himself." I look away, trying to stop the tears that come welling to the surface.

I shouldn't be saying any of this to Ethan. This is so embarrassing.

"Has he ever… attacked you before?" Ethan asks gently.

"No," I answer honestly. "He wants to get back together, and I kept telling him no and that it's over. But he just wouldn't listen. And then he…" My hands fall to my neck, where Colton's hand had been, as I feel the hot tears streaking down my face. I move to stroke my hair back, but feeling my scalp so sore makes me wince, only adding to the pain of this moment.

Why would he do something like this?

In all the years I have known him, Colton has never acted this way before. He has never been violent toward me or anyone.

What the hell do I do now?

As angry and hurt as I am with him right now, I do not want to feel responsible for Ryan's wedding getting derailed by landing the best man in jail the night before the wedding.

What would my family think?

"Please," I plead to Ethan, "please don't arrest him, he's just not himself."

"Miss Tyler, we can't arrest him." Ethan assures me gently. "We are not the police, if you don't want to file a report, we won't. We will make sure he has calmed down, and safe for himself and others. Then we will let him go," he says, handing me his handkerchief.

"Thank you, Ethan," I say, dotting at my eyes.

"Would you like to head back upstairs?" he asks me with a warm smile, and I nod. However, before we head back to the lobby, I stop to straighten myself in one of the picture mirrors hanging in the ballroom.

I really don't need anyone to see me like this and start asking questions about the nightmare that just took place.

When we reach the elevator, I turn to Ethan, mustering as much of a half-smile as I can. "I think I can make it back upstairs by myself."

He nods. "Charlie will be waiting for you, and anything you need I will have sent up."

"Thank you, Ethan."

"My pleasure, Miss Tyler."

After the doors close, I collapse down on the bench in the

elevator, my mind racing.

What just happened?

But I knew that answer—Colton just *attacked* me. Tears start welling in my eyes again, as the trauma comes at me in waves. I do my best to pat them back, knowing that I am about to come face to face with Charlie, and the thought of him seeing me like this is something I cannot endure. The elevator dings, and I stuff the handkerchief into my pocket as I step out into the lobby.

It's then I see Jaxon Pace standing there…waiting for me.

He stands with his hands in his pockets, and his face dark and full of worry as he appraises me silently for a moment.

"Natalie…" he whispers softly.

Overwhelmed and unable to stop myself, I bolt to the comfort of his arms that envelop me immediately. He holds me against his body so tightly I can feel his heart pounding in his chest. I savor the smell of his cologne, and the warmth of his embrace, as I let him hold me in silence for what feels like an eternity.

"I am so sorry," he finally whispers, as he gently kisses the top of my head. I smile to myself, then pull back to stare up at him.

"What are you doing here?" I whisper.

He looks at me as if he is confused by my question, then he reaches up and wipes a tear from under my eye. "As I mentioned, I had a few meetings here earlier this morning, and I was just getting ready to leave when I was informed of the situation in the ballroom."

His gorgeous face suddenly darkens, his icy blue eyes turning frigid in an instant.

"I can't believe he did this to you," he whispers lethally.

He looks down, and takes a deep breath, before his eyes find mine again. "Natalie, please answer me truthfully, has Colton ever put his hands on you before?" The tone behind his voice is blanketed by an emotion I cannot place.

I shake my head slowly. "No, never. I have never seen him do anything like that. Ever."

I close my eyes, trying to wipe the horrible memory from my mind entirely. But Jaxon looks like he wants to find and murder Colton, so I decide to try and bring the softness back to his face.

"I'm okay," I say softly. "Really."

He momentarily smiles at me, but then his eyes fall to my neck. As he gently pushes my hair back, I see lightning flash in his eyes and his jaw clench again.

"Jaxon, I promise I am okay," I say again, softly touching his face with my hand and staring into his eyes.

"Bullshit," he growls.

Before I register what has happened, I am in his arms, and he is carrying me into the living room. While this feels slightly unnecessary, I don't have the energy to object. Instead, I just wrap my arms around his neck and lean into him. He walks us into the living room and sits down on one of the sofas along the glass window ledge, with me strewn across his lap.

I try to slide off him, but he holds me still, unwilling to let go of me. I lean my head into his chest, and he plants a soft kiss on the top of my head. The way this man is treating me is baffling to me. It's almost as if he sees me as some fragile or precious thing that he does not want to break... or see broken. But I can't object. This is strangely everything I want.

So instead we sit, like this, in silence.

"Do you want to... talk about it?" he asks quietly.

"Not really," I say after consideration. "It was awful. I just really want to forget any of it happened at all."

What would I even say?

That my pill-popping, ex-fiancé attacked me and tried to strangle me because I refused to take him back? It embarrassingly reads more like the latest episode of some trashy reality show, than the kind of thing I wanted to divulge to someone like Jaxon.

"Okay, well, would you like something to drink?"

I can tell by the soft innocence in his voice that Jaxon is unsure of what he should say or do, but he is just trying to comfort me in any way he can.

"You know, a cup of tea actually sounds nice," I say softly as I finally slide off his lap.

He shoots me a half smile and kisses my hand. "Tea it is," he says as he heads into the kitchen.

When he is gone, I lean back against the couch, close my eyes, and take a deep breath. I still can't believe that Colton, a man I had grown up with and known for almost half my life, had actually tried to hurt me like that. I had seen him mad before, but not like this. Never like this. Not once had he ever been violent with me, or anyone else to my knowledge.

He seemed different, almost unhinged.

I wonder now if his drug addiction is starting to affect him. I do remember learning in nursing school that when abused, certain drugs like opioids, can cause intense withdrawal. And if abused for an extended period of time, they could sometimes even chemically alter the personality of the patient entirely.

I'm distracted from my thoughts by the sound of Jaxon opening and slamming cabinet doors in the kitchen, and general sounds of frustration. I look up to see him trying to figure out how to work an electric kettle, and I realize the poor man is trying but has no idea what he is doing. This makes me giggle.

"Lifestyles of the rich and famous, baby."

I remember what he said yesterday at the museum, and chuckle to myself as I get up to go end his misery.

"Apparently I should have just asked for wine," I joke as I walk into the kitchen, and Jaxon looks up from squinting at the back of a tea bag.

"That's definitely more my area of expertise," he says with a chuckle. "And there are definitely a lot less steps involved."

I take the tea bag from him, flip the switch for the kettle, and place the tea bag in the mug, biting my lip in the process as Jaxon looks on with a defeated kind of innocence.

When his eyes meet mine, my entire body warms in the way that is clearly becoming canon for us. He extends his hand to me and when I accept, he pulls me into him once again. His strong arms around me make me shiver compulsively.

I don't know how he makes me do that.

"Natalie," Jaxon whispers against the top of my head, holding me close. "Do you swear Colton has never attacked you before?"

"Yes," I whisper back. "I promise. I had been ignoring his calls and texts since last night, but he surprised me in the ballroom. I tried to leave, and he wouldn't let me. But I never expected he would attack me. I've never seen him so… angry."

"Well, being angry is something that happens to be my area of expertise…" he mumbles under his breath, his voice suddenly dark and heavy again.

"I was actually afraid until your men showed up. They saved me." I look up at him, but quickly hang my head and close my eyes. "I am so embarrassed that anyone had to see that, including Ethan. I feel awful," I say as I blush.

Jaxon runs his finger along my chin and raises my gaze to his.

"Natalie, *that* was not your fault. Ethan knows that as well as I do. Colton had no right to put his hands on you," Jaxon growls. "Apparently, the fucker is just an asshole who has no respect for women."

"He was mad at me," I say softly. "For seeing you."

"Well, then that's unfortunate," Jaxon scoffs, "because I seem to enjoy seeing you quite a bit." He winks at me with a naughty look in his eye that makes me giggle and blush harder. "What do you think, should we blow off our plans and start our evening early?" he says mischievously against my neck. "No? Okay, fine, but we are still on for later, right?"

"I hope so," I say, a smile spreading across my face.

He leans in to kiss me but hesitates, trying to be gentle. I thread my fingers in his hair and press my lips to his, showing him that I am in fact not made of glass. He kisses me back passionately.

When I pull away from him, admiring his beautiful face, I suddenly hear someone clear their throat in the room behind me. Jaxon looks up toward the dining room, and it's then we both see Charlie standing there.

"Boss," he says, nodding to Jaxon. His face is a far cry from his usual bright smile.

With just this one word, Jaxon's body seems to tense, but he still holds me fast in his arms.

"Natalie, I do have to get going, if you are still feeling up to it, I will see you tonight. Just text me when you are headed back to the hotel, and we can coordinate from there."

I nod, and he plants a soft kiss on my lips, before pulling me with him toward the elevators. As the doors open, he cups my face in his hands and kisses me passionately, setting my bones on fire from within.

"Try not to get into any more trouble tonight, eh?" he says, winking at me. I kiss him softly one more time and shrug my shoulders playfully.

"No promises."

He flashes me a quick smile, then steps on to the elevator.

"I'll see you tonight."

Chapter Twenty-Two

JAXON

I'm going to kill him.

Natalie had handprints on her fucking neck.

My blood is boiling as I step off the elevators toward the offices.

"Good to see you again, Mr. Pace." Cynthia, the young blonde desk clerk that I slept with a month ago, attempts to flirt with me as she usually does.

"Move!" I bellow. She yelps and jumps out of my way.

Another time, perhaps I would have welcomed her advances, perhaps even indulged. But right now, I want no part of it. There's only one thing I want.

I want to crack Colton's skull with my bare hands.

However, I find that Ethan must have anticipated this, as I see Josiah waiting for me outside of the security office where they are currently holding Colton.

"Where is he?" I snap.

"Ethan is with him now."

He started without me.

We may not technically have the right to *hold* Colton, but it's likely that Colton does not know that.

And even if he did, it's not as if anyone is going to stop us.

Nearly all the police department, and the chief prosecutor's office were on my payroll. I head into my office where I watch via the security camera the interaction happening in the room across the hall.

"Let's go over this again, Mr. Reynolds. When my men entered the hallway, they heard Miss Tyler screaming. What was that about?" Ethan says calmly, tapping a pen on the table.

"As I've already said, this is all just a misunderstanding. Natalie and I were just having a conversation," Colton says, scratching his neck, and then crossing his arms. "She wanted to sort things out between us. I mean, you know how it goes. *Women*, am I right?"

No, you're not... and you are a terrible liar.

Ethan is not falling for it either. I watch as he narrows his eyes at Colton.

"But you are no longer in a relationship with Miss Tyler, are you?" he asks.

"Well, not officially, but we were trying to work things out..."

"Is that why you reserved *separate* hotel rooms?" Ethan asks, as Colton shifts uncomfortably.

"Well, um, we just didn't want to put any pressure on the weekend, you know."

"Additionally, the front desk also notified us that Miss Tyler had requested a 'DNI' or more commonly known as a 'Do Not Identify' order on her reservation upon arrival," Ethan continues. "Indicating to us that she did not want to be disturbed by another guest. She later told them that the DNI applied *only* to you."

So, Colton was the reason for the DNI.

I smirk to myself, remembering that I thought she had done that to avoid *me*, when all along it was to avoid *him*.

Colton looks almost just as surprised by this information, so Ethan continues, "It just seems to me, Mr. Reynolds, that Miss Tyler was very clear in her thoughts about any reconciliation with you."

"Maybe it looks that way to you, but you're just a casual observer. You don't know us at all," Colton snaps back dismissively. "We have a history, okay? I assure you that we are fine. We just had dinner in the restaurant a couple of nights ago, it was quite cozy and romantic."

"Would Miss Tyler echo your sentiments?" Ethan asks.

I smile to myself.

I know exactly how that 'cozy and romantic' conversation had *actually* gone from the new security cameras I had installed. And speaking of the cameras, I watch now in HD as sweat droplets form on Colton's brow, and he scratches his neck a second time.

Well, well, well, what do you know, Colton is exhibiting all the symptoms of a drug user on a crash.

"Look, as I have already said, we were just having a private conversation that your guys interrupted. You are overreacting."

"Perhaps you're right, Mr. Reynolds," Ethan says, crossing his arms and leaning back in his chair. "However, it seems to me as "just a casual observer" that perhaps after your repeated failed attempts to reconcile with Miss Tyler, she was intentionally trying to avoid all contact with you."

"What? That's absurd, Natalie and I were engaged," Colton scoffs.

"*Were* engaged, Mr. Reynolds, but no longer," Ethan clarifies, an uncharacteristic smug smile crossing his face.

"Now you listen to me *buddy*!" Colton suddenly shouts at Ethan. "I don't know what the fuck you're getting at but—"

"You will not raise your voice at me, young man!" Ethan thunders loudly.

Colton instantly recoils in his seat.

"What I'm getting at, *buddy*, is that I think after Miss Tyler rejected and ignored you, you *stalked* her into that room, and physically assaulted her like a common thug!" Ethan smashes his hand down on the table, making Colton jump. "I don't know where you hail from, Sir, but in this city and in this hotel, we don't allow savages to stalk our hallways… or our fucking guests!"

Colton's farce is gone, and his lip starts to quiver.

Damn Ethan, I gotta say, I kind of like the new you.

However, the crazy look in his eye has me slightly worried that he might snap and actually beat Colton's ass.

Probably time to intervene.

"If you ever lay a finger on that girl again—" I find Ethan shouting in Colton's face when I open the door.

"Thank you, Mr. White," I say, clasping his shoulder. "I think that is quite enough."

Ethan glares at me, before tearing himself away from Colton. He kicks the door open and storms out of the room, his rage radiating off him in waves.

This is something I fully understand, as it's taking every ounce of restraint not to rip Colton's throat out right here.

"My apologies," I say, closing the door. "My head of security is just full of personality."

And I will have to tell him how much I like it later.

"Now!" I clap my hands together loudly, purposefully startling Colton, who is obviously on edge. "Mr. Reynolds, forgive me, I am just catching up. I understand we had some trouble today? Some sort of 'misunderstanding?'"

I sit down on the edge of the table, attempting to take the 'good cop' approach, and see if Colton will bite. And he does.

"Yes, that's exactly what I was saying to, uh, whatever that other guy's name was, but he wasn't listening. This is all just one big misunderstanding."

"That's unfortunate," I say coyly. "And in that case, we should probably get you out of these."

I walk over and unlock his handcuffs. Colton eyes me suspiciously but I just smile down at him.

I kind of love that he hates me for spending so much time with Natalie.

"Yeah. Thanks," he says once his handcuffs are removed.

He immediately begins to rub his wrists, probably for a dramatic effect. I've already anticipated that his next move will be to try and intimidate me. Probably by threatening to sue me, since he will incorrectly assume that I don't know the whole story since I wasn't in the room when he attacked Natalie.

Which is fortunate for him because had I seen it happen, I know I would've killed him.

Fuck their family wedding.

"You know, you should be careful man, you ought to keep those goons of yours on leashes... especially that last guy."

"Well, we tried," I say with a wink. "But he bit the vet,"

Colton stares at me, processing what I said.

"Yeah well, I'm just saying, you should be careful. Nice hotel like this," he shrugs. "You don't want to be sued. All I'd need to do is file a police report, and things could get really bad for you."

He squints his eyes at me, relishing his moment of superficial superiority. But I'm not intimidated. I'm well aware of who has the true power in this room.

And it's *not* Colton.

"You're absolutely right.," I say, clapping my hands together once more, watching him jump again. "How rude of me, I should have offered. Would you like to file a police report? I know the sergeant over at County, we play poker every Tuesday night. The highlight of my week, you see, because he sucks at poker, and he drinks too much vodka—so it's practically highway robbery!"

I slap the table, giving Colton a hearty fake laugh.

"But the guy owes me a favor, and it would be no big deal to get him over here. I can have Ethan pull the surveillance footage from the ballroom and—"

"No, no, that's unnecessary!" Colton says quickly, his eyes wide and his paranoia kicking in.

"Are you sure? It really is no big thing at all. I mean I want to do the right thing here, and you said it was just a 'misunderstanding' so I am sure Natalie would corroborate what you have told us. In fact, we can ask her to come down—" I say moving to the door, pretending as if I'm going to open it and call Natalie.

"No!" Colton says, lunging for me. He puts his hand on my arm, pulling me back in the room. I look down at his hand intimidatingly as he quickly removes it from my arm and stares up at me nervously.

"It's fine. I'm good. If you will just let me go, we can just forget all this shit ever happened," he says, rubbing his forehead.

"Are you sure?" I ask again.

"Yes, yes, I'm sure," he grunts irritably. "I do have places to be this evening."

I smile at him but refuse to move from the doorway, picturing myself smashing his head against the table until it's as soft as a boiled melon.

"Oh? Big plans out on the town?" I ask with a wink, my massive frame dominating Colton's. He looks small and uncomfortable in my shadow.

"Yeah, bachelor party," he says curtly.

He is by far the bravest small-dicked, entitled piece of shit I have ever met.

Or the dumbest…

I step out of his way and wave at the door. "By all means."

"Thanks."

"Oh, Colton…" I call after him as he steps into the hall, and he begrudgingly turns back to look at me.

"Do be careful out there tonight," I glare at him unflinching, my tone darkening. "When the sun goes down, these Chicago streets take on a whole different… *personality*."

He swallows so loud I can almost hear it.

"Yeah, thanks," he says sarcastically, rolling his eyes.

"I mean it!" I snap back with such force he stops in his tracks. "I just would hate for you to fall into any more 'misunderstandings.' There are lots of *monsters* out there." I glare at him lethally, the good cop façade gone. I want him to understand that I am no longer playing nice, I am threatening.

Colton stares at me, his eyes growing wider as he contemplates my backhanded threat. Then he practically bolts down the hallway without another word.

I walk across the hall to my office, where Josiah and Ethan are waiting for me, watching all of this on the security cameras. We watch silently, ensuring that Colton goes immediately to his room, before packing up and heading to Valet.

When we reach the cars, I turn to Josiah.

"You did well today. Stay behind and keep eyes on Miss Tyler until Charlie can resume point." I say quietly. "Make sure that *that* piece of shit stays the fuck away from her."

"Yes, Sir." He nods, a dark smile crossing his face. Then he turns and walks quickly back inside the lobby.

I happen to know that Josiah is the son of an abused single mother, and know he will break Colton's neck before he allows him to get anywhere near Natalie.

"We are taking this one alone. You guys can follow," I say to the rest of my security detail. Once we are in the car, I check my phone and see I have a text.

Charlie
2:43 p.m.: Sir, she passed out shortly after you left and is napping comfortably in front of the fire.

Good, at least she has relaxed a bit.
I look up at Ethan, who is silent, his jaw still clenched.
"That was not like you," I say quietly. "Usually, I'm always the one losing my cool."

"I apologize," Ethan says gruffly. "That asshole attacked Miss Tyler, and all of us could hear her screaming over the walkies. I want to go back there and…" He trails off, breathing heavy.

They heard her fucking screaming.
Hearing this my rage floods my veins. I'm grateful I didn't hear that myself, or I would've actually killed him.

Lord knows, I still want to.
"You don't need to apologize to me, Ethan. Ever. And especially for that. I'm still debating turning this car around and teaching him some fucking manners myself."

"Don't tempt me," Ethan growls.

"He left marks on her fucking neck…" I whisper venomously.

"It was all I could do to keep from ripping his throat out the minute I entered that room."

Ethan shakes his head.

"Men like that," he says furiously, "are the worst kind of men."

"No, Ethan, they're not," I say as I pull out my gun and load a new clip into the chamber. "*We* are."

Chapter Twenty-Three

Natalie

"Allllll right laddiieess!!! Is everybody ready to party?!" Rebecca, the matron of honor, cheers as we gather in the lobby of the hotel.

Spritely cheers erupt from the group, and it's evident that a few of our party members have already started pre-drinking while I was still napping.

"It looks like we are still missing a few stragglers," she says to me as I am the closest in proximity. "But they still have a few minutes before ten. After that, they are on their own."

Ten was the call time we decided upon for our bachelorette celebrations, and everyone was instructed multiple times to meet here in the lobby if they wanted to get in the limo.

"Natalie, would you mind ringing the driver?" Rebecca asks with a smile, and I nod politely. I walk out into the atrium and immediately the cold night air hits me.

Good thing I went with jeans instead of a dress!

"Hi there, I was told to ask for Ramon?" I ask the boy behind the valet counter. His eyes light up and he grins up at me enthusiastically.

"Yes, Miss Tyler! I will have it out for you right away!"

I smile.

At this point, I'm almost getting used to strangers knowing my name around here, especially since the valet guys in particular have seen me so often with Jaxon.

I'm about to head back inside to wait when I notice the bodyguard from brunch standing by a smoking post. He was one of the men who had been there when Colton...

Yeah, we don't need to revisit that again.

Since my nap, I decided that in order to enjoy myself this evening, I need to put the altercation in the ballroom at the back of my mind. At least for tonight.

But, regardless, the man standing here smoking had been extremely helpful, and kind, and I didn't get the opportunity to thank him for saving me.

I walk over to him, noticing him stiffen immediately.

"Hi…" I start slowly. "So, I know we haven't officially been introduced, but you said my name earlier, so I am assuming that maybe you know who I am?"

Was that weird? It kind of sounded weird.

"Yes, ma'am." He shoots me a quick glance before looking away again. "You're Miss Tyler. Personal guest of Jaxon Pace."

Like a loyal centurion, he scans the perimeter. But I still try to catch his eye.

"Yes, and you are?"

"Josiah," he says, directly avoiding my gaze.

"Well, Josiah, I just wanted to say thank you," I say softly. "You know, for earlier."

"My pleasure." He takes another drag on his cigarette, but still doesn't look at me.

I feel awkward, like I am making him restless.

"I'm sorry, I don't mean to make you uncomfortable."

Finally, Josiah's eyes find mine, and for just a moment his hard expression softens. I notice that he has a large scar on the left side of his face, evidence of some past trauma. Serious trauma evidently, as the scar trickles all the way down from his forehead to his chin, barely missing his eye.

"It's not that, ma'am…" he says quietly. "The boss said none of us were to be seen *bothering* you."

He briefly looks as if he wants to say more, but then quickly decides against it. He immediately returns to his stoic appearance, his eyes focused straight forward.

Jaxon told them not to speak to me? Could he do that?

I desperately want to pry further into this request of Jaxon's, but the limousine has pulled up outside, and our group has already started noisily piling into the atrium.

"Natalie! Nat! Come on!" Steph shouts at me between laughs, as she waves and gets into the limousine.

"Well, thank you, Josiah." I smile at him.

"My pleasure," he says again, but he doesn't glance my way again.

In all my years, I have never seen any private security behave like this. It seems slightly odd that Jaxon could command such devotion.

Regardless, I walk toward the limo and climb inside with everyone else. Steph immediately hands me a partially empty fifth of Jack Daniels, with a huge grin plastered on her face.

"You look like you need this."

I take a swig before the door to the limo closes, and I turn around to see a statuesque Josiah diligently watching us pull away.

"I love this song!" Steph yells at me, dancing in the middle of a club floor.

"Me too!" I yell back.

Several hours, half a dozen bars, and too many drinks later, I am lost in the music and cannot remember the last time I have laughed so much. The drama from this afternoon is long forgotten, and it feels incredible to now be happily celebrating with the same people I felt so distant from at the start of this trip.

"I'm thirsty!" she yells, grabbing my hand and pulling me towards the bar.

The handsome bartender hands us two glasses of water along with our drinks and shoots me a wink.

"Oh my God, how did you know I needed this?" I pant, downing the water instantly, as he just laughs and walks away to service other customers.

"He probably saw our drunk dancing and figured we needed to hydrate!" Steph says grinning. "That, or he just thinks you're hot, which is just as likely! I mean look at you, you fine ass bitch!"

I laugh and take a bow. I'm not usually comfortable with compliments, but I have to agree, the outfit I chose this evening is to die for. I made a massive effort to upgrade my whole wardrobe for this trip, blowing almost an entire paycheck and even enlisting my best friend to assist with choosing outfits for me.

Tonight, a black one-shouldered top which accentuated my chest and waist, paired nicely with tight dark blue jeans, and a leather jacket that I decided to leave in the limo. However, I am regretting the five-inch heels I chose, as my toes feel completely numb after hours of dancing.

"Girl, we needed this!" Steph laughs as the two of us stand in line for the bathroom. Finally, it's our turn, and since we find it's a single room, we decide to go in together. When we are alone, she smiles at me as she fixes her hair.

"I mean it, Nat, I swear there's like five guys who have been ogling you all night."

"Really? If that's true, then they have undoubtedly been turned-off by my terrible dancing skills," I say with a laugh, as I apply my lipstick.

"Stop that!" Steph rolls her eyes and starts trying to fix the lipstick I have smudged. "You, my darling cousin, are a *stunner*! You always have been!"

I don't know what comes over me, but I impulsively wrap her in a tight hug. I'm so grateful for her.

Steph has always been my rock, my 'familial best friend' and the only one who made any kind of family functions tolerable after Colton and I split. She never asked me why I called off the wedding, saying that if it was bad enough for me to do that, then that was all she needed to know. She has always been the first to defend me when my family tried to pressure me to reconsider being with Colton.

"Aww Nat, are you okay?" she says, hugging me back and looking at me quizzically. I pull away from her with a big smile on my face.

"Yes, I just wanted to thank you for being you. You've always had my back, and I am so grateful for you."

"Of course, girlie! And you're easy to love!" she says with a grin. "And if you don't believe me, just ask that ruggedly handsome hotel *billionaire* who keeps sniffing around."

"Omgggg stoppp!" I say with a laugh.

I remember that I'm going to see him again tonight, and my

heart skips a beat. I have a million questions about Jaxon, but the mere mention of his name makes my stomach do a somersault in the best kind of way.

"Hey, are you bitches planning to have a Pure Romance party in there or something? Or do you feel like sharing the toilet with the rest of us?!" Some angry jerk shouts from outside.

Steph's demeanor changes in a flash, and her eyes narrow as she swings the door open quickly.

"Yeah, I was just waiting for your girlfriend to show up so she can buy herself a bigger dick!" she shouts unashamedly in his face as we walk past. "Wait, who am I kidding? You don't have a fucking girlfriend!" She flips him the bird, as the rest of the crowd standing in line laughs and cheers along with her.

Semi-drunk me can't stop myself from giggling, even though I know that's probably the last thing I should do in this situation.

"You fucking bitches!" he shouts, as we scramble back to the bar.

However, in our wild escape, Steph suddenly trips on her heels and cries out in pain.

"Ahh, shit!" she says as I clumsily help her off the floor. "I think I twisted my ankle."

I help her onto a barstool and quickly evaluate it.

"Looks to be just a sprain, nothing broken."

I ask the hunky bartender for some ice and finagle a way for her to best elevate it in her situation.

"Maybe that's what I get for talking shit," she laughs at me.

"Nah, he was being a jerk. He deserved it," I reply with a grin. "Fuck that asshole!"

"Oh, myyyy look at you using the f-word, you *bad* girl! I'm gonna tell your momma!" she says with a laugh. "I can count on one hand how many times I've heard you say that word, Tyler. Maybe this Pace guy is good for you!"

She tries to high five me, but evidently shifts her body and ankle, in a painful way and winces immediately from the pain.

"Fuck!" she cries out.

The irony of her statement is not lost on us, and we burst into a fit of laughter.

"You know what, I think what we need is another round," I suggest. "Just to help with the pain, of course."

"You know what, Tyler, I think you are correct." Steph winks.

I hand my ID to the bartender, but then I notice Steph is searching in her purse frantically.

"I can't find my ID!" she says, checking her wallet again. "It's not here!" Her face is a twisted mix of pain and worry. "Oh my God, I think I may have left it at the last bar when I started a tab. I have to go get it."

She attempts to get off the stool before I can stop her but winces the minute her foot hits the ground.

"Oh no, Missy, you are not going anywhere."

"But Nat, I have to go get it. I can't be without my license, drinks aside, I need my ID for my return flight."

"I know, don't stress," I say, calming her down. "I have two good ankles and can run back there and get it for you. Just sit tight and elevate your ankle," I say, wrapping her in a quick hug.

"Oh my God, thank you!" she says cautiously. "But also, please be careful!"

I find Rebecca on the dancefloor and update her on the situation with Steph, then head for the door. As I step outside, I briefly consider calling the limo.

That feels a bit excessive to just go a couple of blocks.

Due to Rebecca's clearly mapped out party plans, I know the bar is only a few streets away.

It will just be faster to walk, so I start off quickly down the street. However, I've only made it a few blocks when I'm reminded why they called Chicago the "Windy City."

I left my leather jacket in the limo, and now I'm freezing. I cross an empty street and a gust of wind blows hard against me, almost knocking the wind out of my lungs.

"Yeesh," I say to myself.

I pass an alleyway as I cross over to the next block. The streets are mostly deserted, and the shops have all closed for the night. I have to admit the city feels different at night than it does during the day.

My feet are aching, and I emphatically understand now why these shoes were probably not the best choice for bar hopping.

More like bar hiking at this point.

I grab my phone to check the time as I turn another empty corner, crossing my arms tightly across my body to defend against the wind.

1:44 a.m.

No wonder these streets are so vacant.

As if on cue, I see a text come in from my favorite billionaire hotelier and a smile crosses my face.

Jaxon
1:44 a.m.: Having fun? Where did you end up?

Me
1:45 a.m.: Yes! We are at the TapRoom now and having a blast. Had to take a little detour though. My cousin hurt her ankle and lost her license, so I'm currently hiking back to the last bar to get it. Why is your city so damn cold and windy?

I turn the last corner and thankfully see my destination a few hundred feet ahead. I am grateful, because if it had been any further, I may have turned into a human popsicle.

Jaxon
1:47 a.m.: You didn't take the car? Please tell me that someone at least went WITH you? Chicago streets are not incredibly safe at this time of night.

I roll my eyes.
He is so overprotective. I can handle a short walk, Jaxon.
But I must admit, the bar looks nothing like it did a few hours ago when our crew was here and shaking up the place. It's mostly deserted, with just a few stray men sipping drinks at the bar or playing pool. I quickly explain the situation, and the bartender hands me Steph's ID painlessly, but with a creepy grin that makes me shiver a little considering Jaxon's last text.

I push it from my mind and shoot a text to Steph letting her know that I have her license in my possession. Since it's so damn cold outside, and I need to conserve body heat for the trek back, I put my phone in my pocket and set off once again.

I'm halfway down the block when I notice a couple of men coming my direction on the sidewalk. Both of their towering frames make eye contact with me, and I can't stop myself from shivering.
Just stay calm, you'll be back with the family soon.
I cross in front of another alley, but I notice it's the same alley I passed on the other side of this block. It looks substantially darker than the street I'm on, but it looks like it will save me a good ten minutes of walking, and the narrow walls might provide a bit of shelter from the wind gusts.

Plus, it would also mean I don't have to walk past these two creepy men, who have not stopped staring at me as they continue their approach.

Shortcut it is.

I quickly turn down the alley, picking up my pace as best I can in these horrible shoes. I side-step the puddles, and avoid inhaling near the dumpsters. However, somehow the alley feels thinner than it appeared from the street. And *darker* too.

I am halfway down the alley when all of a sudden three figures step out from behind a dumpster in front of me, making me stop in my tracks.

"Oh my…" one of the men says eerily, stepping into the glow of the only dim bulb hanging on the alley wall. "What do we have here? Are you lost, little lamb?"

His tone makes my skin crawl and my body freezing instantly. He now completely blocks my path through the alley.

Oh fuck… this isn't good.

"No, I'm not. I'm just heading back to my group. So, if you'll excuse me," I say, taking a step forward, trying to move around him.

But he reaches his arm out to block me. I recoil backwards, out of his reach but still trapped. His two friends fan out across in the alley, making it impossible for me to pass.

"What's the rush?" he sneers at me. "I'm sure your bitchy little friend cannot be missing you that much…"

What? Bitchy little friend?

Suddenly, I recognize him. He's the jerk who was shouting at Steph and I outside the bathroom. The same man Steph publicly insulted.

Shit.

"Look, I don't know what you want, but I don't have any cash on me, I'm sorry."

"I don't need your cash, *slut,*" he snaps viciously. "I promise, I make more money than you. But I can't stand snotty little bitches like you, who are used to talking shit. You seem to think you can talk down to anyone you want without any consequences."

"What?" I say exasperated. "I don't know what you're talking about. Please, just let me pass."

I make another advance to try and move past them, but they close the gap even further, making that impossible. The one man reaches for me, although I avoid his grasp and step back further down the alley.

"I think maybe she needs to be taught a lesson, Allen," his friend chimes in behind him, leering at me creepily.

Oh my God. I am in danger, and I need to get out of here immediately.

"Look, I am really sorry for what my cousin said to you. But I promise people will be looking for me, and I need to get back to them, so please let me go."

"Oh, you're not going anywhere, Sweetheart. At least not until I've taught that pretty little mouth of yours a lesson," he says, opening a switchblade and smiling at me wickedly.

"Please, just let me go," I tremble, hearing my voice crack.

But he steps toward me.

I regret volunteering for this mission.

I regret not calling the car.

I regret not bringing anyone with me.

I regret not taking Jaxon's concern seriously.

I don't want to be here anymore.

I need to run, but my fear is making my legs feel as if I'm glued in place, and I'm still wearing these heels.

That is it! These heels!

I know I can't hope to run in them, but I can at least kick them off, and perhaps the stiletto might even work as a weapon.

I slowly, and discreetly, slip one shoe off in the dark alley trying to not draw attention to myself, and not taking my eyes off them.

"Look, you don't want to do this. I need to get back to my family. Can you please just let me go?" I ask, covertly stepping out of the other shoe.

They take another step toward me, and I turn, simultaneously bending to pick up one of my shoes as a defense and bolt back down the alley. But in that same split second, I look up and see a figure emerge from the shadows behind me with a gun drawn.

"I believe I heard the lady ask you a question," the man growls.

As he steps into the light, I see his warm russet colored skin standing in contrast to his black apparel. I recognize him.

Charlie!

His arm steady, he approaches me swiftly in the darkness. His eyes fixated on the men behind me, who instantly halt their advance toward me.

"Charles," the first man growls back, his face growing dark. "We meet again."

What the hell is going on?!

Chapter Twenty-Four

JAXON

"Look at the tits on this one, eh?!" Victor Black wheezes, pointing to the topless girl dancing on the bar below the VIP loft. "Perfect. As they should be, considering I paid for them."

He laughs as he puffs on his cigar.

"Turned eighteen a week ago," he smirks, pointing to the feral men below, howling and flinging cash at her. "Look at that, would ya? An hour up in the cage and the dogs are already chomping at the bit."

Ivan, the unsettlingly pale and incredibly stupid bodyguard known as Victor's 'number two,' licks his lips and growls.

"Woof! Woof!" He barks at her, mimicking the desperate men down on the dance floor.

Rolling my eyes, all I can do is just shake my head.

There was a time when I would have enjoyed this shit. But tonight, I have no interest in naked strip club women, or in strip clubs, for that matter. Tonight the lights, the music, and even women have all lost their appeal. And the smell of Black's cigar is giving me a headache.

Ethan was right. Maybe I am getting too old for this.

I take a sip of the drink I ordered, and then immediately spit it back into my glass.

"What the fuck? Victor, are you still watering down your booze?" I say, after taking a handkerchief from Levi. "This tastes like shit."

"Hey now, I gotta make a dollar where I can," Black says, shrugging and finally turning his gaze away from the stripper and back to me.

"Yeah, well, I'd like to remind you that I'm not a fucking customer," I snap irritably.

"Not anymore anyway," he says with a grin. "Speaking of, where is my missing product?"

"The last shipment is secure, with all product intact," I say, lighting a cigarette and inhaling. "However, the missing product from the first shipment is still that—*missing*."

"So, when am I—" Black starts to ask, but I cut him off.

"You'll get reimbursement when we find it," I snap. "My men are on it. They will get to the bottom of it."

"It had better be soon. I have needy customers, you know." He rolls his eyes and checks out the ass of the waitress bringing him another drink. "Not having a product costs me money, Jackie"

"In the meantime," I continue, ignoring him. "There's this."

However, the moment I reach into the breast pocket of my suit coat, chaos erupts. This simple action causes all three of Black's men, and all four of *my* men, to put their hands on their holsters by instinct.

"Relax, it's an envelope," I say, pulling it out and tossing it on the table in front of Black.

He stares at it for a moment before reaching for it.

"Haha! Look, Boss, she's twerkin'!" Ivan, the giant orangutan interrupts, practically foaming at the mouth.

Black's men forget their posts and move to get a better look, their priorities changed. There is a cheer from below us, howls of delight echo through the packed club.

"You sure you don't want to take a look, Jackie-Boy?" Black sneers with a wink. "Hasn't it been a while for you?"

"It's never that long for me," I grin venomously.

"Oh, that's right, I forgot," He smiles back at me. "This always *was* your type, wasn't it?"

It takes everything in my power not to punch the stupid grin off his face…because he is talking about *Rachel*.

Rachel was a stripper before we met. Something not uncommon in our world, as men who live the way we do, inevitably spend a lot of time in places like this.

Back in the day, Rachel's family had been one of the original mafia families in Chicago. They controlled all the clubs and bars in this section of the Midwest. In a fucked up way, she had grown up in a place like this.

I didn't care about her being a stripper *before* we got together. But *after* we got together, it became a pain point.

I struggled watching other men salivating after her. It caused dozens of fights between us as she didn't want to give up this life. To make things worse, there were rumors that she was still escorting while she was with me. And while I didn't particularly believe these rumors, they still messed with my head. Which triggered more fights between the two of us.

And Victor knew about it all.

I take a drag on my cigarette, glaring at him.

He should pay for that.

However, every move Victor makes is intentional. And calculated. He always knows what buttons to push.

And I know what he really wants: the Don Supremacy.

He's trying to bait me into drawing first blood, which would give him a legitimate reason to fight me and challenge my position at the top of this dirty food chain. But I didn't become the youngest, and most successful, Don in Chicago by flying off the handle whenever someone pushes my buttons.

I did it by being *more* calculated, more intentional, and more lethal than this fat bastard.

This is my city, and I call the fucking shots.

So as much as I want to smash this glass in his eyes, I simply sit back in the chair and cross my leg.

"See, the difference between me and you, Black," I sneer condescendingly. "Is that when I want to fuck, I *don't* have to pay for it."

"You don't pay them to fuck, Jackie, you pay them to leave!" He laughs hard, hitting the arm of one of his oafish goons. "Am I right!!?"

However, his wheezing immediately turns into a coughing fit, making him sound like an eighty-year-old with emphysema.

Jesus Christ. And I thought I was too old for this business.

When he can breathe again, he wipes his eyes and opens the envelope, pulling out the letter. I study his face. I want him to know that Samuel left us this note. I want him to know that we know Sam was using drugs. I want him to know that I know they were his drugs.

"What's this?" Black snorts. "Is it a joke?"

"Well, go on," I say, narrowing my eyes at him. "Be a good boy and follow the instructions. Illuminate it."

"And how the fuck am I supposed to do that? With my dick?"

"Now that would be a party trick indeed," I wink.

He glares at me, a fake laugh escaping his lips.

What's your next move you fat pathetic fuck?

He pauses a moment, then takes his cigarette lighter out and relights his cigar, and starts to hold it to the paper, but I shake my head. He looks at me with an annoyed expression before demanding the flashlight from his bouncers, and shines the light on the page. I watch him read the text and evaluate the message, as I listen to the noisy clubgoers below us continue to paw and cat call the stripper. Finally, he turns off the flashlight and sits back in his chair, puffing on his cigar.

"I don't understand, what the fuck is this?"

"This was found in the pocket of Samuel," I say icily.

"Paranoid enough to search your own men now, huh?"

"I trust my men," I say curtly. "We just happened to find it when we were stripping his body. After he swallowed his own gun, of course."

I now have Black's full attention, as well as the attention of his entire squad.

"Samuel betrayed me," I glare at him. "And when confronted he chose... well, he chose to stop *breathing*."

Leaning forward I take the paper from his hand, putting it back in my pocket.

"But his final act was to make sure we found this message. It was his way of warning us."

"I still don't understand." Black waves his hand in the air, impatiently signaling the bartender to bring him another drink. "What is this Two-Headed Dragon nonsense?"

"Something new," I whisper lethally. "And they want to make a statement."

His eyes meet mine as he takes a puff on his cigar, and his face turns serious.

"But you see, what confuses me," I say, narrowing my eyes and rubbing my chin. "Is that they conveniently knew that *your* drugs get shipped on my boats, and that my boats dock in my yards, and only *my* men can get into my yards. Now why is that?"

"That, uh," he says, swallowing hard. "Is quite confusing."

The waitress brings over two drinks on a tray, and Black takes his before she can even set it down.

Well, well, well. Would you look at that, Black is anxious.

She smiles at me in the way girls do when they find you easy on the eyes, but I wave her off.

"No, I'm not drinking that elephant piss again," I snort.

"Still, Jackie, you're telling me one of *your* men was compromised," Black scoffs, staring into his glass. "Since when is that my problem?"

"Since we found track marks on Sam, and *your* drugs in his system," I snap venomously.

Right now, I want nothing more than to hear his skull crunching under my fist.

Three of my men are dead because of this sack of shit.

"I'm just saying, it's not my fault your men can't cope with the slavish workloads you dish out. And it's not my fault they come looking for *alternative options*," Black sneers, and I see his yellowing teeth through his lips.

The noisy crowd below roars with excitement, causing all of Black's men to turn and look.

I capitalize on the split-second distraction, and lunge for Black. In less than a second, my gun is jamming into his fat gut.

However, there is a gun to my ribs as well…courtesy of Ivan. But then Ethan has a gun on Ivan. So follows the rest of my team and Black's team. Everyone pointing a gun also happens to have a gun pointed at them.

If I shoot him here, all my men are dead, and my daughter is an orphan.

Black knows this truth as well. But, he also knows he is dead in this scenario too. And even if any of us survive, the police station is a half-mile away and gunfire would most certainly mean cops swarming this place in minutes, making escape untenable.

So instead of turning Black's club into the O.K. Corral, I lean in close enough to smell the pickled herring and cigar smoke on his breath, and whisper, "If I find that you have your claws in my men, I will put your fat fucking ass on a hook and drag you up the fucking river."

Black stares back at me almost defiantly. I can tell he is weighing all his options, just as I did, and reaching the same conclusion. Finally he smiles, and gives a short nod, signaling his submission. So I let him go

Time to leave.

"I think we're done here," I snap as I straighten my jacket and turn to leave.

However, our path is suddenly blocked by a large bouncer dragging a man half stumbling up the stairs, with another bouncer in tow. The first bouncer throws the man to the floor in front of Black.

"What's the meaning of this?!" Black shouts angrily. "How many times do I have to tell you stupid fucks not to disturb me when I'm in a goddamn meeting?!"

"This douche asked to buy some pills, but his card was declined. He popped them in his mouth anyway and then tried to run," The bouncer replies angrily. "Thought you should know."

But when the man on the floor slowly looks up, I recognize him immediately. And I wish I *didn't*.

Fucking Colton...

I look down at the party below and realize that *this* is the bachelor party we have been hearing howl all night.

Fuck. Of all the nights and of all the fucking clubs.

My mind starts racing, and I shoot a look at Ethan, whose eyes echo my silent thoughts. Black will kill him for trying to stiff him.

There is no doubt in my mind.

"Tsk, tsk, tsk..." Black sneers, using his shoe to lift Colton's chin. "Don't you know the golden rule, kid? If you want to play at the table, you should never try to stick your dealer."

Colton looks utterly terrified staring up at Black, and then frantically around the room. It's only a matter of time before Colton's eyes meet mine, and I can see the moment of recognition even on his drugged face.

Shit.

"Take him out back and shoot him," Black says flatly.

The bouncers move to remove Colton, but he fights to remain.

"Wait! No! Hey man, don't I know you?!" Colton says to me.

Fuck.

If I say something, I give up the high ground with Black.

If I say nothing, they will kill him.

After I briefly consider that the world *might* be better off without Colton, I realize that Natalie, despite despising him at present, would ultimately be devastated. And I also know that if good-time-best-man Colton mysteriously disappears the day before the wedding, Natalie and her family will break their necks trying to find him.

Fucking hell...

NICOLE FANNING

Black turns to me, "*Do* you know him?"

"Yes," I growl between gritted teeth. "He is a friend of a friend of mine."

For the love of God, Colton, do not mention Natalie.

Considering the letters she's already gotten, I don't need any of these wolves descending on her because of Colton's stupidity. He nods rapidly, miraculously keeping his mouth shut.

"Was this your plan? Did you *mean* to send him here tonight? To try and cheat me while assaulting me in my own club?" Black says sanctimoniously.

"Fuck off, Victor. If I wanted your money, I'd just take it." I snap coldly, pulling out my wallet. "I have no need for a measly couple hundred dollars' worth of pills. What does he owe you?"

"Five hundred," the bouncer replies.

I take four thousand dollars in cash and smash it into Black's hand.

"There. That's more than double for you, your dealer, and *both* your bouncers that had to deal with him."

He stares at the cash for a long moment, then looks up at me and shrugs, pocketing it.

"And, uh," he says, stroking his chin with a smile. "Are you going to guarantee—" He nods towards Colton.

"Don't worry, this one won't say a word," I growl, shooting a furious glance at Colton. "Even if I have to screw his jaw shut myself."

Now it really *is* time to go, especially before Colton says something fucking stupid and gets us all killed. I step past Black while Ethan furiously pulls Colton up by his jacket and shoves him toward the private elevator.

"Wait, what? Screw what?" Colton says frantically. "What's going on?"

Ethan grabs the back of Colton's head.

"Say another word inside his goddamn building, you stupid cunt, and I'll break all of your teeth," he whispers lethally.

Despite being under the influence, he gets the message. Colton thankfully doesn't say anything on our way down, but the minute we step into the alley, his mouth is at it again.

"Hey man, thank you *so* much!" He laughs nervously. "Whew, that was scary. I knew that was you man! Haha! I recognized you from when you—"

Before he can finish that sentence, I grab him and slam him up against the concrete alley wall.

"Shut the fuck up!" I hiss at him.

He screws his eyes shut, reacting to having his head smashed up against the brick.

"Now listen to me you stupid fuck!" I thunder at him. "This is not a game. And you have no idea who you just tried to fuck over! Those men upstairs? Yeah, they would have killed you in a heartbeat!"

"Yeah, I know," he chuckles. "I was just trying to say thanks, friend."

We are not friends.

I smash his head a second time into the bricks.

"Ow, what the fuck man?" he groans. "Not complainin' or nothing, but that *really* hurts, bro."

"As it should. You just cost me a lot more than four thousand fucking dollars!" I shout at him. "I should be kicking your ass myself, not saving it!"

Colton's eyes roll around in his head as he gathers his bearings.

"Dude, I know. I was trying to say thank you."

"Don't fucking thank me!" I hiss angrily. "I didn't do it for your worthless ass, I did it for Natalie!"

Colton's expression changes the moment I say her name.

"That's right, remember her?! Well, let me tell you these men don't fuck around! Did it ever occur to you that they could have come after *her*, or any of the men here with you tonight in retaliation for you running from your bill?!" I roar. "All because you want to get your rocks off on some pills you don't need and clearly can't fucking afford!"

I jam my finger into his chest hard, my voice low and lethal.

"And let me be *absolutely* fucking clear—I know *exactly* what happened today with Natalie. And I promise if you *ever* lay a finger on her again, I will put an end to you myself. Do you understand me?"

"Hey man, hey—"

"I said do you fucking understand me?!" I shout in his face.

"Of course, of course, yeah," Colton says quietly.

I take a few deep breaths, convincing myself out of smashing his skull repeatedly against the bricks.

I can't do that. For Natalie's sake.

Now…what do I *do* with him?

It's clear he's still inebriated. And I obviously cannot return him to his friends *in* the club he just got thrown out of, Black would never allow that.

Ethan takes a call and walks a few feet away.

"Put him in the fucking car!" I snap to Max and Levi.

They grab him aggressively, dragging him towards the Range Rover, just as Ethan hangs up and walks back over to me.

"We have a problem."

"What the fuck now?" I say, trying my best to control the venom dripping from my voice.

"It's Natalie," Ethan says, worry flashing across his face. "She's in trouble."

Chapter Twenty-Five

Natalie

What the hell is Charlie doing here?!

He cautiously steps in front of me, his gun drawn, and his eyes fixed on the three men in the alley.

"I said the lady asked you a question," he says to the men in front of me. "Is there a problem here?"

"The only problem here, *boy*," the man taunts, "is you sticking your big nose where it doesn't belong." The long-haired man spits at Charlie.

"Oh, I see, y'all think you're tough," Charlie scoffs at them.

"Yeah, we are."

"But you know who I am and *who* I work for." He snaps, quickly cocking his gun. "So don't think for a second I will hesitate to dust your racist inbred asses right here."

Holy shit!

"I don't fucking give a shit who you work for, boy. I'm not afraid of your boss. He isn't the only one in this city."

What?

"I'm only going to say this one more time," Charlie speaks slowly, a lethal intensity in his voice. "I need you to back the fuck up and leave the girl alone. She is under *his* protection."

Charlie has now maneuvered himself in front of me, using his body as a shield for mine. I can hear my heartbeat in my ears, but all thought has evaporated entirely.

"You know, I'm not really concerned about what you need, *friend*," the long-haired man replies sarcastically. "And I'm not afraid of your *boss*."

He points to his two friends, sneering at us in the dark.

"I think there are a few more of us than there are of you."

"Think again!" A voice thunders behind me, rattling my bones out of my skin.

Holy crap...I know that voice.

Jaxon Pace suddenly steps into view, his threatening build materializing straight out of the darkness.

"Apologize to the lady and return back to your masters," he demands as he steps in front of me and Charlie. "Or *die*."

"Riley, that is—" Allen, one of the two thugs behind the long-haired man, stammers nervously, but Riley raises a hand to stop him.

"I know who it fucking is," he snaps as he defiantly glares at Jaxon.

However, even in the moonlight he looks paler, his eyes wide with fear and panic.

"Good, then you understand what's about to happen to you if you don't take my generous offer to leave now," Jaxon snaps menacingly, taking another step towards Riley. "Believe me, it makes no difference to me."

No, Jaxon, stop!

My breath hitches in my throat and I silently plead for him to stop approaching the three thugs who were just trying to mug me at gunpoint.

"Did you *touch* her?" Jaxon whispers lethally, his tone sending a chill down my spine.

He takes another step forward, his massive frame now towering over Riley.

Riley's gun hand starts shaking as he nervously tries to think of a response.

But just as he opens his mouth to speak, Jaxon's left hand suddenly clamps down around Riley's throat in a lightning-fast movement, causing the man to drop his gun entirely.

Holy shit!

Reactively, Allen lunges towards Jaxon.

But Jaxon is faster, pulling a gun from the inside of his suit coat and cocking it at Allen. All the while holding Riley off the ground by his throat. Allen raises his hands and takes a step back, watching his friend choking to death under Jaxon's grasp.

Riley's face is turning purple, and he is clawing at Jaxon's hand crushing his windpipe. Jaxon kicks the discarded gun backwards and it skids across the alleyway. It collides with the foot of a man who steps forward from the shadows with his own gun drawn.

Ethan.

When did he get here?

"Did you misunderstand me, *friend*?" Jaxon says in a terrifying whisper, his head jerking to one side. "Are you hard of hearing, *friend*? I bet that's a bad quality to have in your line of work, *friend*."

Then Riley's eyes are rolling back in his head, and for a moment I fear that Jaxon may actually kill him.

"Apologize!" he thunders at Riley.

But he cannot breathe let alone hope to squeak out a word.

"We are sorry!" Allen shouts. "We're sorry, miss whatever your name is!"

Jaxon finally releases Riley, and he crumples to the ground, gasping for air.

Jesus Christ.

"Well, go on!" Jaxon shouts at the other two men. "Pick up your fucking trash!"

He kicks Riley hard in the stomach and he rolls over towards his friends in pain.

Jaxon's voice still echoes against the cold brick walls as the two men scurry forward to collect their leader. They quickly start dragging him down the alley, and it's at this moment I hear Charlie's voice next to me.

"Miss Tyler," he says gently. "Are you okay?"

I can hear him speaking to me, but I feel as though I'm underwater, unable to process everything happening in front of me. My eyes dart from the crumpled man being dragged away, to Jaxon, whose back is now turned away from me.

I watch as he puts his gun back in his suit coat pocket and begins wiping off his hands with a handkerchief.

"Miss Tyler?" Charlie asks again as he steps into my line of vision. "Are you okay? They didn't hurt you, did they?"

"No, no I'm fine," I say quietly, shaking my head.

Charlie visibly breathes a sigh of relief and puts his gun back in the back of his trousers.

Charlie has a gun.

Ethan has a gun.

Jaxon has a gun.

After the muggers load their friend into a black town car and skid out of the alley in the opposite direction, Ethan approaches Jaxon. I can see them talking but have no idea what they are discussing.

Hell, I don't even know what just happened.

"When did you notice they were following you?" Charlie asks me, again breaking my trance.

When did they start following me?

I don't know. But somehow it seems like everyone was following me.

"I'm not sure," I say slowly, finally deciding to focus on Charlie. "But perhaps I should be asking when *you* started following me?" I ask, narrowing my eyes at him.

Charlie recoils a bit. "Miss Tyler, I—"

"Tell me, Charlie, are those the *normal* duties for a 'penthouse butler'?" I demand. "How long have you been following me?"

"Since *I* asked him to," Jaxon snaps from beside me, startling me.

He stands next to me, breathing heavy, his face dark and serious. While I am grateful for the heroic rescue, I *am* still upset that I was being followed without my knowledge.

And now I feel like Jaxon is hiding something from me.

Something pretty significant.

Maybe that's why I'm unable to stop the words that come out of my mouth as my emotions instantly spiral out of control.

"Oh, and that seems like normal behavior to you, Jaxon Pace?!" I snap angrily. "To have me tailed without my knowledge or consent?!"

"If I hadn't, you could be lying in that dumpster, Natalie!" Jaxon's voice thunders across the walls, making me jump.

He has a point.

If Charlie hadn't been following me, I could be dead. Or worse.

Jaxon and I glare at each other in stunned silence, both of us angry, and unwilling to concede.

On one hand, I am furious with him for not discussing any of this with me, and ordering Charlie to follow me. However, I also know that Jaxon, for whatever reason, was just trying to protect me.

Charlie, on the other hand, is innocent.

He had just been doing his job, and doing it *well*. After all, no matter how mad I may be at Jaxon, I was the idiot who decided to walk the unfamiliar city streets alone and take the less-than-safe shortcut through the alley.

I take a deep breath before turning to Charlie, gently touching his arm.

"Charlie, forgive me," I say sincerely. "I didn't mean to sound so harsh. I'm just a bit shaken up, that's all. You risked your life for me, and certainly don't deserve me snapping at you like that."

I look at him apologetically, hoping to wipe away some of the wounded look on his usually cheerful face.

But Charlie shakes his head.

"Don't worry about it, Miss Tyler," he smiles at me. "We are all good."

He turns and walks over to Ethan, leaving me standing alone with Jaxon.

"Now *you* on the other hand..." I say softly, crossing my arms across my body and tentatively looking up at Jaxon through my lashes.

I am not afraid of you Jaxon Pace.

...At least I don't *want* to be.

When his eyes find mine, they are still cold and terrifying. It's clear he's still incredibly angry. Though I suspect he's not angry at me.

At least... I hope not.

"I'm sorry," he says quietly, his voice raw and low.

I swallow hard and look up at him timidly and see him staring at the ground.

"I'm sorry, too," I say softly.

He glances up at me, a bit more warmth in his eyes.

"Ethan," he says, without taking his eyes off me. "Take our party guest home. We will walk."

"Sir, are you sure?" Ethan replies hesitantly.

Jaxon shoots an icy glare at him, indicating to me that he is still a ball of rage balancing on a delicate string for the moment.

Without a word, Ethan nods and walks down the alley with Charlie.

Yeah, I'm pretty confident that I'm safe with the gun-toting, throat-crushing, terrifying billionaire who seems to have an affinity for saving my ass.

Jaxon silently turns back to me, removing his suit coat, wrapping it around my shivering shoulders. His arm snakes around my waist as he gently leads me back down the alley.

Main street is totally deserted, and there is not a car or human in sight.

"Oh my God, Steph!" I gasp, suddenly remembering her and pulling my phone out.

Crap! She has called eighteen times.

"Their driver knows that you're with me," Jaxon says softly, watching Ethan and Charlie pile into the Range Rover just parked haphazardly in the middle of the street. "He was instructed to let them know you were with me, and that I would be bringing you back to the hotel."

"Wow," I say as his eyes catch mine. "That's... efficient."

The frigid look in his eyes has dissipated, but what remains is still indecipherable.

"Still, I should probably message Steph myself, let her know I am okay and that I did find you," I swallow hard. "Well, you know...kind of."

Shooting him a quick smile, I eventually tear myself away and quickly type out a message to Steph.

Me
2:34 a.m.: 1. I have your license 2. I am with Jaxon 3. ICE THAT ANKLE.

Ethan and Charlie drive away, leaving the two of us alone on the deserted sidewalk.

"How far are we from the hotel?" I ask, realizing that nothing around me looks familiar.

"It's about a ten-minute walk from here," Jaxon says quietly, wrapping his arm gently around my waist again and turning me towards the sidewalk.

I relish the feeling of his body close to mine again, and the safety I feel with him beside me

"When did you eat last?" Jaxon asks me.

"Really, Jaxon?" I scoff at him in disbelief. "How is food what you think about? Especially after what just happened back there?"

"Food is what I think about when you're drifting left, and I can smell the alcohol on you," he says a tad sarcastically.

However, I do catch the faint smile tugging at the corners of his mouth, as he pulls me back to the center of the sidewalk.

Oops. I didn't even realize I was doing that.

Suddenly, the gravity of what just happened, and what *could've* happened hits me like a big yellow school bus.

Tears start welling in my eyes, and I start shaking uncontrollably. *I was almost mugged. I was almost…*

But I can't even finish that thought.

"Um well, I ate at dinner before we went to the club, but I don't really remember how much I ate…" I say, trying to hide my voice cracking as I fight the swelling panic attack growing in my throat.

Jaxon stops and turns me to face him. He gently pulls my chin up, causing the tears in my eyes to streak silently down my cheeks. A look of realization floods his face, and without a word pulls me flush against him.

Instantly I fall apart right there on the sidewalk, sobbing hard against his chest.

Damnit!

I hate that I'm crying in front of him, for the second time today, but I am powerless to stop it. Jaxon holds me silently, allowing me to have this moment in the safety of his arms.

Finally, I take a few deep breaths, wipe my eyes, and summon the only fragments of courage and dignity I have left.

"I apologize that you had to see that," I say, staring at the ground. "And yet *again* I have to say thank you for something I could never repay you for."

He gently wipes a tear from my cheek.

"And yet *again*, Natalie, I have to tell you not to apologize to me for anything. Please. I'm the only one who is sorry." He looks away, his clenched jaw twitching as he lowers his gaze to the ground. "This never should have happened to you. Especially here, in my city."

In his city?

"Fuck," I hear him say, and in an instant his hands cup my face, and his lips are on mine.

The same hands that nearly choked the life from my attacker, now cradle my face with gentle reverence and set every fiber in my body ablaze. Jaxon kisses me passionately, urgently, like a man undone.

Finally, he lets me up for air, but he doesn't pull away, keeping his forehead pressed to mine, while I catch my breath.

"I can't imagine what I would've done if something had happened to you."

Whoa…

"I'm sorry that I didn't tell you about the security detail," he says quietly. "Please know that everything I did tonight was for your safety. Because I *need* you safe."

My heart explodes with his confession.

"I know," I say softly, unable to say anything else as my heart hammers away in my chest.

He looks up at me, a raw vulnerability painted on his face. And as I stare into his eyes, I realize that the only real fear I have with this man is being pulled under, deep into their icy depths.

Jaxon may be terrifying, maybe even dangerous, but he would *never* hurt me. Of this I am certain. Further still, he *would* hurt anyone who tried to hurt me, without hesitation. As he demonstrated tonight.

My fear is instantly forgotten, and in this moment I realize that I truly am the safest woman in the city… *his* city.

"Jaxon, none of this makes sense," I say cautiously. "I have a million questions."

"As you should," he says, staring back at me, his expression unreadable.

"Why did you ask Charlie to follow me in the first place? How come the mugger knew you? *All* of you? And what did you mean by 'your city?'"

Jaxon's face is blank, and he looks past me as if he is having a battle within himself.

"I just feel like I am missing something," I say slowly. "And while I trust you, I don't like being left in the dark or left feeling like you might not be being honest with me. I don't handle it well. Especially after what just happened tonight."

He takes a deep breath and rubs his chin, his blue eyes holding me hostage.

"Natalie, I need you to know I haven't lied to you. But…"

"…There's a lot you haven't *told* me?" I finish for him.

He says nothing, but I can tell by his face I'm right. Taking a deep breath, I step closer to him.

"Jaxon, if we're to continue like *this*, you have to let me in," I say, placing my hand on his cheek. "I need you to be honest with me. Completely honest with me. At least about everything orbiting around you, and me… and us."

There. I said it.

Jaxon stares back at me in silence, almost as if he is weighing something in his mind.

Oh no. Have I just requested the impossible?

But just as I am giving up hope of getting answers, he nods, closing his eyes briefly.

"I understand," he says slowly. "But Natalie, I feel like I should warn you that it might be easier for you *not* to know all of the truth about what is orbiting around me, and you, and… us."

Jaxon Pace is giving me an *out*. He is offering me the truth, or the bliss of ignorance. However, I know myself well enough to know that for me, there can be no bliss without the truth.

"We've come this far," I say gently. "Forgive me, but I want the whole picture."

"It's not the prettiest of pictures," he scoffs.

"It's pretty enough," I say, feeling the heat return to my cheeks. "After all, it's the picture of *you*."

He smiles, but this smile does not reach his eyes and for the first moment in the entire time I have known him, this terrifying, dangerous, and intimidating man looks *nervous*.

And then I understand. He's *scared* to tell me.

Jaxon has never hesitated before. The man just exudes confidence from his pores. So therefore, whatever the truth is, it can't be something he is proud of, otherwise he wouldn't be so anxious.

Bliss or truth moment, Natalie.

"Jaxon, I need to trust you," I say, swallowing hard. "I have seen more crazy things happen in the last four days than I have in my entire life."

I take a deep breath, willing myself to keep talking despite feeling my entire body practically shaking.

"And even though I don't understand most of it, I can accept *all* of it," I say softly. "But I can only do that if I know that I can trust you to tell me the truth *when* I ask you. Otherwise…"

My voice trails off, and my eyes drop from his.

I don't actually want to finish a sentence that ends in me saying goodbye to Jaxon. A thought that surprisingly makes me a little nervous.

He considers my words for a moment before he sighs and looks at me with a smirk.

"Fine. I'll do it," he says gently. "On the condition that if I'm going to be baring my soul, it's at least going to come with some fucking food."

He winks at me, a warm smile settling on his face.

Finally I feel as though I can breathe again.

"Fine. But nothing fancy," I say, pointing at him playfully. "I just want normal people food."

"I was thinking tacos," Jaxon shrugs, looking at me with a

mischievous innocence.

"Mmmm *tacos!*" I say biting my lip.

I might be hungrier than I previously thought.

Jaxon laughs, a deep guttural laugh that fills me with warmth as I stand alone with him under these glowing streetlights.

And then it hits me.

He said yes.

This thought overwhelms me, and I pull his face to mine, kissing him hard. His hands wrap around my body again, threatening to undo me right there in the street. I thread my fingers through his hair and kiss him softly once more as he gently pulls back and presses his forehead to mine.

"Thank you," I whisper. "For letting me in."

"I have never let anyone into my world before," he whispers.

"Well, then I will endeavor to be worthy of that," I whisper back.

I kiss him once more, a mixture of passion and gentleness.

His breathing is heavy for a moment, then he steps back with a smile and wraps his arm around my waist, pulling me to him as we start off down the sidewalk.

"Now, let's get some tacos."

Chapter Twenty-Six

JAXON

"Wow, and I thought the view from my room was great…" Natalie's voice trails off as she scans the city skyline.

We sit on a large soft blanket atop the roof of my hotel, a bag of street tacos, and two bottles of water between us.

"Do I need to upgrade you again?" I joke.

"To what? The roof?" She raises her eyebrows at me and takes a bite out of her taco.

I stare at her with a grin, making her eyes go wide.

"Don't you dare," she says nervously with a laugh, playfully slapping my arm.

I laugh along with her.

"Focus. You have guts to spill, mister. Remember?"

"Right, right," I say, clearing my throat. "Real talk, what do you want to know?"

Of all the conversations Natalie and I have shared together; this is the first that feels slightly uncomfortable. While I understand that it is necessary given what she has been through in the last few days, I don't love the idea of putting myself on the table for dissection.

"What do you… *do*?" she asks.

"I do a lot of things," I shrug. "It's just that some of them are a bit more complicated than others."

"Complicated how?"

"Well, I have already told you about my hotel business, as well as my shipping business. I have many others across the country, and the world. Some are various legitimate investments. And some are…" I swallow hard, pausing to think about how to say this delicately.

"Illegitimate investments?"

Natalie finishing my sentence shocks me to my core.

Holy shit.

"Yeah, some of them illegitimate," I say, still utterly stunned. "How did you—"

"Oh, come on, Jaxon," she snorts, interrupting me. "I'm not stupid. In the short time I've known you, your daughter was almost kidnapped. You had a grave situation at your warehouse. You opened a closed public museum for a private tour. You have more money than God and you seem to know everything that happens in this city." She continues counting off on her fingers. "Oh, and you carry a gun in your suit."

Well… damn.

"To be fair, a lot of people own firearms. For self-protection."

"Right, but you look *remarkably* familiar with it," she says, raising her eyebrow at me. "And speaking of protection, you have about a dozen henchmen that appear to have sworn some blood oath to you or something."

"Is it suspicious to hire people who take their jobs seriously?" I say sarcastically, deliberately trying to be a bit facetious. "Isn't it just smart business to hire people with a good work ethic?"

"I'm just saying it doesn't take a rocket scientist to figure out something more complex is going on with you," she finishes softly.

I just stare at her.

She put all of these pieces together on her own.

It's kinda sexy actually.

"Complex is definitely one way to put it."

"The way your men follow you," she says, shaking her head. "It's… a little unnerving. It's almost as if your word is law to them. So, the way I see it, you're either into something illegal, or you're a cult leader."

This time I laugh. Hard.

"Wow, a cult leader, huh?" I say, with a chuckle. "That's a new one. But, no, sorry to disappoint, but I don't have enough patience for that. My men are just loyal to me."

"So, does that mean that you're like a drug lord or something?" she asks, her tone serious and her eyes wide.

"Would that make you run screaming for the hills?"

"Well…" She contemplates, staring at the ground and tucking her hair behind her ear. "I don't know."

"No, I'm not a drug lord," I say softly, crossing my legs. "But I do *know* drug lords. Several, in fact."

"So, you're…?"

"Mafia," I say, realizing there's really no easy way to say this, and I just have to rip this band-aid off.

She nods, and then looks at me again inquisitively.

"When you say Mafia," she says curiously. "Do you mean like *The Godfather* kind of mafia?"

"Well, our lives are not nearly as glamorous as Hollywood makes it appear in that movie, but sure, that is probably the easiest reference for you in some ways."

"Um, I would say your life seems a *bit* glamorous, Mr. Billionaire."

"Fair enough," I chuckle.

She nods, her eyes still wide. She's here, trying to understand, but I am aware that I have just thrown a grenade into the bonfire again. As much as I don't want this to change things between us, I have to acknowledge that if I continue telling her things about my life, it very well could.

"Natalie, if you don't want to know anything else, I would understand," I say, leaning forward on my knees. "I promise I'll give you the truth, but I don't want you to feel obligated to stay because I do. I'm never going to blame you if you suddenly decide to run for those hills."

Even though this is true, I still feel a tightness in my chest at the thought of her leaving. But, I also need her to know she can.

"Do these look like running shoes to you, Mr. Pace?" she winks, pointing to the heels she's discarded.

Whoa…

"Go on," Natalie says softly, looking at me expectantly.

But I just stare at her, unable to say anything at all.

The truth is, part of me was more prepared for her to scream in horror, or leave, than it was for her to stay.

So I certainly wasn't prepared for Natalie to want to know more about my dark and dirty other life. Especially considering the squeaky-clean record *she* herself has.

"Um, I don't know where to begin."

"If you're not a drug lord, then what do you do?" Natalie asks gently, crossing her legs.

Grabbing another blanket from the stack the men brought up from the penthouse, I wrap it around her.

"Technically, what I told you yesterday is true—I work primarily in shipping. Imports, exports, that sort of thing," I say with a shrug. "It's just a bit more complicated than I explained. About sixty-five percent of my cargo is legitimate, and the other forty-five percent is less-than-legitimate."

"Oh… huh," she says, raising her brows.

"What is it?" I ask, confused by her curious expression. "Is that not what you were expecting?"

"Well, not really," she snorts, amused. "I guess I was expecting you to say you did something *really* illegal, like off-market guns, or drugs, or prostitution."

"*Really* illegal, huh?" I smirk to myself. "I'm not directly involved in the day-to-day management of those things. My family learned a long time ago it was smarter to be the transport, not the supply."

"I see," Natalie nods.

"Don't worry, it's still illegal," I wink at her, making her blush. "But it's a little safer to not handle any of the messier bits of manufacturing or selling the drugs or guns. I just control the transport, so my influence is a bit more high level. Except for the sex that is."

"What do you mean?"

"Like I said, every off book product that comes into this city comes through *my* ships, my trucks, or my planes and trains. I am the facilitator, but I don't control the distribution of the majority of those items."

"Uh—huh, and, um, what did you mean about… sex?" Natalie says, her eyes dropping to the ground.

"Prostitution is controlled by another family."

"*Family*?"

"There are different factions, known as 'families' that control other aspects, like drugs or prostitution. Usually it's a family enterprise, passing down control generation to generation."

She nods, tucking her hair behind her ear and staring at me. Her face suddenly turns serious.

"When you say you handle shipping of off book products," Natalie says, swallowing hard. "Does that mean you deal with human trafficking too?"

"Absolutely not," I say with finality.

Her eyes find mine again.

"My ships have never, nor will ever, be used to transport human beings against their will."

"I mean, that's great," she says, tilting her head. "But why is *that* a hard limit but the other stuff isn't?"

"Because it goes against the whole purpose of what we are, and what we stand for."

"What? What do you mean?"

"Just because *some* of what I do operates outside the laws of society, doesn't mean I'm a monster."

"No, Jaxon, I wasn't saying *that*—" Natalie says defensively. "I wasn't trying to—"

"But it's more than that," I say, gently cutting her off. "It was outlawed by my family. We don't condone human slavery, because that's bondage. It might be hard to understand, but the entire purpose of the mafia is freedom."

"You're right, I don't understand."

"So perhaps this is a good place to start," I say softly. "The mafia provides what the government restricts."

"Okay..." Natalie says slowly.

"Certain substances or activities are deemed illegal as such by the government. Meaning that, the powers that be decided that people don't have the right to *choose* certain things or activities for themselves. Yes, they may have good, sound, reasoning for banning those activities or substances, especially when they might be detrimental to a citizen's health or happiness. But, the mafia believes they should still have that *choice*. We feel that if someone wants to buy drugs or sell their body, at the end of the day that's their choice."

Natalie nods.

"My organization does not support human trafficking because there is no freedom of choice there. Women are kidnapped and sold on black markets into the sex trade," I say firmly. "But not here. Not in this city. Not ever."

"I guess that makes sense," Her expression softens. "And a bit of a relief, if I'm honest."

"That's the name of the game apparently," I wink at her.

"So, basically, you are in a mafia family, and handle the shipping of legal and illegal items into the city."

"Technically, I'm the *head* of a mafia family. And I guess more specifically I'm what's known as the Don Supreme."

"The what?"

"Don Supreme," I say, wiping off my hands. "It means everyone, including the dons of the other families, are my subordinates. And *my* family mafia runs the show."

"And because you're the Don Supreme, that's why your men follow you the way they do," she states confidently.

I nod, my heart racing as I wonder if I've said too much already, and should just stop talking.

"So like, how do the cops, or like the FBI, or CIA factor into this? Are they after you?" she asks softly. "Are you on any lists with the government and constantly being watched or something?"

Her question is reassuring to me, because it means that no matter how overwhelmed she might be right now, she's still *trying* to understand the world I am letting her into.

"Not to my knowledge, but I could be," I tell her honestly. "It all depends on how much attention I draw to myself."

"What do you mean?" she says, tilting her head.

"This is going to be the next step of explanation, because this is where the water gets muddy," I say tentatively. "Are you sure you want to continue with this?"

"Yes, I want to know whatever you wish to tell me," she says, tucking her hair behind her ear nervously before looking up at me.

If she is trying. I can try too.

"I feel like I don't know anything anymore. I never would have imagined that 'Mafia Gangster' was a real-life job you could have," she says with a shrug.

I chuckle.

"It's certainly not something you would put on a resume, and I promise it isn't the first choice of occupation for pretty much everyone. But it's very much a real thing. Crime exists in every city in the world. It's a *business*. And it's a business that is vital to any major society."

"What do you mean it's a business?"

"Put it this way, you've been led to believe that if an individual does something illegal that the law infallibly works to ensure justice is swift, and always served, right?"

"Right," she shrugs. "Most of the time anyway."

"What if I told you that it's the exact opposite?" I say, pointing at her. "What if justice is only actually delivered in a *minority* of cases? That more crimes and murders go unsolved than solved, at almost a three-to-one ratio? Does that make you feel better or worse?"

"Um, well, definitely not better," Natalie snorts. "That's kind of unsettling. And a bit depressing."

"And that further still, what if I told you that a lot of your government officials are not only aware of what goes on in the shadows but are occasionally active participants."

"Like, they are part of your organization?"

"Sometimes."

"What?!"

"Shocking right?" I say, watching her jaw hang open. "So how much faith do you have in your judicial system actually dishing out punishment and justice now?"

"Very little, if what you are saying is true…"

"Unfortunately, it *is* the truth."

"So, there's no justice in the world? Is that what you're telling me?" she says, her face obviously disappointed.

"No, there is. But sometimes it's a different kind of justice, and sometimes the mafia is the only way to get it."

"What do you mean?"

"As I said, we represent that vital part in society. We give them the crime they *need* to institute law and order. In exchange, they allow us to operate and manage this world as we see fit. As long as we play our part and keep our 'disturbances' to a minimum."

"So, what you're saying is that you have a business relationship with the government in which the service you provide is crime, and they provide you freedom to run the underworld as you see fit?"

I think she is starting to understand.

"That's pretty close," I say, impressed at how quickly she is picking this up.

"I feel like I still don't understand the whole 'government is in on it' thing though."

"Don't overthink it. Sometimes it's blatant, such as having a few policemen on your payroll, or even the police chief himself," I say, clearing my throat. "And sometimes it's less direct. Sometimes it's a mayor who bases his whole election campaign on being tough on crime. He says he wants to clean up the streets. I mean that sounds nice, right."

"Of course," Natalie nods. "Safety is paramount."

"But how long can you *realistically* clean up the streets? If you really wanted to, with the right task force you could have all the streets, everywhere, cleaned up in a few months tops. However, if that happened, eventually you would run out of criminals to put away. And, Mr. Mayor would have nothing to campaign for again when it comes time for his reelection."

"Oh wow," Natalie nods, raising her eyebrows. "I guess that's true, isn't it."

"This government official realizes that while being a voracious public servant might make him popular for a moment, he *won't* be popular when the streets are all cleaned up. He will be a pariah as soon as he's laying off cops and closing unmanned rehab centers. Doing everything right might get him elected, but it's not *sustainable*. So he realizes that maybe he *needs* a little bit of dirt in the world for other people to clean up. That's how society has always functioned."

"Wow," Natalie says softly.

"But the question is, how does a public servant create the demand, keep the balance, while still maintaining a good public image? I mean, he obviously can't get *his* hands dirty. He's the good guy!"

"Right, okay."

"This is where we come in." I say with a soft smile. "We work with the establishment to preserve the balance. It's like an ecosystem—you need to have both predator and prey. Your city officials need to give the appearance that things are under control. But in order to keep your tax dollars pouring in, they need to have *work* for their police officers and city workers."

"So you're providing the...crime?" Natalie asks.

"Exactly. You can't have state-funded rehabs if there are no drugs. You can't have homicide units if there are no homicides. If all the streets are sparkling clean, and all the work is *done*, there would be a lot of laid off cops and city workers, causing unemployment and poverty rates to soar. Which are harder things to control."

"Let me get this straight. So, what you're telling me right now, is that the police and city officials in power not only know about crime, but actually *sanction* it?" Natalie asks, shock crossing her face. "Off the record."

"Not everywhere, but in most large cities, yes," I say. "Those in power realize that in order to keep the system balanced they have to allow the right people to organize the messier parts and keep it under control."

"Wow." She shakes her head and then looks at me. "So, you can just do whatever you want?"

"Not exactly. Remember it's a very delicate balance. To be in charge, you must stay in charge, and that is hard to do if the rest of the system is out of balance. So too much of a swing in a negative direction and you draw more attention, and more heat—which is not good for anyone. We have to be very decisive about what we do and when we do it. We have to know when and where it's acceptable, or more importantly where it's not," I say with a sigh. "It's why it's important for the right people to be in charge on *our* end too. Even among the bad guys, there has to be some semblance of morality."

"And your family has been in charge of this business for some time now?"

"I was born into it; I am a sixth-generation mafia Don."

"*Don?*"

"Don is just another word for boss. It's more commonly used in families with an extensive heritage like mine that spans centuries of family leadership."

"Wow. I never would have imagined that," she says, shaking her head. "It's like this whole other world is existing all around me, all the time."

"Which is how it *should* be," I say softly, feeling embarrassed now. "Society isn't ready to acknowledge this ugly truth. No one likes to feel like they are just a pawn in someone else's game. It's simply safer for most people to never imagine this at all."

I cannot explain why, but I suddenly feel just the slightest bit ashamed.

I mean, this is what she asked for, and what I do. But next to Natalie's perfect life, I feel almost dirty.

And as I watch her face, I can't help but wonder if it will be too much for her to stomach.

"You said you are in shipping? What do you ship?" she asks, her green eyes finding mine.

"Whatever my clients want," I shrug. "Again, it's a mixed bag. I have a wide variety of clients, the vast majority being legitimate businesses that are unaware of the illegitimate stuff. One week I might ship a container full of children's clothes for the local shopping mall chain I own, and the next week it could be cocaine for a drug boss."

"And do *you*... use drugs?"

Part of me invisibly cringes at this question, knowing that I promised not to lie to her.

"I have in the past," I say, shifting uncomfortably. "But not usually no,"

"In the past" might be a bit of a stretch though...

"I've definitely had more than my fair share of wild nights. But ultimately I have responsibilities, and people who count on me— like my employees or my daughter, who need me sober. And I have a clear head for the businesses I operate—the illegitimate and the legitimate. Drugs make that difficult."

If I felt dirty telling Natalie about my life *before*, it certainly isn't getting any easier.

"Have you killed anyone?" she asks intensely.

Definitely not getting easier.

I sigh, knowing there's just no way around this question.

"Yes."

"That's it?" She asks, raising her eyebrow. "Just, *yes?*"

"As unflattering as that sounds," I say, as I rub my chin. "It unfortunately comes with the territory. But it's not like the movies. I don't have some insatiable bloodlust and wander the streets looking for people to mug and murder. I don't leave unnecessary carnage."

"Would you have killed the man tonight who tried to…" she trails off, her wide green eyes glued to me.

In a fucking heartbeat. Especially if he touched you.

"If it was necessary," I say, tugging at my tie.

"And what makes *you* the judge of when it is necessary to take a life?" she asks.

"Power."

Natalie's jaw drops.

Fuck. Is that the straw that breaks the camel's back?

I stand up and walk over the balcony, feeling anxious.

I sit here, sharing the raw ugliness of my world with someone who probably has never even had a late library book.

The problem is, I've already jumped off the dock with her. And for her part, I can't imagine what this is like to hear for the first time, especially as a regular civilian.

I turn back to face her and find her looking at me expectantly. Deciding that I'm already in too deep, I walk back over to her and kneel in front of her.

"Natalie, look…" I sigh softly, taking her hands in mine. "I realize these are ugly truths that have to be shocking to hear."

Her eyes scan mine, unmoving and unreadable.

"Again, I will not blame you if you don't want to hear anymore. I will not blame you for being overwhelmed or disgusted by the things I am telling you." I sigh deeply. "But I *am* telling you because I have come to respect you as a person, and the only thing you've asked me for is the truth."

I feel vulnerable. As if I really am ripping open my chest and pouring my guts on to the floor. For the first time in my thirty-four years, I could be *unwanted*. For the life I lead, for the things I do, for the people I protect. For all those things, Natalie could decide she does not want anything to do with me. Which would destroy me.

She stares back at me, perhaps weighing her ignorance for bliss at this moment. But just when I think that she has finally had enough, and is going to run for those hills, she suddenly gives me a gentle smile.

"I want to know, Jaxon," she says gently. "Please continue. What did you mean about power?" she asks softly.

Natalie Tyler, surprising me yet again.

I smirk, nodding slowly before standing to my feet again and pacing back to the balcony.

"Power is the only currency in my world," I say, putting my back against the balcony so I can see her face. "It means that you are the one who gets to make the rules. Yes, it means I do some illegal and dangerous things. And, yes, that means I would strangle a man for attacking you in an alley. I have killed and would kill again if necessary."

She nods, her eyes steadily holding mine.

"I won't sit here and tell you I'm a good man, Natalie" I say darkly. "I am by no means a good man. I am a *dangerous* man. But I *have* to be a dangerous man if I am to keep more dangerous and unstable men from taking my place and allowing this city to fall into chaos."

"Well, what do you know, a dangerous man with tons of money, and a savior complex," she says with a chuckle. "Surprising, but sadly not original, Mr. Pace."

I snort.

"What can I say, I'm... complicated."

"That's certainly one way to put it," she scoffs. "And is this the life you want... like, forever?"

Her question catches me off guard. Suddenly memories and demons collide, competing for center stage, again.

"I had an exit strategy," I say, swallowing hard. "Once upon a time."

"What, like some sort of mobster 401K?" Natalie chuckles, raising a brow.

"Kind of," I shrug.

"What was it?"

"Well, you're sitting on it," I wink at her. "We both are."

She looks down, then looks back up at me, confused.

"The hotel," I say laughing. "My hotels are all one-hundred percent legal, and that was my way out."

"What made you start looking for something more than just bullets and bloodshed?"

"Again, bloodshed is never the *first* go-to here," I say with a gentle chuckle. "And it was Jessica, to answer your question. She was the reason I started looking for more than this."

Natalie's face softens, and she looks at her hands.

"When Jessica was born, I realized my own... mortality. I realized that as her father there is only so much I can do to keep her safe. And in this life, as you saw the other day, heirs are never truly safe. The only thing I could do was to maybe make her world safer. So, I started building this hotel empire as a sort of 'Get Out of Jail Free Card.'"

"I applaud your choice of words, Mr. Mobster," Natalie winks at me, making me chuckle.

"When Rachel gave birth I told my father I wanted a way out, something that could at the very least provide Jessica a way out if something were to happen to me."

"And what happened?"

"Something happened to *him*. He was murdered."

"Oh my."

"I knew what needed to be done. Without a leader all of my men were exposed and in danger from other families. I agreed to take over, at first temporarily, until we could peacefully transition to someone else."

"Peacefully transition your organized crime business?" Natalie says sarcastically.

"Limited bullets and bloodshed, if that's easier for you."

"And let me guess, you did such a good job you couldn't leave?"

"Something like that."

"Your family is successful at the mafia thing, I take it?"

"My family is the largest and most powerful in Chicago. Under our leadership, violent crime is the lowest it's been in almost thirty years. We control nearly eighty-five percent of what happens illegally in this city."

"That's why you called it 'your city'," she says to herself. "How many people do you employ?"

"I'm not sure exactly," I shrug. "Probably somewhere near ten thousand."

"Damn," Natalie snorts. "Holy crap."

"Give or take a few hundred. However, you should know that's *all* my businesses combined," I say with a smirk. "I'm not all darkness and debauchery."

"Do you... like the darkness and debauchery?" she asks tentatively, playing with her hair.

"It's just what I know. Again, to me it's just the way of life. It's the life my family has held in various positions, in various countries for centuries."

She nods and sighs, wrapping the blanket around her tighter. I pull out my cigarettes and light one.

Natalie raises a brow at me "And you smoke?"

"After everything I just listed," I chuckle. "And this is what bothers you?"

She folds her arms, disapprovingly.

Damnit, why is she so adorable when she's frustrated?

I flick the cigarette off the roof.

"Technically I'm trying to quit."

"Well, then technically you're doing a shitty job of it." Natalie laughs sarcastically, and I join her.

"We can add it to the list."

"That's quite a list," she says softly, taking a deep breath.

"I know."

This is all I can respond with.

For some reason I cannot explain, I feel uneasy. Probably because I have no idea what's actually going through Natalie's head, but also because I can reasonably *assume* that a reasonable person like Natalie has to be appalled by everything I have just told her.

"Holy shit," she says, looking at her phone. "It's nearly four in the morning!"

"We should probably head down to your suite," I say, rising to my feet. "As much as I selfishly want to keep painfully spilling my guts, you do have a wedding in the morning."

Natalie hesitates a moment, then nods.

I would almost swear that I see a faint look of disappointment cross her face, but it might be just wishful thinking on my part. We head toward the elevator in silence, and I press her floor first, as my thoughts spiral out of control.

I can't believe I actually opened up to her like that.

My body feels cold, and I realize this is probably the end of whatever has been happening between us.

Despite desperately wanting to kiss her and feel her skin under my fingers once more, I make no move on her. After all, I have just handed her a lifetime of red flags and deal breakers. She must be feeling overwhelmed.

… Or utterly *disgusted*.

Still, it's physically painful to fight my desire to kiss her. I can't explain why, but part of me feels as if I would do anything to keep her around. I want her lips on mine more than ever, and I want to know that I *am* going to see her again.

But I also know I *can't* push that on her.

She glances up at me as the elevator arrives on her floor.

Come on, Jaxon. This is not the life she deserves. This is not the life any normal person would choose. Let her go.

Natalie steps into the foyer of the penthouse as I stand in silence, feeling as if my heart is being cracked in half. I try to memorize her face and her features, hoping that maybe I can remember them in case this *is* the last time I see her.

I smile politely, as the doors start to close on their own.

"Jaxon…" she says suddenly, stepping back on the elevator, stopping the doors from closing. "I know this is kind of sudden, but would you maybe want to be my date tomorrow night? You know, to the wedding?"

"What?" I hear myself say, but every thought I have in my head evaporates immediately.

"I mean obviously, only if you're free or whatever." she says nervously, crossing her arms.

After everything I just told her?

Is Natalie thinking clearly?

Hell, am I?

Should I say yes? Should I refuse and just let her go?

"I, uh, will have to think about it," I say, struggling with the war within my head. "I need to see what's on my plate tomorrow."

"Of course," Natalie blushes. "I understand."

She goes to step off again, but this time I can't stop myself, and pull her to me, kissing her hard.

"I will let you know," I say, summoning every ounce of my limited restraint.

She smiles, and my heart swells inside my chest.

"Okay," she says softly, blushing. "Well, then I guess goodnight, Jaxon. Thank you for sharing your world with me, once again."

Her mossy green eyes hold me paralyzed, as I struggle to

reconcile all the different thoughts swirling inside my head.

"Goodnight, Natalie," I whisper as she steps off the elevator, finally allowing it to close.

Even when the elevator reaches my floor, I still have not processed what just happened.

Natalie Tyler is the very first woman that I have willingly let past my barriers, to see into the heart of who I truly am.

And she isn't afraid.

…She is asking for *more*.

Chapter Twenty-Seven

Natalie

Ryan and Michelle's wedding was beautiful, as weddings are meant to be. When Michelle walked down the aisle I cried; watching Ryan's face melt the moment he saw her. It felt as if I watched them fall in love right there at the altar. They were truly made for each other, and I was so excited Michelle was joining our family.

Colton, on the other hand, looked awful. Not that I gave a shit how he was feeling. However, I did enjoy watching his hangover misery a little bit. But only when I was *sure* he was not looking my way.

When it was over, the bridal party left to take some photos around the city, while my cousins and I returned to the hotel to rest and recharge before the reception. We laughed and sang along to songs on the radio the whole way back to the hotel, and it felt as if the last two years of distance and estrangement between us had been but a dream.

As we walk into the lobby, my cousin Bethany—Steph's younger sister, stops suddenly. "Girls, when was the last time *all* the Tyler cousins were in the same place?"

"Um, last night," Steph says sarcastically to her sister, eliciting laughs from the group.

"Ha-ha, very funny, Sis, but seriously! This moment is rare, and who knows when we will all be here again. So, I say we should all have a drink to celebrate!"

"Beth, that's *literally* what we did last night," Steph says, rolling her eyes.

"Yeah, and since when do *you* ever turn down a drink?" Bethany snaps back saucily, making us laugh.

"Fair enough," Steph says, laughing and throwing her hands up. "Hey, I'm in if everyone else is on board!"

Everyone agrees, including *me*. Because for the first time in years, it feels like I am one of the crew again, and I have deeply missed this feeling of connectedness with my cousins.

"Whose room is the *least* destroyed?" Tara asks.

"Why don't we head to my suite?" I offer, suddenly realizing that I probably have the most space for the eight of us in my massive penthouse. "I promise there's room."

"Ooh a *suite*! Yes! Good plan!" Bethany says excitedly.

"We just need to run upstairs to get the booze."

"Actually," I say with a smile, "I think I have that covered too…"

All the girls look at me in stunned surprise, knowing that this is not like me. Steph looks the most surprised of all.

"I can never figure you out Tyler…" she says with a wink.

I roll my eyes innocently and shrug. "This way!" I motion for them to follow me to the private suite elevator. Once inside, the girls murmur amongst themselves about how fancy this private elevator is, and I smile to myself, knowing they have no idea what is waiting for them upstairs.

The doors finally open, and everyone falls silent as we quietly file into the foyer.

"Um, Nat, I don't know if this is…" Steph starts to say before I interrupt her.

"This is my suite."

All my cousins stare at me completely dumbfounded. I tuck a small strand of hair behind my ear bashfully.

"And no, I didn't pay for this, it was a gift for the week."

No one moves a muscle, and they just continue to stare at me. Well, me *and* the giant floor to ceiling windows boasting the Chicago skyline at dusk.

"Well, go on!" I finally say excitedly.

It's as if I have effectively waved the checkered flag. I watch with amusement as they bolt from the foyer and begin excitedly scurrying all over the apartment.

"Holy crap, look at this *view!*" Stacy says, running out to the balcony.

"This isn't a suite, Tyler. This is a penthouse," Steph says, crossing her arms and giving me a sly smile. "Seems like things are getting serious with your rich boy toy…"

I blush, but then instantly feel anxious.

Oh my, how can I explain this?

All my cousins saw Jaxon pick me up from the rehearsal dinner, and they obviously remembered that he gifted us the limo last night, but we have yet to discuss anything about *him*.

So much has happened in the last twenty-four hours, I am still trying to work through all of it. I wonder how on earth I can explain who, or what he is to me when I don't know myself.

And… I haven't even heard from him today…

Jaxon has texted me every morning that I have spent in this penthouse, but sadly no text came in from him today. Not a word since I asked him to be my date to the reception this evening, which was a bit disheartening.

I hope that I did not push too hard last night. However, I was honest with him about my life, so I am not going to feel bad about asking him to be honest, too.

Lost in my thoughts, I am interrupted by the elevator doors dinging. Charlie walks in, carrying a giant white box wrapped in a chiffon red bow. He pauses when he realizes the previously quiet apartment is crawling with girls. All eight of us freeze in absolute silence, until Stacy giggles, causing the rest of us to giggle, too.

My heart soars when I see him, as this is the first I have seen or heard from him since he fended off an armed gunman in my defense last night.

"Charlie!" I wave at him and see my younger cousins gathering around him like a bunch of gawking teenage girls seeing a boy for the first time.

"Miss Tyler, you have guests!" he says, his eyes wide. "And such *pretty* guests at that!"

He smiles, glancing around at all the girls, looking as if he has just stumbled into the Goddess's Temple on Olympus itself. I laugh to myself, watching how infatuated they are with this beautiful man.

"Ladies, this is Charlie. Charlie, these are my cousins. Charlie is amazing."

"He sure is," Stacy says softly.

Charlie glances her way with a wink, and I notice a subtle blush skate across her cheeks.

"What is this?" I motion for the package in his hands.

"This," he says, handing it to me with a huge smile. "Is from Mr. Pace."

The room suddenly goes silent.

"He wanted to make sure that I gave it to you before the reception, and also…" He pauses, glancing around the room again and realizing there is little chance of him being able to say whatever he is about to say to me privately. "He wanted me to let you know that he *will* be in touch. As promised."

A warm feeling floods my body, and I can't help the smile that spreads across my face as I stare at him.

Jaxon had not forgotten me.

Without another word I throw my arms around Charlie, wrapping him in a hug.

"Thank you, Charlie."

For so much more than just this gigantic box.

"Are you going to join us?" Stacy asks bashfully. "We were just going to have a drink to celebrate."

"I would love to, but I do have to be going. I hope I can see you all later."

Disappointed sighs echo around the room, but I catch another stolen heated glance shared between him and Stacy as he heads for the elevator.

As soon as he is out of earshot, all eyes fall on me.

"Well? What are you waiting for, woman! Open it!" Steph says.

"Is this from the guy last night?" Bethany asks excitedly.

"How do you know him again?" Stacy chimes in.

The questions are coming at me so fast I don't know which to answer first. I head into the living room with the girls in tow, and we settle on the couches. I set the box down on the table and stare at it for a moment.

Good God, I hope this isn't something inappropriate—as I clearly have an audience.

I open the box and find a card from Jaxon.

I couldn't resist.
-J

I pull back the tissue paper to reveal some glittering fabric, and as I pull the item from the box, I realize it's a dress. Not just any dress, but the most gorgeous dress I have ever seen.

It's a cream-colored ball gown, with a plunging neckline over a criss-crossed bodice, that has a white lace overlay with thousands of crystals embedded into the fabric, covering every inch of the dress. The shimmering crystals catch the setting sun, casting the reflection on the walls and ceiling around the room like a thousand tiny dancing stars.

I am speechless.

Stacy catches sight of the tag and her jaw suddenly hangs open.

"$11,000?!" she exclaims, looking at me, my jaw drops too, as I pick up the tag myself.

"No way!" I gasp but see that she is correct.

Holy shit. Jaxon Pace bought me an $11,000 dress.

I feel like I might hyperventilate to death.

"Natalie Tyler," Steph says, stepping up and placing my face in her hands as my heart hammers away in my chest. "You have to calm down." She says

Calm down? How the hell am I supposed to calm down?

The Don Supreme of the dangerous Pace Family Mafia just sent me an $11,000 dress.

"You need to calm down," she says, a smile tugging at her mouth. "Because we are going to need some frickin' answers missy!!"

Laughter and hollering erupts around me while I just shake my head in awe.

I can't believe this is my life right now.

"But seriously girl, what on earth is *all* of this?" she says, motioning around the penthouse.

All the voices in the room fade into a baited silence. I slowly sit back on the couch and take a deep breath.

It hits me like a car crash. I haven't told anyone about what has been going on with me and Jaxon… and I am burning to talk about it. I decide it is time to finally open-up to my family, and hope that they understand.

"In truth," I start slowly, "I don't know entirely. But something… well, something happened the other night."

I pause, trying to choose my next words with care. It's like I can just *tell* them that I've been casually dating a man who is in the mafia. And he is not just in the mafia, but runs the mafia.

Hell, Jaxon practically *is* the mafia.

"But what about Colton?" Chloe chimes in innocently.

Suddenly it feels as if all the air is sucked out of the room. As if everyone apparently remembered that Colton exists, and that we have a history together.

I can feel the familiar panic and frustration rising in my throat, threatening to shut me down again.

Wait just a minute...

The guy I've been dating for the last five days is *in* the fucking mafia. If I am not afraid of him, I certainly don't need to be afraid of this overdue conversation that I have avoided for too long.

I can do this.

And I *need* to do this.

"Actually, ladies," I say, taking a deep breath. "Colton seems like a good place to start this story," I say with a sigh, and a smirk spreads across my face. "There is a lot you don't know..."

An hour later, I've unburdened myself to my cousins.

I walked them through everything that happened with Colton, and the crazy whirlwind of my last five days with Jaxon. I was, however, careful to leave out the attempted kidnapping of his daughter and Jaxon's mafia confession to me last night.

If I had been worried about their reaction to the truth with Colton and the introduction of Jaxon into my life, it felt like it was without merit. I instantly felt an overwhelming sense of support from the people I wanted it from the most. Tears were shed, hugs were shared, and one incredibly expensive dress was tried on for all to see.

But as the sun began to set, and it was nearing time for the reception, Steph sent everyone else away and stayed behind to help me put on the stunning evening gown for real. She also fixed my hair and makeup, making me look like a movie star.

Now as I stand in front of the mirror, contemplating my reflection and the cathartic last hour with my family, I can't help but smile and feel like a massive weight has been obliterated from my life. I almost wish I told them sooner.

"You look incredible," Steph says, stepping up behind me.

"Thank you, Steph," I say, trying not to get emotional again.

"For everything. I don't know if I would have had the strength to tell them tonight without *you*. And if I hadn't, who knows how long it would have taken for me to finally feel... free."

"Natalie, you have always had the courage. It's one of the most beautiful things about you," she says, as she fixes a stray hair on my head and stares at me. "And really, I think you have found *something* here with this man. I'm so happy that you decided to take a chance and explore it. It's been years since I have seen this light in your eyes. It's beautiful, just like you."

Holy shit.

I fight back tears, solely to save the intricate makeup job Steph spent an hour on. But at least I see that Steph is fighting them too, and finally she just shakes her head with a smile.

"Enough of that! Cinderella, it is time to get you to the ball!"

We take the elevators to the lobby and certainly turn a few heads as we cross over to the ballrooms.

"Let them stare," Steph says confidently, whispering so that only I can hear her. "That's what that dress was *made* for."

I smile.

That sounds like a dress Jaxon would pick for me.

Steph and I head into the ballroom and find our seat assignments just as the lights begin to flicker, signaling the arrival of the bridal party. However, as we walk between the tables I feel an incredible number of eyes on me, and hear the quiet whispering. I briefly wonder if wearing this dress was a bad idea, as it clearly is drawing a lot of attention.

I'll have to remember to thank Jaxon for that. Whenever I see him next.

But as I find my seat, this thought is weighing on my mind.

Jaxon has not answered my invitation, and despite Charlie's promise that he would 'be in touch', I still have not heard from him at all. Even though he sent me this bombshell dress, it felt strange that *he* has not made any mention of actually *seeing* me tonight.

Had I been too forward in asking him to join me for this wedding?

My thoughts are interrupted, however, by the entry of the bridal party, as they make their way into the ballroom. One by one each couple enters, dancing along to the upbeat background music as the MC introduces them.

I also find myself immediately grateful for the fact that the bride apparently insisted on a formal bridal party table.

This is good news for me, because it means that Colton will be expected at the head table and will not have the ability to harass me during dinner. Which was something I was slightly concerned about when I noticed the seat next to me was still unoccupied after the lights came back up.

I carefully avoided Colton's gaze as dinner began but continued to keep tabs on *where* he was at all times during the meal itself. The seat next to me still sat unoccupied, I didn't want him to see the open seat as an opportunity to join our table, as it would utterly ruin any chance of me enjoying this evening at all.

However, as dinner concludes, I find myself engaged in a riveting conversation with my table about politics, and suddenly realize I have neglected my watchfulness, when I see Colton making his way over to my table.

My heart starts racing as I contemplate what I should do to avoid him.

I do not want to cause a scene, as this is Ryan and Michelle's special day, but I am done being manipulated into conversations and situations regarding him.

But just as Colton reaches our table and attempts to take the back of the chair next to me, Steph appears and slips into the open seat before he even realizes what has happened. She smiles sweetly at me, and winks.

Colton opens his mouth to stay something, but suddenly Stacy, Bethany, and Gretchen appear out of nowhere, and step in front of him, effectively blocking me from view.

"Go back to your seat, Colton," Stacy says icily.

"There's nothing for you here anymore," Bethany snaps, her voice is soft, but she punctuates each word.

"There is nothing for you here anymore."

I realize that Bethany is reiterating my last text to Colton, and I also realize that my cousins are literally forming a protective barrier around me—a wall of protection. They are standing up for me, and sending a clear message to Colton, telling him that they know *exactly* what he has done, and that he's no longer welcome.

Colton's face turns a bright shade of red, and I'm not sure if it is from embarrassment or rage. But nevertheless, he turns on his heel and stomps back to his seat.

Once he is gone, a smiling Steph turns to me.

"We got you," she says with a wink, before standing up and walking away.

It's then that I feel it. A shift has taken place. Small as it is, I can feel it in my bones. A surge of confidence floods my veins and courses through me for the first time in a long time.

I see now that I do not need a man at my side to protect me from Colton. I simply need to remember who I am, and where I come from, and tap into the people I once trusted most in the world. My family.

My family loves me, and they *will* support me. I am not alone.

The lights dim.

"Ladies and Gentlemen, I would like you all to welcome to the dance floor, for the very first time, the newly married Mr. and Mrs. Tyler!" the MC's voice rings out over the crowd.

All the wedding guests make their way over to the dance floor. We watch as my cousin pulls his beautiful new bride into his arms for their first dance. Everyone in the room can feel the love they share.

That's how it's supposed to be.

That's what I want. One day.

After the first dance concludes, the MC invites everyone else to join them. Couples gleefully fill the dancefloor as the band begins to play.

"Natalie? Is that you?!" My mother's voice speaks from behind me, and I turn to see her staring at me, her eyes wide. "Oh my god, you are a *vision*!"

She lets go of my father's arm to hug me tightly, but quickly steps back to take another look at me.

"My word, that color is simply *divine* on you!"

My father hugs me too, as he rolls his eyes, muttering "*simply divine*" in a high-pitched voice. I giggle, knowing this is clearly meant to be a playful imitation of my mother, who presses her lips into a line and smacks him gently on the arm.

"What a gorgeous day! Everything was simply perfect. And dinner! Dinner was just delicious!" she gushes.

"It really was. The perfect day for the perfect couple." I nod.

We stare at the happy couple, still twirling blissfully around the dancefloor, still lost in each other.

"But, oh my God," she says, turning back to me again, "That dress! Natalie, you look absolutely—"

"Stunning."

A deep voice suddenly speaks from behind me, and I know immediately who has finished her sentence. I knew the moment I heard his voice ringing in my ears.

Jaxon Pace.

I turn and see him standing behind me, raking my body with

a gaze so tantalizing, I can almost hear his thoughts out loud. He looks dashing in a perfectly tailored tuxedo, and his usually messy hair combed back.

"Sorry I'm late," he says, taking my hand and kissing it, while his eyes sear into mine.

My pulse quickens feeling his breath on my skin and I realize that this is not a dream. He is really here.

"Mr. Pace!" my mother says, quickly extending her hand to him. "Please, no apologies necessary. We are so honored you could find time to join us."

Jaxon politely kisses my mother's hand as well, and extends a handshake to my father, who looks genuinely pleased to see him.

"It is a pleasure to officially meet you, Mr. Pace. Glad you could accept our invitation. Thank you again for your help with the band fiasco. My brother and my nephew are in your debt."

Wait, my parents already knew Jaxon was coming?!

"Nonsense," Jaxon says with a smile. He turns back to me and gently places his hand on the small of my back, causing shivers to trickle down my spine. "It was certainly my pleasure. Everyone deserves happiness today, wouldn't you say?"

He smiles down at me, his eyes holding a wicked smile. He is clearly proud of himself for the shocked expression that has to be lingering on my face.

Jaxon secured a wedding invitation from my parents. Suddenly, all of it makes sense. The empty chair, the dress, and the radio silence today—all were done in an effort to surprise me with his answer to my invitation.

That was so sneaky!

"Oh, would you look at that, it appears I am just in time for my song request," Jaxon says with a smile, as I hear *Wonderful Tonight* by Eric Clapton begin to play. "If you don't mind, I would like to steal your lovely daughter away for a dance. Or two?" he asks my parents politely.

"Oh yes of course!" My mother gushes, smiling ear to ear.

"My dear?" Jaxon extends his arm to me.

My blood heats inside my veins as his blue eyes stare me down. I reach for him, and he pulls me close, leading me straight on to the dance floor.

Chapter Twenty-Eight

JAXON

Few moments in my life were such that I knew instantly they would stick with me forever:

The day my daughter was born.

The moment my father died.

And the first dance I shared with Natalie Tyler.

The sight of her standing in the doorway in that dress nearly sent me into cardiac arrest. I had chosen that dress with care, after having Charlie find out her dress size from her closet. It was a perfect fit for her small frame, canvassing around her voluptuous curves—almost as if it were painted directly on her perfect skin.

But the dress was nothing in comparison to *her*.

Never in my life have I seen a woman so beautiful.

I lead her out on the dance floor and spin her into me, my arms settling around her tightly. With a quick nod to the MC of the band I paid for, the main lights dim. This causes the lights over the dancefloor to catch the crystals in the dress, and it sparkles like she was covered in a thousand diamonds.

Exactly as I planned.

I got the idea from a benefit ball I hosted here last year. I remembered seeing the way the dance floor lights caught the light of a wealthy woman's engagement ring, to her immediate delight.

That was why I deliberately chose a dress for Natalie that was covered in crystals, hoping for the same reaction. Protocol be damned, every eye in the room suddenly turns to her, and she is stealing the show.

…Which is exactly what I hoped for.

"Oh my God, Jaxon," she gasps, catching sight of how she lights up the ballroom.

"Do you like it?"

"The dress is gorgeous. But I feel like everyone is looking at us now."

"Not us, love," I say, pulling her ever closer. "Just *you*."

I spin her gently with the music and relish her blushing smile.

"Right, but I don't think we're supposed to take the attention from the bride and groom," she says bashfully.

I chuckle to myself, realizing she is humbler than I am. Her cousin and his wife seem nice enough. But I am not here for them. I am here for *her*.

"Natalie, forgive me, but if anyone is upset about that… fuck 'em," I whisper.

"Jaxon!" she gasps with a smile.

I pull her close and whisper in her ear. "What? Are you nervous, my dear, that maybe just a little indulgence might feel *good*?"

She rolls her eyes at me, a sarcastic smile on her face.

"Jaxon, I'm dancing in an $11,000 dress that I put on in the penthouse suite, gifted to me by the Don Supreme of the Chicago mafia, the day after he also opened a closed public museum for a private tour…" She bats her lashes at me. "I think it is safe to say I have become vaguely familiar with just a little indulgence as of late."

"Fair enough," I chuckle, and watch as the couples joining us on the dancefloor stare at her in awe. I want them all to look at her. I find her to be the most beautiful woman on earth, inside and out, and I want all of them to acknowledge her as such.

But this is where I know we are different. I grew up knowing that because of my family's status, I was different. I was special. When I was younger, I was much more of an asshole than I am now. This was mostly because I hadn't learned that a consequence of unnecessary snobbery and superciliousness could affect my relationships and business dealings.

Over the years, I may have mellowed out a tad in my arrogance, but I still live in a world of excess, whereas Natalie lives in a world of humility.

Which probably explains how she has no idea how beautiful she is.

Natalie Tyler is gorgeous.

A girl like her could make a killing in my world. She's the kind of beauty that bosses, and billionaires married—the *highest* tier. She could live a life where she is pampered every day, enjoying extravagant vacations, driving a Maserati, and wearing a rock bigger than the iceberg that sank the Titanic, on her finger.

But that is not Natalie. Natalie is a nurse for the elderly. She lives simply, and has had one serious relationship, unfortunately with a tool, who just so happens to be in the room. Speaking of Colton, I love the look on his face as I hold Natalie against me. He looks miserable, as though he has just swallowed poison.

I wish, but I'm not that lucky.

"I can't believe you came," Natalie says softly, staring up at me. "I was worried this request had scared you away."

"Do I seem like the type that scares easily to you, Miss Tyler?" I say with a wicked grin.

"No, but when I didn't hear from you, I worried. Needlessly, it seems, as my parents invited you too?"

I smile, as I have been keeping this a secret since yesterday.

"Remember the meeting I had at the hotel yesterday morning? Well, that was because your mother, and your cousin's new wife asked to see me. They wanted to thank me for the help with the band and the bachelorette limousine. They gave me an invite."

"Oh my gosh! Did they also happen to say anything... about us?" she asks timidly.

I smile.

The song changes, but I carry on dancing, twirling her into me, unwilling to let her go.

"They may have commented that you didn't have a plus one at your table."

"So, were you planning to come even before I asked you?"

"No, I didn't want to impose. But when you asked me yourself, then nothing would've kept me away," I say tenderly, looking into those mossy green eyes of hers.

"Wow. Just wow," she says, shaking her head. "Today has been full of surprises."

"I do hope you liked some of them?" I ask, pulling her close.

"I have loved them," she says softly. "But having you here with me is the best of all." She smiles at me, and I have to will myself to keep breathing, as she literally takes my breath away.

"Do you like your dress?" she asks excitedly.

"That is *your* dress, Sweetheart, and yes, it looks beautiful on you."

It really does. That low-cut neckline combined with the way the dress clings to her curves is torture when I have her against my body like this. I would like nothing more than to tear apart the fabric between us and shove my cock inside her.

Come on Jaxon... keep it together, dude.

"But," I say, changing the subject, "what about you?" I buck up and decide to ask a question that's been on my mind since last night.

She furrows her brow and looks at me innocently, clearly not understanding what I am asking her.

"Are *you* scared?" I ask.

"Of what?"

"Being in the arms of a man like me? The big bad wolf?" I whisper softly to her.

"Well, I guess I *should* be," she answers softly. "By all accounts, I should be absolutely terrified of a man like you."

It feels like time stops around us, and I immediately regret asking this question. I instantly feel the same sharp pain in my chest as I did last night, when I thought she might leave.

"I mean, I know I don't fit the mold. I'm definitely not the 'mobster girlfriend' type, right? I'm the girl who always keeps to the safe roads and the beaten paths. I don't usually take risks."

Where is she going with this?

"But this... with you, feels different. No matter what I do, I just can't stop thinking about you, Jaxon," she says, turning back to stare into my eyes, and pulling me back from the brink. She presses her hand to my chest, doing things to my body that feel purely erotic. "And I don't want to stop. I *want* you in ways I don't understand."

Holy shit...

"So, to answer your question, no, I'm not scared of you, Jaxon Pace, or the life you live." She pulls back and stares at me, her words stunning me to my core, and her eyes paralyzing me in my bones. "I'm only afraid of running now, and never getting to fully experience you."

Did she really just say that?

My body reacts to her voice and touch impulsively. Warmth

floods over me, as our bodies mold together, swaying gently to the music. She has one hand around my neck, playing with my hair. I spin her slowly, hoping to release some of the friction between us in an effort to calm my racing thoughts. But when we reconnect, somehow, she is closer than before, and I realize it is pointless to try and fight how I am feeling.

I want her now... right here on this damn ballroom floor.

And by the look in her eyes, she wants me just the same.

"Miss Tyler," I say, clearing my throat and feigning surprise, "are you trying to seduce me?"

"Well... I do have a penthouse," she says playfully and winks at me, making me chuckle.

"That is certainly a trump card in most circumstances. However, I am one of the most dangerous men in Chicago, so I am fairly sure I get to call the shots here."

She shudders and bites her lip, something I desperately want to do myself. But just as I am picturing ripping her clothes off, the look on her face changes from one of lust, to one of sincerity.

"Thank you, Jaxon, for more than just this dress, or the hotel room, or the phenomenal dates. But for your *honesty*."

The look in her eye's chills me, and yet at the same time lights the fire in my veins.

"You owe me nothing," she continues. "You could have just as easily lied to me last night, and I would have to understand why."

"Natalie, you asked me not to lie to you," I counter. "But now that I have told you the truth, I would be lying if I said I'm not worried you are going to come to your senses and still run for those hills. Something I would have to understand."

"On the contrary, Sir," she says brazenly. "Somehow it just makes me want you even more."

Her eyes fall to my lips, and I press them to hers, pouring gasoline on a fire I am already trying to combat.

"You have no idea how much I want you, Natalie, but are you sure?"

"Are *you* sure?" she says with a smile. "Sounds to me like you are nervous... Do I make you nervous, Jaxon Pace?" she whispers tauntingly in my ear, as she runs her fingers along my neck, and I realize that she is teasing me.

Oh, that is a mistake, Miss Tyler.

"Sweetheart, I would take you right here..." I slip my hand down to her ass and aggressively press her body against me, making her feel the rock-hard bulge between my legs. I lean in to whisper against her neck, my lips grazing her earlobe. "with everyone *watching*."

I hear her gasp and feel her shudder, and that only makes me harder. She looks up at me through her lashes once again, and I can tell she is thinking about the same thing I am, which involves ditching all of these expensive clothes.

"Can we... leave?" she whispers, and I feel her heart pounding.

"So soon? Are you not enjoying yourself? Am I being a terrible date?"

"No, you're spectacular," she says with a smile.

"Where would you like to go?" I ask gently.

She blushes, and although she says nothing, I know exactly what she wants. And I want *her* terribly, hopelessly, and immediately, and I can't deny this woman nothing that is within my power to give.

"You know, you're a brave girl," I whisper in her ear. The scent of her perfume on her skin is making me crazy. "Wanting to be alone with a dangerous man like me, with terrible intentions like mine."

"Maybe I have an appetite for something different this evening," she replies, staring directly into my eyes and repeating what I said to her two days ago at the museum. "Maybe I *want* a little dangerous tonight."

All the circuits in my brain fry at the exact same time. I can hold out no longer.

"What the lady wants, the lady shall have."

I stop dancing and cup her face in my hands, kissing her deeply and passionately, in front of everyone. I slowly pull back and smile at her, before wrapping my arm around her waist and leading her off the dance floor.

We are nearly out the door when I hear someone calling our names.

"Jaxon! Natalie!"

I turn, I see the bride heading straight for us, but I refuse to release my hold on Natalie.

"I just wanted to make sure I had a chance to say hello! Thank you again, Jaxon, for the band—they are phenomenal! You completely saved our wedding," she says excitedly, and before I understand what is happening, she wraps her arms around me.

An amused look crosses Natalie's face as she can tell I'm not much of a 'hug' person.

"Of course," I say, tapping her back gently. "Glad I could help."

She eventually releases me, smiling at Natalie.

"Natalie, that dress is unbelievably gorgeous on you. So beautiful. Just like you." She smiles, before saying goodbye to us.

"She's right you know," I say, staring down at Natalie. "You look unbelievably beautiful."

"Thank you. I had hair and makeup help from a cousin, and a dress from a dangerously-sexy mafioso with expensive taste," she says, stepping closer to me and straightening my tie.

"With *good* taste." I wink. I lean in to kiss her cheek and whisper in her ear, "Are you sure you don't want to get some more mileage in that dress before I rip it off of you?"

"Come." She giggles and bites her lip, and gently tugs me toward the door.

Oh, my sweet... that's exactly what I had in mind.

We step into the hallway and find a scattering of people casually chatting and enjoying their drinks. Among them is Colton, who I see talking animatedly with Natalie's father.

"I don't know what to tell you, son. She's an adult."

I smile to myself, wondering if Colton just so happens to be complaining about me being her date this evening.

Unfortunately, Colton notices me approaching with Natalie on my arm, and decides to try and intervene. "Natalie, are you *going* somewhere?" he asks loudly.

I feel Natalie recoil.

My blood boils in my veins. I loathe the immediate anxiety he causes her. Intentionally making her uncomfortable, and purposefully embarrassing her in an effort to stop the two of us leaving together.

I knew I should have just let Black's men have their way with him.

I thought I knew all of the slimiest motherfuckers, but this jackass somehow takes the cake. I cannot fathom Colton's audacity to stand here, talking to her father, after what he did to his daughter.

Natalie ignores him, gripping me tightly, but he starts in our direction.

I'm over playing nice with Colton, and it takes everything in my power not to just grab him by the throat and throw him against the wall. But instead, I pull Natalie behind me, putting myself between her and Colton, and bracing for confrontation.

"Oh no you don't, *asshole*!" I hear a female voice shout.

A short-haired blonde woman in a long burgundy dress comes flying out of the ballroom side door toward us. She angrily steps between Colton and me.

"Oh no…" I hear Natalie mutter, squeezing me tightly.

"Whoa! What's with all the hate tonight Steph?" Colton says indignantly. "What did I ever do to you?"

"It's not what you did to *me* Colton, it's what you did to Natalie!" she snaps. I see the shock on Colton's face as this time *he* is the one to recoil uncomfortably. "Don't fucking play stupid with me, Colton!" she shouts at him.

I don't know who this feisty broad is, but I like her.

"Steph, please," Natalie says softly, trying to calm the woman down, as she glances around the hallway, noticing the people staring in our direction.

"I swear, I don't have any idea what you're talking about," Colton responds to Steph, narrowing his eyes at her.

"What's going on here?" Mr. Tyler asks, now walking over and joining the conversation.

I hear Natalie mutter obscenities under her breath, now clutching on me for dear life.

"Nothing," Colton says innocently, plastering a fake smile across his face and crossing his arms. "Just a misunderstanding."

"Now you listen to me you sack of shit—" Steph starts to say, stepping toward Colton with her fist raised.

I really like this chick!

"Whoa! Steph, sweetheart, let's just calm down, okay?" Natalie's father kindly tries to calm Steph down before she takes a piece out of Colton's face.

"Yeah Steph, why don't you just calm down…" Colton says, a smug smile spreading across his face.

"Don't tell her to calm down, Colton!" Natalie's voice suddenly snaps from beside me, shocking all four of us.

"Natalie?" Mr. Tyler looks at her confused. "What on earth is going on here? Why is everyone so angry? Come on now, it's supposed to be a wedding!" he says with a smile.

However, no one responds to his question.

The feisty chick, known as Steph, is glaring at Colton. Colton is staring at Natalie in astonishment. And Natalie is glancing painfully at her poor father, who is looking at the four of us completely unaware of the whole situation. I'm picking up on the fact that Natalie must have discussed yesterday's events with Steph. And now Steph is determined to defend Natalie from Colton.

It is also clear that in all of this, Natalie is finally starting to stand up for herself, which is something I wholeheartedly support.

So, I decide to intercede, and help things along.

"Forgive me, Mr. Tyler, I'm catching up as well. But it appears Mr. Reynolds here has done something to your daughter that this young lady finds reprehensible," I say, glancing unsympathetically at Colton.

"Listen, bud, why don't you mind your own business," Colton snaps acidly. "You don't even know me."

"Oh, but I do, Mr. Reynolds," I say darkly, meeting his gaze with a smile, silently taunting him to try me. "Remember? From your little 'misunderstanding' yesterday?"

I watch as Colton's eyes widen, shocked that I would call him out. Apparently, he is used to people keeping his dirty secrets hidden for him. Which may explain why he has held this entire family mentally hostage for so long. I, however, will afford him *no* such courtesy.

"I... I'm sure I don't know what you're referring to," he says nervously, realizing he is standing on quicksand.

"I think you do," I whisper lethally at him.

"Colton," Mr. Tyler says, forcing Colton's attention back to him. "What is going on here?"

Colton opens his mouth to resume control of the situation, but he is interrupted yet again.

"He cheated on me," Natalie's voice cuts him off, and I can feel her trembling, although her voice is firm. "That is the reason I called off the wedding two years ago. I found out that Colton had been cheating on me—repeatedly."

Her father steps back in shock.

"That is why I left, why I moved to Miami. And it is why I have kept my distance for the last two years. I have tried to respect his relationship to Ryan and our family, but he has been lying to you. To everyone," she continues.

"He *attacked* her, Uncle!" Steph snaps, glaring at Colton. "He's been stalking and pestering her since she got here! He kept asking for a second chance, and when she refused, he cornered her in the ballroom yesterday, and *attacked* her!"

"Natalie, please..." Colton steps toward her, pleadingly, but I put myself between them.

"Oh, no you don't. You're not getting anywhere near her again in my presence," I say authoritatively. "As I promised."

He looks at me stunned, and I can see the anger behind his eyes as if deciding if he is going to get physical with me. I narrow my eyes at him, wishing he would take a swing at me and give me a reason to kick his ass right here. Nothing would make me happier.

Well... maybe one thing...

Natalie's father looks at Colton, and then to his daughter, his mouth now hanging open in shock.

"Nat?" he asks softly. "Is this true?" He sounds devastated.

"Sir, if I could just—" Colton starts to say.

"I am not speaking to you!" Mr. Tyler shouts at Colton. "I am speaking to my *daughter*!"

Natalie hesitates, before swallowing and nodding her head. "Yes, Daddy. It is," she says quietly.

Colton breathes heavily, visibly shocked. He glares at Steph and I, before trying to mutter a response. "Look, Sir, it's not as bad as it sounds. It was just—"

"You shut your damn mouth, Colton!" Mr. Tyler's voice booms down the hall, and I feel Natalie jump. "You put your fucking hands on my daughter?!" Mr. Tyler shouts, grabbing Colton's shirt in his fist and backing him against the wall.

Colton has turned as white as a sheet, faced with the now terrifying Mr. Tyler. He says nothing as he has apparently run out of words.

"You ran around on my daughter, and then had the audacity to sit at our table and exploit our generosity?! Our sympathy?!"

Mr. Tyler's yelling is causing several of the wedding guests to stare. Josiah and Charlie look at me, silently asking if they are needed to help diffuse the situation, but I shake my head.

This is between the Tyler family and Mr. Tyler has it covered.

"Answer me boy!" he yells when Colton says nothing.

"Yes," Colton stammers, terrified.

Steph walks up and slaps Colton square across the face. "You fucking pig!" she shouts venomously.

Colton holds his cheek, but stares at the ground, unable to meet the gaze of Mr. Tyler, who has become a force to be reckoned with. He puts his face in Colton's and whispers through gritted teeth, clearly trying to hold on to whatever self-control he has left.

"You have five seconds to get out of my sight Colton or I will knock your ass out—here and now!"

I rub Natalie's arm as she settles against me. The truth is out. Colton has finally lost his hold on the Tyler family.

"Leave!" Mr. Tyler snaps, and Colton bolts down the hallway, with the red handprint glowing across his cheek.

Natalie's father glares after him, before taking a deep breath and turning to his daughter, his tone instantly softer and compassionate.

"Natalie…" he says as she moves to embrace him. "I am so sorry. I wish you would have told me."

"I know," she says softly. "But I didn't know how… until now." Her eyes catch mine and I feel them wash over me.

Mr. Tyler follows her gaze and looks up at me. He then kisses her cheek and whispers softly. "We will speak more on this tomorrow."

She nods with a smile, before returning to my side.

"Mr. Pace, I apologize you had to see that," Mr. Tyler says, straightening his jacket. "Our family events are not usually so… eventful."

"On the contrary, Mr. Tyler, I think you handled that better than I would have. As a father myself, I completely understand."

The intention in his eyes is unmistakable—he has just learned of his daughter's pain, and he wants to confirm that I, the newcomer, am not here to cause more of it.

"That is not news I would ever want to hear," I say as I stroke Natalie's arm gently.

"Please, enjoy yourselves," he says, smiling at his daughter. "I am heading to the bar, so I don't end up in jail this evening."

I extend my hand and we shake briskly with a nod before he turns and walks back into the ballroom.

"So…" Steph says, stepping up to me, extending her hand. "You must be Mr. Mysterious." Her face is devoid of the anger she had a moment ago, and now sports a hefty grin as I reach out and shake her hand. "Nice to finally meet you."

"Nice to meet you, too," I say, grinning back.

I feel like me and this girl could easily get along. Especially if I ever needed an extra bodyguard.

"Not *my* type, clearly." She winks at Natalie, wrapping her in a hug. "But I can see it for you. And I approve."

Natalie giggles and hugs her back. Then the feisty girl excuses herself, leaving the two of us standing here alone.

I look down at Natalie as she stares after Steph and her father. Slowly she turns to gaze up at me and I see the smile spreading on her face. Even though this was a dramatic turn of events, she seems to be at ease, and more relaxed. I may not understand completely, but I know this was a big moment for her.

I smile at her and kiss her forehead.

"Natalie, we can do something else entirely if you—"

But she cuts me off, wrapping her hands behind my head and pulling my lips to hers. She kisses me hard, making her intentions and her desires perfectly clear.

"So, your penthouse or mine?" she says confidently.

"Mine," I growl.

Chapter Twenty-Nine

Natalie

My pulse is racing but my mind is silent as Jaxon and I take the elevator up to the forty-fifth floor—Jaxon's penthouse.

He stands, leaning against the wall in the elevator with his hands in his pockets. He lifts his gaze from the floor to match mine, and I feel my blood heat instantly. I can't stop myself from crossing the distance between us and crushing my lips to his, giving into the passion in his kiss and pressing my body against his. In one swift motion, he spins me around and pins me against the wall of the elevator, shoving his tongue into my mouth and pulling my hips to his.

But the elevator doors sound, distracting us from our passion and opening to the lobby of his rooms. I wait to see what he will do, as he stands breathless. He closes his eyes in frustration and pulls himself away, motioning for me to take his hand. Taking it, I step into the lobby, following him into his penthouse.

Jaxon strokes his chin with his free hand but says nothing as we walk into the living room. All I want is for him to go back to ravaging me passionately.

Ugh, why do I want him this badly?

I keep getting the feeling he's holding back with me, which makes my efforts to let loose with him feel so much more exaggerated. I am burning with desire for him, while he is trying to control himself.

This makes me feel a bit awkward, as I am more than a bit unfamiliar with this territory. I want him, terribly, but I am quite inexperienced with being the aggressor when it comes to intimacy. I have only experienced it with one person, and it never felt like this. I have no idea what I am doing. Which makes me nervous, considering that I have been the one pushing for this almost all night, and yet I have no actual idea of *how* to take the reins.

I need a moment of privacy to collect my raging thoughts somewhere else, far from his incendiary gaze.

"May I use the bathroom?" I ask softly.

Did you really just ask him to use the bathroom, Natalie?

"Of course," Jaxon says, quietly. "It's in the hall."

Before he can catch me blushing, I turn on my heel and hurry down the hall. Shutting the door, I stop and lean over the sink, staring at myself.

My body is on *fire*.

I want Jaxon, maybe more than I have ever wanted anyone before. I just want him to throw me around the room and ravage me.

However, he does seem a bit more reserved than I thought he'd be.

Am I coming on too strong?

Perhaps he's used to initiating. And, if I'm being honest, I'm pushing hard for something I've never actually led before. I don't know what I'm supposed to do.

Maybe I just need to calm down and let things play out.

I stare at myself in the mirror, appreciating that this dress really is amazing, and impossibly perfect for my body. I decide to pull my hair out of the gentle updo Steph put it in, letting my golden curls fall around my face. When I decide I have a better grasp on my libido, I slowly grip the handle on the door, whispering out loud to myself, "You can do this."

When I walk out, I find the room is dark, but the gas fireplace flickers silently in the corner, casting shadows on the walls.

Jaxon's suitcoat lays strewn across the couch, and he stands staring out the windows to the balcony. He has a drink in one hand, and the other in his pocket. His tuxedo tie hangs loosely around his neck, and his muscles flex against the fabric of his dress shirt.

In the darkness he looks even more devilishly handsome, testing my resolve. He turns to face me, and I watch a wicked grin spread across his face, as my heart begins to pound.

"You let your hair down," he whispers darkly. "I like it."

I walk slowly into the living room, twirling a strand of my hair between my fingers, understanding that this is a view he enjoys. I stop a few feet from him and watch as his eyes canvas my body.

I stand there, letting him look at me, the act itself feeling incredibly intimate as I savor every moment of his attention. I want to go to him, but I also want *him* in control, and to make the first move in this.

"You are heartbreakingly beautiful, Miss Tyler," he says, interrupting my internal pep talk and causing my cheeks to heat instantly.

"Do you worry that I will break your heart, Mr. Pace?" I ask softly, trying to hide the fact that I am starting to shake a little under his intimidating stare.

"Oh yes," Jaxon says, smiling at me wickedly and taking a sip of his drink. "I'm all but certain of it,"

Oh my god...

"Is that why," I say softly. "You're suddenly so reserved with me now?"

The question slips past my tongue before my brain has officially caught up to this conversation. Jaxon now looks at me with a very confused expression on his face.

"Reserved?" he whispers.

Eeek! I didn't mean to say that!

"It... just feels like one minute you want me, and the next," I fade off, biting my bottom lip and taking another deep breath. "Well, it feels like you're trying to stop yourself. Like maybe you've changed your mind about wanting me."

Jaxon's eyes feel like they are going to stare right through my body, but he tilts his head to the side.

"Wait, Natalie, you think... that I don't *want* you?"

His voice is barely above a whisper, but the power behind it makes me tremble. The blazing look in his eyes threatens to set this whole damn penthouse on fire.

I swallow hard.

"Well, I—"

Instantly, he smashes the glass he is holding to the floor, shattering it into pieces. In the same moment he is on me, cradling my face and crushing his lips and his body to mine—hard.

Every thought in my head disintegrates and I melt into him. He pulls my body against his aggressively, and I feel his hand caress my back, working its way up into my hair. He gently pushes my chin back, forcing me to look up at him. I try desperately and pointlessly to calm my racing heart.

"I want you to understand something, Miss Tyler," he whispers. His voice is raw and dark as he trails gentle kisses down my neck, teasing me with his tongue. "For some reason, you keep telling yourself that you're not enough for me, and that I can't possibly want you. But nothing could be further from the fucking truth. You see, I keep telling *myself* that if I had any decency at all, I would tell you to run far away from me."

As he says this, he kisses the nape of my neck, and I feel my insides tense as my body floods with desire.

"I have already told you, I am not a *good* man, Natalie," he growls. "I am a hard man, and I live in a hard world... and I like to fuck *hard*."

Holy shit. Holy shit. Holy shit.

"If I am reserved with you, my dear, it's because while I can be a gentleman in public, or in front of your family, I am not being a gentleman in my head. I can't stop picturing myself ripping that dress off your delicious body, splitting your legs open on that table, and fucking your gorgeous brains out. So, believe me when I say..." He says as he slips his other hand through the slit in my dress, seductively tracing his fingers against the exposed skin on my thigh and pulling my leg upwards across his body. He slowly kisses up my neck to whisper in my ear, as I stop breathing entirely, "there is no part of me that doesn't *want* you."

I can feel his breath on my skin, and the stubble on his chin as he presses his mouth to my collarbone. He kisses a spot that makes me wet, feeling my groin pressed against his. All I know is that I want him to possess me completely, and immediately.

But then his hand gently touches my face in a way that is so different than how he had just manipulated my body. Kissing me softly, leaving me breathless and staring into his blue eyes, I feel the passion radiating from him. Instantly obliterating every doubt in my mind.

"I want *you* in ways I have never wanted anyone, Natalie," he whispers, trailing his thumb along my bottom lip slowly.

"Then take me," I whisper.

He stares into my eyes long enough for me to see them process what I just said, and for a devilish lust to glaze them over. Then his mouth is on mine again, and in an instant, he wraps his hands around the back of my thighs, and lifts my body in one smooth motion, wrapping my legs around him.

I kiss him back, giving into the passion I am feeling, and biting his bottom lip a little hard.

"Naughty girl," he chuckles. "How do I taste?"

"Sinful," I whisper back.

"I bet you taste better," he says against my neck. "What do you say we find out..."

My heart flatlines.

He carries me into the bedroom, smashing me down on his bed, his body on top of me, and his groin pressed against mine.

This is everything that I want.

I start unbuttoning his shirt, practically tearing at his buttons while shoving my tongue into his mouth. He moans against me, kissing down the plunging neckline of this dress, driving me crazy. He sits back and pulls off his dress shirt, and I find myself stunned at the beauty that is Jaxon.

To my complete surprise, tattoos lace his entire left arm—from just above the wrist until they engulf his whole left pec muscle.

I never had any indication that he even *had* a tattoo, let alone an entire sleeve of them.

But somehow it suits him, a man that has both light and dark inside him. The high-society billionaire, gentleman in the boardrooms, and yet also the rugged, bad-boy mafia Don Supreme in private. This unique duality somehow just makes him sexier to me. That and staring at his perfectly chiseled abs.

I want him. And I am going to have him. Right. Now.

He kisses me passionately as his strong hands knead my ass, gripping my hips and pressing me against him. I moan ready to give myself to him. He kisses down my neck and breasts—that press anxiously against the fabric of my dress. I thread my fingers through his hair, and press my chest hard against his face, pulling him to me.

He looks up at me, his blue eyes smoldering in the moonlit bedroom light, as I feel his hands slide up my back to the zipper of my dress, ready to undress me.

This is it. It's happening.

I close my eyes and wait, breathing heavily.

And keep waiting... but nothing happens.

When I finally open my eyes and look up at him, on top of me, I see that his face is livid. However, he is not looking at *me*. Instead, he is focused on something outside the window.

Before I can even wonder what could possibly be so interesting outside at one in the morning, he gets off of me and steps onto the floor.

"How the fuck…" I hear him mutter angrily under his breath.

"Jaxon?" I ask softly, confused. "What is it?"

But he says nothing. A terrifying and inexplicable rage now blanketing his face. I turn quickly to glance out the window, but see nothing, apart from some lights turning out in the building opposite ours. But when I turn back around, Jaxon has grabbed his shirt off the bed and has already stormed out of the room.

"Ethan, they just fucking made contact! Meet me upstairs in five minutes," I hear him say, obviously on the phone.

When did he have time to make a phone call? What the hell is going on?!

"Damnit!!"

I hear Jaxon yell, followed by glass breaking in the kitchen.

I take a deep breath and pull myself off of his bed. I slowly walk to the kitchen where Jaxon stands hunched over a table facing the windows, his shirt hanging unbuttoned on his torso. Broken glass lays shattered across the room, where it was obviously thrown.

"Jaxon?" I ask nervously, wrapping my arms across my body. "What's wrong? What's the matter?"

As he slowly turns to face me, I see his face is empty of the passion we shared a moment ago, instead now heavy with frustration.

"Natalie…" he whispers, hanging his head and looking off into the living room, swallowing another outburst. "I'm so sorry. Yet again something has happened, and I don't want to worry you, but I have to leave. Immediately."

"Immediately?" I gasp incredulously. "What?!"

He cannot be serious.

"You're kidding, right? Please tell me you're kidding?"

His eyes implore me, as I feel the rage and disappointment mounting in my chest.

"Did I," I ask breathlessly. "Did I do something *wrong*?"

"No! Not at all! This—"

"Then what the fuck is so important that you have to leave me? Now?! Again?!" I say, feeling myself shake in disbelief.

I'm aware how desperate and devastated I sound, but right now I do not care.

Jaxon had the wheel, and this was about to actually happen. But now he's suddenly decided to take a detour and I don't understand at all.

He stares at the floor, trying to find an answer.

Fuck this.

"Fine, forget it. I'll go!" I snap angrily, fighting back tears.

I turn and head toward the elevator.

"No wait, you can't," he says, reaching out and catching me in his arms, pulling me to him.

"*Excuse me*?!" I say, pushing him off of me.

"Natalie, listen to me. Remember how I told you that we aren't the only mafia family in Chicago? That there are other players in the game? Well, one of those players has just moved a piece."

"Jaxon, I have no idea what the fuck you are talking about! But this is bullshit, and I *am* leaving!" I step away from him, turning to leave.

"Natalie, they just threatened me," he says, his frustration mounting, the words like acid on his tongue. "And *you*."

I freeze on the spot, comprehending what he just said.

"M..me?" I whisper, turning to him. "What do you mean? Who would be threatening me?! I don't know anyone here?!"

"Well, they know you're involved with me," he says apologetically, his tone dark and lethal. "And they've already made it clear they aren't above harming people close to me to hurt me."

What the hell?

"What are you talking about, Jaxon?! I don't understand. You were just with *me*, alone, in your bedroom. How could they have just threatened you?!" I ask frantically, as none of this makes any sense.

Jaxon stares at me for a long moment before sighing heavily. He looks back at me and nods in that direction. I walk over to him, studying his face as he stares out the window.

But just as I turn to see what he is looking at, suddenly all the lights on the vacant forty-fifth floor of the skyscraper across the street from the Jefferson Hotel turn on... and then I see the message painted on its windows facing us.

WHO IS SHE JAXON?

My breath hitches in my throat, and my blood runs cold when I realize that this message was meant for *Jaxon* and I am the, *she*.

"What does this mean?" I choke out.

"It means someone wants to play," he growls. He steps beside me, pulling me to him aggressively and cupping my face in his hands. "And it means that no matter how much I don't want to leave you right now, it's also the only way I can protect you. And get you answers."

I don't have time to object or ask another question, because at this moment the elevator doors open and Ethan, Charlie, and Josiah walk in, accompanied by three men I have never seen before.

The air in the room feels heavy. Ethan looks furious. Charlie's usually cheerful face is solemn and serious. Josiah looks terrifying. They all stand silently appraising Jaxon, waiting for instructions.

"Jaxon, please, I still don't understa—" I start to say, but he kisses me, silencing my mouth but not my pounding, shattering heart that desperately does not want him to leave.

Especially to go somewhere dangerous.

"Listen to me, Natalie. I need you to stay here. Right now, this penthouse is the safest place in the city," he says, his eyes finding mine. "And I *need* to keep you safe."

"Jaxon…" I try to push away from him, but give up as he holds me tightly, his arms still wrapped around me. "I don't like this. I really don't want you to go."

The fear of something happening to him is nearly suffocating me.

"I know, I know," he whispers softly, pressing his forehead to mine.

"I can't believe you're leaving me right now," I say, trying to fight back tears. "This…this just isn't how this is supposed to go."

This night just went downhill quickly, and I feel like I have whiplash. Jaxon gently touches my chin and forces me to look at him. And then, as I see the concern painted on his face, I realize he doesn't want to leave me. But there's no other way.

"I am leaving Charlie and Josiah with you," he says softly. "Promise me you won't leave this penthouse until I tell you it is safe?"

My body is shaking, confused, and traumatized from the last five minutes, and all I can do is nod.

He kisses my forehead tenderly and takes a deep breath before tearing himself away from me, leaving me standing there breathless and broken. He buttons up his shirt, grabs his suit coat, and pulls a gun out of a drawer in the living room.

"Oh my God…" I say, my voice cracking into a soft sob. I turn away, bringing my hands to my face.

I don't want him to leave, but I *really* don't want him to leave and go anywhere that requires him to take *that* with him.

"Hey, hey, hey…" he says softly, walking quickly back over to me, pulling me in his arms again.

"You're taking a gun," I sob.

"I always take a gun, Sweetheart," Jaxon smirks at me, trying to downplay the seriousness of this moment.

"Please, don't go, Jaxon," I whisper tearfully. "Stay with me, please."

I look up at him, seeing my agony reflected in his eyes. He rubs his hands gently on my arms, kissing my hair and whispering in my ear so that only I can hear him.

"Natalie, I have to go handle this. I have to keep them away from you. And then I will come for you. I promise."

I breathe in deeply, inhaling the scent of him, before realizing that he is definitely leaving, and there is nothing I can say to convince him otherwise.

When I look up at him, he stares at me a moment before landing a bruising kiss on my lips, knocking all the wind from my lungs.

"I promise, Natalie," he says determinedly. "I *will* come for you. You can count on that."

"You better," I whisper, as I feel my heart breaking.

And then, before I can utter another word, Jaxon turns on his heel and walks out of the penthouse.

Chapter Thirty

JAXON

"Someone better explain to me what the fuck is going on!"

I at least wait until the elevator doors close and we are out of Natalie's earshot.

"Levi and his team are already in the building, Sir," Ethan responds. "We will know shortly."

I can tell he's just as concerned, and just as *pissed* as I am.

Well, maybe not entirely.

After all, Ethan wasn't half naked with a beautiful girl.

By the time we've reached the garage, I'm seething.

I cannot believe this is happening. I cannot believe these assholes have ruined my night with Natalie. Again. I'm concerned that they found a way to send me a message forty-five floors up to my penthouse. But what's concerning me the most, is the fact that the message included Natalie.

Why are they involving her in this mess?

"Jessica?" I ask Ethan privately as we get into the Range Rover.

"Secure," Ethan says, with a nod.

With this one word, I know that she is safe, and has been moved to the bunker at the safehouse with Old Nan.

My team speeds out of the garage and crosses the street. The building is a massive skyscraper, similar to mine. However, in this building individual floors are rented out by various different corporations.

Since it's nearly two in the morning, the building is obviously closed and locked down for the night. But Levi, my head of tech and surveillance, and one of the best hackers in the world, has already cracked through its security systems, allowing us access.

He's already upstairs, and in the process of surveying and mapping the floor that had the window message, with several other Beta squad members.

I'm angry.

I don't like being on the backfoot, and I don't like being the last one to know what's happening. My team makes it a priority to always be aware of any activity like this, and I don't like being forced to react. It puts us at a disadvantage, and that can make for a whole myriad of problems.

As I explained to Natalie last night, chaos is bad. It can bring attention from unwanted parties, so it's imperative that *we* are always two steps ahead in order to remain in control.

And right now, we are not.

We park just outside the lobby while we wait for the team upstairs to check out the floor, and make sure it is clear for entry.

"Sir, we have a problem," I hear Levi say over the radio.

"What's the problem?" Ethan asks.

"The painted message," Levi says, his voice trembling. "It's not paint, Sir. It's *blood*."

What?

"And," he sighs, heavily. "We have a man down up here."

"Get me upstairs," I growl at Ethan. "Now!"

"We're coming up," Ethan relays back to Levi and the team. "Do an Alpha sweep, *stat*!"

I can't believe this. Another one of my men is dead?!

"Who?" I ask.

"Levi, who is down?" Ethan asks into the radio.

"Sir, it looks like it's—" But there is only static, and then the radio goes silent.

"Fuck this," I snap. "I'm not waiting any longer while we are losing men."

"Jaxon, wait," Ethan says sternly.

But I'm not listening.

I'm out of the car and heading for the elevators within seconds, as my security detail rushes to catch up and run point. When we reach the forty-fifth floor, Ethan practically pushes himself in front of me, battling my stubbornness to ensure that everything is secure before letting me into the room.

Levi meets us in the lobby with the radio.

"Sir, I'm sorry. There is interference of some kind, but there's no signal on this floor," he fires off. "There's no Wi-Fi, hardwire, or any kind of signal whatsoever."

"What?" Ethan asks.

"I know, it doesn't make sense."

"How is that possible? I thought this building was a corporate conglomerate?" I ask.

However, as I round the corner from the elevators and into the main office area, I see that the entire floor is vacant, stripped down the bare bones. Cables and wires hang from the ceiling, various pieces of construction equipment lie scattered across the floor.

"What do we know?" Ethan asks, reading my mind.

"Apparently this space was rented six months ago by a company named THD," Levi explains. "They have multiple construction permits open for the space, but no one in management has seen them on-site in over a week."

"THD," I say looking at Ethan. "How much do you want to bet that it is an abbreviation for our new friends—The Two-Headed Dragon?"

"I would take that bet," he growls.

Jesus Christ.

"Where is our man?" I ask Levi.

"This way, Sir," he sighs, his eyes falling to the floor.

We cross the massive open space, carefully scanning for tripwires as we go.

The dead man's hands are tied, and the toes of his shoes are scuffed. Which means that he was most likely transported here against his will, from another location. When I see his face, I recognize him as Darnell, a fifth year Beta on the surveillance squad.

One of Levi's men.

It looks like he was strangled with a piece of cable, and his throat was cut. He lies in a pool of his own blood. Blood that apparently supplied the killer's choice of paint for the window message.

He was alive when his throat was cut.

"Sir, Darnell was one of two men that we sent in yesterday morning to have lunch and run surveillance at that restaurant near the underground garage," Levi states solemnly. "He is one of mine."

"How did he end up here?" I whisper, rage building in my chest from staring at yet another dead man from my family.

"I have no idea, Sir."

"Well, let's find out!" I snap, unable to control my frustration any longer. "I am so tired of that answer! How does no one know what the fuck is going on?"

I kick a box filled with cables and it skids across the floor.

"Damnit! We're supposed to be better than this! We are supposed to protect these men!" I shout, stepping away.

Calm down, Jaxon.

As frustrated as I am, I know that losing my cool and yelling at my men will do nothing to keep the morale up. And morale is incredibly important, especially after losing a comrade or subordinate.

I have to pull it together and support my team, or we will continue to keep making mistakes.

I rub my eyes and take a few deep breaths before turning back to Levi and the rest of my team.

"Okay, so what *do* we know?" I say, as calm as I can manage. "Walk me through the timeline. What were Darnell's last activities?"

"Sir, he checked in last night after he left the restaurant and went home," Levi says, swallowing hard. "He was off today, so the reason we weren't looking for him is because we weren't *expecting* to hear from him until tomorrow."

"Fuck," I say under my breath, as I start canvasing the floor.

I have to stop the bleeding.

"Put it on the wire," I say, rubbing my chin. "Until further notice, everyone is to check in with their supervisor every six hours. I don't care if they're on duty or not. If they miss a check-in by more than fifteen minutes, I want someone to go check on them."

"Yes, Sir!"

Even though he replies with enthusiasm, I can see in Levi's face that he's visibly shaken too. It's understandable considering this was a member of his squad, and I know that Levi does everything he can to look out for his men.

Since there's no signal, he heads to the balcony to radio headquarters. I follow him, intent on smoking, and trying to console him as best I can.

As the two of us step outside, we notice that the blood message is painted on the *outside* of the windows.

That's odd. It would be easier to paint it from inside.

However, just before we step out from underneath the canopy overhang, and onto the terrace, I notice wires on the ceiling and grab Levi by the arm, stopping him.

I point and he looks up to see what I am staring at. Six wires, leading to six different high-resolution cameras.

…All of which are aimed *directly* at my suite.

Holy shit.

I shake my head, silently warning him not to proceed onto the uncovered portion of the balcony, as it may put him in view of the cameras. Instead motioning for him to come back inside with me.

"Well, I think it is safe to say that you've been under surveillance for some time," Ethan says, rubbing his chin. "We should take those down and review the footage."

"I disagree, Sir," Levi says, turning to me. "I don't think we should touch them until we get you out of here."

"What? What?"

"Because, Sir, they could be explosive. When my team sets up cameras for surveillance, occasionally we set them up rigged to blow."

"Why?" I ask.

"In case their existence is discovered, Sir," Levi continues. "We do this so that no one else can get their hands on the footage we collect. I don't know if the Two-Headed Dragon has the same capabilities, but it's a risk I do not feel comfortable taking."

I nod slowly.

"I think Levi has a point," Ethan says. "They sent you that message to grab your attention, and they had to reasonably assume that once you saw it you'd find a way over here to investigate. This place could be rigged with anything."

"True," I say, thinking out loud. "But they haven't blown us up *yet*. Suggesting that they might not know we're here. If you think about it, they had no idea *when* I would see that message. They were just flashing it every five minutes to get my attention."

"That's true, Sir," Levi says, nodding. "And the blood was painted on the outside of the windows. Which means they clearly wanted us to step outside to investigate the patio. It's likely that we would've stepped in front of the cameras in the process. But we saw the wiring first, and didn't cross the line of sight or disturb them in any way."

"So, they may not know that we are here," I say, the wheels turning in my head as my team catches up. "At least not yet."

I glance around.

"Levi, you are sure there are no other cameras or tech on the interior of this floor?"

"Confirmed, Sir," he says. "We did a full sweep, and found no tech of any kind."

"And what are the chances that we could hack into those cameras remotely?" I ask. "To minimize the risk?"

"We can certainly try to break into their firewall," Levi says, following my train of thought. "I can have my team at the manor get to work on that."

"We have another development," Ethan suddenly says, staring at his phone. "Apparently the Pilgrim's Echo device just pinged."

Well, well, well.

"Where is she? Is she at least stateside?"

"She's closer than that," Ethan says, his face a mixture of confusion and caution. "She's in *our* harbor, trying to dock at the Rueben Warehouse,"

"Just a week late," I say softly. "Did they give a reason for their tardiness? Was there an issue or a holdup somewhere?"

"We don't know yet, Sir," Ethan says, reading the report. "Our warehouse team says the crew of the Pilgrim hasn't actually said anything over the radio. They're just repeating the docking request over and over…almost robotically."

"That's…odd."

I find it interesting that a ship would go missing with no communication, only to show up a week late, asking to dock where she was scheduled as if nothing were out of the ordinary.

"Allow her access," I growl. "But tell the team they are on high alert. No one enters or leaves that ship until I get there."

"Yes, Sir. I will also request backup."

"No," I say, shaking my head. "We're already stretched thin as it is, and all we have left to spare tonight are recruits. They are too green. I can't lose anyone else tonight."

"Levi, have your team start working on hacking into this camera system," Ethan says, turning to Levi. "But since we're already down a man without Josiah, I think you should come with us."

The mention of Josiah makes me think of Natalie and briefly wonder if she actually stayed put in the penthouse like I asked her to.

Charlie would surely tell me if she tried to leave.

…And he would stop her.

"Have someone bring Darnell back to the manor for a proper burial," I say to Levi as we are walking out the door.

"Yes, Sir!"

For the first time tonight I see the light return to Levi's eyes.

Good. I need him to be sharp and focused.

As we head down in the elevator, I take out my phone and see that I have a text from Natalie.

Natalie
1:49 a.m.: For the record, I'm still furious with you for leaving me. TWICE. But please be careful, Jaxon.

I didn't want to leave you either… but I had to.

I stare at the message but cannot think of a reply. I'm nowhere near the mindset to text right now. My head is wrapped up in dead soldiers, surveillance footage, and a prodigal ship filled with hallucinogenic drugs finally coming home to her moorings… a fucking week late.

As we get into the Range Rovers downstairs, I put the phone back in my pocket. I'll have to respond later.

Natalie would not approve of what I'm about to do.

I know the man I need to be tonight.

When we reach the warehouse, my anger has reached a fever pitch. We were notified that the ship entered the warehouse a few minutes before our arrival. No further movement from the crew has been detected. In fact, no crew have been *seen* in the ship, even when they were navigating her into the hold.

As Ethan opens the door into the warehouse, Wesley scrambles to meet us. I can't help but think he looks so young, reminding me of what happened to Bruno at this very warehouse, and making my stomach churn.

"Sir, we have secured the vessel and advised them that they are to remain in place until otherwise instructed!" he says quickly, albeit a little nervous.

However, his attitude is much more important than the lackadaisical one he was sporting yesterday morning.

Ethan's reprimand must have hit home.

"Good," I say as I walk past him. "Any movement?"

"No, Sir. When the ship navigated into the harbor, we got a docking request, which sounded like a male," he says quickly. "But not a peep since. They haven't attempted to communicate since the docking."

Interesting.

"Get me the intercom," I say to Wesley.

As he runs off to find it, I take off my jacket, rolling up my sleeves. Then I survey the scene as I walk around the front of the ship, canvasing the massive warehouse.

This warehouse is a one-of-a-kind facility. The dockside portion has a retractable floor that allows the ship to pull inside completely inside the warehouse. The floor basically works like a reversed garage door, retracting when in use, and sealing securely when empty.

This amenity was meant to accommodate offloading in bad weather. But given the 'wandering' of the ship as of late, and the obscure behavior of the crew tonight, I've asked my men to allow her inside and close the door. She is now fastened in place with the dock clamps, sitting silently.

Around the warehouse, stacks of pallets are neatly arranged, and two large yellow cranes sit on either side of the dock, ready to remove the heavy shipping containers.

Even though my crew has managed to scrub the place down since the incident a few days ago, I still feel uncomfortable glancing up at Max positioning himself on the catwalk.

…The same catwalk where Bruno died.

As for the rest of my men, I have Ethan, Levi, and Travis as my point team, as well as Wesley and a handful of the Beta warehouse team on hand, with guns at the ready.

"Travis, join Max and be my eyes in the sky," I say. "Bring one of the Betas with you."

"Yes, Sir," he says obediently.

Wesley returns moments later with the intercom on a portable disk. I turn on the microphone, purposefully allowing the feedback to squeal loudly through the building, knowing it echo loudly in the ship.

I want their attention.

"Good evening, Pilgrim," I say into the microphone. "We are glad to see you finally found your way home."

There is no response from the ship. Not a single sound.

"You are now hereby ordered to disembark, one at a time from the port-side exit only. Once you are on the deck—"

Machine gun fire suddenly rips through the air from the deck of the Pilgrim, cutting me off.

Instinctively my men scramble to find cover. One of the men on the scaffold above screams out in pain, taking a bullet to the leg. Ethan and Levi take cover behind one of the massive cranes, and I flip the table next to me and crouch behind it. However, the table I have propped up behind me takes two bullet holes without putting up much of a resistance, so I know I need to get better cover.

"All hail the Two-Headed Dragon!" I hear someone shout from the deck of the Pilgrim.

Jesus Christ...

I see a stack of crates next to a metal staircase and decide that is my best bet given the proximity. I take off running and almost make it before a bullet grazes my left arm.

"Fuck!" I shout, as I hunker down quickly.

"Sir! Are you okay?!" I hear Wesley yell, and I look up to see him behind another stack of crates a few yards away.

I panic momentarily, seeing him contemplating running to me.

He won't make it without getting hit. I must stop him.

"Wesley, I am fine, it's just a scratch. Listen to me, stay exactly where you are! Do not come to me! Do you hear me?!"

"Yes, Sir!"

I turn my attention back to the boat. The port-side exit is open now and there are two men trying to exit down the ramp. There are also two men on the deck of the ship providing cover, and I suspect one of them was the one that hit me. My arm is bleeding, but the wound isn't too deep. Ethan and Levi are still well protected. Max has made it to the foreman's office and has taken cover, but Travis is still on the scaffold, trying to get the injured man to cover in the foreman's office. They are sitting ducks.

Fuck this. I am not watching them die.

I take a deep breath and open fire on everyone near the ship. Round after round, I pepper the four men I see. One of my bullets hits a shooter on the ramp in the neck and he immediately drops, blood spraying everywhere.

One down.

But my success angers the other guys on the deck, motivating them to take direct aim at me. To make matters worse, I am nearly out of ammo, and I see four more men come barreling down the ramp and take cover. Now we have eight active shooters.

I need to get out of this location, and I need to get to the locker room where we have more appropriate weapons stashed. But that means I will have to cross over to the direction of the crates Wesley is hiding under.

"Wes," I shout at him between shots. "I am coming to you! I need you to cover me! Now!"

"Yes, Sir!"

He stands up, unloading the payload of his pistol towards the ship. As he does this, I sprint as fast as I can over to him, luckily making it to him without taking another bullet.

"Wesley, I need to get into that locker room where the machine guns are!" I say, trying to catch my breath.

"Fuck!" I hear Levi cry out, and I turn to see that he has taken a ricocheted bullet to the side.

I have to act quickly before all of my men are completely slaughtered.

"How many bullets do you have left?!" I shout to Wesley.

"Twelve, Sir!" he says, evaluating quickly.

"Okay, now you have seventeen!" I say, handing him the five bullets I have left in my gun. "We just have to get from this spot to that room! But every single bullet needs to count!" I say carefully.

I hate the idea of having this kid as my protection, but I have no choice. This is slipping out of my hands quickly. My Alpha Squad is outnumbered, and I know there is an AK-47 in the lockup, which is about ten yards from here, but it's a handprint lock.

"Are you ready?!" I ask, taking a deep breath.

"I got you, Sir!" he says confidently, a wild look flashing in his eye.

"Okay, Kid. I'm counting on you!" I count to three in my head then shout, "Now!" And at this moment Wesley and I take off for the locker room.

Time slows, and I count as Wesley fires off each of the seventeen bullets. One of the shooters screams, before falling lifelessly over the edge of the ship into the water below.

His bullet found its mark!

We slid into the locker room just as the dead man's brokenhearted pal opened fire on us with his semi-automatic. Closing the door behind us and getting out of harm's way. I immediately find the weapon lock-up and grab a bulletproof vest, the AK-47, and wrap a bandolier of ammo around me. I grab two extra pistols and a knife, before turning back to Wesley.

"Good shootin', Tex," I say, slapping my hand on his shoulder. Wesley beams with pride.

But then, all of a sudden, he collapses to the floor.

What the fuck?!

"Yo, Kid, you okay?"

But when I see the dark red stain down his left leg and understand that somewhere in the shootout Wesley took a bullet. His adrenaline must have carried him onward, but now it's likely wearing off, and he is starting to feel the weight of his injury.

Fuck me, he's losing a lot of blood.

Instinctively I take off my belt, quickly wrapping it around his leg in a tourniquet. He says nothing but he starts to tremble, a smile creepily plastered across his face.

Shock. He is going into shock.

"Hey! You stay with me, okay?!" I shout. "Just stay the fuck with me!"

He nods, but I see the panic in his eyes. I have seen it before. I pull the tourniquet tighter, trying to stem his blood loss.

"This is your first gunshot wound, isn't it, Kid?" I ask, already knowing the answer. Wesley's eyes fall to his leg, and I see the panic flash across his face again.

"Hey!" I say, snapping my fingers and trying to pull his attention off of his bleeding leg and back to me. "Don't look at that. Eyes up here with me. Stay with me. Is this your first gunshot wound?"

"Yes," he says warily. "It is...Oh God. That's a lot of blood. Is there supposed to be that much blood?"

No... not really.

"Yes, this is totally normal," I lie. "It's not that bad. You are going to be fine."

I need to keep him calm.

"Deep breaths, okay? That is going to help keep you conscious."

I can still hear the gunshots in the warzone outside the door, and I know my team needs me. However, I need to make sure Wesley is stable first. I grab my phone from my pocket and dial headquarters.

"Sir, Ethan already alerted us, and we're on-site, pulling into the parking lot now!" one of my backup Beta squad answers.

"How many of you are there?!" I shout into the phone.

"Sir, there are two of us arriving now, and another ten enroute!"

"Be advised: use the back entrance, we are taking heavy fire in the loading bay, and we have at least two men injured—one needs medical attention immediately! I need you to come directly to the locker room, and you will need medical evac!"

"Copy that, Sir, we are coming in now!"

"You hear that kid?" I say to Wesley, keeping his eyes focused on me. "They are already here, and they're going to get you patched up. So you can't quit on me now."

"Yes, Sir."

He looks up at me, sweat dripping down his brow. I can see the shock threatening to take over, his eyes starting to roll back in his head.

"Listen to me, Wesley, you did good, okay? You did really fucking good! So I need you to stay alive, because I'm going tell everyone back at base *who* saved my ass tonight, okay? I can't do that if you are dead, so you have to hang on!"

A glimmer of recognition flashes in Wesley's eyes. "Yes, Sir!" he says, mustering a grin.

I hear the back door open, and I immediately point my gun in that direction

"Identify yourself!" I shout.

"Beta 238 and 321, Sir! Code: Islamorada!"

These are my men.

"Hurry up! The kid is down! He needs medical transport back to base immediately!"

"Yes, Sir!"

Both of them reach Wesley, and immediately get to work.

He might have a shot at surviving this.

"Don't you die on me, Wesley," I snap. "That's a fucking order, do you understand?"

"Yes, Sir!" He smiles.

I turn to the two men who are here. "Get him back to base, go now! Then send the medical transport back with whatever replacements you can find! If any of us survive, I guarantee we're going to need it."

They nod.

I turn my attention back to the gunfight happening in the loading bay.

I kick open the door, and squeeze the trigger on my rifle.

Levi is pinned down and severely outgunned or out of ammo. I pump several rounds into the man shooting at him before sliding over to Levi. I hand him one of the extra pistols and clips I grabbed from the lock-up.

"Where's Ethan?!" I shout.

"There!" Levi point. "He took out one of them!"

I see Ethan crouched down with blood on his neck.

Is that his blood, or someone else's?!

I have no idea, but at least he's alive. However, he can't have many bullets left.

"Ethan!" I shout to him. "Here!"

He turns to look at me, relief flashing in his eyes. I slide one of the other pistols across the floor to him. Once he's reloaded, the three of us take aim at the deck shooters once again. Providing enough cover that Levi and I can make our way over to Ethan.

"Where the *fuck* is the calvary?!" Ethan shouts angrily. "Did they stop for fucking takeout?!"

"They're almost here!" I shout back.

"Good, because we're almost dead!"

"How about we end this?!"

A devilish grin flashes across Ethan's face, and he nods.

"Levi," I shout. "Now!"

All at once, the three of us go on the offensive. I turn my attention to the scaffold, where one of my men lays motionless.

Travis and Max are taking fire from a man in an all-black jumpsuit.

The man from the video the other night.

As I open fire, I see the man clad in black scramble, knowing he will be an easy target no matter which way he chooses to run across the scaffold. The man grabs the railing of the scaffold and flips himself over it into a pile of crates on the floor. I fire several rounds at him on his way down and see him crumple and fall into the stack of crates messily.

Well, that's the end of him!

Next I focus on the two other men on the deck of the ship. Two rounds and one is dead.

Now we can move about more freely.

We still have two active shooters, but we are resupplied, and back-up will be arriving any minute. Ethan takes out one of the remaining shooters on the deck with a well-placed bullet right between his eyes. Levi does his part by putting a bullet into the back of one of the other gunmen, as he tries to take cover behind a stack of crates.

As I head towards the ship, scanning for the final gunman, I find that one of my earlier bullets must have found its mark. As I find the last shooter with a gunshot wound to the neck. He lies paralyzed on the floor, dying slowly.

I step over him, leaving him to die.

He will get no fucking mercy from me tonight.

"I have six confirmed!" Ethan shouts to me.

"Seven!" I shout back, glancing around for the man who fell

from the scaffold. "One is missing!"

The gunfire ceases, and the warehouse becomes eerily quiet, but my ears are still ringing. My attention turns to the ship, as Ethan approaches me quickly.

"We need to sweep the ship." I say breathing heavy.

"Right behind you," Ethan says, reloading his gun with a new clip.

"Levi, check on our men up top!" I say, pointing to the motionless man on the scaffold. "And if anything else kicks off, stay down and just wait for back-up!"

"Copy that, Sir!"

Ethan and I head up the ramp, slowly and meticulously scanning all around us, making sure we have not missed someone. As we enter the ship, we see all of the cargo intact, but also various communication devices and computers have been set up inside.

This is strange...

The thin hallways are quiet as we move, the only sound is that of the ship groaning in her hold.

Whoever took over The Pilgrim had to be aware of the cargo.

There's no doubt in my mind now that they had planned to bring the ship here. They planned for this bloody fight to ensue. The Pilgrim had simply been a Trojan horse.

I silently point to Ethan, motioning for him to sweep the back of the ship, as I take the front. As I make my way, I see the computer screens begin flashing, and beeping with indecipherable coding. And then I hear shuffling ahead, each movement echoing loudly down the metal hallway.

There's someone else.

Not wanting to give away the advantage of surprise, I continue on alone, heading to the bow of the ship. I see the door to the bridge is open, and there is someone inside, frantically typing on a computer.

I bet he's trying to delete the data!

"Freeze motherfucker!" I yell, kicking the door open, aiming my gun at his back.

The man freezes.

It's the man in the black jumpsuit...who killed Bruno.

Slowly he starts to turn around.

"I said freeze!" I shout.

"Is that you, Jaxon?" he says in an effeminate voice.

How does he know it is me?

"I said freeze asshole! Or I'll dust your ass right here!"

"No, you won't do that," the man teases. "I know how much you love to play *games*, and the game isn't over yet. Not even close. You still don't know the rules."

"I make the rules, motherfucker. And since you and your pals decided to shoot up my warehouse and my men, I can't wait for you to tell me alllll about it!" I reply venomously, moving closer to him.

"Oh, you think I'm going to let you beat and torture me to death?" he says sarcastically. "Yeah… I think not."

He whips around, kicking me in the ribs and lunging at me with a tactical knife, slicing my arm and stabbing at my ribcage. I double over as he makes contact between my vest. He kicks the gun from my hands and slashes at me several more times, leaving more gashes on my skin. I kick him in the stomach, causing him to stumble, but he quickly recovers.

"Arrrrgh!" he growls, lunging at me once again.

I swing at him, punching him in the ribs. However, he grabs my arm, knocking me off balance while somehow managing to slip a nylon cord around my neck.

Fuck!

I frantically try to work my fingers behind the cord, trying desperately to prevent him from strangling me, but he has the upper hand now.

"You know what your problem is, *motherfucker*?" he asks, pulling the cord tighter around my neck. "You have always been too fucking confident for a man who knows nothing about anything! I had no idea you were going to show up tonight, and it technically *isn't* time to kill you yet. But I guess sometimes exceptions need to be made!"

I struggle against him, but can't get enough leverage to free myself or strike back. I'm slowly losing oxygen.

I am going to die here.

I think of my daughter, and how I will never get to hear her laughter again. I continue fighting, but my consciousness starts slipping under the strangulation.

I think of Natalie, and how I will never get to hold her again and or see her smile.

No! I'm not ready to die. I have so much to live for!

I need to see my daughter again. I need to watch her grow up and go to college, or become an artist, or even fall in love! And Natalie, the recent but powerful glimmer of hope in my dark world. I need to feel her soft lips and hear the sound of her voice.

If I am gone, who will protect them?!

No! I am not fucking dying today!

Reminded of all the reasons I have to fight, I summon all my strength and place my foot on the wall and push back as hard as I possibly can.

"Arrrgh!" I grunt, smashing my attacker into the control panel desk. He doesn't let go, but his grip loosens, allowing my hand underneath, and allowing me to grab a full breath. Then I pull the knife out of my pocket and jam it upwards behind my head.

It connects hard with his face, and hot blood sprays the back of my head and neck.

"Ahhh! My fucking eye!" He screams, releasing the cord and recoiling backwards. Blind and bleeding he bolts from the room, smashing into the walls as he scrambles down the hall.

Grabbing my gun I point it after him but hesitate, knowing that shooting aimlessly in a metal ship could cause the bullet to ricochet. And before I can get a clear shot off, the bleeding masked man disappears out of sight.

I stumble, trying to breathe and struggling to get my bearings now that oxygen has been restored to my lungs. I somehow manage to open the window in the bridge and yell out to my team, my voice hoarse and raspy.

"We have another gunman on site! He has knives!"

No sooner do I say this is when I suddenly hear gunfire again in the loading bay, as well as shouting.

"He is heading for the yard!" Someone yells.

More gunfire, more shouting, but my ears are ringing. I collapse onto the floor, and then everything goes dark.

Chapter Thirty-One

Natalie

I sit on the balcony, wrapped in a thick fleece blanket until I lose track of time. Only when Charlie steps outside to light the fireplace am I reminded I'm not alone.

"Miss Tyler?" he asks softly. "Are you okay? It's a little cold out here. Would you like to come inside?"

I wipe my eyes and turn to him but say nothing. I don't know what to say.

Charlie's brown eyes scan mine, ultimately deciding against whatever he had been planning to say. Instead, he just walks over and sits down next to me. We sit like this for several minutes, saying nothing, just staring at the fire.

At least it's nicer than being alone.

"I can't imagine what you're thinking," He says softly. "About all of…this."

"You're right Charlie," I say softly. "You can't. I'm not sure anyone can. One minute I feel like I am going insane, and the next, I feel like I am already there," I say under my breath.

"This life," Charlie sighs, "Well…it just isn't for everyone."

My eyes fall to my lap. That's what I have been sitting here thinking about for hours. Jaxon, Ethan, Josiah, and even Charlie— all of them live a life I could not comprehend.

"But it isn't as bad as you might think it is," he continues. "At least, maybe not as bad as you think it is right now, at this moment anyway."

"What do you mean? I've only been around a few days, and I feel like I've been in danger nearly the whole time. And now Jaxon has run off *toward* the danger, and I don't know how to make sense of it… or why I'm worrying for him."

I try to stop my voice from cracking, but I can't. Nor can I stop the tears that well in my eyes again. Charlie hands me his handkerchief and gives me a look of pity.

"What am I doing here, Charlie?" I dab at my eyes. "I mean, I barely know Jaxon, and yet I have all these feelings and I'm sitting in his penthouse worrying about him. How can I feel this way about someone I barely know? What is wrong with me?"

I feel so ridiculous. Charlie puts his hand on mine.

"There is *nothing* wrong with you, Miss Tyler. Sometimes our hearts do things that don't make sense to our heads. But, you shouldn't be ashamed that you care for Mr. Pace. There is nothing wrong with that. It's beautiful."

"*Beautiful*? Does this look beautiful to you?" I say incredulously, motioning to my tearful pathetic self.

"Yes," Charlie smiles softly.

Shaking my head, and snorting to myself I sit back against the couch, feeling pathetic.

"How is *this* beautiful?"

Charlie takes a deep breath then turns to face me.

"Miss Tyler, I know there's nothing I could say to make this better for you," he says, swallowing hard. "But, could I perhaps tell you a story?"

What?

I look up at him, attempting to control the shock on my face, especially knowing how hard it was to get him to tell me anything about his life before. So instead, I just nod.

"My father died when I was only three-years-old. I barely remember his face, let alone his voice or his laugh or anything about him," he says as he sits forward with his elbows on his knees, rubbing his hands together and staring at the fire. "But my *mother* remembered. She'd tell me stories about my father, and she'd laugh and smile as she told them. It might sound silly, but it felt like he came back to life… if only until the end of the story."

He smiles, closing his eyes and taking a deep breath.

"My mother told me of how my father used to make her laugh until she cried, and how she always felt safe with him, no matter what was going on in their lives. It was her way of remembering him, while also making sure that I never forgot him."

I smile, unable to look away.

"But my favorite story of all, was the story of the day they met. She told me when she saw him, and he saw her, it felt like two planets colliding. She'd never met him before that day, and yet she felt an instant connection to him that seemed to answer every question she had…before she could even ask it. She said it was as if every step she had taken in her life had been secretly bringing her closer to that moment, and to *him*."

Wow…

"She said it was *magic*. Like she knew the moment she met him that she was meant for him, and that he was meant for her." Charlie smiles, lowering his gaze to the ground. "I may have no real memories of my father, but I've never doubted my mother, or the love she carried for him. I believe in that love."

"That is beautiful Charlie," I say softly. "It's incredible."

"But you're missing the point, Miss Tyler," Charlie says, putting his hand on mine again. "When I see you and Mr. Pace, I see my mother's story come to life. I see what she was talking about, in your eyes when you talk about him…and when *he* talks about *you*."

I think I have stopped breathing. In fact, I am sure of it. I am just sitting here frozen, staring at Charlie.

"I know our life might seem crazy or overwhelming as someone who is outside of our world, but love," he pauses as his eyes scan mine, "*real* love doesn't care where two people come from. Only that they somehow find each other. And when they do it is pure magic."

Charlie smiles warmly at me.

"I've been with Mr. Pace for a long time now, and I have never seen him act this way with anyone. I don't think he even realizes it. And, if he does, he certainly does not have a clue on how to handle it."

I smile too, wrapping my arms around my body.

Now that's probably true.

"I'm sure he's struggling with how to let you into his world. But he *is* trying," Charlie says, his eyes filled with sincerity. "And he's trying for *you*. He cares for you, Miss Tyler, and I know you care for him, too."

I can't fight the tears welling in my eyes.

"But… it feels so overwhelming," I whisper.

"It's supposed to be. It's supposed to be fireworks and magnetism. Passion and panic. It's supposed to make you feel alive."

I feel myself shaking, Charlie's words lingering on my heart like the fog after a soft rain.

"I *do* care for him, Charlie," I say softly. "But how do I know I can handle the life he lives? All of *this*?" I stand up and walk towards the balcony. "I mean, even if what you're saying is true, and he does feel the same way, how do we even do this? And how often will he be leaving me to go running off *towards* danger?"

I bite my bottom lip, trying to stop it from trembling.

"This is terrifying. And I…" I say, hearing my voice crack. "I just don't know if I'm brave enough to handle this."

I brace myself against the edge of the balcony and stare off towards the building where the message had been painted.

Am I brave enough to handle that?

"In my experience, sometimes you don't know until you know," Charlie says behind me. "You'll have a choice to make, and you'll know then if you're going to stay and fight, or if you *can't*."

I turn to face him.

"All I can tell you is that real love is rare, and that once you find something that sets your soul on fire… you'll never be the same."

My heart aches.

I don't know how to feel right now. I definitely feel that passion with Jaxon. I know the pull I have to him that I cannot explain, and the desire to be with him every waking second.

But can I reconcile the life he leads with the life I have?

My thoughts are interrupted, however, as Josiah suddenly steps outside onto the terrace.

"Charlie, we have a problem," he says, looking nervous.

Oh no. If Josiah is worried this can't be good.

"What kind of problem?" Charlie asks, as we both immediately head inside. Josiah hands him an iPad, with what appears to be a security camera viewing two men standing in an elevator.

The *private* elevator.

"These two guys are on their way up. They have our uniforms, but I do not recognize either of them, and no one said anything about sending replacements."

"Please don't leave me," I say, grabbing Charlie's arm. "I know you both, I trust you, I don't want to be left alone with men I don't know."

"Oh, that won't happen, Miss Tyler," Josiah says, as he takes his gun out of his suit coat and heads towards the foyer.

"But just in case, you need to get out of sight," Charlie says to me. "At least until we can verify who they are and what is going on."

He walks quickly to a cabinet and pulls out a gun, handing it to me and pointing towards the main bedroom.

"Lock yourself in the bathroom—it doubles as a safe room. This gun is loaded, and you turn the safety off like this," he says, demonstrating for me. "If anything should happen to us, you stay in the bathroom until Ethan or Mr. Pace comes for you. Got it? No one else."

"What about you?!" I ask frantically, my hands shaking around the gun.

I don't want to leave Charlie and Josiah alone.

"Five seconds!" Josiah says, staring at the tablet.

"Go!" Charlie whispers. "We'll be fine!"

My heart is racing as I sprint for the bedroom.

I turn off the lights, cracking the door just a few inches in hopes to hear what happens next.

But instead of heading into the bathroom like Charlie instructed, I pause, peering through the crack in the door. Josiah is poised directly opposite me, his gun concealed inside his suit coat, while Charlie leans against the kitchen island facing the foyer. He shoots a look towards the darkened bedroom, just as the elevator dings.

I tighten my grip on the pistol in my hands.

I've never even fired a gun before… could I really do it?

"Good evening, gentlemen. Can we help you?" I hear Charlie say, and I stop breathing.

I see through my peephole as the men slowly walk towards Josiah and Charlie. They indeed are wearing the same attire as all of Jaxon's men. One of them has his hair tied back in a ponytail on top of his head, and the other is a shorter man with a buzz cut.

"We were sent here for Miss Tyler," the ponytail man says. "We're here to relieve you."

"Sent here for Miss Tyler?"

I don't like the way he said that.

And the idea that Jaxon would send someone to replace Charlie and Josiah, after only being gone an hour, seems certainly suspicious.

Charlie is apparently not falling for it either.

"Ah, well that's kind. But as you can see, we have the situation totally under control and we are wide awake. So, you're not needed," he says, clapping his hands together.

"Where is she?" the shorter man asks, glancing around the penthouse. "We are supposed to verify she's here."

"I'm afraid she's already turned in for the night," Charlie lies smoothly, and points to the guest bedroom at the opposite end of the penthouse. "And as I already mentioned, we're all set here."

"That's not up to you buddy."

"You know, I didn't catch your name. I'm not sure I have seen you around before?" Charlie asks, narrowing his eyes at the man.

"You haven't."

"What are your verification identifiers?" Charlie asks.

But instead of answering, the man suddenly takes a swing at Charlie, cracking him upside the head with his gun. At the same time, his friend attacks Josiah, trying to get his gun from his hands and smashing his head into the wall in the scuffle.

I hear a shot go off and see Josiah fall to the ground.

Oh my god! Josiah!

I gasp softly and cover my mouth with my hand. The man races down the hall towards the guest bedrooms, while his friend holds a gun on a recovering Charlie, who has fallen to his knees.

"Don't move a fucking muscle asshole," the buzzcut man says. "Drop your gun."

Charlie obeys slowly, placing his weapon on the ground and raising his hands in the air. The man steps on Charlie's gun and kicks it behind him. I watch as the ponytail man kicks open both doors to the guest bedrooms and switches on the lights...searching for *me*.

Holy shit!

My heart is pounding in my ears. I look towards the bathroom, knowing I should lock myself in there. But my feet will not move.

I cannot just leave Charlie and Josiah to die here.

"Okay asshole, nice try," the man with the ponytail says as he approaches. He pulls out his gun and points it at Charlie. "Let's try this again. Where is she? I'm not going to keep running all over this place looking for her."

Charlie will not give me away. This I know.

He will die here, in front of me...he will die for me.

"You'll have a choice to make, and you'll know then..."

Charlie's words from earlier seem profoundly pertinent right now. I look down at the gun in my hands and flip the safety, making my decision.

I might not succeed, but I sure as hell have to try.

Time slows and I suddenly feel every movement my body is making.

I open the door and point the gun at the man, squeezing the trigger. The gun goes off and recoils painfully in my hand, causing it to sting and tingle. The bullet hits the man's shoulder, and the impact causes him to recoil backwards, flailing his arms about. The momentary look of surprise on Charlie's face disappears, and he immediately overpowers the falling man and disarms him. He fires two shots, killing him instantly. He straddles the buzzcut man, and I see the two of them wrestling until I hear the sound of snapping bones.

His neck is broken. He is dead.

I finally lower the gun, dropping it to the floor and race towards Charlie, who slides off the lifeless man. A streak of blood trickles down his forehead from where he was struck, but he looks at me, relieved.

"Miss Tyler, that was an excellent shot!" he says, his eyes wide. "But I told you to lock yourself in the bathroom?"

"Yeah well, then I guess you're lucky I don't listen very well," I say sarcastically, trying to ignore the fact that there are two dead bodies lying on the ground next to me.

Focus on Josiah. Josiah needs help.

Fortunately Josiah is starting to regain consciousness as I kneel beside him. He has a gunshot wound to his leg, and there is a puddle of blood around him. But it's clear that the bullet didn't hit a major artery or he would be dead already.

Even still, he is bleeding heavily, so I press hard on the wound.

"Charlie, we need to get him to a hospital!"

Charlie pauses, and a pained look crosses his face. Suddenly Josiah puts his hand on mine as I press on his wound.

"Miss Tyler," Josiah says softly. "We can't leave until Mr. Pace gives us the green light. No exceptions."

"Are you serious?!" I ask exasperated. "Josiah, you got shot! This is serious. You could die!"

I look at Charlie, but the look on his face tells me they will not disobey these orders.

"Fine!" I snap, frustrated. "Are there at *least* any medical supplies in this penthouse?!" I ask quickly.

"Yes, in the bathroom, I will get them!" Charlie says, and races down the hall.

I turn back to Josiah, who is trying to stay alert.

"Ma'am?" Josiah asks me. "How bad is it?"

"You're okay, Josiah. You've been shot, but it's not too bad. We are going to get you fixed up, okay?"

I see him wince with pain but take out a hand-held radio. He breathes heavily as he tries to sit up.

"Eagle's nest to base. We've had two intruders in the penthouse. Shutdown the elevator access immediately until further notice."

"Roger that. Any casualties?"

"Not ours," he grunts, as he tries to sit up and maneuver himself to a more comfortable position.

"Josiah! I need you to stop moving!"

I feel bad for snapping at him, but I need to make sure he doesn't shift the bullet into a worse position than it's already in.

His eyes find mine and he smiles.

"My apologies, Ma'am."

"Here you are, Miss Tyler," Charlie says, handing me the first aid kit.

I look at what he gave me and realize it is nothing more than a typical drugstore first-aid kit.

"This is it? This is all you have here?!"

Charlie looks confused.

"Charlie, this is useless. I can't put a band-aid on a *bullet wound.*"

"I'm sorry, Miss Tyler," Charlie says. "But this is all we have here at the penthouse."

"Jesus Christ. I can't believe that living the dangerous life you guys live you don't even have a real medical kit anywhere! You're going to need to get mine from my room."

"But you can't take the elevators," Josiah says, wincing. "I just had the base shut them down so that we don't have any more unwanted guests."

"I'll take the stairs!" Charlie says, turning for the door.

"Charlie," I say before he leaves. "Please also grab me something…um…more *appropriate* to put on."

I realize this is a personal request, but I already have blood all over this expensive gown, and it's not very functional.

"Yes, Ma'am!" Charlie says as he darts out of the room.

"Josiah, you're very lucky. It doesn't appear to have hit your femoral artery."

"I don't know what that is," he says with a chuckle. "But consider me grateful."

"Are you conscious enough to put pressure on this wound while I get some supplies? Can you do that?"

"Yes, Ma'am," he nods.

Leaving Josiah, I run into the bathroom and grab as many towels as I can carry. Then, having remembered seeing Jaxon's office, I head in there and snatch a pair of scissors off the desk.

As I head back into the living room, I see Jaxon's bar across the room.

"What's your poison, Josiah?" I ask quickly.

"Ma'am?"

"Whiskey? Bourbon? Vodka?"

"Um, whiskey, ma'am," he says, a very confused look on his face.

I grab the bottle and head over to him. I unscrew the lid and take a swig, bracing myself for what will come next.

"Here," I say, handing the bottle to Josiah. "Since we can't get you to a hospital, this is the only other anesthetic we have. I'm going to have to fish that bullet out… and I promise that is not going to feel good. So, I recommend taking a big healthy drink."

"Roger that." He takes a few huge gulps out of the bottle.

"More," I say, pushing him.

"Ma'am, I—"

"I know it probably doesn't taste great," I say, shaking my head. "But the less you feel—the easier this will be."

"Oh, it's not that, Ma'am," Josiah chuckles. "It tastes great. But that's probably because you grabbed the *expensive* scotch."

"Oh…oops."

He tries to hand it back to me.

"No, no, you have to drink more. I'm sure Mr. Pace can afford another bottle," I say with a slight smile. "And if he has a problem, he can take it up with *me*."

Josiah smirks and nods before downing the rest. A few minutes later Charlie arrives with the supplies.

"We need to clear off the kitchen table."

As I look over, I just happen to notice there's blood splattered on the white roses sitting on top. It jars me, seeing these beautiful flowers, the same kind Jaxon sent me, covered in blood.

But I can't delay.

Taking the clothes Charlie brought me I quickly change in the other room.

As I am changing, I try to talk myself down.

I have to put everything that just happened in the last ten minutes out of my head and simply remember my medical training. I have to at the very least stabilize this man enough until we are free to leave this penthouse.

However, this also reminds me that I am *not* free to leave the penthouse.

Now that is something I will be taking up with Jaxon.

But I have to focus on Josiah.

I walk back out, and Charlie helps me get Josiah up on the table, where I use the scissors to cut open Josiah's pant leg to give me better access to the wound.

"Thank you, Miss Tyler," Josiah says groggily, the booze starting to kick in. I shoot a nervous glance at Charlie.

"You can thank me when you no longer have a bullet lodged in your leg, Josiah." I say softly.

I sip a glass of whiskey at four-thirty in the morning as I stand on the balcony of Jaxon's penthouse. I never thought I would start a morning off with a cocktail, but it has been an exceptionally long night. I've never had a night quite like it.

Charlie has gone to fetch me another *fresh* set of clothes, as the set he brought me earlier is covered in blood. But at least Josiah is resting comfortably with a bullet-free leg on the couch in the living room.

An $11,000 ball gown lies in the bathtub of one of the guest bedrooms, completely ruined.

The two dead men have also been moved into the other guest bedroom, obviously for sanitary reasons, but also so I didn't have to look at them anymore.

My hands have stopped shaking only because I am numb and exhausted... and there still has been no word from Jaxon.

Charlie knocks gently on the penthouse window, and I head back inside. The two of us exchange a glance but say nothing as he hands me my clothes. Despite everything, I am grateful for Charlie. He has been my rock tonight. I don't know what I would have done without him.

"Why don't you go relax, Miss Tyler," he says softly. "Lay

down for a few hours?"

"No, I'm fine," I say, shaking my head. "I'm going to go take a shower though."

But there'll be no sleep until we hear from Jaxon. I know this.

"Still nothing?" I ask him.

But Charlie shakes his head. "Not yet."

I head towards Jaxon's bathroom, before silently and robotically starting the shower. The minute the hot water hits my skin, I sink to the floor. The tears hit me like a freight train, and I begin to cry.

No, not just cry…I *sob*.

I have seen more tonight than I ever expected to see in a lifetime: I shot a man. I watched two men die. I had to stabilize another so he *wouldn't* die.

And the man I care about left hours ago, with a gun, and has not phoned or texted since.

Overwhelmed is an understatement, but it is the only word I can think of at this moment. So I just sit here on the floor of the shower, in my little ball, sobbing.

How is any of this possible?

And how did I somehow get wrapped up in all of it?

I just wish I could escape from all of this, but now I feel trapped. And what is worse is that even if Jaxon called right now, and told me I *could* leave right this minute, I wouldn't.

I must know what has happened to Jaxon.

I am trapped by my own emotions.

I sigh, acknowledging my own part in this mess. But eventually I realize that just sitting here on the floor of this shower is doing me no good.

Maybe I should go lay down like Charlie suggested.

Finishing my shower, I step into the bedroom. But when I see the sheets, disheveled from our impassioned 'almost' hookup, I realize I don't want to be in *Jaxon's* bed without Jaxon *beside* me.

Quietly I step into Jaxon's walk-in closet. Instantly his scent hits me as I stare at all his clothes. His taste is simple and clean. His shirts and suits are pressed and hung, and beautiful watches sit in a display case, while ties and shoes sit perfectly arranged on shelves.

Jaxon may not *be* here, but this room smells and feels like him.

I open a drawer and find a navy long sleeve t-shirt that is so soft to the touch, I take it out and put it on. Feeling something of his around me, here in this closet, surrounded by his scent, offers me the first comfort in hours. I lay down on the floor in the closet, wrapped in his shirt, and as soon as my eyes close, I am asleep.

I'm not sure how long I was asleep, but a short while later the sound of my phone ringing wakes me.

Momentarily confused by my surroundings, I shake it off and scramble to get my phone out of my pocket, hoping that perhaps it's Jaxon.

My *mother* is calling.

Shit! They are leaving today.

I let the call go to voicemail, unsure of how to address this situation. I know she will want to see me, especially since my father has likely told her the truth about Colton.

But I cannot bring her *here*. And, I cannot leave.

Wait a minute, I'm a grown ass woman! If I want to leave, I can leave, and no one can stop me.

I refuse to be a prisoner.

Quickly I head down the hall and into the kitchen where I find Charlie and Josiah, enjoying a cup of coffee.

"Hi. We need to talk."

They turn to face me, and a nervous look suddenly appears on their faces as they try to stand up, but I wave them off.

"At ease boys," I say sarcastically. "Stay where you are."

I cross my arms and stare them down as I summon all of my courage for what I plan to say.

"We have a problem," I start cautiously.

"What is it, Miss Tyler?" Charlie asks.

"My family is checking out of the hotel today, and I was supposed to be as well."

Charlie looks concerned. He opens his mouth to say something, but I beat him to it.

"I don't necessarily *have* to leave today, but my parents do. And my mother is going to want to say goodbye to me."

"But, Miss Tyler—"

"Look," I say, shaking my head. "I understand you two have orders. I also understand that you'd be breaking those orders if you let me leave and go see her. However, we obviously can't bring her here with dried blood on the floor and two dead men in the guest room. I mean, this whole penthouse is practically a crime scene."

That's a sentence I never imagined I would say.

"But we have to figure out something. A compromise," I say, looking at Charlie. "So, what if we just go back to *my* penthouse. My mother can come to visit me there and say goodbye. You guys can camp out in the guest bedroom until she leaves."

"Miss Tyler…" Charlie starts to object. "I don—"

"Please know, I'm not really asking," I say firmly. "This is my family, Charlie, and if that alone is not *enough* for you, then please remember that I shot a man to protect you and dug a fucking bullet out of Josiah's leg. I think I have earned the right to call this one."

I am not messing around.

Charlie and Josiah pause for a long moment, then shoot a look at each other. Josiah nods to Charlie.

"Okay, Miss Tyler," Charlie says with a nod. "You win."

Really?! Oh my God!

"Good," I say simply, maintaining my stoic facade. "Well then, let's get moving."

After Josiah gets the elevators turned back on, Charlie and I help get him into the elevator and into my penthouse. A sense of calm fills me, as I step back into my temporary space.

At the very least, there's no corpses of dead mafia men here.

My mother calls again, but *this* time I answer. I was correct in my assumption about her wanting to say goodbye. I ask her to join me in my suite.

I'm locking Josiah and Charlie in the guest bedroom, when I hear the elevator ding.

"Oh, my goodness…" I hear her say as she takes in the view. "This is *incredible*."

"It is beautiful, isn't it?" I smile, stepping into the foyer.

My mother takes a long look at me and then immediately wraps me in a hug. She pulls away with a smile.

"Is this from…?" Her voice trails off.

"Yes. It was a gift for the week," I smile. "From him."

"Wow."

She sets her purse down, still looking around the gorgeous penthouse space in awe.

"Would you like a cup of coffee?" I ask, and she nods.

We head into the living room to sit in front of the gas fireplace. My mother sips her coffee silently, glancing at me nervously. Finally, she finds her words.

"Natalie, I wanted to see you to obviously say goodbye, but I also wanted to see you because," she starts slowly, "well, because I want to apologize."

She sets her cup down, her expression suddenly solemn and sad.

"I promise I didn't know about Colton," She whispers, lowering her eyes to the carpet. "Here I was, pushing you to be with him, and I…"

She suddenly looks up at me and I see the tears now welling in her eyes.

"I'm so sorry, Natalie. I feel terrible about it!" She sobs.

Oh my...

I set my cup down on the table and move closer to her, taking her hand in mine.

"Mom, it's okay, really. If anything, it's my fault for not telling anyone the truth about what happened."

"No," she says, wiping her eyes, tears still streaming down her face. "It is not okay! You needed me to support *you*—my daughter. Not some fluffed up relationship. I needed to be a mom. Or at least someone that you felt you *could* talk to about what happened, and I wasn't."

I feel myself choke up a bit.

"I should've supported you, just you, from the beginning as soon as you left Colton," she continues. "I should've trusted that it was for good reason, and even if it wasn't, it was still *your* decision. I should have supported and respected that. And I'm just...so deeply sorry, Natalie. I really am."

We are both crying now.

This moment is so special to me in ways I cannot even comprehend. I feel as though I just got my mother back.

"Mom, it's okay," I say, swallowing hard and wiping my eyes. "There is nothing to forgive, but if that is what you want, then of course, I forgive you."

"I'm just so disappointed in myself," she says, closing her eyes. "I let you down. I won't do it again, I promise."

I smile softly, unable to say anything.

"And I told your father that if I see Colton before we leave, I'm going to punch him!" she says, anger flashing in her eyes. "Or maybe I'll just hit him with the car!"

Seeing her get so mad makes me giggle a little, as she looks kind of adorable all riled up.

"What's so funny?" she asks with a smile. "I'm telling you, if I see him I will give him a piece of my mind!"

"I appreciate that," I say, now laughing harder. "But it's not necessary. I think... I've finally let it go. All of it."

My eyes drift to the vase white roses on the table in the foyer. The one with the bright red bow.

Jaxon.

My heart pings a little, still desperately longing for confirmation that wherever Jaxon is, he's at least okay.

He is. I know he is. He has to be.

"I'm okay, Mom," I say with a smile. "I'm happy."

My mother nods.

"And, would that happiness have anything to do with all this?" She waves her finger around the room. "You know, that devilishly handsome man who just couldn't seem to keep his eyes, *and hands*, off of you?"

My cheeks heat and I bite my bottom lip.

"Uh huh," she winks at me.

"Perhaps a *little*, but not entirely," I say, playing with the sleeve of Jaxon's shirt. "But actually, letting go of Colton has been a long time coming. Jaxon is just kind of the catalyst I needed."

"Needed for what, sweetheart?"

"To find *my* voice again," I smile. "I was so worried about how devastated everyone else was going to feel, that I put myself on the back burner. And I suffered because of it."

I look up at my mom and swallow hard, wanting to finish what I feel I really need to say.

"You guys are my family. I love you all so much," I say softly. "I just need to work on loving *myself* that much too."

"Yes," My mom nods. "You do. Because you deserve that too, Natalie."

I wipe the tears streaking down my cheek. She reaches over and grabs my hand.

"And you know," her face suddenly serious. "If this Mr. Pace doesn't treat you right—"

"Don't worry, he is," I chuckle. "Even if I still have no idea why a guy like *him* is interested in me of all people."

"I do," my mother says immediately. "You're beautiful, kind, thoughtful, and smart. Any man who doesn't see what a catch you are is an idiot. And that Mr. Pace doesn't seem like an idiot."

"No, he's definitely not," I blush.

"However, he does seem very into you," she winks at me. "Are you two...?"

"We're just taking things slow for now," I say politely. "I might stay a few more days. I don't have to go back to work *right* away."

She smiles.

"Well, if you're happy, then I'm happy," she says. "You two just go at your own pace. You don't need anyone, and you don't need anyone telling you what to do. Including me. You've got this, Nat. All on your own."

It's true. Jaxon hadn't been the *reason* I finally spoke up about Colton. I'd done that all on my own. Jaxon had merely been the supportive *push* I needed to remember my own strength.

But I was enough, and I was enough all on my *own*.

We say our tearful goodbyes, and I walk her to the elevator, stealing one last hug before the doors close.

"You guys can come out now, she is gone," I shout, walking towards the guest bedroom.

"Miss Tyler! I've just had the call!" Charlie says bursting open the door. "Mr. Pace is alright! They are sending a car for us now!"

Oh, thank God! Jaxon is safe!

I feel the weight lift from off my shoulders, and finally feel like I can breathe again.

But then all of a sudden, the gravity of the last few hours hits me like a car crash. And I realize something:

I'm actually *angry*. At Jaxon.

Not only did Jaxon leave me here, to run off and fight bad guys, but he also kept trapped in this penthouse until *he* gave the order.

And I am *done* being ordered around.

"When can I see him, Charlie?" I ask.

I have some words for you, Jaxon Pace.

Chapter Thirty-Two

JAXON

I'm awake. And I'm being carried.

I feel myself being jostled into the backseat of a car, and hear men shouting.

But the next thing I feel after I awake is the *pain*.

There is a horrible burning sensation on the left side of my ribcage, and I am suddenly very aware that someone is pressing on it. Hard.

"Fuck off, that hurts!" I snap as the pain drags me into complete consciousness.

"Thank Christ!" I see Ethan's face above me. "He is awake! The boss is awake!"

He's the one pressing on my abdomen.

"Can you lay off a bit?" I ask, trying to sit up, wincing, but Ethan presses me back against the seat. "That hurts."

"I don't doubt it. You've a nasty cut on your side. It's pretty deep. Luckily it didn't hit any of your vital organs."

"Yeah, but right now *you're* hitting my vital organs, Ethan. And I can't fucking breathe," I say, wincing again and pushing his hand away. "What the fuck happened? Did we get him?"

Ethan's face turns dark, the blood splatter on his neck and chest making him look murderous.

"He got away," he growls, handing me another towel to stop the bleeding. "The fucker made it through the yard, and into the canal. Max says he hit him, but until I see a body, I don't believe it."

"Yeah, I wouldn't either," I say, finally managing to maneuver myself upright. "I thought I had him too. I shot him off the balcony. I watched him fall."

"You also got him in the eye," Ethan says with the smallest hint of a grin. "That's something."

"He still got away," I say, grabbing a water bottle from the front seat. "How many injured?"

"Almost everyone got hit, so about eight."

Fuck!

"Casualties?" I ask tentatively.

"Ryder. He was on the scaffold... he didn't make it."

"What about Wesley?"

"He's back at base, and he's stable," Ethan says with a nod. "He said you saved his life."

"No," I say, shaking my head, "The kid saved mine. He had my back tonight." Despite the pain I feel, fury erupts in my chest. "None of this was supposed to happen, Ethan. How did we walk into a fucking warzone tonight? And for what? Some computers? Please tell me we at least know more than we did before we all got shot to hell?!"

"Well, we're scanning the computers and the hard drives, from both locations now."

"And?!"

"We will know shortly."

"I'm really getting tired of being the last to the party," I growl. "We need to be on the offensive, and soon. Before this starts to interfere with more than just our warehouses."

"Agreed," Ethan says, wiping blood from a cut on his brow. "Levi is working on a miracle."

"What do you mean?"

"Well, that man who sliced you up was trying to delete whatever information was on the boat," Ethan says. "However it appears you got to him before he could. Levi's team is on-site deciphering everything."

"Let's hope he gets something," I mumble, tossing the bloody rag on the floor. "Otherwise this was a mistake, and a total waste of time."

"Better it was us than one of the unsuspecting Beta Squads working the warehouse shift," Ethan shrugs. "Had it been, they all would've been massacred."

He's not wrong. Even if I hate that he's not wrong.

I look at Ethan. The poor man is covered in blood and grime, and has deep bags under his eyes from what I can only assume is a lack of decent sleep.

Fuck, he looks so banged up right now. And old.

"You need a vacation," I say to him. "You look rough."

"Says the guy sitting here with his guts practically hanging out," Ethan chuckles. "I'll take a vacation when I don't have to worry about your punk ass doing something crazy."

"I can handle myself," I say, wincing.

Ethan looks at me and raises his brow. "Yeah... I can tell," he says sarcastically. "Besides, you have *other* people to worry about now."

He's referring to Jessica and Natalie.

"Are the girls okay?" I ask.

Ethan's face grows dark, and I immediately fear the worst. "Jessica is still safe in the bunker."

Thank God.

"...But your *girlfriend*, on the other hand, apparently shot a man tonight," Ethan continues. "*And* fished a bullet out of Josiah's leg by hand. There's also two dead imposters in your penthouse, we don't know who sent them."

"*What*?!"

"I talked to Charlie a little while ago," Ethan says, turning the corner. "Apparently, two men dressed in *our* uniform showed up and tried to relieve them from duty."

"Jesus Christ..."

"Naturally, Charlie refused, but they overpowered him and shot Josiah in the leg."

"Then how..."

"Natalie," Ethan grins. "Apparently, she shot one of the guys in the shoulder and saved both their asses."

I am speechless.

How the hell is that possible?

"I keep underestimating her," I whisper, as I shake my head. "And she keeps surprising me."

Ethan says nothing.

But this time he doesn't even try to hide this smile.

Pace Manor is bustling with action when we arrive.

Four of the men injured had substantial injuries. However, thanks to the efforts of Dr. Franklyn, my long-time private physician, they are stabilized relatively quickly.

With *suspicious* wounds like these we cannot risk going to the hospital, so this is the best option we have. But Dr. Franklyn is only one man, and there are a lot of us.

My men are my priority, and did not deserve the blood bath they survived this evening. So after determining that my injuries aren't completely life-threatening, I insist that Dr. Franklyn attend my men *first*.

I've set the more seriously injured men up in the bedrooms upstairs, as I have plenty of rooms to go around.

This is where I find Wesley.

He's in the middle of drinking a Coke and watching TV with his leg propped up when I walk in the room. He practically spills his drink on himself trying to get up, but I wave him off. I grab a chair and bring it around to the side of his bed.

"Wes, I just wanted to stop by," I say, clearing my throat uncomfortably. "And say thank you."

It still feels somewhat foreign to me to express emotions or gratitude with my men, as I don't currently have this kind of relationship with them. But I'm working on it.

"Sir, it was my duty…" Wesley says, his eyes wide. "No, no… it was my *honor*!"

I smile politely. "Well, you did a hell of a job kid. And I will make sure that everyone knows it."

I see Wesley's face light up.

"Are you comfortable?" I ask.

"Oh yes, this bed is incredibly comfortable!" He says excitedly. "I mean, definitely compared to the one I have at home, it's like sleeping on a cloud!"

His enthusiastic oversharing makes me chuckle.

"I'm glad."

I'll have to buy the kid a better mattress.

But then I find myself sitting there awkwardly staring at him, unsure of what to say next.

Maybe that's enough socializing for today.

"Well then," I say as I stand and head for the door. "I'll let you get some rest. Let me know if you need anything."

Wesley nods.

But just when I reach the door, I hear him clear his throat.

"Sir?" he says, and I turn to acknowledge him. "I want to apologize, in person, for what I said… the other day."

He looks to the floor, remorsefully, and even though it takes me a second, I suddenly understand.

He's asking forgiveness…for his comment about Natalie.

"It's in the past. I'm sure it won't happen again."

"No, Sir."

"Then we're good," I say quietly. "Alright?"

"Yes, Sir," he nods.

"Get some rest," I say, closing the door behind me.

I head down the hall to my bedroom where I take a seat on the bench at the foot of my bed.

Forgiveness is not usually in my repertoire. But, even an oak bends in the wind occasionally. And my men, especially Wesley, fought very hard for me tonight.

They deserved more. And, occasionally, if the situation warranted, maybe even forgiveness.

Speaking of forgiveness…

I pull my phone from my pocket.

I've already sent Ethan The Jefferson to fetch Natalie, as well as a team to handle the mess in my penthouse. But still, I know I have to beg forgiveness from her. Especially for leaving her a second time.

I've apologized a lot to this poor girl in such a short amount of time.

I rub my chin gently, trying to think of what to say.

Me
11:15 a.m.: Ethan is coming to pick you up.

Natalie
11:16 a.m.: …and bring me where?

Me
11:17 a.m.: To me.

Natalie
11:17 a.m.: Do I have a choice this time? Or am I just to obey?

Yeah, I think it's safe to say she's still very pissed.

Me
11:18 a.m.: Natalie, there is so much I want to say, but I know it should be said in person, I hope you will give me that opportunity.

I wince again. The cut on my side is perhaps the biggest of many slashes and gashes all over me, and is still bleeding. I have pain radiating from so many places on my body I can hardly think straight.

I wait for a response to my text, but after a few minutes I realize a response is not coming.

Natalie is mad, and I cannot say I blame her.

But right now, I need her. I cannot explain how or why, only that I do. So all I can do is hope that she answers my request, and comes back with Ethan.

Chapter Thirty-Three

Natalie

Ethan stands before me, looking quite disheveled.

"Miss Tyler, Mr. Pace has requested that you come with me."

Everything I had wanted to say, all the resolve I had built up, folds like a house of cards around me when I see the look on this seasoned bodyguard's face. Because right there I know two things without Ethan saying a word:

Something terrible happened last night.

…And Ethan is worried about Jaxon.

So, despite my perfectly crafted plan to chew-out each of these men the next time I saw them, the response that escapes my lips is simple.

"Okay," I say quietly. "Give me two minutes."

I rush into the bedroom, quickly ripping off Jaxon's shirt and changing into one of my own as all the worry from earlier comes flooding back to me.

What had happened to him?

My hands are shaking as I grab my purse, my phone, and my jacket. Charlie helps Josiah into the elevator with Ethan, and I am halfway out of the door when I remember something and run back to the kitchen to retrieve it.

"Miss Tyler?" Ethan asks softly, holding the door.

"My medical bag. Something tells me that I might need it," I say, walking back to the elevator and shooting a scrutinizing look at Ethan.

His head tilts to the side, and his eyes confirm what I already know.

Soon we are in the lobby of the hotel, but unfortunately for me, so is *Colton*. We have clearly interrupted him flirting with the front desk clerk, but I couldn't care less. His eyes meet mine, and I frigidly turn away, ignoring him. But he immediately rushes over to us as we walk across the lobby.

"Nat, I've been trying to call you, but it keeps giving me a disconnected signal?" he says confused. "I'm leaving today, and I just wanted a chance to try and make things right."

"I don't want to talk to you Colton," I say dismissively.

"Well, then I think you should at least know a few things about your new *manfriend*," he says irritably, while looking cautiously up at Ethan, and struggling to keep up with us as we pass through the lobby.

"Colton, I don't want to talk to you," I snarl at him. "Especially about Jaxon."

I really am not in the mood for his shit today.

"No, Nat, listen he's not a good guy…"

"Enough Colton!"

"Nat—" He persists.

"The lady said enough!" Ethan explodes on Colton.

"Why don't you mind your fucking business old man?!" Colton shouts angrily back at Ethan. "God, I'm so sick of this! Fuck you people! And fuck you too, Natalie!"

But in a blink of an eye Ethan, Charlie, and the limping Josiah step in front of me. They stare down at a dumbfounded Colton, baiting him to say another word and looking as though they are going to rip him to pieces on the spot.

But this time I'm the one who speaks first.

"Enough Colton!" I snap. "Seriously, enough! I've asked you multiple times to just leave me alone! I don't want to speak to you, and I don't have to give you a chance to apologize or explain! I owe you *nothing*, Colton! And just so we are clear, whoever I choose to spend my time with is absolutely none of your fucking business!" I shout loud enough to turn a few heads in the lobby, but I don't care.

Colton's jaw drops… but he says nothing.

Finally, his obnoxious mouth is speechless.

I turn on my heel and head for the doors. Charlie holds it open for me, a smirk plastered on his face as he glares back at Colton. Even Ethan winks at me before opening the backseat door of a black Range Rover. Once inside, I take a deep breath, proud of myself for finally putting my worthless, sociopathic, and nosey ex-fiancé in his place.

As the car pulls away, it occurs to me that I've just hopped into the backseat of a car with three big, scary, and frankly dangerous men, without even asking where they plan on taking me. And even though I know they would never harm me, it still kinda feels a little bold…even for the *new* me.

"Ethan, where are we going?" I ask.

"We are headed to the Pace Manor, Miss Tyler," he says softly. "Mr. Pace's primary home. It's just outside the city."

"I thought," I say cautiously, "Jaxon does not bring women to his *home*."

"No, Miss Tyler, he does not," Ethan says, his eyes catching mine in the rearview mirror.

Holy crap. Am I ready for this?

After twenty-five minutes of driving down quiet streets lined with picturesque trees displaying their early fall colors, we stopped at a house with a tall iron gate, the entrance to a long driveway. The tall iron fence lines the whole property and the lawn sprawls upwards towards a fountain on a hill. It is so big that no house can be seen from the road. I notice that at least four security cameras are pointed directly at the car.

"Occupants?" A female voice on the intercom asks.

"White, Baptiste, Eton and Tyler." Ethan states, placing his hand on the intercom, initiating a fingerprint scan.

"Cleared for entry," the voice says. "Report to Ops immediately."

There is a buzzing sound, and then the gate slowly starts to open. As we drive past, I realize that both the gate and the fence are nearly six inches thick.

Who on earth needs a gate that thick?

Mafiosos apparently.

And speaking of mafiosos, that was definitely a *woman* who answered on the intercom. Which I guess means that Jaxon must employ female employees in his mafia business.

Hey, at least he's an equal-opportunity gangster.

Trying to fight my own pettiness, I briefly wonder if *that* technically counts as bringing women back to the house. But deep down, I know it doesn't, and isn't anywhere close to the same thing. I'm being ridiculous, and I know it.

However, I do feel a slight sprinkling of jealousy topping the great big pile of emotions I'm already currently sitting on.

Damn Jaxon for all these stupid... feelings.

The car curves down the long driveway, next to the sprawling lawn that I see contains a beautifully maintained garden, with statues and a reflecting pool. Hundreds of gigantic pine trees line the property, and the branches of connecting maple trees cover the entire drive, boasting their Midwest beauty.

Suddenly the house comes into view, and completely takes my breath away.

Nestled on a bluff overlooking Lake Michigan, it stands majestically against the Great Lake like it was plucked from a postcard. Huge white pillars adorn the front of the house, and the brick paved driveway circles around a fountain as big as a car. The huge stone house with its black framed windows fans out in either direction, opening into huge east and left wings.

To my left, a helicopter pad and garage sit unoccupied. To my right, a large greenhouse with windows lined in decorative stained glass, guards the entrance to yet another garden with meticulously trimmed hedges, fountains, and winding paths.

Pace Manor is absolutely gorgeous.

...And I haven't even gone inside yet.

Ethan parks our car, and Charlie opens the door for me. I follow Ethan up the steps and find myself in front of a gigantic twelve-foot door, a modern combination of dark wood and iron—reminding me of a medieval castle.

Despite desperately wanting to feel the contrary, I cannot help but feel a little intimidated.

I suppose that's the purpose of a house like this.

It feels like a fortress. Clean. Traditional. Foreboding.

It feels like Jaxon.

The right side of the door opens and a tall, burly man nods at Ethan before welcoming us inside.

"Miss Tyler, may I take your coat and bag?" He offers.

"I'd like to keep my bag with me," I say politely. "But you can take my coat, thank you."

I hand him my jacket and then turn to Josiah, who is being helped into the building by Charlie.

"How is it feeling?" I ask.

"Honestly, it's not too terrible, Miss Tyler. I'm even starting to put some weight on it." Josiah smiles up at me.

"That's great!" I say with a smile. "Take it easy though, don't go too hard all at once. Take some ibuprofen, and keep ice on it, that will keep the swelling down. If you start to feel feverish, let me know. That is the first sign of infection."

"Yes, Miss Tyler."

"*Natalie*," I say softly to both Josiah and Charlie. "I know you have your rules, but I think we've been through enough together now for you both to just call me Natalie, okay?"

They both smile, giving me a slight nod.

"You saved my life." Charlie says. "I don't know how to thank you."

"Well, you saved mine too, remember?" I smile back at him. "That's what *friends* do."

The young man who opened the door for us clears his throat, possibly uncomfortable with our casual exchange.

"Bring Mr. Eton to Dr. Franklyn on the veranda," he says, looking at Josiah. "The Boss wants him looked at immediately. Pretty sure he's almost finished with Travis."

Charlie helps Josiah down the hall to my left. When I turn back around, I notice I'm alone, as Ethan has stepped into a room just off to my left, and I can see him inside talking in hushed tones. I glance cautiously in the room and see about two dozen people on the phone, scanning security tv's, or buried in computers. When one of these shadowy figures sees me, he promptly closes the door, effectively blocking my views.

They don't want my prying eyes in their business.

I turn my attention back to the atrium. A gas fireplace greets me, and two colossal, circular, white marble staircases, lined with dark metal banisters that curve upwards on either side of the foyer. Three stories above me a gorgeous mid-century chandelier illuminates the room, while subtle contemporary artwork lines the walls.

If I thought the house was big from the outside, it feels even bigger from the inside. The first floor seems to extend out so far that I cannot even see all of it. To the right of the fireplace, I see what appears to be a huge kitchen, with a brick masonry oven, formal dining room and sitting area, leading outside to a huge patio and pool. Beyond that, the most breathtaking view of Lake Michigan I have ever seen.

The house is absolutely beautiful.

I'm just moving to glance into the kitchen when the door to the computer room opens and Ethan emerges, followed by a pretty brunette with a tightly pressed bun and a tightly pressed face. She dramatically appraises me up and down, a judgmental frown plastered on her small face.

"I'm sorry, but Mr. Pace is not receiving anyone at this time," she says resentfully.

She sounds like the woman that spoke over the intercom.

"He *asked* for her, Marta," Ethan snaps, crossing his arms.

"And he needs to rest Ethan!" she snaps back, clearly annoyed with Ethan's statement. "You saw him yourself; he is in no condition to be..." She trails off, waving her hand at me.

Perhaps it is my lack of sleep, or the emotional roller coaster I've been on for the last twenty-four hours, but I am not accepting this.

"Listen lady!" I snap. "I don't know what you're implying, but I definitely do not appreciate your tone. Jaxon requested that I meet him here. So here I am! And I don't give a shit what condition he is in, but if you think I'm leaving here *without* seeing him, you must be out of your fucking mind!"

"She stays," a thundering voice says from behind me, atop the stairs.

Jaxon.

I try desperately to control the way my breath hitches in my throat, but it's no use. I slowly turn around towards him.

"But, Sir..." Marta protests, but Jaxon raises his hand to stop her.

"Leave us," Jaxon commands from atop of the balcony as his eyes meet mine, paralyzing me in place.

When I hear no movement from Marta to my left, I tear my eyes away from Jaxon, and see her struggling with her desire to protest again.

"I'm sorry, did I stutter?" he replies in a lethal whisper, glaring at her with a look of fury and exhaustion.

She turns a bright shade of red, but begrudgingly obeys this time and storms off down the hallway.

When she is gone, I look back up at Jaxon, who starts walking down the stairs towards me, without taking his eyes off me.

When he finally steps off the staircase, he stops just a few feet away from me. For some reason, he looks nervous, almost as if he thinks I'm going to bolt for the door, and he will need to catch me.

I briefly consider it, realizing this might be my last chance to run, before I am officially in too deep with this man.

But after worrying about Jaxon all night, my body betrays me, and I run straight into his arms instead.

This is real. He's alive. And I'm here with him.

I inhale his scent, squeezing him tightly.

Suddenly, I hear him wince. I release him immediately, pulling back to fully survey the damage.

The same man, who had looked so devilishly handsome in an impeccable custom tuxedo last night, stands before me now looking like a different person.

…And like he is lucky to be *alive.*

The same collared shirt I had unbuttoned for him is sliced in multiple places, its tattered carcass hanging limply from his body. He's covered in cuts and bruises, and there's dried blood on his forehead. He winces again, presses his right hand to his side, and that's when I see the massive blood stain, which looks far too fresh for my liking.

My stomach twists.

Jaxon looks as if he had left me to go fight in a war.

What the hell happened last night? How the hell did he survive this?

I feel the tears welling in my eyes, and my emotions spiraling out of control. And before I can even register what I'm doing, I slap Jaxon square across his face.

Chapter Thirty-Four

JAXON

"How dare you, Jaxon?!" Natalie shouts at me, tears streaming down her cheeks. "How dare you leave me like that, to go handle business like *this*!"

"Natalie, I—" I try to say.

"Do you have any idea what I have been through tonight?!" She interrupts. "Do you know how fucking worried I've been about you?"

She pushes away from me and steps toward the door, as my heart starts pounding in my chest.

I cannot let her leave. I just got her back.

"Hell, I...I... don't even know what I am *doing* here!"

Without thinking I step forward and hook her around the waist, pulling her back to me and wrapping her in my arms. The poor girl immediately bursts into tears, yelling some indecipherable things against my chest, while gently slapping at me.

Despite the pain from the multiple knife wounds all across my chest, I refuse to let her go. Instead I press my lips to the top of her head, kissing her softly.

"I am so very sorry, Natalie," I say, struggling to keep my own emotions in check. "I never intended for any of this to happen to you."

"To me?" she asks, pushing back to look at me. "Wait, do you honestly think I'm upset about what happened to *me*?"

I thought things were starting to calm down, but she suddenly looks pissed again.

Maybe I really do need a manual for dealing with women.

"I'm not mad about what happened to me!" she yells at me. "I'm mad because I spent the last twelve hours worried that I lost *you*, Jaxon!"

Is she for real?

From what I understand, this woman was nearly abducted, shot a hitman, and saved two others. Yet here she stands, more upset about what happened to *me*.

I know emphatically that I could live a thousand lifetimes and never fully understand Natalie Tyler—or deserve her.

"I barely know you, Jaxon, but I have all these fucking feelings for you!" She continues yelling at me. "And then you left me, at the worst possible time, trapped in your penthouse while you run off to fight bad guys and nearly get yourself killed!"

"Well, I don't think it was ever that bad—"

"Look at yourself, Jaxon! You look like you've been through a war! Like you're lucky to be standing here!"

"You should see the other guys," I wink, trying to diffuse the situation a little and make her smile.

But it doesn't work.

"That's not funny, Jaxon!" she yells, bringing her hands to her face and sobbing again. "Fuck you! Fuck you, and all these stupid feelings!"

I pull her back into my arms, and this time she does not fight me.

She's here. I have her in my arms, again.

There was a part of me that was truly afraid I'd never get the chance to hold her again.

And it had been that fear, combined with my insatiable desire to spend every available second with Natalie, that had ultimately saved my life.

I kiss the top of her forehead again, and we hold each other in silence for several minutes. When I happen to look up, I realize that Ethan must've walked back into the foyer at some point, and now stands in the doorway, smiling.

I bet he enjoyed watching me take that ass kicking.

"*Thank you.*" I mouth at him silently.

"Thank you, Ethan," Natalie says against my chest, somehow aware of his presence as well. "Thank you for bringing him back in one piece."

"More or less," Ethan says, winking at me.

Natalie chuckles, still without looking up.

"Oh I see," I say teasingly. "So *his* joke was funny?"

Ethan chuckles to himself but heads into the command center, leaving me alone with Natalie.

It's clear I wasn't the *only* one who was worried that I might die last night. Natalie had been worried, too. Very worried. I'm not sure I can ever tell her how close I actually came to that threshold.

At least not anytime soon.

But...She has feelings for me. A lot of them apparently.

Natalie gently pulls back and wipes her eyes, appraising me warily.

"Holy shit..." she says, shaking her head.

"I know," I say quietly. "I promise I'm alright though."

She looks me over, shaking her head again.

"You can keep being mad at me if you want," I say, brushing a piece of her hair from her face. "But I'm going to kiss you now."

I lean in and kiss her gently on the lips.

"I'm so sorry, Natalie," I whisper. "For leaving you. For the chaos in your life. For all of it."

She looks up at me, her green eyes still puffy.

"But I'm so happy to see you. And to have you here."

I hesitate, hoping that she will say something.

But instead she steps forward and kisses me, far less gently than I just kissed her, making my heart rate soar.

"Thank you for coming back to me," she says quietly.

And suddenly I have to stop myself from telling Natalie everything. About how she had been a light at the end of a tunnel for me, and how I would've gone through hell and back just to have her kiss me one more time.

Okay. That's a bit much.

Perhaps I should cool it with the confessions of affection for the time being. After all, I don't really want to scare her off yet.

...Or make her start yelling at me again.

"Would you, uh," I say, clearing my throat. "Would you like a tour of the house?"

"No," she says firmly. "What I'd like is to get you patched up. Immediately. From what I can tell, some of these cuts need stitches, and I've already almost lost you once, I don't need you turning septic."

"This is the priority?" I ask with a smirk.

"Yes," she says firmly. "Because you look like you were thrown into a woodchipper, Jaxon." She takes another look at me and shakes her head. "And please tell me you have a better first aid kit here than you have at the penthouse?"

"What's wrong with my first-aid kit?"

"Jaxon, those kits are for knee scrapes and bug bites!" she says. "Men in your line of work don't need butterfly bandages, they need stitches and actual wound care."

"I happen to like the butterfly bandages, thank you very much," I say, biting my lip to avoid breaking into a laugh.

And despite her stern tone, Natalie fights a smirk too.

"I think there should be some supplies upstairs. Dr. Franklyn keeps the place well stocked."

"Good. Take me to it."

I take her hand in mine and kiss it, before turning and heading for the staircase. But then all of a sudden, I feel her stop in her tracks.

Shit…is she having second thoughts?

"Jaxon, you should probably get a bottle of scotch or bourbon, or whatever you Dons like to drink, too. Unless you want to feel me sewing your skin back together *sober*."

As she says this, I finally see a flash of humor in her eyes, and the beginnings of a smile tugging at her lips. I step forward, cupping her face with my hands and kissing her deeply. And for the first time in hours, I don't feel any pain.

I only feel *her*.

"Yes, Ma'am," I whisper against her lips. "Whatever you say."

It is no secret my feelings for her have developed quickly, but it makes me feel… *alive*. In a way I have never felt before.

Yes, I crave and want her, but I also respect her. I want to protect her. I want to cherish her. I want to spoil her.

However, it's even deeper than that.

In my line of work, sometimes I hurt people. Sometimes I hurt people who deserve it, and sometimes it's by accident. But for the first time in my life, I know that I never want to *hurt* Natalie Tyler. Intentionally, or unintentionally.

Even if I'm terrified that *she* could hurt *me*.

But over and over again, she's had the opportunity to leave, and legitimate reasons to do so. Yet chose to stay. For me.

She is more woman than I could've dreamed of. She rescued my daughter. She saved my men. She cared for me and chose to take a chance on me, above everything familiar and easy.

All of these things were the reason I decided to bring her here, to my home. No matter how terrified I was of my impending vulnerability, if she was willing to take a risk to be with me, then I am willing to tear down whatever walls it takes to keep her in my life for as long as I have her.

"Are you okay?" Natalie asks me, interrupting my thoughts.

"Marta," I call from the stairs, knowing that she is eavesdropping. "Please bring my scotch to the bedroom."

"Yes, Sir," she calls from around the corner.

I smile and take her hand, leading her up the staircase. I lead her down the first corridor of bedrooms, and a few of my men pass by, presumably after checking on the men recovering inside.

They nod silently in respect, but I notice the unmistakable look of surprise on their faces as they see Natalie—here.

The only women in this house these days are staff.

Aside from the cleaning staff that I never see, there is Jessica's nanny, Old Nan, who is an older woman who has been part of this family since I was in diapers. And Marta, who is part housekeeper and part secretary, though I suspect she wants to be more.

Natalie is the first *girlfriend* I have allowed inside my house since Rachel passed, and for the first time in years, I am nervous.

I mean, hell, I don't even know if she is my girlfriend yet.

It's crazy to me to even consider something like that so quickly. We have undeniable chemistry, sure, but we haven't even fucked yet, which is usually the *first* thing I do with a woman.

Although to be fair, that wasn't for lack of trying, and I probably could have saved myself a lot of misery had I just ignored the message on the windows last night and instead buried myself inside *her.*

But last night showed me something I was not expecting. Last night, with my back against the wall, the only two thoughts in my brain were of my daughter… and Natalie.

I was not ready to lose either of them.

It had been enough to push me forward and keep me alive in the process. It gave me a new perspective. Ethan had been right. No amount of brute strength could ever compete with the strength derived from having something, or someone worth fighting for.

So, despite my hatred for openness, despite my inexperience with actual dating, and despite the horribly crippling feeling of vulnerability. I am determined to *try* with this incredible woman, who has proven time and time again to be worth every effort.

We finally reach my bedroom doors. I pause, internally addressing the gravity of this moment for me, and look at Natalie. Her silent, but empathetic expression, somehow assuring me she knows that this is foreign territory for me.

"Jaxon, if you don't want to do this here, we can always find a room downstairs, I'm sure there's like a million of them," she says gently.

She does know. Can women do that?

I stare at her, convinced that even though she is most assuredly exhausted and emotionally drained, she is still the most beautiful woman I have ever laid eyes on.

My mother used to say that effort was everything.

And if it takes me making an effort to allow Natalie into my life, my home, and my bedroom to show her I want her around, then I am prepared to do exactly that. I pull her flush against my body, feeling the surge of electricity, and kiss her… *hard.*

"I want this," I whisper, then slowly open the door.

Chapter Thirty-Five

Natalie

Of two things I am acutely aware.

First, Jaxon's bedroom is bigger than the entire first floor of my house. And two, I know this because I am standing *in* Jaxon's bedroom.

The significance of this moment is not lost on me.

This is the same man who revealed to me less than three nights ago, that despite his never-ending trail of girlfriends in the past five years, none of them have ever been allowed in his house. And perhaps I shouldn't necessarily call them *girlfriends*, but regardless, none had set foot in this room.

But here I stand, with his hand in mine, and I know that he is letting me into his *world*, not just his bedroom.

I hear an audible gasp from behind us, and turn to see Marta, holding a tray with Jaxon's scotch, standing in the hall. She looks just as shocked as I am. Out of instinct, I move to drop Jaxon's hand and step away, but he holds me fast, unwilling to let go.

"Thank you, Marta. You may go," he says politely, taking the tray from her with his free hand.

But Marta is frozen in place, her face a mix of emotions too difficult to read. Jaxon pauses a minute longer, assumedly waiting for Marta to leave, but she stares at him, dumbfounded. He takes a deep breath and lets out a sigh, his posture slightly more rigid than a moment ago, before looking at her coldly.

"I said you may go, Marta. I wish to be undisturbed." His voice is low and steeped in dominance. It is clear from his tone he will not be repeating himself a third time.

Something I've learned he does not appreciate.

Just as I am starting to become concerned, she seems to wake from her trance and nods silently, before walking off quickly towards the stairs.

I shake my head.

Just another woman swooning over him.

Not that I blame her, or *any* woman for that.

Jaxon finally releases my hand and shuts the doors to the bedroom, as I casually glance around. The room feels like a marriage of turn of the century luxury, with modern minimalistic features. It's both old and new.

Which I suppose is a bit like Jaxon, too.

The fourteen-foot walls in dark gray wainscotting, sit against a palette of clean cool colors, providing the perfect backdrop for a collection of eclectic artworks. Above me, an Edison-bulb chandelier sits between two gigantic wooden beams, while soft cove lighting lines the ceiling's exterior molding.

Beyond the sitting area, and yet another gas fireplace, a colossal king bed faces outward towards the cliffside.

Inexorably, the minute I lay eyes on his bed, images of him throwing his glass on the floor, and his unbridled passion ravaging me last night come back to me. I impulsively feel my heart rate climbing, and the overpowering desire I have for him threatening to take control of me.

Natalie… He looks like Swiss cheese. He needs your help.

"Where's the bathroom?" I ask, doing my best to get my selfish desires in check.

"This way," he says as he pulls me past the bed, and around the wall with the fireplace. There Jaxon opens the door to the most majestic bathroom in probably the history of bathrooms.

On my right, an impossibly long granite countertop runs the length of the room until it touches a massive glass walk-in shower, with a slate rock wall. A smaller room sits further still, situated behind a gigantic standalone tub, marble steps leading down into a built in jacuzzi tub, surrounded by four large stone pillars. On my left, five spectacular floor-to-ceiling windows boast the bay view in all its splendor.

"The windows are tempered glass, so no one can see inside," he says quietly. "I hired the same team who built the Bellagio."

"I think all you're missing is the fountain," I say sarcastically.

"Jealous?" he says, winking at me.

"Uhhhh, yeah. Shamelessly," I say with a laugh. But as I turn back around to look at him, I'm reminded that even though he is smiling, he is still covered in open wounds and must be in agony.

"Time for scotch," I say warily.

He sets the tray down and pours a shot into the glass. The only glass that is, as it is apparent that Marta *forgot* a second glass.

How convenient…

However, I stop him before he can bring it to his lips, taking the glass from his hand, and replacing it with the entire bottle. Jaxon stares at me confused.

"This is going to hurt," I say, taking a sip from the glass. "A lot."

Jaxon nods, and takes a giant swig of the scotch, but his eyes never leave mine. They call to me, and I am helpless in their wake.

"Now, take off your shirt," I say, clearing my throat while taking another sip of the scotch and remembering immediately how much I enjoyed this view last night.

Jaxon smiles, with a smoldering intensity.

"Now we are talking. I like bossy Natalie."

He swallows another big gulp of scotch, cringing slightly from the bite, then sets the decanter down on the counter and reaches for his top button.

"Fuck!" He recoils almost instantly, doubling over in pain.

"What? What is it?"

"It feels like a red-hot poker was just jammed into my arm!"

He slowly steadies himself from the wave of pain on the counter and I step up to see what the issue could be.

"It did not hurt this bad earlier."

"Let me help," I say, reaching for the top button.

My eyes meet his, and I have to force myself to focus on the task at hand. My closeness to him makes my breath quicken, and my body floods with warmth. Despite being covered in sweat and blood, I can still smell the faint traces of the cologne lingering on his body, making me shiver.

I swallow hard, looking into his eyes as my fingers gingerly continue all the way down the front of his chest. If it were not for the immense amount of pain plastered on his face, undressing him slowly would be incredibly sexy.

I mean, it's Jaxon, so it still is sexy.

But Jaxon is visibly in agony; although I suspect he is trying to contain it for my sake. I gently help him out of the tattered shirt, tossing it to the floor.

"Jesus." This is all I can say as I look upon his bare chest and shoulder.

He is covered in stab wounds, and dried blood. I slowly walk around him, surveying the damage. From my immediate assessment, Jaxon has at least six cuts that need stitches, in addition to a deep gash on his right side. The left side of his abdomen is purple and blue already, evidence of trauma to his ribs. Then there is the hole in his shoulder, which is swollen and hot, evidence that something is there that should not be, causing severe inflammation.

"Gunshot," Jaxon says. "The bullet passed through."

"Not entirely, I think. You may still have a bullet fragment still lodged in there, Jax," I say, gently examining the wound in more detail. "Which is causing all the swelling and pain you suddenly feel. We need to get it out, quickly."

Then I turn and grab one of the black chairs along the counter and pull it over to the center of the room, under the best lighting.

"*Jax?*" he says with a smirk. "That's…different."

My cheeks flush instantly, and I turn away from him and back to my medical bag to start pulling out my tools.

"I'm sorry, I didn't even realize I said—"

"No, I like it," he says amused. "I don't remember the last time I had a nickname from an adult."

I bite my bottom lip.

"Plus," he says, taking a seat on the chair, "if you're giving me a nickname, that means you've got to be closer to forgiving me."

I steal a glance at him in the mirror, catching the wicked grin painted on his handsome face.

"Oh, it means nothing of the sort, Sir," I say, looking at him in the reflection, raising my brows and deliberately pulling out my needles and Metzenbaum scissors, and holding them up in the air so he can see them. "But I have a few ideas on how to exact my revenge."

As I turn around and head toward him, I see a look of panic flit across the face of Jaxon Pace.

"What does that mean?" he says nervously.

I ignore his question and press firmly on the bruise on his ribcage.

"Holy shi—" Jaxon winces, putting his fist in his mouth and gasping for air. "Fuck, Natalie, is this really necessary?!"

A facetious smile tugs at the corners of my mouth.

"Mostly," I say, winking at him through my lashes. "But lucky for you they feel bruised, not broken."

"Yeah," he gasps, trying to catch his breath, and immediately reaching for the decanter again. "Lucky that I have *lots* of scotch."

The bullet fragment was easily retrieved, at least for my part. However, I ended up having him bite down on a hand towel to stop him from screaming in a houseful of heavily armed mafia men, sworn to protect their leader.

I gave him a break from what he coined my 'merciless torture' and allowed him to explain the events of the evening after he left me in his penthouse. He told me as much as he could remember. Even the part about what he found in the building where the message had been written on the windows.

By the end of his recollection, even I had poured another shot, as this was intense. This war with the other mafia clan was real, and the man I was growing to care for, my only protection from this dark world, was lucky to be alive.

As I fished the bullet out of his arm, he sat in front of me, naked from the waist up, covered in blood, both his own and that of his enemies. I understood now that the bullet wound, and the gashes all over his body were made with the intent to *kill* him. He had killed men last night. And as he had already said, it was not his first time. He had been honest with me that night on the roof. Jaxon Pace was certainly a dangerous man and every fiber in my body should be afraid of him.

But I am not afraid of Jaxon.

It was true, so much of his world was clouded in darkness. He did illegal, dangerous things with dangerous people. He had lost people he loved because of this life. The same life he was born and bred for, where power was the only currency, and sometimes justice can only be achieved by the damned.

But despite all his darkness, he had light in him too.

Jessica for one, was the center of his universe. Whenever he spoke about her, his whole demeanor changed. The biggest, scariest mafia gangster in Chicago was at the mercy of his sassy little six-year-old daughter. Who loved Dora the Explorer and gave him funny kid nicknames like 'Mr. Unicorn Fluffypants.' Jaxon wanted so desperately for her to have no part in the mafia life. He was determined to find a way out for her, even if that meant the end of his family's dynasty as the leading mafia clan in the city.

Jaxon also had Ethan, who seemed to be the closest thing Jaxon had to family. I saw Ethan as a kind of father figure. He was just as big and scary, just as violent and dangerous. But he cared for Jaxon and would do anything for him. And while he took his oath of service seriously, and would certainly take a bullet for Jaxon, it was clearly deeper than that. Ethan was the one person brave enough to say the things most would not *dare* to say to the Don Supreme, because he was the one person Jaxon trusted the most.

And Jaxon wasn't as rigid as I thought he might be. He was open to negotiations. After seeing him carved to pieces, I may have tapered it back a bit from my morning resolution, but I still ripped him a new one. I explained he had no right to *demand* I stay in the penthouse, or demand Charlie and Josiah keep me there. I knew his actions were well-intended, but I told him I was not going to be ordered around like the men who followed him. He apologized and insisted that he only did so to keep me safe.

Which I already knew.

Yes, I should run. I should leave Chicago and run far away from all of this. Chalk it up to a great week-long adventure, and just go about the rest of my life, remembering the great Jaxon Pace as the generous and sexy enigma he was.

But I don't *want* to.

I *want* to feel the way he makes my body tremble with a look, and the way his voice sets my veins on fire. I want to feel the heart-pounding, room-spinning, incomparable and completely overwhelming way that only *he* makes me feel, as often as I can, for as long as I can. Jaxon has awakened a part of me that I never even knew existed and made me feel alive for the first time in my life.

"Fireworks and magnetism. Passion and panic. Life in your bones."

Exactly as Charlie described it to me last night.

All logic be damned.

Jaxon finishes a much-needed cigarette from the bedroom

balcony and walks back into the bathroom, jolting me from my selfish thoughts.

We may have to work on that too.

He said he is trying to quit, and as a nurse I cannot support a habit that I know is slowly killing him. Especially considering the fact that everything else in his world is already trying to kill him.

He looks visibly tired, and he has to be exhausted. This had not been a pleasant process for him. We had retrieved the bullet, and fixed the wound on his scalp, but there is still much work to do.

"So, what is next?" he asks me warily.

"Okay, so as much fun as I am having torturing you," I say playfully. "I still have all of these wounds to clean before I can stitch you back up."

He laughs, resting his arms on the back of the chair and hanging his head for a moment in resignation. He looks back up at me, squinting his eyes.

"Remind me to hire *you* to extract confessions the next time I'm in the market for a torturer," he says with a wink.

"You couldn't afford me," I say sweetly, batting my lashes at him as I clean my tools.

"You're probably right," he replies with a chuckle so infectious it makes me chuckle.

"In all seriousness, though, what I'm saying is that individually this process will be long and painful. Unfortunately, wound cleaning... sucks." I say.

"I thought we just finished the long and painful?!" He laughs nervously, shaking his head.

"Sadly, we are just getting started."

"Jesus..." He sighs, heading back to the scotch on the counter.

As I watch him move, and appreciate the gloriousness of his half naked body, a thought suddenly pops into my head. One that is equally as efficient as it is... sinful.

"Well, there is another idea..." I say slowly, swallowing hard. "Perhaps we could clean them all in one go."

I tuck a strand of hair behind my ear, debating if I really want to say this out loud.

"I'm listening," he says, throwing back another drink. "What do you have in mind?"

I pause a moment, feeling my breath hitch in my throat.

"Maybe you could just get into the shower, and we could blast these wounds, with soap and water, all at once."

I try my best to say this in a medically professional tone,

ignoring the fact that I instantly feel warmer at the possibility of seeing him completely naked.

I see Jaxon freeze as he puts the scotch back down on the counter. He turns to look at me, sending shivers down my spine.

A wicked grin, the intensity of which I have never seen, spreads across his face, making him look positively terrifying and deliciously tantalizing at the same time. He steps toward me, his eyes staring straight into mine.

I suddenly feel like the lamb who has mistakenly wandered into the wolf's den.

"Let me get this straight," he whispers, his voice low and dangerous. "You want me to strip down, and get in the shower? Here, now?"

"Yeah, just to clean your wounds... all at once," I say, hating how breathless I sound. "Purely *medicinal*."

He takes another step towards me and unbuckles his belt buckle, as my heart threatens to come hammering out of my chest. His eyes are fixed on mine as he unzips his pants and steps out of them, inching ever closer to me. He now stands before me in nothing but his black boxer briefs.

"Purely, Miss Tyler?"

He reaches for my hand, kissing the inside of my wrist and looking up at me with those piercing blue eyes. Every thought I have mulling around in my brain evacuates like a bomb went off.

Despite willing myself not to look down, I fold, taking in the full beauty of Jaxon. I assumed he would be physically fit because of the lifestyle he led and the way his clothes always seemed to cling to his body. But seeing him now, in his practically naked glory, I realize I was wrong.

He is perfection personified. An Adonis in human form.

"Deal, on one condition," he says, his face inches from mine.

He runs a finger along my chin, tilting my head back to look in his eyes. My heart is pounding so loud I am sure he can hear it.

"Which is?" I whisper.

He sits down on the chair behind him and pulls me down so that I am straddling him. I can feel his arousal between my legs, separated only by just a few thin layers of clothing. He threads his fingers through my hair and lands a bruising kiss on my lips. Every cell in my body is immediately set ablaze.

I press my hand gently to his chest, reminding myself that this is not a dream, and give into his passion, pushing my tongue inside his mouth. He matches my fervor, pressing me against him, and his erection, and prolonging the magic between us. I pull away breathless, and it's then I can feel his heart racing under my hand. With his fingers still in my hair, he gently tilts my head back and places three tantalizing kisses on my collarbone.

"Alexa, start the shower and dim the lights," Jaxon speaks to his virtual assistant, against my neck.

I feel his nose trail my neck and his lips gently kiss my earlobe, as I hear him inhaling my scent, making me warm between my legs. Behind me the shower turns on, and I see the lighting decrease to a gentle ambiance as I start to tremble.

"What is your condition?" I whisper.

However, I am convinced now that no matter what he asks of me, I will certainly agree. He releases my hair and kisses me gently on my lips, then pulls back, forcing me to stare directly into his breathtakingly blue eyes.

"My condition is," he says commandingly. "That you are getting in *with* me,"

Fireworks erupt in my stomach, instantly obliterating any hope of intelligent thought. Almost too intoxicated to respond, my brain speaks slowly, as if on autopilot.

"Jaxon, this is supposed to be about what you need," I whisper. "You're the one who is hurting right now."

He smiles, his eyes fervent and wild.

"Natalie, I've been hurting since I met you. I just didn't know what for," he whispers, his voice seductively low. "I want you, desperately, and right now, the only thing I need is *you*."

He says this as if he is a man on fire, gently gripping my chin in his fingers, while pushing my hips down harder onto his erection.

"Baby girl, I know full well I don't deserve you. But, if you let me, I will *worship* you."

I am done for. I want him… and I am going to have him.

"Yes," I breathe.

Jaxon stares into my eyes, then cups my face with his hands, kissing me slowly and ardently. Then he pulls back, resting his head against mine, his chest breathing deeply. He slowly reaches for the top of my black button up, his eyes locked on mine, with a look that will be etched forever on my soul.

This is happening.

Time slows, and I can feel the breath shared between us. He gently undoes the first button and traces his fingers along my neck and collarbone. A quiet moan escapes my lips as he presses his lips delicately to my skin. Suddenly, I hear the tearing of fabric, as I realize he has ripped open my shirt, unable to wait any longer. I melt watching his eyes pour over my exposed chest and feel his hands slide up my back, squeezing me against him, and pressing his hard cock against me. My breath hitches, and I am shocked at his aggression, but I am certainly not objecting.

"Yes," I repeat softly, looking into his eyes, begging him to continue. "Please, don't stop…"

He hesitates no longer, and buries his face in my fully exposed neck, kissing me passionately, as his hands travel along my ribs and up the front of my chest to the front clasp of my bra.

"I want you to understand, Natalie, this is *everything* to me," he says, his eyes holding mine.

Jaxon unclips my bra, exposing my breasts and letting it fall to the floor. His eyes ravenously rake my body, cupping my breast in his hand, and with the other leaning me back.

He kisses down my neck and breasts, stopping only to firmly place his mouth around each of my erect nipples, teasing them with his tongue, sucking and pulling, causing an incredible sensation in my stomach.

"Jaxon…" I moan, feeling his tongue tantalizing me, his other hand holding my ass hard against his bulging erection.

I am lost in this—in him.

"I've never needed anyone," he whispers, his cock throbbing against my clothed pussy, and his mouth instantly returning to his relentless pleasuring of my nipples. "But I need *you*, Natalie."

The way he says my name sends me over the edge and I lose all control.

"Oh my God, Jaxon…" I mumble incoherently. "Yes."

He pulls away to look at me, the wildly wicked look in his eyes returning with smoldering intensity.

"I was right…" he teases, cupping my cheek and kissing me hard. "That *does* sound better in person."

In one swift motion, Jaxon stands with me still straddling him, my legs wrapped around his waist and his hands around my thighs, holding me tightly. With his mouth on mine, and his tongue in my mouth, he walks both of us into the already heated shower.

Water pours over my body as he pushes me aggressively against the shower wall, pressing his groin between my legs and making me moan. He continues to kiss down my neck and breasts as the water flows down between us. Placing me on my feet in front of him, his hand reaches down my body, cupping my pussy in his fingers, touching me gently.

"Fuck..." I mumble, electricity shooting through my body as his fingers massage and tease me.

Jaxon's mouth is all over my neck and tits, squeezing them with the rhythm of his fingers between my legs. His fingers reach for the edge of my leggings, and his eyes meet mine. Neither of us say a word, but I can tell he wants to see my face as his hand slips underneath the fabric, and his fingers gently brush softly against the lips of my pussy.

"Jesus Christ..." he whispers, visibly faltering. "You are so fucking wet."

He steadies himself against the shower wall behind me, as I moan against him, feeling him gently caress me, and gasp out loud as he slips a finger inside me.

"Yes, you... did... this..." I whisper breathlessly, as my body convulses in pleasure.

"Oh, sweetheart," he growls heavily against my neck, sucking on my earlobe. "I am *just* getting started."

He brings his fingers to his mouth and sucks them, his eyes burrowing into mine.

"You taste fucking incredible."

Jesus Christ.

I'm certain I am no longer breathing.

He kneels in front of me, hooking his fingers under my leggings and underwear, gently pulling them down. He silently helps me step out of them and tosses them in the corner. I stand before him, completely naked now, and breathing heavily, realizing his face is just inches away from my throbbing pussy.

His eyes find mine, and then I understand that Jaxon is doing something he doesn't usually do...he's asking for *permission*.

"Don't stop, Jaxon," I breathe. "Please."

Before I can process another thought, his face is against my pussy. He presses hand on my abdomen, pinning me against the wall and exploring the most sensitive parts of me. My body shudders and seizes as I cry out in pure ecstasy.

"Holy shit..."

I'm in heaven as his tongue probes and encircles me, sending rapturous shock waves throughout my body.

Now who is torturing whom?

Just when I feel like my legs might give out, he relents, kissing up my body. He gently helps me to the stone bench in the shower and motions for me to sit. I can feel my clit pulsing, dripping with desire and wanting more. Almost as if he can read my thoughts, he kneels back down before me and pushes two fingers inside me.

"Oh my God!" I moan, as his eyes find mine. I push myself up off my elbows and further against his hand.

His fingers gently start pushing and pulling inside of me, almost as if he is beckoning me to him in a 'come hither' motion. His eyes canvas my body reverently. He takes my leg in his hand, kissing my calf just behind my knee and making me shiver. Everywhere he touches sends waves of goosebumps across my skin.

I can barely form coherent thoughts, but luckily, Jaxon speaks for both of us.

"I don't know what it is that you do to me, Natalie, but fuck, baby, I want you."

Ummm, yes. Exactly that.

"I want you, too, Jaxon," I whisper, watching the water streaming down his face.

He stares at me, placing his hands on my knees and slowly spreading my legs further before him. I breathe in quickly, tensing as I realize how vulnerable my position is. Somehow, I'm now naked, wet, and spread-eagled in front of this dangerous mafia boss, who is asking to worship me.

He kisses along my thigh before staring deep into my eyes and biting his lip, a look of wanting I have never before seen on a man.

Holy. Shit.

I feel so wonderfully exposed, so devilishly naughty watching him look at me with such desire.

"You are so beautiful," he says softly. Then all at once, he buries his face in my pussy.

"Oh my God!!" I cry out, grabbing the back of his hair.

His tongue circling my clit, he continues his relentless rhythmic torture with his fingers inside me. The sensations wrack my body, thoroughly catching me off guard and making me cry out again.

"Fuck me!" I moan, lost in pleasure.

He smiles up at me, still moving his fingers inside me.

"Oh yes, baby, trust me, I am going to fuck you senseless," He places his thumb on my clit and my body responds, giving him complete control of my body. "But first, I want to taste your cum."

Oh, my God!

"And this time there will be no fucking interruptions," he growls, pulling my legs towards him.

Wrapping his hand under my thigh, he pins me beneath him, maneuvering my legs over his broad shoulders and giving him better access to all of my most sensitive areas.

Then presses his mouth back to my pussy, continuing *his* steady and merciless torture, even when my legs start to shake.

I'm helpless, the pleasure is almost too much. I'm falling apart, inching ever closer to the edge, as he continues relentlessly. My orgasm builds inside me, the sensations of his fingers and tongue connecting and merging into one. And then suddenly the climax hits me like a freight train.

"Jaxon!"

My body seizes, the warm tingling sensation permeating every fiber of my being.

Jaxon gently slows the rhythm of his fingers inside me, a satisfied grin on his face.

I must kiss him. Now.

I sit up quickly, landing a passionate kiss against his lips, pushing my tongue into his mouth, still feeling the blissful waves of pleasure. When I pull back, pressing my forehead to his, the devilish grin on his face has only intensified.

"You see how good you taste?" He whispers. "That's why I couldn't get enough."

Holy shit! Did he really just say that?

"Jaxon, that was amazing," I whisper between labored breaths.

"As I said, baby girl, this is only the beginning," he whispers, kissing my neck. "I've waited so long for you and I am going to savor every single bit of you I can have."

"You," I say, kissing him again. "You can have all of me."

Lightning flashes in his eyes, and he kisses me again.

"Good. Because I want it all," he growls.

His finger gently strokes my extremely sensitive clit, making me jump.

"But now you are ready for all of *me*."

Before I can respond, he uses the other fingers to spread my pussy lips apart. I squirm, my body shaking as he groans, licking his lips and practically staring *inside* me.

Jesus Christ, this is vulnerable.

Jaxon removes his boxers, fully baring himself to me.

Holy shit...he's huge!

He stares at my pussy while he strokes his sizable length. My heart starts racing and I can feel my cum trickling down my body. His eyes meet mine, and I feel my feverish need return.

I've only had a piece of him, but now I want *all* of him.

"Jaxon..." I whisper, channeling every ounce of temerity I possess. "I'm yours. Take me."

My statement registers in his eyes and without another word, he grabs my hand and pulls me up with him. In a flash he picks me up, grabbing my legs just below my ass, and pinning me against the wall. The cold wall, mixed with the fact that his erection is no longer clothed, and is touching my pussy delivers shock waves across my body.

His lips find mine, passionate and ravenous. He presses his forehead pressed to mine, breathing hard.

"You want this?" he whispers softly.

"Yes, Jaxon," I breathe against his lips. "I want you."

With that Jaxon presses his face to my neck, pushing his cock inside me. My already throbbing and swollen pussy expands around him as he thrusts inside of me. He moans, a guttural symptom of his need and pleasure.

"Holy *fuck*..." he whispers, thrusting slowly into me again, causing me to convulse and grip him tightly. "Oh my God, Natalie, you are so incredibly tight."

His breath hitches as he thrusts in again and presses his lips to mine, pushing his tongue into my mouth.

"Fuck..." he groans.

"Oh God," I moan loudly. "Jax, that feels so good."

"Yes, baby..." he whispers again.

I feel him swell inside me, my pussy contracting around him. With every thrust I stare into his gorgeous blue eyes. His rhythm is steady and strong, and I bury my face in his neck as sounds of passion erupt from me.

His pain is forgotten, and my insecurities are forgotten too. In this moment between us, nothing else in the world matters.

We are simply two souls, *burning* for each other. My hands are in his hair, and his are squeezing my ass, pulling me down on his cock. He sucks on my neck, causing me to tense and shiver against him.

And then, out of nowhere, a second orgasm hit me.

"Jaxon, I'm...I'm...cuming!" I cry out as my pussy immediately squeezes and contracts around him, relishing the feeling of him filling every inch of me."Yes! Fuuuuck!"

"Good girl," he whispers against my lips, his eyes closed and his rhythm increasing. I squeeze him tightly as waves of delight crash over me.

He kisses me hard, and I cup his face in my hands, watching as his climax nears. But just before, he releases me carefully and pulls out of me, continuing to stroke himself while kissing me.

He's just going to jerk himself off after that? No. Fuck that!

"No," I say, holding his gaze while taking his cock in my hand. "Let *me* do this."

I resume his rhythm, stroking his length and squeezing the head of his cock.

"Cum for me, Jaxon."

"Fuck!" he whispers as he reaches the pinnacle of ecstasy, exploding in my hand. He presses his lips to mine as his body shivers, before pulling me into his arms. I press my forehead to his, the two of us lost in our bliss…and each other.

Chapter Thirty-Six

JAXON

"I like this one," Natalie says, twirling around in my closet in one of my t-shirts.

"Then it's yours," I grin.

"Now I think I just need pants," she says, biting her lip.

But when I see her perky nipples pressing against the thin fabric, and the immaculate curve of her ass poking out the bottom of my shirt, I decide otherwise.

"Nah, I don't think so," I growl, pulling her to me and pressing her against my throbbing erection. "I think I might just ban you from wearing clothes all together,"

She giggles, kissing me hard. "I'm not opposed."

I'm about to take her right here in the closet, but then a knock sounds at the bedroom door, distracting us both from our little tryst.

What the hell? I specifically told Marta we were not to be disturbed!

"I can get it!" Natalie steps toward the door. "It's just Charlie, I asked him to see if he could find and bring a couple of things up here to—"

"Whoa, hold up there, tiger," I chuckle, catching her around the waist. "You, my dear, do not have pants on, remember?"

"Whoops," she giggles bashfully. "But this shirt is basically long enough. It is just Charlie."

"As a truly *impartial* judge, I'm pretty sure the "butler" has seen more than enough of you already, missy."

Stepping in front of her, I snag the opportunity to gently swat her fine naked ass, barely hidden under my t-shirt.

"Naughty boy!" she laughs as we both step into the bedroom. "Well then, *Your Honor*, I humbly ask for that incident to be stricken from my record."

"On what grounds?"

"On the grounds that he's not *really* a butler," she says innocently, leaning against the wall behind the door.

"Perhaps," I wink at her.

I exhale, trying my best to put on a more serious face when dealing with my men, before opening the door so that it discreetly hides Natalie.

"Sir," Charlie says, "here are the items Miss Tyler requested."

"Thank you, Charlie." I nod, taking the glass bottles from him. "Have someone retrieve Miss Tyler's belongings from The Jefferson," I say, trying to hide my smirk. "She won't be returning."

At least not if I have any say in it.

"Already done, Sir," he says, shooting me a cheeky smile.

"Good."

Unable to hide it, I smirk back at him as I close the door, deciding I will allow it from Charlie, who was anything but subtle regarding his approval of Natalie.

Seems like Natalie is stealing the hearts of my men.

"I'm not returning to The Jefferson, eh?" Natalie says with a smirk, raising a brow at me. "And here I thought we agreed you weren't going to try and hold me hostage anywhere anymore."

Rolling her eyes with a smile, she trots off toward the bathroom.

"If you will recall, Miss Tyler," I chuckle. "I believe I agreed I wouldn't let anyone *else* try and hold you hostage. I said nothing about making you my personal prisoner."

I roll the two tiny glass bottles filled with clear liquid around in my hand. For the life of me, I don't have any idea what these things are, or why Natalie would have asked Charlie for them.

"Are you trying to get out of our deal on a technicality? That is a dirty trick, Mr. Pace!" she calls teasingly to me from the bathroom, as I hear her shuffling about in there.

"Well, dirty *is* my favorite."

I sit on the bed, putting my hands behind my head and purposefully positioning myself so that when she returns she is greeted with a full "crotch view."

She appears with her medical bag, a bowl of water, and a few hand towels.

"Hey Baby," I say, raising my brows at her with a goofy exaggerated cockiness. "Like the view?"

"Oh Lord," she giggles, rolling her eyes. "But yes."

She throws her hand on her hip and just shakes her head at me, paralyzing me with that addictive smile of hers.

"So, what are these exactly?" I ask, placing the two bottles in her hand. "I tried to read the labels, but they are indecipherable as if they are in French."

"Well, this is Penicillin, it is to prevent infection," she says, holding up the first.

But I've already stopped listening.

The sunset over the bay is casting a radiant glow across her face. Her hair is a wavy mess, and her tits are still poking through my t-shirt. My shirt, which barely covers her curvy thick ass, is held up by those long legs of hers.

God she is pretty.

I reach forward and stroke the outside of her naked thighs, feeling her beautifully soft skin again under my fingertips, and feeling my desire igniting in my blood.

"And this is Lidocaine," she says, holding up the second bottle. "It will numb the area surrounding your wounds so you will not feel anything while I'm stitching you back together."

"Wait… this was an option the whole time?!" I say incredulously. "As in, we could've done this *before* you dug that bullet fragment from my arm?!"

"Technicality," she winks at me.

I laugh, a big hearty laugh, and Natalie does too.

Unable to resist her beauty any longer I seize this opportunity to pull her down on top of me again, kissing her deeply and staring into her mossy green eyes.

"You," I say, gently placing my hands on the outside of her thighs.

"You," she whispers. She leans forward and kisses me, still chuckling against my lips.

"How did you even get your hands on these?" I ask.

"Well, you mentioned something about Dr. Franklyn's stash, and I remembered hearing his name when I arrived with Charlie and Josiah," she shrugs. "Since I do house calls with my job I just correctly assumed since he was *here* that perhaps he might have one or both on hand. So, I just texted Charlie to go find them and bring them to me."

"Just like that?" I chuckle, impressed.

"Yup," she says, beaming at me.

"Miss Tyler, you constantly find a way to surprise me," I say, sitting up and cupping her face in my hands. "How do you keep doing that?"

"Oh, I am full of surprises," she says, biting her lip.

"Is that so?" I ask, pushing my growing erection against her pussy. "Shall I endeavor to find out more of them?"

I am eager to get inside of her again. And by eager, I mean fucking impatient.

Natalie's pussy felt incredible and I want more.

"I hope you do. And I will let you," she says, kissing me passionately. But just as I slip my hands up her body, she pulls away quickly. "*After* I close up these wounds, of course."

I collapse back on the bed in defeat. "More merciless torture… and you call *me* a sadist."

"I think I called you a masochist, actually," she says, using a syringe to draw out the Lidocaine. "And this should help make this a more merciful kind of torture. I promise."

"Fine, but *you* are not going anywhere," I say, placing my hands on her hips again. "Whatever you need to do, you can do it just like this with you on top of me. This works for me."

"Fair compromise, sir."

It beats any alternative. Well, maybe not any.

Over the course of the next hour, Natalie worked on sewing me back together.

She was right, the Lidocaine made it tolerable.

And, true to her word, she sutured each wound while straddling me across my lap.

Surprisingly, having her body so close to mine, but not actively fucking, was strangely intimate and comforting. We took the opportunity to continue to get to know some random little facts about each other.

I learned that Natalie hates pickles, but she loves classical music and the theater. She tells me about her favorite sports teams, and how she's always wanted to see the northern lights.

In turn I tell her about how I grew up listening to the oldies, and can't stand twangy country music. I even swallow my pride and confess that I don't follow any particular sports teams, and that despite being pretty good with a firearm, I'm absolute garbage when it comes to playing video games.

As I periodically run my hands over her naked thighs, we also discuss the more serious issues as well.

Everything from the harsh realities of the life I live, to our views on family and children.

"I loved being an only child, but I was lonely sometimes too," Natalie says softly. "So I'd probably say two."

"I love my daughter," I say as she bandages the gunshot wound on my shoulder. "But I'd love to have a son too."

"For your legacy to continue?" she asks.

"No, because then I'd have the best of *both* worlds," I grin, putting my other arm behind my head, resting comfortably. "It's funny how things change. Before Jessica was born, I didn't really want to have kids. In fact, I was adamantly against it. Perhaps I just wasn't ready to process the responsibility of fatherhood."

Natalie smiles, continuing her sutures.

"But after she was born," I say, shaking my head with a smile. "Man, I was done for."

"You were smitten, huh?"

"Completely. She was the most perfect thing I have ever seen," I say quietly. "I will never forget how incredible it felt, holding her for the first time. Knowing she was part of *me*."

I sigh, swallowing hard.

"I just wish she hadn't been born into this life," I say quietly. "She deserves the world, and I…well, I feel like I'm letting her down. I never know if I'm doing it *right*."

"You really are, Jaxon. Jessica is an incredible kid," she says with a smile. "She is smart, and *brave*."

Natalie glances at me and then bites her lip.

"I don't want to bring up a sensitive subject," she says cautiously. "But I've never met a six-year-old who could stand her ground like Jessica. I guess she has her father's fierce personality. As well as his good looks."

She winks at me, and I smile.

God, she's amazing.

I continue stroking Natalie's thigh under my fingers, and decide to ask the question I've been avoiding.

"I suppose I'm a bit late in asking this question, but are you on any kind of…birth control?"

She injects the last wound on my pec muscle with the anesthetic, and I wince.

"Sorry, I promise it's the last one," she says, carefully threading the needle. "And yes, I am on the pill. I've actually been since I was sixteen, because unfortunately I had horrible migraines as a teenager."

I nod, chuckling to myself.

"Funny, I'm actually a stickler for that kind of thing. But with you, I didn't even think about it. And, even if I had, I don't think I even *have* any condoms in this house. I've never needed them here."

Natalie gently uses her forceps to place the last suture, glancing up at me cautiously. "Do you *usually* use condoms?"

"Always," I say, looking at the ceiling. "I have to."

This was true, I never would sleep with a woman without using protection, as that was a massive risk I did not need in my life. However, for some reason, when all this went down with Natalie today, I hadn't been the least bit concerned.

Perhaps it was naive, but knowing what I know of her, I actually believed what she had told me about her limited sexual history.

But now that I think about it, maybe *I'm* the bigger risk.

After all, I'm the one who has been far more sexually active than Natalie.

And if the roles were reversed...

My eyes find hers, and I wonder if she can hear my thoughts.

"Natalie," I say, clearing my throat. "It just occurred to me that I...well, maybe I was a little bit selfish today."

"What?" she asks, confused. "What do you mean?"

"Well," I sigh, searching for the right words. "When everything happened between us there, I got so caught up in the heat of the moment, and I just *trusted* you. Which is weird for me, because I hardly trust anyone."

I take a deep breath.

"I guess part of me assumed you would've said something if you were at all uncomfortable. But, looking at it now, I'm sorry if my actions were selfishly motivated without considering *your* concerns."

Natalie smiles.

"I'm truly honored that you trust me, Jaxon," she says softly. "But..." A soft blush settles across her cheeks as her gaze breaks from mine.

She looks down at her hands, biting her lip.

"But...*my* lifestyle makes you nervous," I finish for her.

She nods gently, but I see the tentative look in her eyes.

Sitting up on one of my elbows, I use my other hand to cup her face, my thumb stroking her cheek.

"Natalie, if you are *ever* unsure about anything please do not hesitate to ask me," I say, waiting until her green eyes find their way back to mine. "Always tell me anything that is preying on your mind. I promise to give you the truth."

I kiss her softly, taking my time and savoring her soft lips.

"Yes, it is true, I've had a crazy go of things for a few years, with a few…partners," I say gently. "But as I said, I'm always careful. And I always see Dr. Franklyn afterwards, just as a precaution."

"That's smart," Natalie says, leaning her head against my hand.

"And, please know, I never would have initiated sex, without protection, if I knew there was *any* risk to you. I respect you too much to ever do something like that to you."

She smiles, leaning in to kiss me again, lingering this time on my lips.

"I know," she whispers against my lips. "You've only ever protected me, and been honest with me, no matter how hard it was. So, in that moment, I guess that I just decided that I trust you too."

Her words stun me to my core.

There is no way for her to know, nor could I ever hope to explain, the emotions this simple sentence makes me feel.

Natalie *trusts* me.

Somehow I, Jaxon Pace, the asshole, the gangster, the combatant, have earned the trust of the most incredible woman I have ever met. And this woman, who is so far above me in more ways than I could ever count, has taken a leap of faith…on me.

Natalie actually trusts me.

This time I cannot stop myself. I sit up to kiss her and flip her over onto her back on the bed, landing another bruising kiss on her lips.

"I will endeavor to be worthy of that," I whisper to her, as I gaze upon her mossy green eyes. I kiss her passionately once again, fully intent on making love to this woman until I collapse from exhaustion.

The sun is shining through my windows.

Um, that shouldn't be happening?

I guess that somehow the nightly housekeeping staff forgot to set them to 'Evening' mode before they left for the night. But as I come to consciousness, I remember I had no maids in here last night…because I was with Natalie.

I yawn and roll over slowly, my body aching, protesting after being stitched together by a sexy half-naked nurse.

A nurse who is evidently *not* in bed next to me. And as I finally wake up completely, she's not anywhere to be found.

She's probably in the bathroom.

"Natalie," I call out softly. "Are you okay?"

But no response.

She must've not heard me.

I yawn again and look at the clock.

9:00 a.m.

Considering I normally can't sleep past 7:00 a.m. I'm admittedly a bit shocked. However, my body is in shambles and probably needed the extra sleep today.

I rub my eyes a few times before crawling out of bed to use the bathroom, my body objecting painfully with every single movement.

"Hey, Nat?" I call softly, knocking on the door. "You in here?"

But again, no response.

This time I open the door, and realize she is not in the bathroom either. I look around the room and listen for any sign of her.

But she's not here. Neither is her purse or phone.

Natalie is *gone.*

Forgetting my need to piss, I scramble to throw a pair of sweatpants on, my heart pounding in my chest.

Shit. When was her flight? Had she gone back to Miami?

However, just leaving in the middle of the night, without saying goodbye, doesn't seem like something Natalie would do at all. And especially after the incredible night we just had.

I try to talk myself out of it, but I cannot stop the tightness growing in my chest.

We had sex for nearly seven hours straight last night, each time better than the last. At least, it had been for me. But perhaps it hadn't been for her? Had I done something wrong? Was she upset with me?

But still, what the fuck?

Why would she just leave without talking to me?

Shirtless and furious, I yank open the door to my bedroom, intent on knocking the head off the first person I see for allowing Natalie to just leave without *telling* me. I feel like a fucking idiot for letting my guard down.

How did this happen?! Again?!

However, I hear nothing in the hallway. In fact, I hear no sound in the entire east bedroom wing of the house. Which seems incredibly odd considering how many injured men are currently occupying these rooms.

But when I reach the stairs, I hear voices. Lots of voices, coming from somewhere downstairs.

What the hell?

I fly down the stairs, realizing that the sound is coming from the kitchen. As is an enticing aroma.

Is that…bacon I smell? It can't be. The chef leaves at 7:30.

However, the moment I storm into the kitchen, I freeze.

Two dozen of my men, several still in bandages from yesterday's fight, are scattered around the kitchen. They are drinking coffee, eating… and laughing. Charlie is sitting at the island slicing and juicing oranges while chatting with Josiah. Ethan is talking with Levi in the corner. And Max and Travis sit at the breakfast bar, eating pancakes.

And in the center of all of this, standing behind the giant stove, flipping those pancakes, and frying bacon… is *Natalie.*

What in the…

I am still processing the sight before me when the room suddenly grows quiet. Suddenly aware of my presence, my men begin to stand to their feet, their jovial and relaxed expressions fading instantly. Before long, the room is completely silent, except for the sound of frying bacon.

"Jaxon! You're awake!" I hear Natalie exclaim from across the room. "Alexei, could you take this?"

She hands the pan in her hands over to Alexei, one of Levi's men, before rushing over to me and placing her hands gently on my bare waist.

"I didn't want to wake you," she says with a smile. "You needed your sleep, so I was just getting ready to bring you breakfast in bed!"

I stand frozen, too stunned to move, my brain sluggishly struggling to catch up.

"What—" I start to say.

"Sir," Ethan says, his hand clasping my non-bandaged shoulder as he steps up beside me. "Good to see you got some rest. Forgive us if we woke you. When she realized the cook had already left, Miss Tyler raided our pantry and spoiled us this morning."

Knowing that Ethan would never speak to me in such a cavalier manner in front of my men, tells he is only doing so to give me a moment to process, before I say something I shouldn't.

Natalie is beaming from ear to ear, and instantly my anger evaporates, realizing my panic was completely unnecessary.

"We can leave, Sir," Wesley, who is sitting at the giant kitchen island chimes in, reaching for his crutches. "If you prefer."

Silently my men begin to make a move for the door, and somehow this is what finally shakes me from my trance.

"No... please," I say, shaking my head. "Don't go anywhere. Enjoy yourselves."

For a moment my men observe me hesitantly, unsure if I actually *mean* what I said.

"Please." I nod sincerely. "As you were."

Slowly they begin to take their seats again, and the room soon begins to buzz again with conversation.

"How are you feeling?" Natalie asks, gently placing her head on my forehead.

"I'm... better," I answer honestly, wrapping my arm around her tiny waist. Her mere presence calms my racing anxious heart.

She's still here. She didn't leave.

"Are you hungry?" she asks, her eyes quickly flitting back to the stove. "There are eggs, bacon, pancakes, and fruit! Whatever you want!"

"Sure...any of that sounds great."

"How about you take a seat, and I'll just make you a plate?" she says enthusiastically, and I nod, watching her walk back to the stove.

I stare around the room, taking in the entirety of this scene. My kitchen has not had this many people in it since my mother died. All around me, my men chat amongst themselves, eating their breakfast or drinking their coffee, discussing football and music.

Have I ever seen any of them look so relaxed... or happy?

I walk slowly toward the stove, where Natalie is quickly frying up a couple of eggs in a pan. I lean against the counter, watching her fussing about preparing food for me.

I feel like an idiot for assuming she would just leave without saying goodbye. Or maybe I just feel like an asshole.

I always assume the worst.

Even though it was in contrast to everything I knew about her, I still immediately *thought* she might've just picked up and left. But instead, she came down here, and decided to cook breakfast for me and all my men.

The men definitely needed the morale boost.

"Breakfast!" Natalie appears next to me with a piping hot plate of food.

"Thank you," I smile, taking the plate from her and sitting down at the island.

She looks so adorable. Her hair in a messy bun, her eyes bright with happiness.

"Now, do you want coffee, or fresh squeezed juice?"

"Coffee sounds great."

"Coming right up!"

I'm still somewhat in shock, but the plate in front of me smells incredible. It tastes incredible too. And when Natalie reappears with a cup of black coffee, I've already plowed more than half of it.

"I wasn't sure how you take it?" she asks me quizzically, referring to the coffee cup in her hands.

"Just like this," I say, pulling her into my arms and resting my forehead against hers, inhaling her scent once more, overwhelmed with gratitude for her as a whole.

I kiss her cheek and whisper in her ear softly. "Thank you, Natalie, for all of this."

And for not leaving without saying goodbye.

"You're welcome," she says with a smile. "I hope I didn't scare you. You just looked so peaceful this morning, and I knew you needed to rest. I figured a good meal might help you get back on your feet."

I take a sip of my coffee and look her over, staring at the way her leggings curve around her ass, and her midriff peeks out from my t-shirt she has knotted up around her waist.

I suddenly feel a shift in what I desire.

"That's funny," I say, leaning in and kissing her earlobe, making her shudder and giggle softly. "Because I rather intend on keeping you off of *yours*."

I decide I am no longer hungry for food. Instead, I scoop her up in my arms, tossing her over my good shoulder.

"Oh my God, Jaxon!" she gasps, astonished, as some of the men in the room turn to look at the commotion.

"As you were, gentlemen," I say, heading towards the staircase, hearing a faint chuckle erupt in the room behind me. I almost wish Natalie could see the wicked grin spreading across my face.

Chapter Thirty-Seven

Natalie

I lay strewn across Jaxon's chest, feeling him breathe beneath me. My head is curled comfortably in his shoulder, as he kisses my forehead softly. He takes my hand in his, and this is how we stay, both of us coming down from the high we just reached together. The last of many.

"Did you call Mel?" he whispers, his lips still pressed to my skin.

"Yes, I talked to her this morning. I let her know I moved my flight to tomorrow." Although, the thought of leaving Jaxon is already beginning to form a pit in the middle of my stomach.

"I bet she is missing you," he whispers softly, his voice is raw and tinged with an emotion too hard to place.

"Actually, I think she is more upset about having to give Cyclops back to me," I say, kissing his chest. "She always enjoys her time as an auntie dog sitter."

I turn against his body so that I can see his face, which looks strangely sad. "I am not nearly as important as Cyclops."

He smiles back at me but says nothing, his fingers softly caressing my hair. I am convinced he is the most beautiful man I have ever seen. Even now, with the new stubble lining his chin and his hair a mess, he still looks like a god.

"What are you thinking about?" he asks me inquisitively.

Shit. Busted.

"I just cannot believe that I am here with you," I say. "No matter how many times I prepared myself for this trip, I never could have imagined any of this... or you."

I tear my eyes away from his, second guessing whether that was too forward, and trying desperately to fight the welling tightness in my chest. Jaxon raises my hand to his lips, and I look back up at him, a smile brightening his face ever so slightly.

"I know exactly how you feel." He kisses my hand again as his eyes hold mine. "I keep thinking this must be a dream, and I am going to wake up at any moment."

"I still cannot understand why you chose to waste your time with me," I say, holding his gaze. "Especially with all of the Colton drama that went down this week."

I cringe. It really had been incredibly embarrassing to have my life play out on the public stage like that. I shudder, silently wondering how on earth I stayed with Colton for as long as I did.

"Natalie, not one second of my time with you has been wasted," Jaxon says softly. "I don't give a fuck about Colton. I only ever cared about you."

When he says this, I want to swoon, but I still have a million doubts and questions. I have no idea what comes next for me and my complicated CEO of Crime.

"Why are you crying?" he asks softly, wiping my tears away and turning on his side so that he is facing me.

He wraps his arms around my naked back and pulls me flush against him. I take a deep breath, unsure of the right way to address all these secret fears spinning in my head.

"It has just been... so much in such a short amount of time," I whisper, trying to keep my emotions in check. "I guess part of me is intimidated by what I... feel for you."

"That is comforting," he says with a chuckle. "Because I am absolutely terrified." His soft blue eyes burrow into mine. "You were a stranger to me a week ago, and now you have seen parts of me and my life that I keep successfully hidden from the rest of the world," he says, touching my cheek. "Now, I don't know how I return to that life or being that person...once you are gone."

"Once you are gone."

My stomach tightens even more. That is what I am dreading most. Of course, I want to get back to my dog, my home, and my patients, but that means I have to leave Jaxon.

What becomes of us then?

Realistically, long distance relationships are hard, even when you are a billionaire. And that is assuming Jaxon even wants to continue to see each other. He certainly has no shortage of available and eager women here, desperate for the chance to spend even just a night with him, as I just had.

But as my anxiety, and overactive brain threatens to overthink this situation to pieces, Steph's words from the other day come back to me with haunting relevance.

"Don't be so quick to judge a painting while the artist is still holding the brush. Or you might miss out on something beautiful."

She is right. No matter what comes of Jaxon and I, the painting is still being painted, and at the end of the day it is still beautiful, no matter what.

I knew what I was doing when I said yes yesterday.

I knew that there was a chance that whatever this was could just be a moment in time, and I accepted that. I had no regrets then, and I will not tolerate any now.

Because the truth is, I would rather live in a world where I had one incredible moment with Jaxon, than live in a world where I did not. Even if this only becomes a memory. And despite all reason, here in Jaxon's arms, I feel like I am exactly where I am supposed to be at this moment.

I sit up on my elbow and kiss him slow and deep, taking my time to linger on his lips, and feel his body tense beneath mine. Pulling back, I run my fingers through his messy hair. I watch him close his eyes and lean into my touch as I canvas his entire face, wanting to imprint it to memory.

He is beautiful. This is beautiful.

And I decide that I am going to spend every single second with him, appreciating this beautiful moment in time. Until I have to leave.

He opens his eyes, and I am aware that I am smiling.

"My God, you are beautiful." he says with sincerity.

I giggle to myself, considering the irony of the internal conversation I just had with myself.

"What?" He is confused, but a playful smile crosses his face.

"Nothing." I chuckle to myself and kiss him again. "Nothing at all."

Suddenly I feel his body shift, pressing us closer together. His hands slide down my back and settle on my hips.

Oh my...

"Jaxon..." I say sheepishly. "As much as I want to do that again, I don't know if I can. I don't know if I can even walk," I finish with a giggle.

"Fair enough," He smiles up at me and nods. "Fuck, why do I want you so badly? All the time?" he says in disbelief. "I can barely move myself and yet..." He motions to his waist, now clearly erect, and I giggle again.

"Maybe I've cast a spell on you..." I narrow my eyes at him and wave my fingers around in the air mischievously.

He smiles with a wolfish grin in his eye. "Is that so?" he growls at me. "I should have known you were up to some voodoo, devil woman." He tries to pin me beneath him, as I scramble out of the bed with a mirthful laugh. But he follows quickly, playfully stalking me into the closet and catching me in his arms.

"Eek!" I shriek with laughter, as he kisses me softly.

"I'd believe it, you know," he says as he pulls away from me. "There is something enchanting about you. Some kind of magic."

I blush, but I revel in the bliss I feel right now compared to a few moments ago.

Jaxon claps his hands together. "Okay, so what would you like to do today?"

"What are my options?" I ask as I walk over to my suitcase. I pull a pair of dark jeans and a casual gray sweater.

"Anything you want," Jaxon says, pulling on a pair of underwear. I savor the view of 'the goods' before it is clothed.

Holy crap! I cannot believe I had that inside of me.

"Are you peeking, Miss Tyler?" he says as he sees me staring. "I thought you needed a break, but I will take these off in a heartbeat if you change your mind." He grins wickedly.

I blush, but shake my head. "How about a tour of this gorgeous house? I have only seen your bedroom and your kitchen so far."

"We can do that," he says, raising his brows in a lighthearted shrug. "Hell, it has been a while since I have seen most of the house myself. I probably have forgotten parts of it." he chuckles.

I chuckle to myself, wondering what it is like to have a house so big you forget parts of it entirely.

As I watch him pull a gray t-shirt over his perfect abs, I resist the urge to reach out and touch them. It seems he feels comfortable showcasing part of his tattoos now that I've seen them in their full naked glory. I smile to myself.

"Do you mind?" I ask, as I purposefully put on a bra that has a back clasp. I pull my hair off to the side, and look over my shoulder to him, now pulling on a pair of blue jeans.

The moment he looks up at me I hear him breathe heavily and move towards me slowly. This is an intentional move on my part. I am giving him a little tease, hoping to drive him wild. But then I feel his lips touch the skin on my neck and feel his hot breath, immediately making me shiver at his touch.

Oh no... what have I done?

Jaxon kneels behind me and runs his hands slowly along my backside and hips, taking his sweet time on his way up my back. He places a trail of kisses up my spine, making me shiver before very slowly clasping my bra together. His hands hook into the belt loop on my jeans, and he turns me to face him.

"Why is it that if I give you an inch, you take a mile, Mr. Pace?" I smile slyly at him, and run my fingers through his chestnut hair as he presses his lips to my abs.

"Well..." he says, placing a kiss dangerously low on my stomach. "I did promise you, Miss Tyler..." he whispers against my skin, kissing me again. "That I would worship you," he says, raising his face slowly so that he is between my breasts.

Jesus Christ...

I fear I might spontaneously combust as he slowly kisses each of my breasts, and then my collarbone.

He continues this onslaught as he stands up and kisses my neck, then he cups my face in his hands. "I intend to keep that promise."

Oh my...

My heart explodes inside my chest, overwhelmed by this statement. Jaxon kisses me softly, tucking my hair behind my ear.

"But you *have* seen more than enough of my closet." He winks at me and then settles on the bench and begins to put on a pair of boots.

Damnit! My plan to tease him completely backfired on me!

Now my skin and body are burning for him, and I almost debate jumping his bones again here and now but decide that I do want to see the rest of his house. We can always come back to *this* later.

Pace Manor, as it was known in the time of his father and grandfather, is magnificent.

The mansion hosts twenty-two guest bedrooms sprinkled across the east and west wings, and over a dozen separate areas of the house dedicated to entertaining guests, including a formal ballroom. Additionally, it has all of the modern amenities as well, such as a movie theater, indoor gym, and racquetball courts.

But by far, my favorite room of all, was the three-story library off the back of the house. This glorious respite was replete to the brim with immense collections of books and original manuscripts, all of which had been painstakingly collected by his family over the last six decades. And if this room wasn't beautiful enough, the back half of the library facing the bay opened into a colossal eighteenth century iron solarium, allowing the sun to brilliantly filter into half the room during the day.

I was smitten. If given the opportunity, I could happily spend hours in there, just reading Shakespeare in the sunshine.

But this estate, although still maintaining its original charm and grace, was intended to be more than just a beautiful piece of architecture. It was also constructed to be a *fortress*. All the exterior windows were bulletproof glass, and there were multiple secret passages in the house leading to various exits.

On top of that, beneath the sprawling lawn, gardens, and stables existed a full underground *bunker*. This bunker came complete with a command center, three bedrooms and all the modern comforts and supplies to last up to six months.

And as a last resort, in the event of a full-scale evacuation, there were the tunnels. They snaked down the cliffside to the cove at the bottom, where in theory a boat could be waiting to spirit any evacuees away. However, thankfully, this provision had yet to be necessary for any of the Pace family.

The house had been maintained to an incredible scale, with several massive renovations over the last thirty years, updating the security and fortitude each time.

It was certainly a home fit for a mafia boss.

A little after one we conclude our tour, landing on the patio, where we help ourselves to a bottle of wine, and enjoy the warm late summer sun. Here I sit, admiring the look of blissful relaxation on Jaxon's face. His body no longer rigid and tense, he almost looked like a different person altogether.

But still just as beautiful.

"Sir," Ethan says, gently interrupting our conversation about sailboats as he walks outside. "I just want to let you know that all of the men are on the mend, and Dr. Franklyn has shipped off. Therefore, I am on my way to retrieve Miss Pace, as we discussed."

"Ooh! Jessica!" I say impulsively.

Jaxon told me last night that she was tucked away in a safehouse with her nanny a few miles away. Just a precaution until all of his men had been tended to by Dr. Franklyn and the scene at the house was no longer one of carnage. I cannot deny that I am excited to see her sweet face again before I have to leave.

Jaxon glances between Ethan and myself, slowly a bemused expression settles on his face. "You know what, Ethan, why don't we join you?"

"Yes, Sir," Ethan says with a grin.

It feels so good to see Ethan smiling.

I follow Ethan and Jaxon to the two Range Rovers outside.

"We will take this one alone," Jaxon says to his men, and Ethan, Charlie and a man named Levi pile into the other SUV.

Once we are on our way, I find a station on the radio playing music from the seventies, remembering that Jaxon prefers the oldies. Jaxon takes my hand, as *How Deep Is Your Love* by the Bee Gees comes on the radio, and I lean back in the seat, smiling to myself.

Perhaps that is the beauty of living in the moment—it allows you to experience everything around you to the fullest capacity. We drive in silence along the quiet streets of Winnetka, the autumn colors on full display.

Soon we reach another iron gate, with a long driveway. But instead of pulling up in front of the large house, Jaxon takes us to the pool house in the back.

"The house is vacant. It was owned by a friend of the family, it now belongs to my estate," he explains, as we walk to the back yard. "The land, the permits, everything is in a trust in that family's name. Meaning that no one knows I own the property, which increases its security as a safehouse."

However, when we walk inside the pool house, it is empty. I look around slightly confused, until I see Jaxon remove a picture from the wall, revealing a screen on which he places his hand for a fingerprint scan. A soft buzzing echoes in the room, and a large panel on the floor opens slowly revealing a staircase, leading underground.

Holy shit! This is incredible!

The technology may be amazing, but I am not at all surprised by the level of detail Jaxon has applied surrounding Jessica's safety, as everything Jaxon did was done to the highest efficiency. And this was the security of his daughter. Ethan stays behind in the pool house as the two of us descend the narrow staircase.

"Who is that?" I hear Jessica say, and before we can even reach the bottom of the stairs, her cherubic face appears in the doorway, and the biggest grin erupts on her face. "Daddy!" she squeals with excitement.

Jaxon picks her up into his arms as we step into the room.

The living area of the safehouse is about the size of a small studio apartment, but it looks as if an effort has been made to make it feel less like a bunker, and more like the bedroom of a six-year-old girl. Jaxon had mentioned to me yesterday he never wanted her to be afraid of coming here to the safehouse in case it was an imperative last-minute decision he had to make. Therefore, he made sure to have the designers mimic her room at the manor.

"Miss Natalie!" Jessica says from her father's arms.

"Hi there, troublemaker!" I smile.

"Did you get all your homework done, Jessibear?" Jaxon asks.

Jessica adverts her eyes and scrunches up her face. "Most of it…"

"Most of it, huh?" he asks, maneuvering her in his arms so that she has to look at him.

"Okay…" she confesses with a sheepish giggle. "Just a *little*."

"That sounds more accurate," he laughs heartily.

"Are we going *home* now?" she asks.

"Yes."

"Can Miss Natalie come too?" she whispers to her father, putting her finger to her nose, glancing at me.

Jaxon pauses for a moment, pretending to consider her request while she waits with anxious excitement.

"I suppose," he says finally, a smirk blanketing his face.

She squeals with delight and wiggles out of his arms to collect her backpack from her nanny, the shy older woman they affectionately refer to as Old Nan.

"Well, that was surprisingly easy," Jaxon whispers as he steps closer to me.

I wink at him, but then feel him cop a very sensual feel on my backside and squeeze it tightly. "And I certainly plan to make Miss Natalie *come* again this evening," he whispers in my ear. "*A lot*."

Oh my…

"I'm ready!" Jessica says, running back up to us. "I can walk on my own, Daddy."

"Well, okay then, big girl," he smiles, waving his silent thanks to Old Nan.

Jaxon starts up the stairs, and it is then I feel a little hand slip inside mine. I look down to see Jessica standing next to me with an adorable, semi-toothless grin.

She chose me.

Jess and I head up the stairs and out to the car. But the moment we step outside, Jaxon's jaw nearly drops. Jessica refuses to let go of my hand until it is time for her dad to lift her into her car seat. As the two of us pile into the front seat, Jaxon looks at me and smiles broadly.

"Some kind of magic…" he whispers.

He shoots me a wink as he fires up the engine and looks at Jessica in the rearview mirror.

"Tell you what," he says with a wild grin. "Given the last two days, I think we need to make a pitstop… for *ice cream*."

"Yesssssssss!" Jessica squeals excitedly, making the two of us laugh.

Jaxon gently takes my hand in his, and the three head off on our adventure. And as far as moments go, this might just be one of my favorites. *Ever*.

Chapter Thirty-Eight

JAXON

I carry an exhausted and drooling six-year-old wearing a Halloween costume to her bedroom. She is out.

I have never heard that child laugh that much.

We had ice cream, followed by an *actual* dinner, followed by a dramatic reenactment of her favorite cartoon superhero, and ended the evening with a movie she chose in the home theater. All of this ultimately resulted in her falling asleep between Natalie and I ten minutes into the movie.

But it was perfect. All of it was perfect.

After all, there was a moment the other night when I thought I might not see either of them again.

After putting her to bed, I walk back down the staircase, and I see Charlie and Ethan chatting softly outside the surveillance room.

"Sir," Charlie says, nodding to me.

"What's the word on that garage in Chinatown?" I ask Ethan softly, glancing towards the kitchen, confirming that Natalie is still in there, where I left her.

I want to keep this worry from her if I can.

"We just heard from our men underground. They confirmed

that they've found the garage entrance to the subway. I called our people on the city transit authority, they shut down all the trains that run through that part of town, under the guise of 'renovations.' So, we have a team down there now posing as a construction crew and gathering intel. I have also requested the city blueprints for that entire section of tunnel." he says.

"Good," I say, rubbing my chin. "Perhaps cutting off their supply lines will slow them down a bit while we calculate our next move."

"Agreed," Ethan says. "The team says they are using an old out of service platform just outside of Chinatown as an entrance into the tunnels. They have actually dug out some of the tunnel floor to give them more room between the wall and live lines to move about more freely."

Smart. Less likely to get electrocuted. Or decapitated.

"Who are these people?" I sigh.

"Sounds like there are two bosses and a bunch of pawns," Ethan says. "Intel says none of the workers we've identified are notable in any way, other than the fact that most of them are ex-cons, with a pension for violent crimes."

"So, new bosses, and an army full of grunt workers with rap sheets," I growl to myself. "That's not a healthy combination. We can't have a bunch of unstable and unhinged violent criminals flooding the streets and causing a scene, or we will lose our leverage with the city council."

"Charlie, have we heard anything from IT on the tech we found?" Ethan asks.

"Sir, Levi just cracked past the firewall on the cameras viewing your penthouse an hour ago, he is currently in there poking around and reviewing the footage as we speak," Charlie says. "He's had the IT team working round the clock shifts to decipher the encryption codes on the computers we found on the ship. We should know more shortly."

"Okay, just keep me informed, I'll keep my phone on me." I start to walk away before I stop.

Charlie.

"Charlie, I just want to tell you that you did a hell of a job protecting Miss Tyler the last few days," I say with a nod. "I don't think I could have done it better myself."

"Thank you, Sir."

His face remains stoic, but I can see the smile tugging at his eyes, and Ethan smirks his approval.

Not wanting to hover, I head back to the kitchen. However,

again I find that Natalie is nowhere to be found.

But I bet I know where she probably is, though...

As I walk down the long hallway toward the east side of the house, I eventually see light pouring out from the half-cracked library door and I realize my guess was right. I could tell she loved this room when I gave her the tour. I pull the door back silently, peering covertly inside.

The chandelier is only dimly lit, but I can still see Natalie, gingerly trailing her fingers along the bindings of books on the second floor.

"Somehow I had a feeling I'd find you here," I say, sitting down on one of the couches. "Oddly enough, this was my mother's favorite room, too. I never understood the appeal myself. You can read a book anywhere."

"Well, your first mistake is assuming that it was ever about *reading* the book in the first place," I hear her say softly. "Instead, it is about losing yourself in another world altogether."

She tears herself away from the books and starts down the spiral staircase.

"You are right, you can read a book anywhere. But there is something truly spectacular about finding a quiet, tranquil place where you can be undisturbed—and just *escape* into a book for a few hours." She wraps her arms around herself as she walks towards me. "The truth is your body will age and fail, but your imagination will stay young forever. Books are just sustenance for the soul."

She sits down on the couch with me, her eyes still canvasing the books on the shelf with delight. I wrap an arm around her, pulling her to me and breathing in her scent.

"Come to think of it, my mother would come in here for hours on end," I say, remembering my childhood. "Some days she would even go as far as to lock the door."

"I'm sure only on the days you drove her crazy, right?" Natalie teases.

"Which was every day," I chuckle. "I was a handful."

"*Was?*" Natalie says, raising a brow and winking at me.

"Never a dull moment with me hotcakes," I say, kissing her gently.

As I do, my eyes catch sight of my dad's old Victrola in the corner behind her, and the large cabinet with all of his records.

Hello there...

I remember listening to these old records many times as a child.

My earliest memories as a child were in this library. My father would often find my mother in here after a long day and slow dance with her to the old records for hours. It was all they listened to, which meant the same for me.

Which is probably the reason it is still the kind of music I prefer to this day, since I don't really have time to listen to music much anymore.

I stand up and walk over to the cedar cabinet, bursting at its seams with records from the fifties, sixties, and seventies. I find the one I am looking for and put it on the Victrola, thinking to myself that it has been nearly twenty years since I have touched this thing, and shocked I still remember how to use it.

Lucky for me, the old girl fires right up without missing a beat, and a mournful *Unchained Melody* by The Righteous Brothers begins to play, one of my absolute favorites.

Walking over to Natalie, I extend my hand to her, pulling her to me effortlessly. She folds into me as I wrap my arm around her waist. Her eyes find mine, and neither of us say a word as we just hold each other close and sway along to the music. The glow from the dimly lit chandelier makes the shadows dance around the room and casts a gentle light on her face.

"I don't want you to leave," I whisper against her ear. "I can't seem to get enough of you."

As the words pass over my tongue, I release the tension in my chest, surrendering to the impossible vulnerability I feel. None of that matters right now. In this moment, I just need to say it.

"I know," she says tenderly, reaching her hand to my cheek. "I'm kind of getting used to this."

I spin her softly, and when her eyes meet mine, I am helpless.

"So... what now?" I say softly.

This is it.

My heart begins to pound in my ears, and I'm grateful for the music, as the fear of what she *could* say next nearly paralyzes me in place. I know that she deserves more than this life. She deserves more than what I can give her. But that does not stop my selfish heart from wanting to keep this tiny piece of happiness I have found with her to myself.

Natalie Tyler has brought the sunlight back into my life, and now I find myself fearing the night that follows when she has to leave me.

"You mean... after I leave?" she asks as soft as a whisper, as she lowers her gaze to the floor. I nod, unable to speak.

"Well, if we think about this rationally, one could make the argument that this week has been incredibly intense, and perhaps we have just been swept up in its current," she says, unable to meet my gaze.

"Agreed," I choke out.

"And we live over a thousand miles apart."

"We do."

"And we both admittedly have a significant amount of baggage when it comes to *trust*."

"Surely."

"But..." she whispers, tightening her hold on me and unknowingly pulling me back from the brink of destruction with those mesmerizing eyes of hers and just one word. "...for you, Jaxon, I would be willing to *try*."

This moment is incomparable. Relief floods my body like a dam has broken. I can finally breathe again. Time seems to have slowed, and the last five years of my life pass behind my eyes.

I swore I would never let these walls down for a woman.

I swore it was something I didn't need.

I swore that it could only ever be a distraction.

I swore that it could not be good for Jessica.

I swore that I could never give a part of me away.

But I lied.

Because right here in this moment, every self-protective oath I have ever sworn to myself shatters into a thousand pieces on the floor.

And I could not be happier.

I do not deserve this woman, but by some inexplicable divine intervention she has come into my life. She is the undeniable catalyst that has changed so much around me in such a short amount of time, and I know that I will never be the same.

I kiss her softly, deeply, and fervently feeling the electricity crackle between us.

"I am yours, Natalie Tyler," I say tenderly.

Her eyes sparkle in the shadows, and her smile could light up the whole damn sky. "It might not be easy," she says softly.

"Nothing ever is," I say, squeezing her tightly.

"And at least we have tonight," she whispers against my ear, planting a tender kiss on my earlobe. I cup her face in my hands, memorizing every part of her face and landing a bruising kiss on her lips.

"Let's make the most of it."

It is just after midnight when I step out onto the balcony, with a cocktail in each hand. Natalie is standing against the railing, dressed in only one of my long sleeve t-shirts.

One that I was convinced I had left at the penthouse...

I smile to myself, realizing that perhaps a little thievery had taken place. But I am not upset about it in the least. She wants to take a piece of me *with* her, and I find that adorable.

And I kinda like it when Natalie is a bit of a naughty girl.

"Aren't you cold?" I ask with a smile, stepping up next to her, handing her one of the drinks. It's less windy tonight, but still a little cool, and she is only half-clothed.

"After what we just did?" she asks, looking up over the edge of her glass. Her eyes are bright and playful. "Hell no, Sir. I am out here just trying to cool down."

I laugh and take a drink. It is true, and we had just finished fucking our brains out for the tenth time in the last twenty-four hours.

Or was it the eleventh? Fuck... I really can't remember.

All I know is that I have spent more of my time awake buried inside of Natalie than doing anything else combined... and I want to keep it that way.

"I shall take that as a compliment."

"You should," she says, her gaze bashfully looking away from me. "Speaking of, may I ask you a question?"

"Always," I nod, appraising her carefully.

"Is it... always like *that?*"

"No," I chuckle. "It's definitely not."

"Oh," she smiles, biting her bottom lip.

I reach up to cup her face, stroking her soft lip with my thumb tenderly.

"I know that I have a bit more experience in this department than you, but I can say with confidence that I have never felt *that*, ever, with anyone."

She smiles, leaning into my hand and looking up at me with such intensity, that my veins feel as though they are catching fire within me.

She is so fucking sexy.

Natalie has this adorable innocence paired with a wild, fiery passion that creates this impossible combination of sensuality. And I, the adrenaline charged mafia Don that I am, find it positively addicting.

I step behind her, burying my face in her neck, and cupping her ass cheek in my hand as she looks out over the water.

"Do you like what I do to you, Αγαπημένη?" I growl in Greek sensually in her ear, making her giggle.

"Yes," she gasps.

Unexpectedly, I slip my hand between her legs from behind, feeling her soft pussy lips in my fingers. She is still wet from our previous adventures, dripping with need.

…Which I find *incredibly* hot.

"Jaxon…" she moans driving me wild.

"Yes, baby?" I whisper softly, kissing her neck and rubbing my fingers against her sex.

"What if someone sees us?" she replies, her voice trembling nervously as she glances around.

I grin.

I know that no one is on the grounds in the back of the house, and I know that my team would never dare to watch us on the security cameras.

Not if they valued their eyesight anyway.

But Natalie doesn't know this… which could be fun.

"Well, then I would suggest you keep quiet," I say, suddenly slipping a finger inside her, feeling her shudder. "We do not need to draw any attention to us, do we?"

"Oh, my God… maybe we should go back inside?" she whispers trying to move, but I grip the railing on either side of her, pinning her between my arms.

I kiss her cheek and return to what I was doing, slipping a second finger inside her, listening to her moan out loud as she throws her head back against my chest.

I gently wrap my free hand around her throat tilting her face up to me and kiss her lips.

"Now, now, you *must* stay quiet, Miss Tyler," I whisper wickedly in her ear. "Because we do not need the whole house knowing how fucking *wet* you are right now."

Her breathing increases and I feel her insides clench tighter, the prospect of being caught clearly elevating her experience.

"Holy fuck…" she whispers as my fingers explore and penetrate her, over and over, teasing her relentlessly.

"Now I want you to listen to me carefully," I say softly.

"Yes…"

"Do not move." I release my hand and kiss her neck gently, without stopping the motion of my hand. "And you need to keep your voice down."

"I don't know if—"

"You can. And you must," I growl sensually.

"Oh my… okay."

"Now, spread your legs."

She gasps, and I respond by moving my hand faster, calling to her with my fingers inside her, and solidifying my control over her body.

"Spread. Your. Legs." As I make my demand, I kiss her earlobe, commandingly accentuating each word. Slowly Natalie obeys and moves her legs just slightly apart. I kneel behind her, kissing both sides of her voluptuous behind, now directly in front of my face.

"Eyes forward," I say authoritatively.

"Oh, my god… Jaxon!" she exclaims.

"You had better stay quiet, Miss Tyler… unless of course you want an audience."

Obviously I'd never allow that, but this harmless 'threat' does its job to set the scene and I can instantly feel her pussy contract around my fingers.

"Now, bend over for me."

Natalie's legs shake as she slowly spreads them further apart.

"Good girl," I say, tantalizing her clit with my fingers. "Now I think it is time to inspect my work…" I spread her pussy lips apart and shove my tongue between them.

"Oh fuck!" she exclaims out loud as my tongue licks her clit."Jaxon! Oh my god!"

I briefly pull back, listening to her breathing and watching her legs tremble.

"You have to stay quiet," I say again, now using my fingers to spread her ass cheeks apart, giving me a glorious view to *all* of her and makes my cock swell immediately.

"Eek!" She breathes. "That's not easy to do! It's so sensitive from behind!"

"That's the point," I press my fingers back to her clit and slip just one finger inside of her. "But you are clearly loving this. So, go on baby, spread your fucking legs for me."

She whimpers in ecstasy, biting her bottom lip and moaning softly, desperately trying to keep her voice down. I press my tongue against her soft pussy, tasting her juices and pushing it inside her, assaulting her sensually. I feel her legs begin to tremble uncontrollably and her breath quicken.

"Jaxon... I can't... I can't take it anymore..." she whispers desperately. "Please..."

She is remarkably close, but I want to be inside her when that happens, so I continue my onslaught a moment longer before untying my robe. My cock has been throbbing the entire time. I stand up and waste no time pressing it gently to the outside of her pussy. I wrap my arms around her waist, pulling her ass against me and burying my face in her neck.

"You did well... very well..." I say, rubbing myself against her sex, teasing her.

I gently grab her chin and pull her face to mine, landing a bruising kiss on her lips.

"Shall I reward you?" I say against her lips.

"Yes...yes *please*," she says breathlessly.

"What do you want Natalie?" I ask, stroking my cock against her, teasing her entrance.

"I want you," she breathes, desperate for me.

"And you shall have me," I say, pushing inside her.

"Oh, my God... Jaxon..." she breathes as her body takes my full length inside of her. She grips the railing, her legs shaking and trembling as I find a rhythm. Slow and steady and first, I continue to thrust into her, filling all of her and feeling her swollen pussy clench around me, and her desire dripping down my leg.

"I am going to..." she whispers, her voice catching. "I am..."

"Come for me, Natalie," I say, feeling my own intensity building. Then I feel it happen.

She moans, her voice strangled as she tries flutily to restrain herself, and I feel her pussy tighten around me, and her orgasm flooding beneath me.

I am undone. I explode inside of her, feeling the cataclysmic passion, blinding both of us in a moment of exceptional bliss.

Chapter Thirty-Nine

Natalie

I look down at my hand inside Jaxon's. I have been dreading today, more than I ever thought I would. But the day has come, and it is time to go home.

Of course, I am excited to go back to my house, my dog, and my city. I have missed all of these things terribly as I knew I would when I left town for this wedding.

But what I never could have imagined, is sitting next to me in the backseat of a Range Rover, with his arm around me.

Jaxon.

He hit me like a hurricane. Terrifying. Intimidating. Dangerous. Devastating. Powerful. Breathtaking.

There was no part of me that ever expected to fall for anyone on this trip, let alone a scary billionaire mafia lord. But Jaxon is more than any of those things combined. He's also kind, generous, and thoughtful… and utterly intoxicating. All the things that drew me to him like a moth to a flame and made him impossible for me to deny. From the angry first meeting in his office, to the spectacular dates and the last two days of passionate, sensual bliss, I am completely consumed.

I couldn't deny that there was a part of me that feared how

quickly things had developed between us. One week, one blisteringly insane and spellbinding week was all it took for me to fall hard for Jaxon Pace… and for him to fall for me.

And now here we are.

It was no secret that this was going to be complicated. Both of us were somewhat terrified of how we would be able to actually make this work. Neither of us had the best luck in our previous relationships, and trust was difficult.

Understatement.

And if that was not enough of a challenge, the fact that he was the leader of the largest Chicago mafia, was something I was still wrapping my head around. The last few days have held the most terrifying experiences I had ever survived, with the kidnapping attempt of his daughter, the muggers in the alley, and the men who came for me the night of the wedding.

But they had also held some of the most incredible experiences of my life. The nine-hundred white roses, the yacht dinner, the private museum tour, and the dress he gifted me for the wedding. Not to mention the last forty-eight hours of orgasmic ecstasy.

Jaxon may be complicated, but he had opened his heart and his life to me, trusting me the way I was trying to trust him—openly and completely. And as unlikely as all of this is, somehow we've agreed to give long distance a shot. It is complicated, yes. It is also the most alive I have felt in my entire life. So I know it's worth the effort to *try*.

I look up at him as he stares out the window, his arm gently pulling me into his side, and his hand stroking my shoulder.

He is dangerously handsome.

A little stubble, from a day of being too occupied with our 'extracurriculars' to shave, lines his defined but currently clenched jaw. He seems just as disappointed as I am that our time, secluded in fantasyland, is ending.

At least for now.

I watch as Ethan turns off on the exit to the airport.

"Are you sure I can't convince you to just take my jet?" he asks softly. "There is still time for Otto to make a flight plan for Miami, and I would feel so much better about your safety," Jaxon asks, his voice soft but raw.

I smile, turning my head into him but keeping my eyes and my voice low.

"No Jaxon, I appreciate the offer but that is really unnecessary," I whisper back to him. "I already paid for this ticket, and it is only a three-hour flight."

I look up into his icy blue eyes, that stare at me now with fervent intensity, and he sighs.

"At some point, I think you are going to have to get used to a little 'unnecessary', Miss Tyler," he says with a smirk. "I'm not going to have my girlfriend always flying coach on commercial airlines." He gently kisses my forehead.

Girlfriend. Holy crap!

"So, when will I see you next?" I ask softly, swallowing back the sweet mix of bliss and sadness that wells in my throat.

"If everything goes according to plan, I will wrap up what I have going on here, and hopefully I can come down by next weekend."

This cheers me up a little, as it was sooner than I anticipated for someone with a grueling schedule like his.

"You and Jessica are more than welcome to stay with me," I say with a smile. "…and Cyclops."

Jaxon smiles, the first real smile he has had this morning. "That is a tempting offer, my dear, and I am sure Jessica will love Cyclops. She loves dogs. Although, my shepherds seem to scare her." He brushes a strand of hair from my face and looks at me reverently. "But you know I have a house there, right?"

"Ummm, how would I have known that?" I chuckle. "Where is your house?"

"Oh, it is just a little place on Miami Beach," Jaxon says with a wink, as he looks out the window.

I find his use of "little" suspicious. Nothing about this man was little.

Of that, I am certain.

"Uh huh, and um, how often do you visit your 'little' place in Miami Beach?"

"Hopefully, a lot more now," he growls playfully against my neck with a trail of kisses, before sighing deeply.

"I like that plan," I smile as he cups my face and kisses me gently. "I'm going to miss you."

"I wish you could stay a little longer…" he whispers so that only I can hear him. Shamelessly, I melt.

"I know, I do too," I say, pressing my forehead to his. "But I *do* have a job I have to get back to."

"You don't have to get back to your job, you know. You are with *me* now," he says, his face now scrunched in sarcasm. "I don't want you to do anything that doesn't make you happy."

"My job *does* make me happy, and I have patients that depend on me. Plus, I have a house and a dog and responsibilities," I say.

I pull back to look him in the eyes, gently stroking his cheek with the back of my finger.

"I like you, Jaxon Pace, a lot. But I have no interest in becoming just your little penthouse pet," I say, rolling my eyes at him sarcastically.

"None?" he growls naughtily in my ear. "You seemed to enjoy being my *pet* last night... over and over."

His hot breath on my neck, and the tempting sound of his voice are momentarily distracting. He has a way of doing this to me, and it threatens to derail my entire thought process.

"Yes, I did," I whisper back to him. "But I can barely walk straight today."

"Forgive me, I don't see how this is a problem?" he says darkly, narrowing his eyes at me.

"Moderation, Jaxon. Everything is good in moderation."

"I've never been a fan of moderation," he whispers, putting his hand on my thigh and squeezing. "I prefer *indulgence*."

Oh, God... I need to regain control here.

"Clearly. But you also said you've never felt *this* before with someone, right?" I look up at him, batting my lashes and slyly disarming him with a tender kiss on his lips.

"No, I haven't," he says, with a smile.

"Uh huh, and why do you think that is, hmm?" I ask softly, kissing him again and knowing that I now have his complete attention. "Because I, Mr. Pace, am the whole package. And if you truly say you want me—"

"You know I fucking want you," He growls wickedly.

"...Then you have to take all of me," I say, raising my brow at him. "Including my career, which I just so happen to love."

"Fair point, Miss Tyler, fair point," Jaxon chuckles, surrendering to me, and realizing I've outsmarted him and his sexy tactics. "You win."

Suddenly he cups my chin gently and pulls my face up to look at him, kissing me hard.

"Please forgive a desperate man for being selfish and wanting to keep you all to himself."

Damnit... well, I had the upper hand.

To add to my sadness, the car starts to slow down and comes to a stop. We have finally arrived at the airport, and my heart sinks instantly.

Is it too late to change my mind?

Charlie and Ethan hop out of the car, leaving Jaxon and I staring at each other, hopelessly unprepared to be parted. I cup his face in my hands, kissing him with the same fervor in which he just kissed me. His tongue is in my mouth, his hands wrapping dangerously around my body, spiking my blood, and setting me ablaze.

But when the trunk opens, and the men start removing my bags, Jaxon and I pull back, staring at each other in silence.

"Are you sure?" he pleads.

"No," I whisper back. "But I have to."

He nods, sighing deeply and straightening his suit coat. He takes my hand in his and kisses it tenderly.

"It's just a week," he says with a smile. "It'll go quickly."

Then he opens the door and helps me out of the car and onto the sidewalk outside the terminal.

"Have a safe flight, Miss Tyler," Charlie grins. "Try not to get into too much trouble, okay?"

I walk up to him and move to hug him, but he steps back, shooting a look of concern at Jaxon.

Seriously? He risked his life for me but can't even hug me goodbye?

I turn to Jaxon, lifting my sunglasses. Jaxon chuckles to himself and nods his concession, turning around. I wrap my arms around Charlie.

"Thank you for everything Charlie," I say softly. "Really, thank you."

"You are welcome, Miss Tyler," he says warmly.

"Okay, okay," Jaxon says from behind me teasingly. "No need to push your luck kid."

I chuckle, knowing that Mr. Overprotective is going to have to get over it because I fully intend on hugging Ethan and Josiah too.

"Thank you Miss Tyler," Josiah smiles after the world's fastest hug. "For everything."

Jaxon clears his throat, and I just roll my eyes as I release him and turn lastly to Ethan.

"Ignore him," Ethan says as he hugs me tightly. "That's what I usually do."

"It was really nice meeting you, Ethan," I smile. "Do me a favor and try to keep him in one piece for me until next weekend, okay?"

"I will try, Miss Tyler."

"Are we done?" Jaxon asks, looking at me over the top of his sunglasses.

"Yes, your *Highness*," I tease as he walks towards me.

"Mmmm, so sassy, Miss Tyler," Jaxon says, suddenly scooping me up, spinning me around and pulling me into his arms as mine settle on his hard chest. "Perhaps I'll have to do something about that next weekend," he whispers lethally in my ear, as he sets me back on my feet.

"Oh, I hope you do, Mr. Pace," I smile defiantly and narrow my eyes at him. "For 'you have no idea what I'm capable of...'"

He laughs. Moments like this, where he is just a regular guy, not the foreboding, demanding, intimidating and frequently bossy CEO Mafia King... are my favorites.

"What?" he asks inquisitively, pressing his forehead to mine. "What are you thinking?"

"You," is all I say, as I smile and shake my head, admiring his beauty.

"You need to tell me, Αγαπημένη," he says with a wink.

"What does 'ah-gapi-menos' mean?" I ask, trying to say it back to him. "I keep meaning to ask you."

"Oh, so you like it when I speak Greek to you?" he says, pulling me close and nuzzling me until I giggle. "Fine, I'll tell you, but only if you tell me what you were thinking.".

"Fair compromise," I laugh.

"Αγαπημένη, means *sweetheart*," he says with a smile.

My heart swells past the breakers, and now I definitely don't want to leave him.

"Now, Αγαπημένη, tell me. What were you thinking?"

"If you must know," I say, touching his suit coat and pulling him closer to me. "I was just thinking that seeing you happy *like this* makes me happy. And, that this has been a crazy week, but it has also been the most incredible week of my entire life."

I run my fingers through his hair, watching him close his eyes and lean into my touch, before pressing my lips to his, and kissing him deeply.

"I miss you already," he whispers to me. "Saturday can't come soon enough." He cups my face in his hands and kisses me again, this time tenderly. This is our final goodbye.

"I'll see you later," I say with a wink. "Goodbye Jax,"

"Until next time, Αγαπημένη," he says with a smile. "I will see you soon."

And with that, I say goodbye to Chicago's Don Supreme and head inside.

"Have a nice flight, Miss Tyler." the ticket agent says as she hands me my first-class ticket.

I should've known Jaxon would pull something like this.

I don't know how, but somehow Jaxon Pace managed to upgrade *my* plane ticket from coach to first class. Without my knowledge.

I honestly was anticipating more of a struggle after I turned down his private jet, repeatedly. But there was no way I was going to allow that to happen.

However, it's becoming increasingly obvious that Mr. Jaxon Pace does not like being told *no*. I'm not mad at him, though. I know his intentions were thoughtful, and he just wants to make me happy.

I shoot him a text to say thank you and then put my phone away as I head off to security. I've nearly reached it when I hear someone say my name.

"Hey Nat."

I turn to see Colton, standing beside me with a small over-the-shoulder bag and his jacket across his arm. My whole body instantly tenses.

But even though I despise him right now, when I look at him now, I find it is not hatred I feel for him any longer. It's *pity*. He looks terrible and exhausted. His eyes are sunken and red, his skin looks sallow and pale. And I cannot be sure, but he also looks as if he has a few bruises on his neck and arms.

Perhaps he injured himself at the bachelor party.

I for one knew how rowdy and occasionally dangerous those can be.

Maybe better than anyone.

"Colton," I say, swallowing hard. "I didn't think you were still in Chicago. Thought you said your flight was Sunday?"

"Yeah, I was supposed to," he says softly. "But I got caught in traffic on the way to the airport and I missed my flight entirely. This was the first flight I could get out."

"I see."

"Look, um," he says, scratching his head and making eye contact with me briefly. "I just want to say I am sorry for how

I treated you the other day, in the ballroom. And, obviously, for calling you a bitch."

I shift, crossing my arms.

"I think you know, I was not... in the right place mentally," he says, looking at the floor. "And you don't have to believe me, but I'm really ashamed of how I've behaved. And for Emily, and just for hurting you the way I did. You have every right to hate me for it."

I stare at him in silence. I'm still furious with him, and I know I have every right to be. But I also know that his behavior as of late *isn't* like him at all. For all his faults, Colton had never been violent or aggressive with me. Which made his actions this week all the more shocking.

"Look," I say, taking a deep breath. "You're right, I *am* still incredibly angry. And hurt. I need you to understand I don't love you like that anymore."

Colton hangs his head in defeat.

"But I don't *hate* you," I say flatly. "And, considering your apology, perhaps I can forgive you, if you promise to accept that and never ever lay your hands on me again."

"I can...I mean, yes, I accept," He nods, looking up at me expectantly.

"That does not change the fact that you need help, Colton," I whisper firmly, while still trying to be compassionate.

He looks at me confused.

"I saw the texts on your phone from Edgar, Colton," I say with a sigh. "I know you were not asking me and my family for pain medication because of an injury. You were asking because you have an *addiction*."

He looks at me, sighs and then looks at the floor.

"I know," he whispers. "I guess I just got involved with the wrong people."

At least he is acknowledging this. That's a start.

"We all make mistakes. But just remember that your mistakes are not what defines you," I say gently, touching his arm. "It's whether or not you can own that mistake, and take the steps to make it right *afterwards*, that does."

When his eyes find mine again, he looks sad, practically a shell of the human he was just a week ago.

"I accept your apology. Now, maybe when you get back home, get yourself in a rehab or something. Get yourself some help," I say with a slight smile, slinging my bag over my shoulder. "You can fix yourself. It's never too late."

"I think it might be Nat," he says, swallowing hard, his eyes wide.

"It's not," I say, forcing a smile. "You're strong. You'll figure it out, get help, and this will eventually be water under the bridge, okay?"

I glance at my watch, realizing I spent a bit longer than I should have saying goodbye to Jaxon and need to hustle to make my flight.

"Listen, I've got to run to catch my plane," I say, adjusting my bag over my shoulder. "I hope it all works out for you."

He looks at me and shakes his head. "Nat, I am so sorry."

"It's okay, Colton, I said I forgave you," I say, trying to be polite. "We're good for now."

"No, not for that," he says, shifting. "…For *this*."

I hear the gun cock before I see it.

Hidden underneath his coat, I see the barrel of a handgun. A handgun that Colton is pointing directly at *me*.

"Col…" I start to say, but my throat goes dry, and my ears start ringing.

Oh my God…is he going to shoot me?! Right here?!

"Natalie, listen to me carefully," Colton says, his eyes wide and panicked. "Don't struggle. You need to come with me. Now."

All I can focus on right now is Colton's face, which still looks just as sad and sickly as before, but a new emotion appears in his eyes—*fear*.

Colton is afraid. But…of who?

I consider screaming, but decide instead to try and talk him out of whatever ridiculous plan he's concocted.

"Colton…" I whisper shakily as I stare at the cocked gun pointing at me. "Do you have any idea what you're doing? In the middle of an airport? You can't actually be serious!"

"Oh, he certainly is," a man's voice speaks forcefully beside me, low and lethal. "So, if you want to survive this, don't make this difficult. Because unlike this pathetic little boy toy here, I'm not afraid to shoot you."

I hear the cocking of another gun… but this time I feel it press into my ribcage.

"What do you want?" I choke out.

"You're coming with *us*."

Chapter Forty

JAXON

A feeling of uneasiness settled on my skin after leaving Natalie at the airport. I decided to drive, wanting to feel like I was in control of something. I grip the steering wheel tighter and reach into my pocket looking for my cigarettes.

But I cannot find them.

I check the rest of my pockets, but alas, they aren't here. Somehow I must've left them at home, which is something I never do. For the last five years, I haven't left home without them and yet I don't remember even thinking about them when Natalie and I left the house.

Come to think of it, I have not really thought about my cigarettes the entire time Natalie was *at* my house.

But now the minute she's gone…

My God. I'm not this pathetic. I'll see her in a week.

"Here," Ethan says from the passenger seat, passing me one of his.

I take it without saying a word, annoyed that I feel so out of sync.

How the hell can a woman do this to me?

The car phone rings, distracting me from my pity party.

"Ethan, go ahead," Ethan says, answering the phone.

"Sir!" Levi's voice rings out loudly in the car, frantic and panicked. "Tell me that you still have Miss Tyler with you?!"

"Um, no? We just dropped her off at the airport," I say, confused, feeling the hair on the back of my neck stand up. "Why? What's going on, Levi?"

What did she forget a hair dryer or something?

"Fuck!" Levi shouts. "No!"

Instantly, I feel my heart start pounding, a sickening feeling twisting my stomach from just the tone in Levi's voice.

This is something more serious than a hair dryer.

"Tell me what's going on, Levi?" I growl.

"Sir, we made a mistake," Levi says, "I was just reviewing the last of the footage on those cameras. You know, the ones we thought were pointing at your penthouse."

"And?" I ask anxiously.

"They're not pointing at *your* penthouse, Sir," Levi says. "They were pointing at Miss Tyler's."

My blood freezes in my veins.

"All the footage from this week, well, it's all *her*. They've been watching her all week."

"What are you saying?"

"Miss Tyler is a target, Sir," Levi says anxiously into the phone. "She may even be *the* target."

Instantly I veer off the road and slam on the breaks, coming to a screeching halt. My body's numb besides the suffocating fear growing in my chest.

"Sir, I can't get her on the phone," Charlie says from the backseat. "It just keeps going to voicemail."

I slam the car into park and jump out walking out into the field that lines the highway and yanking my phone from my pocket. I dial Natalie, trying to swallow the feeling of dread rising in my throat.

Please, for the love of God answer, Nat. Please.

Voicemail.

Fuck!

I text her, my shaking hands making it difficult to type.

Me
2:49 p.m.: Natalie, do not panic, but you are in immediate danger. Find somewhere quiet and call me ASAP. Please. Trust no one.

"I've contacted airport security," Ethan says, jogging up to me. "Natalie checked into her flight, and got her boarding pass but she's not answering pages at the gate."

I look up at him, unable to think or breathe or speak.

My head is spinning.

"Look, let's stay calm, and head back to the airport," Ethan says carefully, motioning back to the car. "Her flight does not leave for another forty-five minutes, we can be back there in ten."

We have almost reached the car when my phone rings.

Video Call-Natalie.

"It's her!" I say, relieved.

Oh, thank God!

"Nat! Are you there?" I answer the phone, waiting for the camera to focus. "Nat?"

But when it does, my heart stops. For it's not Natalie who greets me. Instead, to my horror, it's the masked man. The same man who shot up my men and nearly killed me on the ship two nights ago. Except that now, his eye is bandaged.

He has her phone.

"Hello…" I hear him say slowly. "I was wondering when you would call, Jaxon. I really thought we had a special connection."

My chest and stomach tighten around me.

"But I think someone else wants to say hello," he says. "Say hello to Jaxon, Sweetheart."

What I hear next makes my blood run cold.

"Jaxon! Jaxon!" Natalie screams, terror in her voice.

He laughs, panning the camera to her face. Tears, and mascara stream down her cheeks, as he grabs her by the shoulder, holding the camera in front of her.

"Natalie!" I shout, my heart breaking.

"Talk to your boyfriend, dollface," he says as she struggles to get away from him. "Tell him how much you miss him."

"Jaxon!" Natalie screams and I watch as she sobs loudly into the camera.

"Jesus Christ," Ethan whispers quietly beside me. "*Charlie, call Levi!*"

"That's enough! Shut the fuck up bitch!" The man suddenly screams at her.

"I don't know who the fuck you are," I growl lethally. "But I'm warning you, if you harm a fucking hair on her head—"

"Tooooooo late!" The man laughs in a sing-song voice, viciously grabbing Natalie by her hair and forcing her face into the camera again.

I am seething.

"What the fuck do you want?!" I shout at him. "She can't give you anything!"

My stomach twists as he steps behind her, grabs her chin and whispers in her ear, pressing his lips to her skin.

"Oh, I think she can…" He sneers at her. "And a *lot* more."

"The only reason you went after her is because of me!" I shout at him. "So, what do you want from me?!"

"Well, oddly enough, it has always kind of been my luck in life, you know, stuck playing with other kid's toys."

What the fuck is this asshole talking about?!

"But *your* toys are particularly nice," He smiles at me

Natalie whimpers as he strokes her face intimately.

Fuck! I hate watching him assault her like this!

"Now you listen to me—" I start to say.

"You don't get to give me instructions, Jaxon Pace! I am the one giving the fucking instructions!" The man suddenly shouts, his eyes suddenly angry and wild. "Or do you need a reminder of who is really in charge right now?!"

I watch in horror as he slaps Natalie across the face, and then again.

"Stop!" she screams. "Please! Stop!"

"Okay! Okay! I'm listening!" I shout back. "But you still have not told me—what do you actually want?!"

He growls at her, barking like a crazy person, before laughing and then shoving her again out of frame.

"What do I want, Jaxon dear? I want vindication… for the life you fucking *stole* from me."

What the fuck?!

"What are you talking about?!" I shout angrily.

"*Levi is tracking the call*," Ethan whispers, stepping away. "*Keep him talking!*"

"You had everything. And yet you *still* took everything from me. So, now I'm going to take everything from you."

"I don't know who you are, or what you are talking about, so how the fuck am I supposed to give you retribution?" I ask, anxiously trying to keep his focus on me as Ethan works with Levi to trace the call.

"Retribution?" He laughs. "I don't just want retribution. I want revenge…with interest."

"Is there a point in this phone call where you actually tell me what the fuck that means, or are you going to continue speaking to me in riddles?!" I snap at him, my blood boiling.

"Listen here you cocky fuck!" he suddenly roars. "You will watch how you talk to me, or you'll get this pretty little 'toy' of yours back in *pieces*! Do you understand?!"

Natalie's silent and tear-stained face is pulled back into frame. Blood dripping from her lip, her eyes screwed shut.

I stare at her, feeling whatever is left of my heart shatter.

"I will give you *whatever* you want," I say, choking back my emotions. "Just please, don't hurt her."

"Much better," he says, stroking Natalie's face with the back of his hand while she flinches—repulsed by his touch, and terrified he's going to hit her. "Do you hear that, sweetheart? Your little fancy rich boyfriend has decided to play the game."

I want to rip his throat from his body. I want to pop his eyes from his skull with my fingers. I want to...

"I want your fleet, Jaxon," he says, smiling.

"What?" I ask, confused.

"You will hand over your entire fleet to me. Tonight, by eight p.m."

"That's impossible..." I whisper in disbelief.

"What was that?" he whispers back. "Did you say *impossible*?" he hisses, holding a gun to Natalie's throat.

I stop breathing.

"Go on then, tell *her* that, Jaxon!" He shouts, pressing it into her neck. "Tell her it is impossible and that you are the reason she is going to die!"

Natalie starts silently crying again on camera and I feel as if I am losing my mind, but I don't know how to make that happen.

"Fine I will do it! I'll figure it out!" I snap. "Just stop! Stop this! This does not concern her! Your revenge is with me!"

"That's true. But I mean look at her..." he says, licking her face sensually, making Natalie recoil in absolute disgust.

"You fucking monster!" I shout at the phone, as he laughs manically.

I feel like I'm going crazy watching this play out in real time and being helpless to stop anything being done to her.

I decide to speak directly to her, "Natalie, baby, listen to me! I will get this done, okay?! Just stay strong! I will get you back! I promise! I will get you back!"

"Oohhhhh!" The man says, laughing. "Listen to that! All the *feelings*! God, that is amazing! How things have changed. You know, you were never one for making promises, Jaxon. I sure hope you are better at *keeping* them! For her sake anyway!"

He shoves a whimpering Natalie out of frame and looks back into the camera.

"Oh... I am. And I promise you, I will make you pay severely for anything you do to her," I growl lethally.

"Shivers! That was almost believable! But how about this, since we are making promises, how about I make you one in return?" he says, stroking his chin.

"How about this: If your fleet is not *in* my possession by eight tonight, I will start taking it out on *your* possession. For every hour you delay, I will take another *piece* of the lovely Miss Tyler."

"Where are we making this transaction?" I snap at him.

I have to keep the focus on us, and our deal. For my own sanity in this moment, and because Ethan and Levi have nearly locked on his signal.

"Well, since I've spent so much time at your warehouse, why don't we just agree to meet there? If you ask nicely, I might even let you say goodbye to all your ships."

"I will do this, but Miss Tyler is *not* to be harmed, agreed?"

"Tick-tock, Jaxon!"

"*Jaxon! Keep him on the phone, we need more time!*" Ethan whispers forcefully to me.

"Agreed?!" I shout back to the man.

"Tick...Tock..."

The call ends.

And all I see is red.

I ran every red light all the way home, and the moment we reach Pace Manor, I'm out of the car before it even stops moving. I smash through the front door of the house with such rage, I nearly break the damn thing off its hinges. Charlie and Ethan are quickly on my heels, presumably to stop me from killing anyone in the immediate vicinity.

"Levi! Josiah! Max! Study now!" I thunder.

The men assemble, closing the door behind them, just as I turn around.

"Someone needs to explain to me," I hiss, my voice low and lethal. "How the fuck this happened..."

But no one speaks.

I snap. I move to my desk and shove everything on its surface onto the floor violently. Then I pull out my gun and aim it at the floor.

"I said someone better fucking tell me how they have Natalie, and how we are so fucking behind the mark! *Again*!"

Ethan clears his throat.

"Don't start with me Ethan," I growl, unable to even look at him. "I have love for you, but I won't hesitate to shoot you in the fucking face if you try to lecture me right now. Don't test me."

I cock my gun.

"You five men are my Alphas. You're the only ones who can give me answers. So, someone in this room better give me answers now or everyone in this room dies here and now."

I'm done being polite. I'm done being calm. I'm done fucking around.

I am furious.

"Sir," Levi says quietly, "when we broke into the cameras last night, we saw that they've had them operational for at least eight days. Each day was its own file."

I say nothing.

Levi swallows hard, but continues.

"But because we did it *remotely*, each file had to be accessed and assessed individually, so it took us a moment to review the footage in its entirety. That's why it took so long."

"Go on..."

"For the *first* two days the cameras were focused on your apartment. I've had someone on my team reviewing the footage, around the clock. But it wasn't until about an hour ago, we moved onto the next day's footage, and that is when I realized that it had suddenly switched from being footage of your penthouse to becoming solely focused on Miss Tyler's penthouse." I hear him clear his throat. "But I realize this is not an excuse." He says quietly. "I'm sorry, Sir."

"You are the bravest man in the room, Levi," I say slowly, uncocking my gun and putting it away. "Your head is safe. I trust you will rectify the problem."

"The question remains," Charlie says. "Why would they be after her?"

"We are still deciphering the information we retrieved from the ship computers, but…"

I look up from the floor and my eyes find Levi finally.

"…but we are still working on placing a motive."

"I think we can safely assume the motive is they are using her to get to me," I say flatly. "He made that abundantly clear on the phone. She's a hostage. Natalie has nothing to offer him outside of that."

Which means I need her out of danger. Quickly.

"My question is how? *How* did they get to her? And how have they been one step ahead of us this entire time?"

"Who knows when they got to Sam, and what information he had been leaking to them, for God knows how long," Max says. "Who knows what they know."

"Sam may have been on Alpha, but that was only a recent advancement. Meaning his access to intel was limited to little more than Jaxon's schedule," Josiah counters. "That's not it."

"But your schedule has been a big factor this entire time," Charlie says, looking at me. "And it's pretty full, Sir. But every move they've made has been conveniently when you're *not* in the picture."

"He did say to me the other night at the wharf that he, 'did not expect me to be there,' when that ship came into dock," I say rubbing my chin.

"They assumed that you'd be preoccupied with Miss Tyler, and even if you weren't, then you'd be at the building across the street from your hotel, far away from the wharf." Charlie continues.

"That makes sense. If the ship just arrived exactly at its destination, that wouldn't be suspicious enough by itself. Ships are late for any number of reasons. It's unlikely the team would alert you, and even if the team did, it was even more unlikely that the Don Supreme would physically waste time to go there himself," Ethan says. "And if not for the echo software, you may not have even been alerted *at* the moment, seeing the coincidence and connecting the two."

"Which means you would've been out of the picture when this happened," Max adds. "Which would also look suspicious. Especially with the men."

"Wouldn't that make it look as if this happened without his knowledge?" Charlie asks him.

"Possibly to the papers or the cops, but not with the men, or the other clans," Max says. "I mean, nothing happens in this city without us knowing about it, right? And if a robbery happens at your warehouse, that's not that uncommon either. But, if a *second* shootout at your facility takes place, it could seem like you were *purposefully* out of pocket and avoiding the carnage." Max finishes firmly.

"From what we saw, they probably would have overpowered and murdered all the unexpecting staff there and staged the same kind of scene they did the other night: Dead men, and a freighter full of drugs." Levi says.

"Exactly," Max continues. "And no matter how loyal the men are, I'm sure a second occurrence would have created doubt amongst your men, putting their loyalty to you in jeopardy. And your safety."

"All it would take would be a few pictures conveniently making it across some eager newspaper or city official's desk," Ethan says, looking up at me. "Enough to make them question your hold on the city. Shifting the tide."

"Basically, they're just creating chaos," I growl. "Calculated chaos."

"Perhaps that's the goal?" Charlie says. "Perhaps they are trying to cause a ruckus and tip the scales?"

"It's possible. If they wanted to take control of the city's underground, taking *you* out is the first step. And since it is incredibly difficult to get close enough to *kill* you, creating problems and killing your relationship with the city council would be next." Ethan agrees. "Drawing more attention to our activities."

"Offsetting the ecosystem…" I whisper.

"What else did he say on the phone?" Ethan asks.

"Something about how I took everything from him," I say, walking to my bar and pouring myself a drink. "And he said he wants revenge."

"That could be anyone who has tangled with us," Max says.

"Any number of people could want revenge," Ethan says gravely. "But not everyone has the *resources* to make a move like this."

"And this *quickly*," Charlie says, and all of us turn to face him. "Think about it. It's been decades since this city saw a new mafia clan of any kind. And there's protocol for joining. They just arrive on the scene, and somehow, they can make a move like this, this fast?"

"They have access to subways…" Max tries to interject.

"I get that, but you said it yourself, we have eyes and ears all over this fucking city, little moves without our eyes on it," Charlie counters. "So how can a new player emerge on the scene with this much intel and this much muscle this fast?"

"He would need a guide... a *partner*. Someone who could feed him information and help place him in the most effective locations to shatter my hold on the city, and my reputation," I say, starting to see the pattern emerge from the woodwork. "As well as my commitments to my 'customers.' Which could sour if I couldn't get their shipments to them on time."

"*Victor Black*," Ethan says angrily.

"Black knows me, he knows my staff. He would've known Sam was the newest member of Alpha, and therefore the easiest to manipulate. He also specifically knows when and where my drug shipments come in for him, and he could easily pick out which shipments he wanted the Two-Headed Dragon to seize. Further still, Black knows I have few weaknesses," I growl, "He'd quickly deduce that a woman in my life could be a..."

I close my eyes, unable to even finish the thought. The image of Natalie, sobbing and assaulted on camera will be permanently seared to my brain.

I have to get her back. And fast.

"He also realistically knows he could never beat you in a straight fight for this city with the control we currently have over it," Ethan suggests. "He knows he'd need the support of the rest of the clans."

"And he would *get* that if he had a substantial reason to suggest our leadership is failing," Levi interjects.

"So, he props up a new pawn, helps them cause all kinds of problems for us, then gets himself elected as the new king of the mountain with the other clans," Charlie finishes.

We all stand in a stunned silence.

Now that I see the way the pieces fit together, it makes a disgusting amount of sense.

The door suddenly bursts open, and Travis comes barreling in, carrying what appears to be a stack of blueprints.

"Sir, we just got the airport footage!" he says breathlessly. "And we believe we have located Miss Tyler!"

"On screen," I demand.

Levi pulls up the footage.

"Colton..." I say, watching closely as Natalie's demeanor changes from one of comfort to one of fear. "...and *Ivan*."

Ivan, the giant goon, and Black's second in command. I watch as he forces Natalie outside to a burgundy Mercedes.

"There's more," Travis says excitedly. "Our new cameras in Chinatown clocked that vehicle entering the parking garage about a half hour ago. So I had our people pull the building blueprints."

"She is there," I say, my heart rate increasing.

"Yes Sir," Travis says.

"Then *that's exactly* where I am going."

Chapter Forty-One

Natalie

"Get the fuck off me!" I scream, attempting to hit and scratch at the massive hand of the giant man dragging me down a hallway by the arm.

I am forced into a small concrete room with a single lightbulb overhead. The room is little more than a large closet and seems to have been converted fairly recently, evidenced by the fresh concrete and fencing to house two cages.

"Move bitch!" The large ginger man from the airport shoves me into one, and I fall to the ground painfully.

"Let me out of here you assholes!" I scream back at him, launching myself at the gate, trying to attack him through the fence.

"Jesus Christ was she always this feisty?" The short, thin, one-eyed monster who slapped me around on the video call, asks with a sickening laugh, as he enters the doorway behind him. "I am sure that must have made sex *very* exciting."

"Natalie, please… just stop struggling," Colton pleads, stepping forward from his place beside The Monster and the giant Gorilla Man who threw me in here. His tone is apologetic, but the very sight of him enrages me.

"Fuck you Colton!" I scream at him, tears streaming down my cheeks. "How could you?! I forgave you!"

Of all of the horrible things Colton has done to me, this by far is a new low, even for him.

"Natalie, I don't want to see you in here," he says, his eyes imploring mine. "Jaxon just needs to do as he is told, and they will let you go."

I spit in Colton's face. Both The Monster and Gorilla Man laugh.

"Go to hell, Colton!" I shout angrily at him. "Go to hell and take your new buddies with you!"

The Monster starts clapping, still laughing in a way that sounds almost twisted. "You know, I can almost see why Jaxon likes you so much," he says, stepping closer to the gate that I'm rattling aggressively.

I glare at him.

"I'll admit, at first I really did not get it, but now... so much spirit!"

I do not like the creepy way this pig is looking at me with his one eye, and I take a step back from the bars.

"You're not going to hurt her, right? That is what you said, that was the deal," Colton says, grabbing The Monster's arm.

"Deal?" he asks, looking down at Colton's hand on his arm, and then back at him slowly.

I happen to catch the brief glance he makes to the giant Gorilla Man, but Colton does not, and suddenly finds himself being manhandled by the big man.

"I do not remember making any *deals* with *you*, Sir."

"No! Wait! The other guy! The other guy said we had a deal!" Colton protests and I watch in shock as he is shoved into the makeshift 'cell' next to me. "I was supposed to go free, that was the plan!"

"Plans have changed." The man shrugs, unemotional.

"No! Stop! This is not what I agreed to! You said you just wanted me to bring her to you!"

"You fucking asshole!" I scream at Colton from my cell, punching through the gate between us and almost hitting his shoulder.

Colton keeps protesting but the man just smiles. He lights a cigarette and then steps up to the fence surrounding Colton's cage, just far enough away that Colton's arms cannot reach him.

"Let me go! Please!"

The man blows smoke through the bars at Colton. "Hmm, I

think not," he says with a smile. "We are going to hold on to *both* of you for the time being. When her new boyfriend comes through with his end of the bargain, then maybe we can talk deals. Until then…" he says, glancing at me but whispering to Colton, "why don't you two love birds get reacquainted, eh?"

He chuckles to himself as he walks out of the room, with the large man shutting the door behind him.

"Please! Please! Come back!" Colton yells after him. Colton rattles the cage door, frantically trying with all his weight to pull it open. "Come back! Please!"

"He's not going to come back you *dumbass*!" I yell at him.

"You don't understand, he said we had a deal! Natalie, he said that they just needed you as leverage to get Jaxon, to negotiate for something, then he would let us both go!"

"Oh, you mean your new underworld buddies lied to you, and double-crossed you?" I shout at him sarcastically. "Shocking Colton! Fucking shocking! You know, you're the worst human being alive, and the dumbest!"

I crumple to the floor, my legs, arms, and body shaking entirely from the adrenaline. Colton stares at me, as if he is just now understanding the royally screwed predicament, we now find ourselves in.

"Fuck!" he yells, pulling at his hair.

I wrap my limbs around my body, placing my head on my knees, trying to keep myself mentally together.

"I will come for you, baby… I promise."

Jaxon's words ring in my head. The faint glimmer of hope in this increasingly dark situation.

Jaxon will do everything in his power for me, I know that. However, I now understand something that Colton is just learning the hard way: *These* men were not going to keep any of their promises… to anyone.

This meant that Jaxon was walking into a trap, and it decreased the likelihood that *any* of us would be walking away from this alive.

"Holy fuck… Holy fuck…" Colton cries, as he collapses in the back of the makeshift cell. "Oh, my God… I'm going to die here."

I look up at his delayed realization and subsequent panic attack, tears welling in my eyes and a rage building inside me.

"No, *we* are going to die here," I hiss at him from my cell. "You have killed us both, Colton."

"I didn't mean to!" he yells, his voice cracking. "They promised me that it was just a power play!"

"*Who* promised you?" I snap. "And what did they offer you in exchange for bringing me here?!"

Colton looks up at me, almost considering answering, but then he looks at the floor quickly. "Nothing," he whispers, looking away.

I knew it.

"Colton," I whisper, "if there is anything that I have learned about this world of theirs, it is that no one does anything for *nothing*. So, they must have offered you something!"

"Listen to you, Nat! Do you even hear yourself?! 'This world of theirs!' Since when do *you* know anything about 'this world of theirs?!' Who dragged you into that world, huh?" Colton snaps. "Your new criminal boyfriend? Well, it seems if it were not for him, none of us would be in this fucking mess! So, if you are looking for someone to crucify, blame him!"

I stare at him, my rage reaching a fever pitch at his audacity to once again try and skip responsibility for his own actions.

Slowly I stand, feeling the gloves finally come off.

"No," I hiss at him acidly, my nostrils flaring. "Jaxon would never put me in any danger. He's only ever protected me from danger. Unlike you! The cheating, lying, pill-popping, pathetic excuse of a man who betrayed me and sold me over to the fucking mafia! For little more than what I'm sure is just another fucking fix of whatever drug you're hooked on!" I shout at him furiously, my rage mounting so high Colton cowers in the corner.

"Nat…"

"Get my fucking name out of your mouth Colton!" I shout. "I know exactly what you are, and that is not even a fraction of the man Jaxon is! And I'm not going to sit here and listen to you try and pass the buck for your own fuck up this time! So, yes, you are right. You *are* probably going to die here tonight! But I want you to know that you're already fucking dead to me!"

Colton stares at me, a look of utter defeat and fear skating across his face. I walk over to the corner and sit down, turning my back to him entirely. I curl my legs into my body and place my head against the wall.

Jaxon… please hurry.

Sometime later I look up to see that Colton is sitting in the corner, holding his knees, and rocking back and forth while he mumbles to himself.

If he is faking a mental breakdown, he's doing a good job.

I look down at my watch and touch the screen.

6:37 p.m.

Suddenly, it hits me like a car crash.

Oh...My...God... my smart watch!

The giant man had taken my purse and my other belongings, but he had neglected to take my watch from my arm. Which was probably because it did not look like a typical smart watch. It wasn't as bulky and obvious as the older versions and had a screensaver that looked convincingly like a real watch. A fact, I remember, that was a selling point for me when my best friend and I got one on our pre-wedding shopping spree.

I press on the screen with my shaking fingers.

6% Battery.

I have no phone signal, but the Wi-Fi bar keeps appearing and disappearing, which means it was right now picking up an occasional weak Wi-Fi signal.

I might be able to get a message out to Jaxon and pin my location!

I open our text thread—finally seeing his last pleading message coming across the screen and feeling my heart ache.

Whatever had happened, had evidently happened *after* the Gorilla Man took my phone. I type out my message, deciding that I should try and send it to Charlie and Ethan as well, hopefully increasing my chances that maybe one of them would see it.

Me
6:45 p.m.: Jax-do not call or respond-they have my phone-sent from my smart watch. They brought me back to the city, to some parking structure and dumped me in a small room, or closet of some kind, about 8 feet wide. Please be careful. I think it might be a trap.

I pin my location, close my eyes, and press 'send' watching as the bar loads.

MESSAGE FAILED.

Internet Connection Unavailable

Damnit! It did not work.

3% Battery.

I feel the panic rising in my throat and the overwhelming feeling of defeat threatening to take over.

No. I can't stop trying. And because the Wi-Fi keeps appearing and disappearing, that means there must be a faint signal in here somewhere. I take my watch off my hand and hold it up in every direction trying to find a signal and resend the message.

2% Battery

Shit! I am running out of time!

It suddenly occurs to me that the three of them brought me down a lot of stairs on the way to this room.

Maybe if I can get closer to the ceiling, I'll be closer to the signal!

I climb up the flimsy fencing, stretching my arm through the fencing to the corner of the room. Just when I am on the verge of giving up, I feel it vibrate on my wrist.

SENT.

Holy shit! It worked!

"Yes!" I yell.

But just as I do, the corner of the hastily constructed fencing that I am clinging to cracks the concrete that holds it in place, bends under my weight, sending me crashing to the floor with pieces of busted concrete.

"Ouch." I say, pulling myself up.

I dust myself off and look over at Colton, who is still rocking back and forth, mumbling to himself.

However, getting that text message out had lit a tiny little flame of hope in my heart that perhaps someone might find me, and I might make it out of here.

What else can I do?!

I now turn my attention to the bent corner of the fencing. I wonder if I could break more of that concrete frame and bend the fencing, creating a gap big enough to squeeze through?

It's worth a shot!

I climb back up and give it my best effort, pulling as hard as I can. But the rest of the concrete frame around my fence cage is unwilling to give at all. I collapse back to the floor, feeling the sinking feeling of defeat.

And since my watch died after I sent the message, I have no way of knowing if anyone actually *got* my message. Which means I have no way of knowing if anyone is actually coming to my rescue.

The tiny futile hope of escape or rescue evaporates.

This realization feels absolutely crushing. So crushing, in fact, that I cannot even cry. I simply crawl into the corner and lean my head against the wall.

I hear footsteps in the hall and my heart starts pounding.

Are they coming to torture me? Or did they somehow see my text?!

I scramble to grab the biggest piece of the concrete that fell from the wall and tuck it into the back of my pants.

If I'm going to die, I'm at least going to put up a fight.

My legs are shaking, as I brace for the worst when I see the door open slowly, but instead of the giant Gorilla Man, or the small, thin Monster, I watch as a woman walks inside, carrying a bottle of water and a small bread roll.

"Thought you might be hungry," she says softly, but then a wicked smile skates across her face as she winks at me but nods at Colton. "What do you think, you two want to fight for it?" She places the bread and water within arm's reach on the floor outside the cells. "I do love a good cock fight."

Jesus Christ. These people are twisted.

I remain silent, watching her carefully. I watch her eyes appraise Colton, now curled tightly into a ball in the corner of his makeshift cell, hiding his face.

"Well, that didn't take very long…" she says sarcastically, her face almost disappointed. "But look at *you*… at least you still have your wits about you."

She smiles, crossing her arms.

"I bet it felt good to break him down like that… especially after what he did to you. You know, betraying you and all."

"He deserved what he got," I say icily. "Trusting people like *you* is something only an idiot would do."

"I'll give you that. It would be unwise to trust anyone in this cruel line of work," she says with a nod.

I fold my arms across my chest and look away.

"And yet *this* doesn't feel just a little cruel to you?" she says, motioning to Colton.

"What do you care?" I scoff out loud, watching as she narrows her eyes at me.

"I don't," she says with a smile as she steps back, leaning against the wall. "I've just said for ages that women are more ruthless than men, they can be cold-hearted bitches when they need to be. And pushing your ex-lover into a mental breakdown while you're both being held prisoner? Now that's *cold*. So, you proved me right."

"You're trying to guilt trip *me*? That's fucking rich." I laugh sarcastically, as I narrow my eyes at her. "Let us not forget it was you and your asshole brigade that threw him in there. The same upstanding citizens that abducted me as leverage in some stupid business deal with my boyfriend." I snap.

I walk back to the wall and sit down.

"Don't try to lecture me on being *cold*," I hiss acidly. "You can save your fucking breath, bitch."

"You know, you really are a brave little thing."

I ignore her.

"Oh, my God..." she whispers, sitting up and walking towards me as if I am some sort of zoo exhibit. "Holy shit. I get it now... that's it! You still think *Jaxon* is going to come for you, don't you?"

What?

I look at her, but quickly look away, trying not to fall for her taunting tone, dripping fake pity.

She suddenly laughs loudly.

"So, let me get this straight. You actually believe that a *billionaire* mafia don is going to go back to his mansion and transfer ownership of his entire shipping fleet, just to rescue *you*?" She giggles.

Her words are like knives through my heart.

"And that he, Jaxon Pace, the ruthless, cruel man that he's, is going to sacrifice the empire that has been in his family for generations... just to save *you*?" She laughs.

As she says it out loud... it hits me. It does sound ridiculous. My stomach flips, as her words weasel past my mental defenses.

"Huh... that's disappointing." She steps away from the cage, a look of judgment plastered on her face as she stares at me teasingly. "Funny, I could've sworn you just said trusting someone like *us* was something only an idiot would do," she says mockingly. "And here I thought you were smarter than that."

No. What Jaxon and I have is real. He will come for me.

"I have no reason not to believe that," I snap back at her, trying to stop my hands from trembling. "I know how he cares for me. And he promised he'd do whatever it took to get me back. And from my experience, he always keeps his word."

I choose to trust Jaxon's promise.

"In *your* experience?!" She says, laughing acidly. "Your extensive experience? Girl, that is laughable," she says sarcastically. "Wake up! You barely know him! You've known him what... a week? At that? But let me guess, you feel that what the two of you have is so *special* and *different*?" She laughs again.

Her vicious words launch another attack against my fragile optimism, which dangles by a thread already.

"Let me tell you what the *rest of us* know about Jaxon Pace," she says, glaring at me. "Your boyfriend has got a reputation in this city. He's not the knight in shining armor you seem to think he is. He's the devil in a fucking human suit."

I look away, trying desperately to tune her out.

"Do you even know what happened to his last girlfriend?"

"Yes, I do actually," I snap, failing to ignore her. "Jaxon told me all about it. She died in a horrible accident."

"It wasn't an accident!" she shouts, making me jump. "She was murdered! By Jaxon!"

"No," I say, shaking my head. "You're lying."

"I assure you; I am not. I was very close to her."

"I don't believe any of that!" I shout at her, unable to contain myself any longer. "You're a liar!"

"Oh, I'm definitely a liar, but not about this. Trust me, or don't, but you know nothing about Jaxon Pace. But *I* do. A lot of people in this town loved that girl…" she says, heading for the door. "…and we haven't forgotten what he *did* to her."

She opens the door but suddenly stops and turns to me before walking away.

"Tell me, Natalie… does it *still* feel good?" She glares at me venomously, and then glances towards Colton. "Now that you know how it feels to have the last tiny piece of hope ripped away from you?"

I swallow hard, fighting the tears welling in my eyes.

"We're leaving in thirty minutes." She closes the door and is gone.

Chapter Forty-Two

JAXON

Travis spreads the blueprints out on the table.

"Jaxon, I think we need to pause and think this through before you go putting yourself in the line of fire," Ethan says quietly. "There has got to be another way."

"There isn't," I say, looking over the dusty garage blueprints as my men gather around the table.

"Levi, I need you and your whole team on tech. We are going to have one chance at a surprise approach. Our advantage is that we know the location they are holding Natalie," I say, staring him down, and start circling the areas that have surveillance cameras. "I want to come up through the tunnel entrance, and for this to work we will need to hack every surveillance camera on the way to keep them blind as long as possible. Both exterior and interior in real time, can we do that?"

"Yes, we can," he says determinedly.

I nod and turn to Josiah.

"And to keep them unaware of our movements, and stop them from fleeing, I am going to need a diversion of some kind at the garage entrance, here," I say, pointing to it on the map. "Josiah, I don't care how you do it, but I think we need a fire or an explosion—something that would close it off and stop them from leaving."

Josiah's face lights up. "Oh, I can definitely handle that, Sir."

"Max, I do not want to put our men in the tunnel at risk, so let's pull them out. We have to move quickly, so call it in now."

"Roger that. I am on it, Sir." Max acknowledges and then walks out of the room dialing his phone.

I turn to Charlie, who has been incredibly reliable to me in the last few days. I know this rescue is now personal to him.

"Charlie, you're going to be my transport. I also need you to run point, and relay to the team back at base what we need."

"Yes, Sir!" he responds enthusiastically.

"I also have no idea what we are walking into," I say, staring out the window and feeling my stomach twist. "So, Travis, let's make sure to have medical evac on standby too."

"You got it, Sir."

God knows what they are doing to her right now.

I have to shake this thought from my brain before it completely shuts me down.

Lastly, I turn to Ethan, who stands with a complicated expression of concern on his face.

"Jaxon, let me go in after her instead," Ethan says gently, his tone serious. "I have reviewed these blueprints; I know my way around them, and we can't risk you—"

"Ethan..." I say, locking eyes with him, acknowledging his unspoken reservations but also indicating I am not changing my mind. "I need *you* here. If something should happen to me, you are the only one who knows what to do."

Ethan knows I am referring to Jessica.

I have discussed my emergency plans for Jessica's care and safety in length with him and he is the only person on earth that I trust with her.

However, the pained look on his face now is one of concern and worry that something might happen...to *me*.

"Jaxon, the text from her phone said it might be a trap. And we have no way of knowing if that text was even from *her* at all," he says.

"It was," I say with a smirk. "I'm positive she added the 'Jax' on purpose so that I would know it was from her."

Which was a very smart move on her part.

He opens his mouth to protest again, but I shake my head. There is no arguing with me about this, my mind is made up. And he knows it too.

"Ethan, you've reviewed the blueprints, and it's likely that nothing besides a headset will work down there, so I won't have a GPS. I won't know my way around, and I won't have time for maps. You'll have to be my eyes and ears. I need you to help me get to her." I place my hand on his shoulder and look him in the eyes. "I will get to her, and then I will get out, I promise. But I *will* get to her."

And I will kill every motherfucker who stands in my way.

The look on Ethan's face is heartbreaking. I glance around quickly before stepping closer to him, whispering so that only he can hear me.

"Look, you told me once, that when the day came, I would have the courage I need to fight for the things that matter. That I'd be able to protect something worth fighting for. Natalie is worth fighting for, Ethan," I say, my eyes imploring him. "And I know you know it too."

"I know," he says, closing his eyes with a sigh. "I just need you to come back too. And your daughter needs you."

"I will," I say, slapping his chest, seeing him nod. "I always come back."

"Are you sure you don't want me to come with you?" Charlie asks ten minutes later when we pull up outside the tunnel. "It could be a bloodbath in there, boss."

"With any luck, Charlie," I say, loading the clip into the last of my pistols. "It fucking *will* be."

I didn't want to say it to Ethan, but part of me knows that he already knows I'm here to settle a fucking score.

I want blood. And I *will* have it.

Watching what that man did to Natalie, and being unable to do anything about it, ignited a rage in my blood that I have felt very few times in my life.

I'm no longer a man tonight. I am a fucking Don. I'm not here to try and negotiate. I'm here to viciously eliminate every last one of these cockroaches living in my city, permanently and without mercy. Tonight, I'm judge, jury, and executioner, and I'm going to enjoy exacting my vengeance for what was done to Natalie.

Due to Max's intel from our people on the ground, I have a fairly good idea of how to get access to the tunnels underground. The path is marked out for their grunt workers with small pieces of reflective tape, spread out every ten to thirty feet, but with no clear order to its placement. It could be on the walls, the floor, the ceiling, and this meant that unless you knew specifically what to look for, it would be incredibly difficult to notice a pattern.

"Levi, do you have control of the tunnel surveillance cameras? Are we in and have we taped over?"

"Yes, Sir."

"Good man," I say, cocking my gun, and smiling to myself.

As I come around the corner of the tunnel to the area that has been dug out to avoid the close proximity to the train lines, I am grateful the trains are not in operation. When they were live, anyone traveling this path would need to immediately hit the deck in order to not be decapitated by the train. There's simply not enough room to move along the wall.

I've also made sure that all of my gear tonight is black, to allow me to move and work from the shadows.

"Talk to me, Ethan," I say into my earpiece.

"You're about thirty meters from the junction. Once you reach the junction there is a long platform that is going to be on your left."

"How many do we have in the area?"

"I see four, smoking on the platform."

I move slowly along the dugout tunnel, and as I approach the corner Levi speaks again in my ear.

"Sir, I have you in our sights you're nearing the junction."

"Are they still distracted?"

"Yes. And we've hijacked the security cam."

Perfect.

I've caught them with their pants down, and as far as their surveillance knows, I'm not here at all. I exhale deeply, then whip myself around the corner and deliver six well placed bullets into these four men, dropping all of them.

As I walk up to each corpse, I fire another bullet through the head, guaranteeing they are all *really* dead.

"Jaxon." Ethan's voice admonishes in my ear.

"Yes, dear?" I say sarcastically. "Do you not approve?"

"I don't necessarily think you need to administer a double-tap. Perhaps it would be wise to *conserve* bullets since you're on your own."

"Don't you worry, Sweetheart," I say darkly, pulling a walkie off of one of the bodies. "I brought *plenty* of bullets."

Every single man I see is going to die today. Because to me, all of them had some part in Natalie's abduction.

"Okay, Sir, you've reached the doors," Levi says, "and we have their interior cameras, you can proceed."

"Ethan, where am I going?" I ask, pushing the bodies off the platform and into the tunnel.

"You're going to go through the doors and up a set of stairs. Then you'll have a long hallway to your left and then you should reach the stairwell."

"How many targets am I looking at between here and the stairwell, Levi?"

"Sir, we have three more cameras between the stairwell and your location, and it looks like you have six more men."

"Copy that," I growl.

"Sorry, Sir, make that *ten* more men. Four in the hallway before the stairwell, and six on the stairwell itself." Levi corrects over the phone.

"And they also appear to be heavily armed."

"Well," I say, putting my pistol in my vest, "good thing I am too."

I pull my AUG off my back and attach the silencer.

I've always liked this gun, and never get to use it.

I also make sure my hand grenades are easily accessible, just in case. I open the door, following Ethan's direction up the staircase. When I happen upon the four unsuspecting men in the hallway, I ruthlessly obliterate them all, and reach the stairwell fairly quickly.

"Did you hear that? It kind of sounded like... screaming, didn't it? Like, lots of it?" I hear a man sitting in the bottom of the stairwell ask.

Unfortunately for me they don't make silencers for humans.

"Virginia Team, over?" he asks over the walkie.

But he will not be receiving a response, as I just remorselessly cut their entire "Virginia Team" down.

"Virginia Team, status, over?" he asks again. "I'm going to go check and make sure they have their damn walkies on."

He starts heading up the stairwell and I open fire, picking them off one by one as they are all gathered together in the tightly packed stairwell.

That makes fourteen.

"Where to next?" I ask.

"Based on the size of the room she described, and these blueprints, there is only one room it can be."

"Talk to me," I say.

"You need to take that stairwell down to the bottom. Once you go through the door, you should see a short hallway a few paces to the right, follow it until you get to a set of double doors. Go through and turn left. It should be the only room in that hallway but be advised you'll be directly next to another stairwell."

"I have one man coming down that stairwell," Levi says cautiously.

"Jaxon, it looks like Ivan, he is heading down," Ethan interjects.

I check my watch.

7:45 p.m.

They are getting ready to leave for the warehouse.

They are coming for her.

"Josiah, can you hear me?" I ask, reloading my rifle.

"Loud and clear, Sir," he responds.

"Give them hell."

"Yes, Sir!"

I race down the stairwell and through the doors. Three seconds later I hear a boom and the walls around me vibrate and shift. A second boom echoes through the halls, dust falling from the ceiling as all the lights flicker.

"All the targets have been hit," Josiah says excitedly through the mic. "And the front exit is blocked."

"Sir, Ivan is—" I hear Levi say on the radio, but then nothing. All the lights flicker again, and then go out entirely.

"Levi... Levi!" I shout, but with no response. "Ethan...?"

Shit! The explosion must have knocked the power and communication down.

This means I must continue in darkness, with no direction from Ethan... and I will have no idea where Ivan is.

But I have to get to Natalie first or I will have no idea where they are taking her.

I race to follow Ethan's instructions, pausing shortly at the double doors. I watch for any kind of movement from the other stairwell Ivan was seen coming down when I last spoke to Levi, but I see nothing. No movement.

Silently, I push through the doors and down the hallway

cautiously, my heart pounding every step of the way. I keep my gun pointed at the stairwell as I approach the room that they are holding her, aware that at any second it could open.

Suddenly, I hear Natalie shout, and the sounds of a struggle. My worst fears realized: Ivan is *already* in the room with her.

Fuck!

"Get the fuck off of her!" I shout, kicking the door, with my gun drawn.

But what I see in the darkness nearly makes me drop my gun. Natalie scrambles to her feet, a large concrete rock in her hands, and Ivan lays face down on the ground, a pool of blood forming under his head.

Natalie has *killed* Ivan.

I stare at her, too stunned to move.

"Jaxon?" she asks, dropping the rock. "Is that really you?"

What the hell?

"Yeah, I'm here to… rescue you," I respond, still in shock. "But it seems that you did that yourself."

"Jaxon!" she shouts tearfully, and then she launches herself at me. Relief floods my veins as I wrap her in my arms.

She is alive. And she's in my arms. I was not too late.

"I knew you would come!" She weeps against my chest.

"Of course, baby," I whisper to her. I cup her chin, kissing her deeply, feeling her wet tears, her body trembling against me.

"We need to get out of here," she suddenly says. "Colton was here too, but that big ginger guy came and took him first. I have no idea where they took him. But I knew he was coming back for me, and I didn't know what I was going to do. But the moment he unlocked my cage, all the lights went out, and I realized I had an advantage so I…"

She suddenly looks down at the concrete rock on the ground, covered in blood and she gasps, bringing her hands to her face.

"Oh, my God…" she says trembling, the horrific realization apparent on her face. "I… I… *killed* him," she whispers. "I… killed… Oh, my God…"

Natalie starts to hyperventilate. Her breathing is strangled, and her body starts shaking uncontrollably as she points to Ivan on the ground.

Shit. She's panicking.

Your first kill is something you simply never forget.

But we cannot delay, for anything. I assume they'll not abandon her as a prize, so I must get her out of this labyrinth as quickly as possible and I won't be able to do that if she's debilitated with shock.

I need to bring her back to me.

"Natalie, baby, listen to me, okay?" I say gently, as I cup her face in my hands, forcing her eyes to mine.

She looks up at me tearfully, her whole-body trembling in horror.

"I know this seems awful, but you did what you *had* to do to survive. And trust me, that man would've done the same to you, or worse," I say firmly. "But we still need to *survive*, okay? We need to get the hell out of here, so even though I know it is really hard, I need you to pull it together, okay?"

She nods, but her eyes start to drift back to Ivan.

"Αγαπημένη, look at me," I say gently. "Just me."

Slowly her eyes find mine.

"Do you trust me?"

She swallows hard, then nods.

"Take a few deep breaths, okay?" I instruct her to inhale and exhale deeply, slowly watching as she starts to get control of her breathing. Her mossy green eyes finally focus on me, indicating she is back with me in the present.

"We are going to be alright. I promise."

Natalie nods quickly.

Pulling her to me once more, I land a hard kiss on her mouth. "I'm going to get you out of here, and then I'm never letting you go again."

"Okay," she says, managing a soft smile.

"That's my girl." I say, winking at her. "Keep an eye on the door for me." I say, maneuvering her to the doorway. "If you see any movement from either direction, say something."

Deliberately, I wait until her eyes are focused on the hallway, before reaching down and instantly searching Ivan's corpse. I find a flashlight, a cell phone, and a set of keys on his person.

That and his weapon, of which *he* has no further use for. And oddly enough for a gangster, it is a semi-automatic pistol.

Which will work for Natalie.

I stand back up and present her first with the flashlight.

"This is your job," I say slowly. "We've knocked all the communications and power out, which unfortunately means, it's going to be dark, the whole way."

"Jesus…" She shudders.

"I know, but we have no choice," I say gently. "You're going to stick to me like glue and let me do the rest."

She nods, taking a deep breath.

Then I hand her the gun. "This gun is a semi-automatic. It'll fire one round every time you press the trigger," I say slowly, watching her take another deep breath. "This is only a precaution. It's just extra protection, okay?"

She exhales deeply, then takes the gun in her right hand and looks up at me with a nod.

"Let's get the fuck out of here," she says resolutely.

Chapter Forty-Three

Natalie

If anyone would've told me a week ago that I'd be scurrying along darkened concrete hallways, a hundred feet below the city, with one hand on a flashlight, and the other on my rifle-wielding, mafia boss boyfriend, I would've laughed at them.

But this is exactly where I find myself. We open a stairwell door and start down a long and darkened hallway approaching a tunnel intersection. I turn the flashlight to glance behind us, I faintly hear voices in the distance.

"Do you hear that?" I ask, nervously.

"Yes, it's coming from up ahead," Jaxon whispers, as he pushes me back against the wall. "Turn that off."

Oh, my God...

I click the flashlight off, and my heart starts pounding. Jaxon pulls something from his pocket, fidgets with it for a second, before throwing it down the hallway to his right. As soon as he does he whirls around, forcing me to the ground, and covering me with his body. I am confused until an explosion detonates, and flames illuminate the intersection. Intense heat funnels down the hallway, fanning out in every direction.

All of this is followed by the horrifying sounds of men screaming somewhere ahead.

"Cover your ears," he whispers, and I obey.

Jaxon then yanks the massive machine gun off his back, and opens fire for a few seconds. When he stops, the sound echoes painfully off the walls, the smell of gunpowder and blood lingering in the air.

There is no more screaming. Because everyone is dead.

Jaxon is unfazed. Calm and calculated, the man is a machine, briefly scanning our way forward with his night-vision binoculars, before taking my hand and pulling me forward. If I wasn't completely terrified that *we* were about to be viciously shot or blown up ourselves, his stoic resolution might be incredibly sexy.

It is slightly comforting to know I'm *with* Jaxon though. The man with the plan. Because even though I was able to take out Ivan on my own, I have no idea where we're going, and I never would've made it this far, especially with so many armed men down here...presumably all looking for *me*.

But I'm with Jaxon. And he came for *me*.

As we make our way down the tunnel, it becomes harder to see, the smoke burning my eyes. But in the faint flickering of a few dying flames scattered around the rubble, I can make out two massive double doors ahead of us.

"Take my hand, and watch your footing," he says as we approach the smoking doorway. "But try as hard as you can *not* to look down."

I'm about to ask why, until I feel *flesh* press against my shoe and smell the metallic scent of fresh blood. With every step I take toward the door, I hear the crunching and squelching of the dead men under our feet.

We are literally stepping through a pile of bodies.

My stomach lurches.

This cannot be real life.

Something brushes my leg and impulsively I shine the flashlight, illuminating a faceless man tugging at my leg.

"Jaxon!" I scream, nearly falling over.

He whirls around, firing a bullet into the faceless man's head. Hot sticky blood sprays my face as the corpse sinks back into the pile of dismembered body parts.

Horrified, I run, launching myself through the doors, sure that I have somehow stepped into a nightmare itself. Safely on the other side, I brace myself against the wall willing myself *not* to vomit, my entire body shaking.

That really just happened.

Then the tears take over, and unable to hold back any longer, I collapse to the ground. Jaxon is immediately by my side, trying to comfort me.

"Natalie…" he says gently.

Well, as gently as one *could* say after they just murdered a dozen people, and casually walked across their corpses.

"I'm fine," I say reassuringly, trying to steady my breathing. "I'm fine."

I am not fine.

I'm so far from fucking fine.

I'm quite literally in hell. And the worst part is that despite wanting to curl up into a ball and cry, I know I can't. We have no choice but to continue this hellish crusade, or we'll be trapped in these tunnels forever.

Jaxon pulls me up and into his arms.

"I know, this is awful," he says, wiping my face. "We are almost to the subway, and that's the finish line."

Closing my eyes against his tactical vest, and feeling his strong arms around me, I take a few deep breaths trying to calm my racing heart.

"I promise we are almost done," he says encouragingly. "But we *have* to keep moving."

"Okay, I'm ready," I say, taking a deep breath.

Jaxon takes my hand, and the two of us continue our slow and steady progress. Finally, I see lights up ahead through the windows on a small set of beat-up red doors.

The subway!

But before I can celebrate, two shots rip through the air.

Jaxon and I duck down, but we quickly realize that the gunshots are on the *other* side of the subway door. We hear another two gunshots, followed by the distinctive and disgusting sounds of flesh hitting the floor.

The door opens and a man's voice echoes down the tunnel.

"Levi, I just dropped all three of the fuckers, but I still can't reach the boss. No, I'm not waiting anymore. I'm going in."

"Jaxon," I whisper in the darkness. "That sounds like—"

"Charlie?!" Jaxon shouts down the hallway, finishing my sentence.

"Sir?! Is that you?!" I hear Charlie exclaim in relief. "Oh, thank God! Ethan! Levi! I found him!"

Charlie is here too!

I run to him, throwing my arms around him.

"Miss Tyler!" He says, hugging me tight. "I'm so glad you're alright. Thank God you're both alright."

"I thought I told you to stay back," Jaxon says, but his voice is laced with more surprise than admonishment.

"You did, but when Josiah shot off the rocket launchers, it somehow cut all the communications to the tunnels," Charlie explains with a shrug. "We tried everything we could to reach you, but when we didn't get a response, we started to fear the worst. And I'm sorry, Sir, but I just couldn't leave you in here blind."

Jaxon clasps Charlie's shoulder with a smile, his unspoken gratitude evident on his face.

"Rocket launchers?!" he says with a surprised chuckle. "Jesus Christ!"

"Well, you *did* give him free reign," Charlie says with a smile. "Pretty sure Ethan is *still* yelling at him."

A small sense of relief floods me, one I cannot describe.

Jaxon. Charlie. Josiah. Ethan. Levi.

They'd all come... for *me*.

"Well, let's *actually* get out of here," Jaxon says, nodding to Charlie and wrapping his arm around me. "Be alert, this place is crawling with grunts that somehow have military grade artillery."

"Good thing you do too," I say softly.

I look up to see a small smile on Jaxon's face as he looks down at me. I cannot stop myself. I cup his face and kiss him. No matter how scary or even deadly this man may be, he cares enough about me to risk everything to save me.

"Take me home," I whisper against his lips.

"With pleasure, Αγαπημένη," he whispers back, pressing his forehead to mine.

We turn around and proceed toward the doors, my heart minutely lighter than it has been in hours.

I am safe now.

...Or so I thought.

The moment we step through we are met with a gruesome sight: The Monster stands in the middle of the tunnel...holding a pistol pressed to the back of Colton's head.

Charlie and Jaxon draw their weapons and I feel my stomach drop through the floor.

"Well, well, well..." The Monster says, looking up at the three of us. "So nice of you to join us, Mr. Pace. And look, you even brought a plus one to the party."

"Yeah, you know, I think I've had enough of your fucking party," Jaxon snaps. "I think I'll go now."

"Before you do," the man teases, pulling at his mask and tossing it to the ground. "Perhaps you'd like to meet your host."

The look on Jaxon's face is completely indescribable.

"...*Michael*?" Jaxon chokes out, barely more than a whisper.

"Oh, so you *do* recognize me. How touching!" The monster named Michael continues. "Forgive me for thinking a decade of silence might have erased me from your memory completely."

Charlie's face holds a darkness I have never seen. It's clear they *both* know who this evil man is.

"How did you—"

"Escape? From the *prison* you locked me away in for nine years? That really is quite a story actually. But one for another time I think." Michael says, cocking his gun behind Colton's head.

"No!" I lunge forward, only to be stopped firmly by Jaxon's arm around me. I watch as tears stream down Colton's face and despite all of the anger I feel for him, I don't want to see him murdered.

"Michael," Jaxon says rationally. "You needed help. I got you help."

"Is that really what you tell yourself Jaxon?!" Michael shouts. "That locking me away in some looney bin, having doctors come in, poking and prodding every fucking day and trying to dissect my mental state like some science experiment—was kindness?!"

"Michael, listen to me. I did what Rachel asked me to do," Jaxon says calmly, but still firmly holding his gun. "She didn't want to see you end up in prison for your crimes."

"Don't you dare speak for *me*, Jaxon Pace," A woman's voice suddenly echoes through the tunnel.

Slowly, I watch as the dark-haired woman, the same woman who visited me and Colton in the cells, emerges from a tunnel door, walking towards us.

"Rachel?!" Jaxon's voice rings out from beside me.

Wait...what did he just say?

I must have misheard him.

But Jaxon looks as though he has seen a ghost.

"You look surprised," the woman says.

Jaxon says nothing, he just continues to stare at her in disbelief. And the longer I look at her, the more I see the resemblance to Jessica.

That's when I know.

Holy. Fucking. Shit... this is Rachel.

This is the dead mother of his child. However *she* looks very much alive.

What the hell is going on?!

"How? You... are dead?" Jaxon says, his voice sounding strangled.

"Funny, I don't *feel* very dead," she says venomously. "Which I guess means you must've been unsuccessful in killing me!"

"What?" Jaxon whispers, confused. "What are you talking about? I didn't try to *kill* you?"

I'm too stunned to speak, in fact I'm nearly sure that I'm hallucinating this entire experience.

"Why do you look so confused? This was all your doing." She walks over to Michael, tucking his hair behind his ear. "After all, you're the one who locked my brother in a mental institution, took over my family's fortune and legacy. You made my life a living hell, Jaxon! And when I finally tried to leave, *you* tried to have me murdered!"

"Rachel, that is not true. That is *not* what happened," Jaxon snorts, confused and frustrated. "I tried to—"

"Oh just shut the fuck up!" Rachel shouts. "I know what you did. You tried to wipe the Valentines off the map! You tried to take everything from us! But it clearly did not work."

"Rachel, I promise, that's not at all what—"

"Oh my god, enough!!" Michael yells, pushing the gun against Colton's head harder. "I don't care for this pathetic lover's squabble! We had a fucking agreement, Jaxon!"

"Let Colton go, Michael," Jaxon says, trying to remain calm. "We can talk this out. I know we can."

"Talk? This from the man who just broke into my facility and killed dozens of my men," Michael laughs. "All to rescue his latest little *whore*."

His eye falls to me.

"No. I don't feel like *talking* to you, Jaxon. But you know, I did make you a promise."

"Michael..."

"Jaxon, I am going to tear your world apart, piece by piece, until there is nothing left," Michael whispers venomously.

"Starting with *this* bitch!" Rachels snaps, stepping past her brother and pointing a gun at me.

I hear the shot ring out. In an instant, Jaxon's body is on mine, and we are falling to the floor. I hear more shots and yelling...and then there is silence.

Jaxon slides off me and I'm finally able to look around. Michael and Rachel must've taken off, leaving a distraught, but breathing, Colton sitting in the middle of the tunnel.

But then Charlie appears beside me, looking panicked, grasping at Jaxon.

"Get me medical evac in the fucking tunnels now!" He shouts into his earpiece. "The boss is hit!"

What?

That's when I see Jaxon lying on the platform, and realize that he didn't slide off of me.

He took a bullet…meant *for* me.

No. No. No.

I'm on him in a heartbeat. There is a bullet hole in his abdomen, and he's bleeding heavily. He's conscious, but only barely. His hand reaches for me.

Oh my God! No! Please!

"Jaxon! Jaxon!" I scream frantically, touching his face trying to keep his eyes on mine. "You're going to be fine! You stay with me? Do you hear me? You stay with me damnit!" I sob, my voice cracking.

"Goddamnit where are you guys? I said we need evac now!" I hear Charlie shouting into the phone.

Jaxon's eyes roll around in his head, trying to find me. "Natalie…" he whispers, reaching for me again.

"Jaxon! Baby, stay with me! Don't you leave me!" I choke out, my voice strangled. "Please. Jaxon. Please!"

I hear movement on the platform behind me.

I hear myself shout his name.

But the world around me is completely silent as I watch helplessly as Jaxon Pace slips behind the veil to the unconscious.

I instinctively start compressions to keep his heart pumping…as *mine* shatters into a thousand pieces.

I'm sure this is a dream. None of it seems real.

I am alone, sitting on the bottom step of the staircase at Pace

Manor, cradling my head in my hands. Hands that are covered in the dried blood of Jaxon Pace. I know that I should wash them, but part of me is unable to move, and the other part of me is unwilling to part with him.

Any part of him.

Flashes of my relentless chest compressions in the back of the ambulance play behind my eyes, and the echoes of the defibrillator that we used several times still echo in my ears.

Jaxon is *alive*. But barely.

I guess that's a phrase I never thought I'd have to say to myself twice in a week.

He is still unconscious, but he is alive.

His men rush in and out of the study on the first floor, where Dr. Franklyn and I have rapidly set up a makeshift mini hospital for him. We chose the study as it was on the first floor and close to the door, which proved useful considering how his pulse was touch and go for a while.

Colton is in a room upstairs under guard and sleeping off a sedative that Dr. Franklyn forcefully gave him. But he is relatively unharmed.

Ethan is camped by Jaxon's side.

"Miss Tyler," I hear Charlie's voice. "I was able to locate your belongings."

I want to say thank you, but all I can focus on are my hands, which are still caked in Jaxon's blood.

"Miss Tyler?" Charlie asks again, gently. "Why don't you take a minute. Would you like help upstairs?"

I say nothing, but shake my head, shooting a glance to my comatose boyfriend in the study, feeling the tears welling in my eyes again.

"*Natalie*," Charlie says softly.

I'm finally pulled from my silent apocalypse by the fact that for the very first time, Charlie said my *name*.

"Natalie," he says softly. "You've done all you can, which as I know from experience, is more than enough."

Tears now streak down my face and I swallow hard, wiping them away, but also realizing that he's probably right. Dr. Franklyn has Jaxon stable, and I'm accomplishing nothing just sitting here covered in blood.

Charlie still hasn't moved. He stands here, patiently waiting for me.

"Here, let me help you," he says gently, helping me to my feet.

"I'll bring your stuff upstairs for you."

Slowly I nod, my eyes finding Charlie's.

Without another word, he carries my bags upstairs and sets them inside Jaxon's bedroom. The moment I step inside, however, Jaxon's scent hits me hard and not a second after Charlie closes the door behind him do I hit the floor, sobbing uncontrollably.

What the hell had just happened?

Had I been abducted by a lunatic and held prisoner?

Had I bludgeoned a hitman to death with a rock?

Had Jaxon broken into the facility, killing 'dozens of men' on a rampage to rescue me?

Had I learned that his ex, Rachel, was still alive, and apparently convinced that Jaxon tried to *murder* her?

And had Jaxon taken her bullet to save my life?

Yes. All of those things had happened.

I had witnessed all these things and now I am broken.

For the second time in under a week, Jaxon has almost died, and even now he lies under a mountain of tubes clinging to life. So here I sit. Sobbing. I sob until I feel the well dry up entirely. And somewhere in that agony, I feel a quiet creeping numbness enter my body. Too many crazy things have happened for me to comprehend.

So, I decide I won't comprehend or feel.

Cleaning myself. This is something I can handle.

I stand to my feet, willing them to move to the bathroom. As I start the shower and step inside, I feel the tug of my emotions, wanting to remember the beautiful memories with Jaxon in the shower, but I force them down.

I cannot handle that.

Instead, I force myself to focus on savoring this simple task as something I at least understand, in a world where nothing makes sense anymore.

An hour later, after scrubbing the blood and dirt from my body, I changed my clothes and sat down on the edge of Jaxon's bed, staring off at nothing. Sleep feels necessary, but impossible, as I am trying to focus on my own emotional preservation.

Maybe I should pay Colton a visit.

The very thought of him jolts me from my numbness a little and makes my blood boil. But I still want to make sure the asshole is alive and has come to his senses. Perhaps this whole experience has shocked him back to reality.

As I walk down the hallway towards the room where he is

being held, I find Josiah sitting in a chair outside the room. We say nothing to each other, but I place my hand on his shoulder. He silently places his hand on top of mine, and nods.

Somehow I appreciate the hell out of his usually quiet demeanor tonight, because anything regarding Jaxon feels like agony.

But Colton, on the other hand, requires no feeling from me. *None whatsoever.*

I open the door, and step inside the room, with Josiah following close behind me. I find Colton awake and sitting up in the bed, his fingers fidgeting with the edge of the comforter. He looks up to look at me, and instantly his eyes go wide with fear.

"Why are you here?" he asks, terrified. "Are you coming to kill me?"

"There's over a hundred men in this house that want to kill you," I say emotionlessly, as I pull up a chair to his side of the bed. "I'm here to see if you can give me a reason why they *shouldn't*."

He stares at me, processing what I have just said to him. But he's part of the reason that Jaxon is fighting for his life, and I want to hear him acknowledge it.

"I can't," he says, lowering his head. "I know all of this is my fault. I deserve to die."

I look up at Josiah, silently having an entire conversation. He nods.

"Perhaps," I say slowly. "Perhaps not."

Colton slowly looks up at me.

"But that depends on how honest you want to be with me, and if you can finally leave the arrogant narcissist behind in those cells."

This is Colton's last resort. An option to come clean. But only if he wants it. For I am too numb to care what happens to him anymore, since he doesn't seem to care about himself.

"Yes," he says softly, "I can."

"Prove it," I whisper.

I cross my legs and stare at him in a way that suggests I am in no way kidding. At any moment, I could choose to have Josiah rip Colton's head from his body, and it still would not be the worst thing I have seen tonight.

But Josiah is also perhaps the only person in this house who understands the mind of an addict, having watched his mother struggle with addiction. Jaxon told me about it. However, Jaxon told me that Josiah also saw her get *clean*. He is here to evaluate whether Colton is being honest, or whether he's still playing games and is beyond hope.

"I guess I should start by telling you what happened," Colton says.

For the next hour, I sit and listen to his story, learning what his experience had been since he missed his flight Sunday night.

The taxi he hailed from the airport back to the hotel, didn't take him to the airport. It took him up to the parking garage instead. Once inside the garage, Michael and an older fat man with a cigar got into the car with him. The cigar man showed Colton pictures of him buying drugs from some of his dealers during the week, and at one of his clubs the night of the bachelor party. He also said that he knew that Colton was familiar with me and with Jaxon, explaining that this put him in a unique position to assist them.

Michael then explained that the pictures of Colton buying drugs would be mailed to his employer if he did not comply with their instructions. Instructions that were to assist with *my* abduction. Colton was assured by the cigar man that no harm was to come to me, and that this was simply to have temporary leverage over a business discrepancy he had with Jaxon Pace.

"That's everything," Colton says softly, after finishing his story. "That's the whole truth."

Josiah nods silently, both of us feeling that Colton is at least being honest with us now.

"Doesn't it feel good?" I ask softly. "Telling the truth?"

"Nothing feels good right now," Colton says, settling back into the pillows behind him. "I really am a disaster."

I am angry with him, and I am disappointed in his weakness. But I am *not* heartless.

I might've been harsh, but tonight, in the cells I held him accountable for putting me, Jaxon, and everyone else that has been circulating around him, in danger for his own selfishness, and I refuse to feel bad about that.

"Colton, what I said to you this morning at the airport," I say, finally looking him in the face, "is true."

He looks at me confused.

"You need to get *help*."

"Yeah, I know I do."

"This person you've become, someone that would do the things you've done—lying, cheating, manipulating, and betraying the people in your life... this is not you," I say sternly, but then soften my tone. "At least, I hope not."

Colton's head tips to the side and he shoots me a look of utter defeat. I stand to my feet and walk to the side of the bed.

"At least it is not who you *used* to be," I say softly, watching his lifeless eyes, now filled with tears. "I remember a much different version of you. One I actually liked and respected. Before all of this ridiculous other stuff took over."

"I don't know if that guy exists anymore," he whispers softly.

"I think he does. But I think the first step in finding him again, is being honest… with *yourself*."

"I am sorry, Nat," Colton says, and a single tear streams down his cheek, but he makes no movement to stop it. "For all of it."

I believe him. But more importantly, I know that if there is any hope for me finding any peace in all of this chaos, I need to close this door for good.

"I forgive you," I say, squeezing his hand.

"Do you think that we could be… friends?" he whispers.

"I don't know, Colton," I say. "I think the jury is still out on that one, and I think the possibility of our friendship cannot be a priority for you right now. You have a long way to go in your own healing."

I take a deep breath, trying to make this about my healing, too. "But I don't wish you evil, and I don't want to carry around anger towards you. I've had enough of that to last a lifetime."

He nods. "I understand."

"I want to release you from the burden of our failed relationship, so that you can stop carrying it around like some sort of failed penance, and actually get the help you need. Maybe to finally start living a life that makes you happy. Without the drugs."

"Thank you," he says, wiping his eyes.

"I'll see you around," I say softly.

Josiah slowly opens the door and I head toward it before a question pops into my head, causing me to turn around.

"Colton," I say, turning to him., "do you have any idea how those two men who abducted you, would have *ever* connected you to Jaxon? And me?"

Colton looks at the floor trying to remember. "Well, the night of the bachelor party, my card was declined for the pills I tried to buy. The bouncers dragged me upstairs to meet the cigar man. We ended up interrupting some meeting he was in that night with *Jaxon*."

I pause, confused.

"Wait… so, Jaxon *saw* you there that night? Buying pills?"

"Yeah," Colton says, taking a deep breath. "He actually paid them for what I owed and got me out of there before they killed me. He saved my life." Colton finishes, looking a bit annoyed. "Twice now it seems."

This is *news* to me.

Why wouldn't Jaxon tell me that?

"Thanks, Colton," I say as I nod and exit the room.

As I walk past Josiah and down the stairs, my mind is overwhelmed with information overload. I find myself standing outside the doors of the study.

Jaxon.

My heart breaks at the sight of him. He is intubated and his motionless body is a mess of tubes and IVs connected to beeping machines. Dr. Franklyn is fastidiously checking all of Jaxon's vitals, and Ethan sits watching him like a hawk. When he looks up at me, his face warms slightly. I wrap my arms around myself and walk into the room. As I approach, I realize that Ethan is also still covered in Jaxon's blood.

He arrived on the scene with Jaxon's private medical team, and he'd been with me in the ambulance. But I barely had a memory of that. I barely had a memory of anything outside of the relentless compressions I was ramming into his chest, trying to keep him with us.

"He's stable, but still out," Ethan says quietly, his eyes still focused on Jaxon. "Dr. Franklyn here says that is on purpose."

"Yes," I say, my body responding mechanically. "To reduce the swelling to his brain caused by lack of oxygen."

"I don't like it," Ethan whispers.

I lean on the desk behind me and squeeze Ethan's shoulder. We say nothing, but after a moment I feel his hand on mine.

"But he is alive because of you," he says softly.

"No, Ethan…" I say whispering, my emotions welling to the surface again. "He almost *died* because of me."

"This," he says, his voice low and raspy, "is not your fault. But rest assured, I'm going to find out whose fault it *really* is."

His threat gives me shivers. But then it occurs to me that Ethan might not know.

"Ethan," I say slowly, watching him turn to face me. "Rachel is alive."

He looks confused, a mix of shock and disbelief in his eyes.

"Her brother, Michael, is the one who abducted me. As we were escaping, Jaxon and I reached the subway, but Michael and Rachel were waiting for us. Rachel said something about Jaxon trying to have her killed, and Jaxon tried to deny it, but she wouldn't listen. She shot at me, and Jaxon put himself in front of the bullet."

"That is not possible…" he says, looking at Jaxon. "Rachel

is..."

"Dead. I know. Except she's *not*. She is very much alive, and she very much shot at me, and Jaxon very much took a bullet for me," I say, my voice cracking. "But do you see now? This is my fault. This is all my fault. He is lying there *because* of me!" I crack into a soft sob, putting my head in my hands.

I feel tears streaming down my cheeks again.

"No, Natalie, it's not," he says, putting his hand on my back. "Even if everything you are saying is true, I was *there* tonight. I tried to get him to let me come after you instead. I promise you, there is nothing that would have stopped him from getting you to safety tonight... even a *bullet*." His eyes drift to the floor. "Believe me."

His words make my heart crack even more.

"But Rachel being *alive*," he says slowly, "is a lot of new information."

He stands to his feet, and then turns back to me. "I need to make a few calls. Are you alright to...?" He points to Jaxon.

I nod slowly, wiping off my face. "Yes, I can stay with him for now."

He walks away, leaving me alone in the room with Jaxon. I take his limp hand in mine, pressing it to my lips.

What I wouldn't give to have him back right now. I feel so adrift in this situation without him. I desperately want him to wake up and tell me this is all going to be okay. To feel the same security, I felt in his arms, even tonight in the dark and nightmare filled tunnels of the parking garage.

My heart is breaking, overwhelmed by what I feel for him.

And as my eyes settle back over his lifeless body, I feel my brain struggling to make sense of what I am feeling... and thinking.

How can I feel like I know him one minute, and like I don't the next?

Rachel had been right about one thing:

I have only known him for a *week*. An insane week to say the least. And to that end, Rachel, who is the mother of his child, is still alive.

And convinced that Jaxon had intentionally tried to kill her.

Could she be right about that too?

No. That can't be true. I really don't believe that.

Rachel and her brother demonstrated tonight that they could not be trusted in any way. On top of kidnapping me, they lied to Colton, and Rachel herself had admitted that she *was* a liar.

The way Jaxon reacted tonight, when she made her accusation, was authentic. He truly had no idea what she was talking about. And regardless of what she said about Jaxon, it didn't add up to the same man who risked his life and braved those hellish tunnels to save me tonight.

But, speaking of the tunnels... he could be violent. Really violent.

On two separate occasions, I have now seen him brutally attack men. However, Jaxon *had* been honest with me about this, from the start. He'd told me he'd killed people, and he'd always told me that he was a dangerous man. And, both times I had witnessed it, he had acted to protect or rescue me. I refused to take issue with that.

But, even still, I don't really believe that he would ever try to *kill* the mother of his child, no matter how angry he was. He had never been violent with me, not even when he *was* angry. He had only ever been incredibly gentle and protective.

He promised he would never hurt me and had thus far kept all his promises to me no matter how impossible. I trust him.

He protects me. He keeps his promises. He tells me the truth.

But why didn't he tell me about Colton buying drugs?

Jaxon saw Colton at the bar the night of the bachelorette, attempting to buy drugs, but neglected to tell me about it. But it wasn't like he was obligated to tell me, and that night *had* been very eventful. We had discussed a million different things, so maybe it just slipped his mind. Or maybe he just had not gotten around to doing so yet.

I just have so many questions.

All these things *combined* make me feel a bit uneasy.

All of these things, *separately*, however, seem to be totally reasonable and explainable.

But sadly, Jaxon is not able to give me any explanations.

I need to calm down, be patient, and wait for Jaxon to wake up.

Then we can discuss them all, and he can put my anxieties to rest. But that is easier said than done.

I should put my thoughts on paper and address each one individually.

I used to make these lists when I needed to make an important decision, or when I felt torn and overwhelmed by the thoughts in my head. I just need to find pen and paper, and it occurs to me that I am in Jaxon's office, and his desk is right behind me. I walk around to his desk chair and sit down.

In the center drawer, I find a pen, and on top of the desk I notice a notepad. It sits atop a small stack of papers that seem to have been shuffled off to the side, presumably to make room for the machines now keeping Jaxon alive.

I pick up the notepad, but when I do, the item underneath it immediately catches my eye.

Tyler, Natalie

My name, written on a manilla folder, sits on top of the stack of papers on his desk.

What the...

I gently pick it up and set it before me. My heart starts pounding in my ears, and I stop breathing. I open the folder and am greeted with my picture.

My senior picture.

My social media profile picture.

My work badge identification picture from my hospital.

A Tyler family lineage report.

My birth certificate.

Transcripts from college.

A copy of my engagement announcement with Colton.

A letter to my caterer announcing the cancelation of my wedding.

My latest tax return, and a copy of my social security card.

My mortgage statements.

An analysis of my banking and investment information.

What the fuck?

I realize that my jaw is hanging open.

...And Ethan is standing in the doorway.

Chapter Forty-Four

JAXON

My name is Jaxon Pace.

I am awake and I have made a few necessary observations.

One—There is a loud beeping sound every three seconds.

Two—My throat is on fire. I mean on fucking *fire*.

Three—I am unable to sit up.

Not because I am restricted or confined in any way, but because my body is not responding to my desires. I want to sit up, but I simply cannot. After some serious concentration, I can move my arm to my face and that's when I realize that there is an IV attached to it.

Holy shit... I must be in the hospital.

But as I look to my left, I realize that I am not in the hospital, but rather I am in a hospital bed... in my bedroom.

My bedroom at Pace Manor.

I use my arm to gently pull myself up ever so slightly and that is when I see Ethan step into the room.

"Morning gorgeous," he says sarcastically. "Is that really you this time or are you still sleeping?"

"Fuck... off..." I groan, not in the mood for his humor.

God, my throat really is burning. Why?!

"Well, I'll be, it *is* you," he says with a smile. "Sit back, don't waste your energy."

He walks over and starts raising my bed. I release the bar on the bed and fall back against the pillows, breathing heavy and hurting all over.

"Jesus Christ, why do I feel like total *shit*?" I ask, my throat dry and sore.

"Well, for starters you got shot, and your insides got all rearranged," Ethan grabs a cup of water and holds the straw to my mouth. "And you've been in a coma for nearly a week, so I imagine your body is still stiff and catching up."

Holy shit.

I look down at my stomach and lift my t-shirt, revealing a massive bandage on my left side.

"And my throat?" I ask, motioning for more water.

"You were in a coma for a week, bud. You were intubated."

"I don't know what the hell that means, but I feel violated," I groan. "It does not feel great, I can tell you that."

Ethan chuckles softly. "You almost came to yesterday, but you kept slipping back to sleep. So, Dr. Franklyn started reducing your pain medication to see if that would prompt you out of slumberland and back to the land of the living."

Suddenly, everything in the land of the living hits me at once. Images of the garage, and Michael... *Rachel...* and Natalie.

I glance quickly around the room.

"She's not here." Ethan sighs deeply, his eyes hitting the floor.

But somehow, I knew that before he even said it. Her presence no longer lingered around me, and everything felt cold.

"Where is she?"

The tightness in my chest is growing more painful than any of the injuries to my body.

"She's fine... she went back to Miami." His voice is grave and tinged with sadness.

"So, you just let her leave?!" I snap angrily, trying again to sit up. "They kidnapped her and—"

"Don't worry, she's safe. I have Charlie covertly watching her house, But, well... she found the file, Jaxon. *Her* file."

Oh...shit.

I sigh and close my eyes, collapsing back against the pillows.

"How fucked am I?" I ask, my eyes still closed.

"Well... considering that she found the file, after she found out Rachel is still alive and apparently convinced that you tried to have her offed?" Ethan asks, raising his brows. "I'd wager pretty fucked."

Fuck.

I'd planned to tell her about it, and then to destroy it. But never got the chance. Now I am kicking myself, because there is nothing I can do now to explain its existence to Natalie.

"But not entirely," Ethan whispers softly.

What?

I look back up at him.

"She was pretty upset about the file. And naturally very confused about Rachel," Ethan says, crossing his arms. "But she didn't say she hated you. She just said that it was clear you had a lot to deal with on your own and did not need her around right now."

That could not be farther from the truth.

I would give anything to see her.

The pain I am in suddenly seems to intensify.

"There was nothing any of us could do to convince her otherwise. Believe me, we tried. All of us tried," Ethan says quietly, and I stare at him, unable to speak at all. "But that's where I could tell she still had feelings for you."

"If that's true, then why would she leave?" I whisper, my words strangled.

"I think she just needs time, Jaxon," Ethan shakes his head. "The girl has been through hell. But I wouldn't have let her leave if I thought for one minute that she was not still holding a candle for *you.*"

I lock eyes with Ethan.

"Well, you know," he says, cleaning his throat. "Only because of everything she knows and has seen here."

"*Only?*"

But I'm grateful, even if I wish I were still asleep still and unaware of my entire life falling apart.

"I promise, there is still time for you to fix this. But Natalie does have a point, Jaxon. There *is* a lot to sort out here," Ethan sighs. "Black is still a problem. The city is asking questions about the explosions and the collapse of the subway tunnel under the parking garage. There's also rumors of the FBI being involved. And we still have Michael, Rachel, and their growing army of goons to contend with. We have a lot to do."

Rachel. Rachel is still alive.

"Rachel and Michael fled... I think they have gone west from what I can tell," Ethan says. "But we can assume they will return."

All of this still feels so surreal. I shake my head and sigh.

"Jaxon…" Ethan says slowly, "how is Rachel alive? And why does she think that you tried to kill her?"

"I have no idea," I say honestly. "I could barely believe it when she walked out in front of me, and I had no idea what she was talking about when she started accusing me of trying to kill her."

Ethan sits down on a chair next to my bed and rubs his chin.

"So, Rachel and Michael are alive, and they're working with Black," he says, shaking his head. "I mean, it's true that we never found her body in the wreckage. But coming *back* from the dead is not nearly as difficult as pretending to *be* dead for five years. Where has she been all this time? What has she been doing?" he asks.

"I don't know. I don't know anything anymore. How could she do this, Ethan? To me and to Jessica? I mean how could she have just abandoned us for this long?" I say angrily.

I feel my rage and confusion bubbling at the surface, but unfortunately it is making my head hurt. I grab my forehead and rub my eyes.

"I think that keypad on your bed has a morphine button you can press if you're in too much pain," Ethan says, pointing.

"No, I don't want to get high," I say. "I need to focus. I need answers. I can't do that drugged up."

"Right, but you were *shot* Jaxon. That doesn't heal overnight. I think in this instance, it's allowed."

I stretch out my fingers, trying to get more feeling back in them. I reach for the water, and Ethan gets up to help me.

"When I saw her gun," I say, remembering, "I just reacted." As I'm replaying my foggy memories in my head. "I just *knew* where she was aiming. Even though this had nothing to do with Natalie, I knew she was gunning for her. She was always jealous."

I close my eyes and slam my head back against the pillows.

"I could barely comprehend seeing Rachel myself, I can't even imagine what Natalie was thinking. And then I was unconscious, so I didn't even get a chance to explain anything to her." I whisper. "Natalie has to fucking hate me,"

My life feels as though someone had just dropped a *bomb* in the middle of it.

"I promise, that girl does not hate you, Jaxon," Ethan says slowly, a faint smile crossing his face. "Otherwise, she wouldn't have asked me to text her when you came to."

Suddenly, a glimmer of hope erupts in my chest.

And an *idea*.

"Have you… done that already?"

"No…"

"Good, let's hold off on that."

I stare at him a moment longer, a plan beginning to formulate. Then I turn my attention to my hand, still connected to tubes and wires. In an instant I start ripping them out of my skin, one by one, much to Ethan's obvious shock and horror.

"Whoa there! What the fuck, Jaxon?!" he says, lunging forward to try and stop me. "What are you doing?!"

At this point Dr. Franklyn also comes rushing into the room, presumably hearing all of the machine's malfunctioning.

"You said there was still time," I say, looking up at Ethan.

I swing my legs off the side of the bed and sit trying to get a better handle on my vertigo and my breathing.

"I don't want to waste anymore of it," I say heavily. "I need to go get my girl *back*."

Epilogue

Natalie

"You're all set, Miss Tyler, here's your headset. You're at station six," the nice woman at the gun range says to me.

"Thanks," I say with a half-smile.

She smiles back as I put my wallet and sunglasses away.

"Is this your first time?" she asks. "Using a firearm?"

"No, it's not." I instinctively tug at my sleeve that covers the only bruise on my arm that is still visible after a week.

The most *miserable* week.

That had followed the most unforgettable week.

I pull my headphones over my ears and start off down the hallway to my station.

Out of habit, I reach into my purse and grab my phone. Still no word from Jaxon. Or anyone for that matter. I feel a tinge of longing, but quickly admonish myself, focusing instead on loading bullets into my gun.

I have no business lingering on fantasies.

Especially when I have learned there actually are *real* monsters in this world, who actually want to harm me.

If the last two weeks have taught me anything, it is that I cannot rely on Jaxon for my protection.

I cannot rely on anyone. I can only rely on myself.

So that is exactly what I intend to do.

And if any monsters decide to come for me a second time, then they best believe *this* time I am going to be ready.

Natalie and Jaxon's story continues in

Ignite

Heart of the Inferno Series
Book II

Out now.

About the Author

Award winning author Nicole Fanning lives on the east coast with her husband, three dogs and her cats. She has a background in marketing, and Human Resources. She has often found that the human element is by far the most colorful, complex, and most interesting in the world.

As a child Nicole devoured every book she could get her hands on, and spent her free time writing fictional short stories to share with her friends. This led her to writing her debut series Heart of The Inferno.

She writes dark and sexy thriller mafia romance; Heart of the Inferno is an action-romance about a dangerous mafia lord and his girl-next-door paramour. Written from both male and female perspectives, and with a few crazy twists and turns Catalyst certainly isn't your standard mafia romance novel!

You will often find Nicole cuddled up in her writing cave, when she isn't writing you'll find her spending time with her friends and family.

Acknowledgements

Jennifer & Mark: Thank you both so much for your friendship and support in this creative process, and for your enthusiasm to read my scribbles.

Jackie, my twin flame: Thank you for staying up way past your bedtime to talk fiction and life. Your words are poetry for the soul.

Charly : Thank you for being amazing and making this work of mine as beautiful as it possibly could be.

Shavonne & The Discord: Thank you for lifting me up, especially when I was struggling, and for constantly looking out for each other.

Mickey: Thank you for believing in my story and helping to make it the best it could possibly be.

To the Brunch Crew: Thank you for backing me up no matter what.

To The Goddess Lo: Thank you for spitballin stories with me and helping me grow. Love you lady.

To all the Fans: You are the flame that brings Heart of the Inferno to life. There are no words to express my gratitude.

Keep In Touch

To keep up to date with Nicole Fanning, you can follow her on:

Tiktok:
@AuthorNicolefanning

Instagram:
@AuthorNicoleFanning

Author reading group
Nicole Fanning's Reader Group

You can also subscribe to her newsletter at:
Authornicolefanning.net/

Made in the USA
Las Vegas, NV
18 April 2024

88854806R00277